I'm Sorry

Anna O'Malley

POOLBEG

Published 2004
by Poolbeg Press Ltd
123 Grange Hill, Baldoyle
Dublin 13, Ireland
E-mail: poolbeg@poolbeg.com

© Anna O'Malley 2004

The moral right of the author has been asserted.

Typesetting, layout, design © Poolbeg Group Services Ltd.

1 3 5 7 9 10 8 6 4 2

A catalogue record for this book is available from the British Library.

ISBN 1-84223-123-5

Typeset by Patricia Hope in Palatino 9.6/13.5
Printed by
Litografia Rosés S.A., Spain

www.poolbeg.com

About the Author

Anna O'Malley lives in the west of Ireland with her dog, and now writes full time.

Acknowledgements

Thanks to: Katy Egan, my first reader and harshest critic. To Mikey for the dope stuff, to Damien for the Football stuff. To Gaye Shortland and Paula Campbell at Poolbeg and, last but not least, to Elaine and Breda for their constant support.

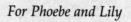

For Phoebe and Lily

Chapter 1

"I'm sorry."

No *"Hi, babe"*. No *"Love, Mark"*, just – *"Mark"*.

"I'm sorry . . . Mark"

Curious. She couldn't remember having had a row, or even a minor disagreement come to that. But then Mark wasn't the easiest to have an argument with. Arguing with Mark was like arguing with a bowl of water. He hated confrontation, preferring to sulk, which drove her crazy.

Weird.

More weird was the fact that this had to be a first. Mark was never the one to say sorry. He was a stubborn bastard and it was usually left to her to make things right; so after a couple of hours of stand-off, of stony silence or crashing things around, for the sake of peace she'd give in and do the apologising thing. Then he'd say something like "Me too" or "Ditto" or on rare occasions "It was my fault", then she'd reclaim responsibility and they would kiss and make up or make love, and that would be that.

1

It hadn't really struck her before, but seeing the phrase on the screen caused her to reflect that in the two years that they'd been a couple, she'd never heard him actually say those words aloud. Ever. It left her feeling vaguely irritated.

"*I'm sorry.*"

For what? If he had gone so far as to apologise, to say the words, well, type the words, the least he could do was specify what it was he was apologising for. She perused the message again.

From: Mark Beyer
To: Maggie Fortune
Sent: Wednesday March 13th. 2002. 12:15
Subject:–
Nothing. Subject left blank.

It was a mystery.

Picking up the phone she hit speed dial, but his phone was powered off and she was put straight through to his voice-mail. She broke the connection without leaving a message, then, putting his email to the back of her mind, opened Lily's email.

"*Could eat a child's arse through a chair,*" it read. "*You're buying.*"

She looked through the open door of her office, and spied Lily Keane dramatically sprawled in her chair in reception, tongue lolling, apparently having lately expired from the hunger.

She replied: "*A nun's arse through a convent gate maybe – O'Neill's?*", hit *send* and, as an afterthought, reopened Mark's email and replied: "*What for, babe?*"

The clock on her computer read 12.59. Saving the finished script of a fifteen-second radio ad for a package-holiday promotion, she clicked off her computer and headed out for lunch.

The day was unusually sunny and mild, almost balmy for March, and a welcome relief after a lengthy, horrendously wet and miserable winter. As they strolled along by the river towards the pub, the Liffey sparkled in the spring sunshine and Dublin City council workers were in the process of sprucing up the streets for the Paddy's Day festival. Along the quays they were erecting banners on lampposts in readiness for the influx of tourists for the parades and gigs and fireworks. The unexpected upturn in the weather seemed to have put a spring in the step of the general population too and an infectious air of good humour was unmistakable.

"Make the most of it," Lily remarked sourly. "It's just lulling us into a false sense of security, so it is. By the weekend it'll be pissing down again."

It was a fair comment. For as long as Maggie could remember, with few exceptions, rain was a mandatory prerequisite for the feast of Saint Patrick. Lily's observation evoked memories of her rural childhood: of tatty and damp crepe-paper-bedecked floats sponsored by the local dairy and animal-feed co-ops, and of huddling in her Irish dancing frock, goose-pimpled and shivering, with half a dozen other small bedraggled girls on the back of a lorry. It was a different ball game now of course. Even if the ubiquitous Celtic Tiger was a smidgen arthritic, the evidence of a still buoyant economy was apparent everywhere, not least in people's expectations. She'd heard her mother comment that even in the wilds of the west of Ireland it was impossible to get a bog-standard ham sandwich any more.

"It's either your *panini* or your *focaccia* or the *ciabatta*," she'd whinged. "And with *pesto* mayonnaise for God's sake! *Pesto!* Isn't it far from *pesto* and the *panini* we were reared! What's wrong with a sliced white loaf and honest to goodness salad cream, I say!"

What indeed?

O'Neill's was crowded and while Lily went off to snag a table, Maggie stood in line at the lunch counter and bought a smoked salmon and cream-cheese bagel for herself and a roast chicken dinner with a side order of fries for Lily (though thin as a whippet, Lily had the appetite of a navvy). To go with it she purchased two bottles of mineral water, glad that her grandmother wasn't around.

"Paying good money for *water*, is it?" Shock, horror.

Scanning the room through the lunch-time throng, Maggie spotted Lily waving at her from a table by the open window overlooking the river. In celebration of the spring weather she was a vision in baby pink today. Pink vintage sixties minidress and matching embroidered cardie with pink kitten-heeled shoes, her wild orange hair struggling to escape from a pink chiffon scarf valiantly attempting to hold it up. Trust Lily the Capable to ferret out one of the better tables in the joint. Jim'll-fix-it wouldn't get a look-in.

"So did you hear the latest?" Ms Organiser personified asked as Maggie set the tray on the table and unloaded the food.

"The latest?" Maggie took off her jacket and sat down,

feeling invisible in her black skirt, black opaque tights, black jumper and charcoal suede boots.

"The new creative director. Domenic's hired yer one – Sally Something. Used to be with BBD&K. D'you know her?"

Maggie nearly choked on her bagel. "Sally? Sally Gillespie?"

Her mouth full of chicken and two veg, Lily just nodded.

"It can't be. Last I heard she was at Penhaligan in London."

"Not from next Tuesday, she ain't," Lily replied, and Maggie's heart sank in tandem with her rising hackles.

Chapter 2

On the face of it, the job with Deadly Inc was a good career move for Sally Gillespie. From senior copywriter to creative director was a step up the career ladder and, although small, Deadly Inc was one of the better, more forward-looking, advertising agencies; but on the other hand, a nagging feeling in her gut told her it was a pace backwards. She'd had such high hopes when she'd headed off to London to her 'Big Job', and now here she was, four years later, back in small-town Dublin with her tail between her legs.

Though she was loath to admit it, Sally knew she had only herself to blame. Handing in her resignation had been a knee-jerk reaction to, as she saw it, an impossible situation – a bluff, a ploy which had backfired badly. Charlie was supposed to have talked her out of it. He was supposed to have reassured her that they were fine, that they had a future. Instead he'd accepted her resignation, muttered about it being for the best and wished her every success for the future. He couldn't get shut of her fast enough.

"No hard feelings, eh?"

"No hard feelings?" No hard feelings that he'd broken her heart? God! That sounded so wet and Sally Gillespie didn't *do* wet, but it was a fact. Charlie Penhaligan had broken her heart.

She'd been aware that the general unspoken consensus had been along the lines of, "Well, serves her right for shagging the boss". But it hadn't been like that. She hadn't intended it to happen. She'd never been one to go for married men, and certainly would have bristled at any implication that it was an attempt to sleep her way to the top. Sally was too sure of herself to even consider that a necessary option. She was good at her job, exceptional, and she had a healthy number of high-profile, spectacularly successful campaigns in her portfolio to prove it. But Charlie's pursuit had been relentless, a roguish charm offensive that had finally broken down her resistance and made her fall madly, deeply and completely in love with him. Looking back, she kicked herself for being so receptive to what she now recognised as his old-married-philanderer guff about waiting until the time was right to leave his neurotic, depressed, frigid, menopausal wife. She'd swallowed whole the fiction that he loved her because by that point she had needed to believe it. What an eejit! Had it been some other sucker, she'd have guffawed with gusto that any women would be so naïve as to buy into it.

Easy to say. Sally felt the grief welling up in her chest again and took a couple of deep breaths. She'd never experienced rejection before. She'd always been a "treat 'em mean to keep 'em keen" kind of gal, looking upon men as a disposable commodity. If she saw someone she liked, even if he was with someone else, she'd get him, then dump him when the excitement wore off – it was no big deal. But she'd never lied to them. Never said, "I love you".

No, she'd been too focussed on her career to even think of settling down. She was by nature a competitive being, so success was important to her, imperative; it had been her priority. The problem was that the clock was ticking big-time and her priorities were shifting. She'd taken a breath and realised that she was ready to settle down. She didn't want to spend the rest of her life alone, but it wasn't just that. Damn it, she wanted to settle down with *Charlie*. She'd been sure that he was the one – her equal, her soul mate – and she had truly believed that he felt the same.

She felt herself flush with humiliation again and, leaning forward, gently banged her forehead against the mirror.

"You stupid, stupid, stupid cow!"

Feeling the hot tears welling in her eyes, she blinked them back.

"You are not going to blub," she instructed her reflection in the bathroom mirror. "You are not going to let fucking Charlie Penhaligan make you blub again."

She swiped away a rogue tear with the back of her hand, then regarded herself, checking for any telltale crow's feet or a sagging jawline. Although she was pushing thirty-five, she'd always looked after herself.

Cleansed, toned and moisturised even after a night on the tear, kept her face out of the sun, spent a small fortune enhancing her naturally luxurious blonde hair, her slender shapely body a testament to a vigorous workout three times a week. But deep down she knew that wasn't it. Nothing so superficial. Give that much to Charlie, he hadn't been after arm candy, but evidently not a trophy wife either. She was an executive accessory. Career, flat, country pile, wife, two kids, designer dog, holiday home in Marbella . . . Power-Mistress. It was what Charlie did. It was the thrill of the chase, a recurring pattern, an ego trip, she could see that now in the cold light of rejection.

It was talk of the big C that had done the damage. Commitment. In theory it was OK, – "I love you, cherub. Of course, I want to be with you . . . when the time's right" – but her ultimatum had scared him shitless. He'd switched off like a light bulb, eyes glazing over with that Bambi-caught-in-the-headlamps stare, roaring a silent "Wooah!". Despite his promises, he'd had no intention of disrupting the status quo. The town flat, the house in Gloucestershire with wifie ensconced. The kids in public school.

It was so humiliating. Now here she was homeless and rejected, back where she started, and she knew beyond doubt that her reappearance in the capital city of begrudgery was bound to prompt knowing smirks and comments.

"Are you still up there, Sally?"

Her mother calling from the foot of the stairs.

"The tea's made!"

As if a cup of sodding tea could fix her life.

"So what's your problem?" Lily asked, conscious of her

friend's lack of a whoop-de-doo response at the news of Sally Gillespie's appointment.

Maggie chewed thoughtfully on her bagel for a moment, then looked up. "What d'you mean, *problem*?"

Lily gave a snort. "Your gob looks like you just swallowed a razor blade, for feck sake."

Maggie sighed. "That obvious, is it?"

"Just a bit. So what's the story?" She leaned forward conspiratorially. "Do tell."

"Not much to tell really," Maggie said, off-hand. "Except to say that she's a self-centred, arrogant, ruthless, devious, flint-hearted cow, generally referred to by all who knew and loved her at BBD&K as SPOD."

"SPOD?"

Taking a swallow of her mineral water to wash away the bile, Maggie looked over the top of her glass. "Spawn of the Devil."

Chapter 3

Maggie had little chance to ruminate over the fact that her new boss was to be the daughter of Beelzebub as she spent much of the afternoon with Tom at a briefing. Deadly were pitching for the I-Sport account, a new isotonic sports drink, and had two weeks to come up with a pitch. The client had very definite ideas, which was bad news, but Paul Brody, the account director, had given them a comprehensive brief which left room for creative manoeuvre. After the meeting she and Tom went off and sat in the sunshine on the boardwalk by the river and tossed ideas around. It was the way they worked best, coming up with their most brilliant ideas brainstorming away from the bustle of the office.

Tom Mulligan and Maggie had worked together as a team, she the copywriter, he her art director, ever since she'd joined Deadly three years previously. He was a mountain of a man in his early forties, married with three kids, overweight, bald as a coot and drank too much, but they'd hit it off as soon as they'd met, sharing the same irreverent, anarchic sense of humour, which was a breath of fresh air after working with her last art director, an anal retentive with an irony bypass.

She'd been headhunted by Dominic Heche while she was still with BBD&K. She'd worked with both Dom and his partner, Leo McKenna, at various stages of her career, and when they had set up Deadly Inc she'd jumped at the chance after Dom had laid out his plans for a small creatively led agency. It was a decision about which she had no regrets as the work environment lived fully up to her expectations. The atmosphere was laid-back, fun and informal, and the agency was on the up-and-up having snagged a number of prestige accounts from the big boys.

At around four-thirty when Tom went off to get a couple of lattes to warm them up (it might have been fine and sunny but the breeze blowing off the river reminded all brave enough to sit out of doors that it was still very much March) Maggie tried Mark's number again, only to find it was still powered off. This time she left a message telling him that she'd be home around six and would bring something for dinner.

Tom returned with the beverages and Maggie wrapped her hands around the carton, enjoying the warmth radiating through the cardboard. Then out of the blue he said, "We've a new CD, did you hear?"

Maggie nodded, her jaw at once stiffening. "Yep. I heard. So what d'you think?"

Tom gave a shrug. "Dunno. Heard she's shit-hot. Was with Penhaligan so far as I know . . ." He glanced in her direction. "Why'd you reckon she'd be coming back here?"

"Probably run out of people to stab in the back," Maggie muttered, not without bitterness.

Tom's bushy eyebrows, which met across the bridge of his nose, shot up his forehead like a levitating caterpillar. "You're a fan, then?"

Maggie took a sip of her latte, then after a pause said, "She was at BBD&K the same time as me. She's a bitch."

Leaning back against the bench and stretching his long legs out in front of him, Tom just muttered, "Bummer."

If Rhona Gillespie had one regret in life it would be that she had given birth to only one son. Not that the one son she had was anything less than perfect – James was a constant source of joy in her otherwise martyred existence. Her regret was the fact that her only daughter was such a disappointment. She'd had high hopes for Sally, particularly in light of James' academic achievements: the highest marks in his class and the only one to get into medicine (a consultant in obstetrics before he was thirty-three). And he had also married Catherine (lovely girl with a degree in Psychology, father a GP) who had produced two perfect grandchildren. A boy, Michael, 5, named after his grandfather, God rest his soul, and a girl, Melissa, who was three.

Sally wouldn't go to college, of course. Well, not *university*. Instead she's done some sort of *course* in advertising, and wrote *advertisements*. What Rhona couldn't figure out was, if she was so good at English, why hadn't she done a proper *degree*? Now here she was back home again, still with no husband, and her nearly thirty-five.

"So what *is* this new job?" she asked her daughter,

who seemed somewhat distracted and had spoken barely a word since her arrival the previous day.

"Creative Director," Sally said, picking up her cup absently, then, seeing it was empty, putting it down again.

"A *director*? Oh." That sounded more promising. "A company director?"

"No, mother. A *creative* director. I'm in charge of the creative department. I have responsibility for the quality of all the creative work in the agency," Sally explained, trying to keep any note of impatience out of her voice.

"Oh. I see." Rhona couldn't hide her disappointment. What kind of a job was it writing ads, for God's sake? If her father were alive he'd be spinning in his grave, and he a dentist with the largest practice in South Dublin.

Rhona's attitude was no surprise to Sally, who had spent her life trying to gain her mother's approval, all to no avail, so she was well used to falling far short of her expectations. But at least she was past caring now. She was resigned to the fact that even if she came home and announced that she'd achieved an Open University degree in rocket science and nuclear physics and was about to be the first Irish scientist to be launched on the Space Shuttle, Rhona's predicted response would be "Oh . . . an *open* university degree?"

Sally stole a surreptitious glance at her watch and, seeing it was past four thirty, felt it was decent to make a move. "Well, must go, Mother. I've an appointment to view an apartment."

Rhona gave a heavily martyred sigh. "I don't know why you have to be looking at apartments and this house empty but for myself."

Sally was ready, mainly because Rhona was nothing if not predictable, but also because the thought of living under the same roof as her was second only in her list of *Things I'd Like To Do With My Life* to pushing hot needles into her eyeballs.

"Nonsense, Mother, I couldn't possibly impose. You need your space after all." All this was said as Sally was in motion towards the hallway. "Anyway, where would Michael and Melissa sleep if I took up a room?"

"I thought you could sleep in the attic," Rhona said, adding, "But I suppose you're right."

It was good to get out of the cloying atmosphere of the house. Sally found it hard to spend time with her mother who, when she wasn't criticising her, would send her on major guilt-trips or suffocate her with sudden and short-lived displays of affection. Her patience reserve was bordering on the red, but equally she didn't want to fall out with her – having lost her father to a heart attack five years before, she was conscious that Rhona wasn't immortal. Though considering the fact she was a hypochondriac and always had some imagined disease or complaint which usually took up the first twenty minutes of any encounter (an innocent "How are you, Mother?" would elicit a veritable litany of pains and aches) it was a wonder that she'd lasted as long as she had. Sally and James had a private joke that their mother's epitaph would read:

"See! I told you I was sick!"

The other reason Sally had had the need to flee was that she was aware of a sudden wave of grief overtaking her again, and she'd rather die than break down in front of Rhona. It came and went in waves, the grief. A sudden rush of pain rising in her chest, then an overwhelming sense of desolation. She felt bereft in the same way as she had when her father had died so suddenly. Her car, a silver VW Beetle, was parked a little way down the street. She hurried towards it fighting the tears that were once again welling in her eyes. I don't need you, Charlie Penhaligan, she thought angrily. I'll get through this. But the overwhelming sense of emptiness, the physical pain in her heart, made her wonder if she could.

Tom and Maggie parted on the quays around five fifteen, Tom to catch the obligatory scoop at the Palace before heading out to the suburbs, Maggie to pick up something in Marks & Spencer's food hall for dinner. She called Mark again to check if he had any preference, but his phone was still off. Irritated that he hadn't got back to her all day she chose an Indian meal for two, knowing that he preferred Thai, then pricked with guilt by her small-mindedness, replaced it and substituted the Thai green curry.

They'd met at a wedding – what a cliché! She was bridesmaid to her cousin Ella and he, the best friend of the groom, best man. He wasn't the usual type she went for. Being tall, five foot nine, Maggie was inclined to go for tall men, but Mark was an inch shorter. He was fair-haired too and she usually went for dark guys. Not the tall, dark and handsome type – her criteria just included tall and darkish, well, not fair – so she was as surprised as anyone when they'd hit it off so well. He was an accountant too which was a joke. Maggie had never imagined herself going for an accountant; accountants were boring old farts. But Mark was different. Not an anorak or suede Hush Puppy in sight and he had a great sense of humour. Within a few months they'd moved in together. This was prompted by the fact that Maggie's housemate had moved out and she needed a lodger to help with the mortgage, so it seemed logical. Mark let his own apartment and moved his things in. At first she'd had some misgivings. It had all happened so swiftly she'd felt as if he'd railroaded her into it, but with hindsight it had worked out really well. They each had a life beyond their relationship and her fear of feeling suffocated hadn't materialised.

Her mother loved Mark to bits too and spoiled him rotten on their trips home to the West, only occasionally drawing their attention to the fact that most of Maggie's schoolfriends were married and producing grandchildren like it was going out of fashion, and asking pointed questions such as, "And is Stella Gibbons thirty-*two* or thirty-*three*," perfectly aware that said Stella Gibbons was thirty-three, the same age as Maggie. Other than that, Anna Fortune didn't overtly nag her daughter about marriage, which was a welcome relief to Maggie. Her father offered no opinion one way or the other which was par for the course. Daniel Fortune wasn't one to talk about feelings. A vet and a racing man, he was more likely to discuss what he fancied in the three fifteen at Chepstow, than to enquire if Mark's intentions towards his eldest daughter were honourable.

The walk back across the Liffey over Capel Street Bridge towards the Liberties, the old inner city area where Maggie lived, was pleasant even though it was just coming on for dusk. The stretch in the evenings was perceptible. Soon the clocks would go on and she looked forward to the long days. She'd bought her terraced house six years before at what she had considered to be a madly inflated price only to see property prices escalate in the intervening years. It had made her feel like a grown-up for the first time in her life which left her vaguely aggrieved. She wasn't sure she wanted to be a grown-up yet, with solicitors and mortgages and all that stuff, but with hindsight she realised that she'd only just escaped missing the boat altogether, for there was no way she could have afforded to buy her house at present values. That was another thing about being a grown-up she resented. All the talk of property prices and pensions plans caused her eyes to glaze over. Buying a house was as far as she was ready to go in the grown-up stakes. Leave talk of pensions and equity to Mark.

As soon as she turned the key in the lock she had a sense that something wasn't quite right. His car wasn't parked and the house was in darkness so she knew he wasn't home yet. She left the front door wide open, clicked on the hall light and her heart almost stopped as she stared through the open sitting-room door.

Chapter 4

Under the circumstances, with hindsight, she felt her initial reaction had been pretty restrained. Well, perhaps less a case of restraint, more a type of temporary paralysis. The room was completely empty except for the bookcase with her books, a few CD's and her elderly VCR, which was sitting forlornly on top of the otherwise empty TV shelf in the alcove to the left of the fireplace. Regaining the use of her legs she ran through to the kitchen. All seemed fine in there with the exception of the empty space on the worktop where the microwave used to live. She took the stairs two at a time and flung open the bedroom door. A rumpled duvet and the bed linen lay in a heap in the middle of the room where the bed had stood only that morning, and on further inspection she realised that Mark's clock radio was missing too. Her heart was pounding to beat the band now, as she stepped over to the dressing-table, but strangely her jewellery was still there. The thieves had taken most of the contents of her sitting-room, a microwave and a bed, for God's sake, but left her easily portable jewellery. It didn't make sense. While retracing her steps downstairs to the hall, almost in a daze, she noted that her old bed was still in the spare bedroom, obviously not to the burglar's taste she supposed.

Back in the kitchen she checked to see if anything else was missing, but the blender, which was relatively new, bought last summer to assist in the making of frozen margaritas, was still in its place and so also was the electric kettle. Her eyes circled the room and she let out a groan. The espresso machine Mark had bought in Brown Thomas at great expense was also gone. Poor Mark! He'd go ballistic.

Rooting her phone out of her bag she dialled his number. The call connected and rang, but terminated and she was diverted to voice-mail. He must be in a meeting, she thought, shit! Then she suddenly was overtaken by an attack of panic and the paralysis returned.

A knock on the open front door and a call of "Hello?" brought her back to reality. She hurried out to see the bloke from next door standing just in the hall. She groped for his name; it wasn't that she was unneighbourly, but he'd only recently moved in. Seeing her difficulty, he gestured towards the adjacent house with a nod of his head.

"Aiden Dempsey . . . I'm from next door."

"Yes, yes, I know . . ."

"Your, um . . . he asked me to give you these." He held out a set of keys. They were on the key-ring Maggie recognised as Mark's.

She was confused. "Mark?"

He nodded. "Yes – he asked me to drop these in to you."

"When?" She didn't understand. "Why?"

"I suppose he thought he wouldn't need them any more." Aiden gave her a strange look. "Seeing as he's moved out, I mean."

It was like a wallop to the solar plexus. "What!?"

"You know – moved out. The removal people came this morning." He was enunciating the words carefully as if they didn't speak the same language. He glanced through the open sitting-room door in an attempt to draw her attention to the fact that the furniture had gone, as if she hadn't noticed.

"Moved out?" Maggie repeated. She couldn't take it in, but was conscious that she must sound like a moron, so she pulled herself together and cleared her throat.

"Moved out, right."

Aiden was staring at her now, and a look of horror spread across his face. "Shit! He's done a runner. You didn't know, did you?"

The look on Maggie's gob must have made that self-evident. She tried to speak but her vocal cords were inoperative. Her head spinning, she sat down heavily on the bottom step of the stairs.

"I . . . um . . ." she managed, but her tongue wouldn't cooperate either, so she gave up.

He closed the front door, and crouched down on his hunkers in front of her. "Are you OK?" He sounded genuinely concerned. She wasn't aware that, apart from the communication problem, her face had gone a colour akin to that of raw pastry, and she was visibly shaking.

"Um . . ." She shook her head and managed an almost silent, "No." Then abruptly she jumped up and stumbled up the stairs to the front bedroom where she flung open Mark's wardrobe. A couple of wire hangers fell to the floor, and a lone denim shirt she recognised as her own swung gently on the rail.

"I don't believe this," she said aloud, staring at the empty cupboard. Wrenching open a drawer of the chest under the window she saw that it too was empty of all Mark's stuff. It was crazy. She heard a cough behind her and turned to see Aiden standing awkwardly in the doorway.

"He took the bed?" He sounded stunned. "Bloody hell!"

"It was his," she said simply.

"And the other stuff?"

Maggie shrugged. "Not really. It was ours. We bought it together." Then it dawned on her. Mark had bought the two suede sofas on his credit card. And the paintings, and the microwave and his precious espresso machine. Technically they were his, despite the fact that they shared expenses, but then Mark was a stickler for keeping accounts – why wouldn't he be, wasn't he a fecking accountant? Shared expenses meant halving the bills. He bought the sofas, she'd paid for their safari holiday in Kenya the previous June . He'd bought the microwave, she'd bought the blender. He'd bought the TV and music system, she'd paid for the skiing break in Andorra in early January.

"Bastard!" she said. His calculated pettiness angered her and she temporarily forgot that he had, as Aiden had put it so succinctly, done a runner.

"I'm sorry."

It made sense now, but was hardly adequate.

"The spineless gobshite!" she snarled, kicking the wardrobe door shut. "He never said a word!"

"Are you serious?" Aiden sounded incredulous. "He just upped and left? Just like that? No warning?"

"Pretty much."

He let out a long sigh. "Bugger."

Strangely, the anger of moments before had evaporated and in its place Maggie felt numb, anaesthetised – later she put it down to shock. She walked towards the bedroom door. "I need a drink," she said. "Fancy a beer?"

Luckily Maggie had bought the six-pack of Miller and the half bottle of tequila she found in the bottom of the fridge, otherwise that would probably have gone too. She plonked a Miller in front of Aiden and dumped two shot-glasses on the kitchen table.

"Tequila chaser?"

Without waiting for a reply, Maggie sloshed the amber spirit into the glasses.

"Shouldn't you call him?" Aiden said, picking up the bottle of beer.

Maggie slugged a mouthful of the cold Miller then snorted. "No point. Bastard isn't answering his phone. I've been trying to get him ever since I got his email at lunch-time 'cos it didn't make sense but it does now 'cos he's a spineless tight-fisted gobshite."

"Say again?"

Hooking out a chair with her foot for Aiden, in an unspoken invitation to sit, Maggie took a seat at the top of the table. He hesitated for a nanosecond than sat also.

"I had this email from him at lunch-time. It said: "I'm

sorry." Just that. "I'm sorry." We hadn't had a row or anything. I hadn't a clue. I tried to get him, I left a couple of messages. To be honest I'd forgotten about the sodding email. I even got him Thai green curry for dinner because I know he doesn't much like Indian, then I came home to this."

Aiden took a swallow of beer. "You'd *really* no idea?" He found it hard to believe.

Maggie shook her head in reply then picked up the shot-glass and knocked it back in one, coughing slightly as the spirit burned the back of her throat, its comforting glow spreading right down to her stomach. She refilled her glass and repeated the operation.

Aiden sat silently sipping his Miller, uncomfortable but unable to leave. He'd seen the removal van arrive and had been aware of a bit of banging about next door that morning but had thought nothing of it. Then the guy, Mark, had knocked on his door around twelve and asked him to give the keys to Maggie.

He'd seen her coming and going since he'd moved in and had a nodding acquaintance with her, but she'd hardly noticed him. He'd thought she was lovely. Tall, shoulder-length reddish-brown hair, great body, though she didn't really dress to show it off, high cheekbones and striking green eyes. He'd felt a little disappointed when he'd first realised that she had a partner.

"So were you two together for long?" he asked to fill the silence.

"Two years," she said, after downing another tequila shot. She picked up the bottle and made a questioning motion at his still full glass. Aiden shook his head and took a swig of beer instead. Maggie refilled her own glass and this time took a sip, made a face and put the glass down, then had second thoughts and knocked it back in one swallow.

"I hate this stuff neat," she gasped when the subsequent fit of coughing had subsided, adding, "But I feel the need to get wasted right now," then slammed another measure.

"You should talk to him," Aiden said. "It's probably one of those stupid spur-of-the-moment misunderstandings that'll blow over."

"But we didn't have a row, I keep telling you," Maggie wailed, frustrated that he didn't seem to get the point. "And I hardly think," she started, swallowing a hiccup, "that booking a removal van and whipping half the contents of my house out would qualify as *spur of the moment*. Seems pretty premeditated to me." The anger was returning, no doubt with the help of the five shots of tequila she'd downed in as many minutes.

"I suppose," Aiden conceded adding, perhaps a tad insensitively, "Is there someone else, d'you think?"

Strangely that thought hadn't crossed Maggie's mind and she'd no reason to suppose it was the case. She shook her head dismissively. "No, not Mark. He's not the type to play away."

"How do you know? I mean has he been acting strangely lately, for instance?"

Maggie refilled her shot-glass. "How do you mean, strangely?"

Aiden shrugged. "I don't know . . . has he been withdrawn, secretive? Have there been silent phone calls, you know, where the caller hangs up without speaking?"

"No! Nothing like that!" Then she paused. "Well, he has been a bit moody lately, but I put that down to pressure of work. He's an accountant and it's the end of the tax year."

"How about the silent phone calls?"

Maggie thought about it, shook her head, then picked up Aiden's full shot-glass and dispatched the contents.

"Has he been working late then?"

"Yes. But it's the time of year." It occurred to Maggie then that she was defending him. "You mean, you think it was just an excuse?"

Aiden shrugged. "Dunno. But it's a thought. You're the one looking for a reason."

Maggie stared at him, noticing that he was ever so slightly out of focus. She blinked and suddenly she didn't feel so good. A clammy sweat had broken out on her forehead and upper lip, and saliva was filling her mouth. Leaping abruptly from her chair, ping-ponging off the table, his chair, then the doorframe, she made a dash upstairs to the bathroom where she threw up in the loo, for once grateful that Mark had left the toilet seat up.

The room was swimming. She felt weak and still very nauseous. She was conscious of Aiden behind her at the hand-basin running the tap. She didn't want to throw up in the company of a stranger but had no choice and wretched violently again. She felt his arm around her shoulder supporting her, and he wiped her forehead with a cold wet flannel, as she threw up again. She felt too atrocious to protest as he handed her the flannel to wipe her mouth when she'd finished.

"Take a sip of this," he said, holding a glass of water to her lips, and she complied gratefully.

The room was still spinning. She tried to talk, to tell him she was OK now and that she'd be fine and "Please leave me on my own," but was having difficulty with speech. She had an almost uncontrollable urge to curl up by the loo and go to sleep but then another wave of nausea overtook her.

Aiden helped her to the spare room and put her to bed, despite her unintelligible drunken protests. He managed to get her boots off but demurred about going any further, pulling the covers over her fully dressed, but making sure she was lying on her side. She was out cold. After that he went back downstairs and returned with a pint glass full of water, a packet of Nurofen which he'd found in the bathroom, and the washing-up bowl, all of which he left by the bed.

"Not a good move to down half a bottle of tequila in the space of ten minutes – and on an empty stomach," he said to the softly snoring figure. "And you'll have the mother of all hangovers in the morning."

He felt sorry for her finding out like that, and wondered what kind of cowardly wimp walks out of a two-year relationship without a word of warning. Though truth be told, the fact that the lovely Maggie was now single was a silver lining.

Chapter 5

Maggie rolled over and opened her eyes. Big mistake. Her head exploded with pain, the early-morning light stung her eyes and she had an epic thirst. She was disorientated in the unfamiliar room and it took her a moment to realise where she was. Stretching out her arm, expecting to find Mark's warm body beside her, she encountered only a cold empty space. Then it all came back to her. He'd gone. Mark had gone. He'd left her. Panic welled in her chest. He can't be gone! her brain screamed. Not just like that. He loves me!

The big question that roared like a cyclone inside her head was, Why?. It didn't make sense. They were fine, weren't they? He hadn't given her any sign that he was unhappy, that he'd stopped loving her. What had happened to make him do it? She racked her brain trying to think of anything, any warning sign, but her brain function wasn't up to much.

Gingerly she eased herself up. She couldn't remember

getting herself to bed. God, but she must have been drunk – her thumping head and arid mouth were a testimony to that. Then her eyes fell on a pint glass of water on the bedside table and a conveniently placed box of Nurofen. For someone who'd downed a bucket of tequila she was impressed with herself for being so organised. She glanced inside the box – she hadn't taken any. Pity I hadn't had the presence of mind to take a couple before I went to sleep, she thought, then noticing that she was still fully dressed but for her boots, realised that it would probably have been asking too much.

She fell on the water and gulped most of the glass, saving the dregs as her shaking hands wrestled with the bubble-pack of painkillers. Once she'd liberated two she threw them into her mouth and washed them down, the effort leaving her weak and sweating. Flopping back against the pillows she closed her eyes, and as she did so the fact that Mark had abandoned her became suddenly all the more real. Hot tears washed her cheeks and she began to cry. Mark used to make sure that she had a big glass of water by the bed when a hangover threatened. He was the one who could always put his hand on painkillers or an Elastoplast or indigestion tablets. She had to talk to him. If there was a problem surely it wasn't beyond fixing? That was Mark's trouble: he'd never talk about how he felt; he bottled stuff up and let it fester. She reached out for the phone, then realised that she was in the spare room.

"I have to talk to him," she said aloud. "If I talk to him he'll come home."

Struggling out of the high pine-framed bed, she landed on rubber legs, grasping the headboard for support until the room stopped rotating, then padded out to her bedroom. The duvet was still lying in a desolate heap, tangled with the bed linen where it had been discarded, but when she looked for the phone it wasn't there.

Of course it wasn't. The bedside phone was Mark's.

Misery gave way to anger again as the calculated manner of his flight became ever more apparent. How long had he been planning it, she wondered, as the venom of his betrayal gathered strength. Had he known in Andorra? Had he shared her bed, made love to her, all the time knowing that past Paddy's Day they'd no longer be together, that he'd be . . . what? With someone else?

Aiden's question raged in her head: "Has he been working late?"

It stabbed at her, prodded her. In the last couple of months he'd worked late at least three nights a week and went into the office the odd weekend too, at least that was where he said he was going.

"Is he seeing someone else?"

Was he?

Had he planned it, or had he decided on the spur of the moment? No, Mark was a planner. He'd taken every last one of (what he considered to be) his possessions so he must have had somewhere to go. Or someone to go to?

Suddenly she was overcome by an attack of giddiness and the strength drained out of her legs so she flopped down on the duvet and curled up, wrapping the soft fragrant cotton cover around herself. Nestling her head in the pillow, she caught a whiff of Mark's aftershave. She wanted to sleep. To forget about it all. Maybe if she just closed her eyes for a while, she'd wake up and everything would be back to normal.

If only.

The persistent ringing of the phone in the hall woke her with a start, and she'd hurtled halfway down the stairs before she realised it.

"Hello?" Her mouth had dried out again.

"That you, Mags?"

Lily. Maggie grabbed her wrist to steady it, then peered at the time. Almost eleven. She'd slept for over three more hours.

"Lily. Listen, I'm sick. I can't come in," she muttered through what felt like a wad of cotton wool.

"Oh, poor you . . . you sound awful," her friend replied sympathetically. "A bug, is it?"

It was the heartfelt genuineness of Lily's concern that did it.

"Something like that," Maggie gulped. "Well, no . . . the thing is . . ." Suddenly she was crying again, down the phone, snuffling and sobbing and babbling a string of incomprehensible words devoid of any coherence or even elementary punctuation.

Lily arrived in a taxi fifteen minutes later which was a feat in itself considering the Dublin traffic. Letting herself in with her spare key, she found her friend still sitting on the bottom step of the stairs sobbing quietly, rocking gently for comfort, her arms wrapped around her knees. She hadn't had a clue what to expect from Maggie's garbled phone call, only that she needed help. She'd dashed to

Dom's office and told him that Maggie was really sick and she had to go to her straight away. Dom was on the phone, but, seeing the uncharacteristic panic-stricken look on her face, had made no objection and waved her off.

It took about ten minutes to get any sort of coherent story from Maggie. It came out in disjointed sentences interspersed with hiccups, which, together with the physical evidence of the empty sitting-room, immediately apparent through the open door, gave her the gist of what had happened.

Maggie looked terrible, hair every-which-way, mascara-smudged panda eyes, still in yesterday's clothes which looked slept in. She also reeked of tequila to the extent that Lily wondered briefly if it was oozing out of her pores.

They were sitting side by side on the second-to-bottom step of the stairs. Lily had made coffee but Maggie had been reluctant to move so she'd brought it out to the hall and joined her friend. She was appalled by Mark's behaviour. It was so cold and considered, not to mention spineless, but that aspect of his conduct didn't surprise her. It was common knowledge that he avoided confrontation at all costs. She'd never really taken to him but had kept the fair side out, the way you do. He certainly wasn't her cup of tea, and she didn't understand what Maggie saw in him, but they'd never discussed it, other than the time Mark had mooted moving in. She'd thought it was way too soon and had had a feeling that Mark had some agenda other than a commitment of sorts to Maggie – a suspicion that was confirmed to her when she discovered through a throwaway remark by Mags that he was getting twice as much rent for his upmarket apartment than he was contributing, which more than covered his modest mortgage. He was actually making a profit on the arrangement.

"He must have been planning it for a while," Maggie said miserably after a silence. She seemed calm again, all cried out.

"Looks that way," Lily agreed.

"He even took the sodding bed."

Lily was gobsmacked. "You're not serious!"

"Well, it was his. And his stupid radio-alarm with its irritating beep, beep, beep noise, and the bedroom phone. I mean, how petty can you get?" she paused. "Mind you, I never liked that bed. It was hard as a rock."

"Well then," Lily said, attempting to be positive, "suppose it's as good an excuse as any to get a new one."

Maggie took a sip of coffee. Her face had a bit of colour now, and the pale green tinge had gone. "He's found someone else, you know?"

Lily, who had just taken a gulp of her beverage, almost choked. "What! Who?"

Maggie shrugged. "Dunno. But it makes sense. He must have had somewhere to go. The late nights supposedly working, the weekends he said he was going into the office, it was all lies . . . all the time he was seeing someone else . . . it was Aiden who suggested it."

"Who's Aiden?"

Suddenly Maggie groaned and put her head in her lap. "Oh God!"

Lily had lost track around 'the late nights . . . the weekends'. "Who's Aiden?"

"My new neighbour. Mark gave him the key to drop in to me. Naturally I was a tad shocked and I got completely twisted on tequila and . . ." She closed her eyes. "Oh shit! I threw up in front of him. God! Several times. He must have put me to bed . . ." She let out a long moan. "How embarrassing is that?"

Lily snorted. "I'd say that's the least of your worries. That prick's nicked half the furniture, for feck sake!" Then a thought struck her. "Have you checked your joint account?"

Maggie shook her head, an act she immediately regretted as her brain felt as if it was bouncing loose around the interior of her skull. "No, but I'll put money on it that he'll have calculated his half of the electricity bill and the phone and withdrawn any cash surplus to requirements."

"Bloody hell, Mags. What did you see in him? He's such a mean bollox!" Lily blurted, and Maggie's face crumpled.

"But he was *my* mean bollox," she whimpered. "Honestly, Lil. You didn't know him. He could be so sweet and caring, and – and he loved me."

"Evidently not enough," Lily commented perhaps a wee bit harshly.

"And he has a huge willie," Maggie added, wistfully.

Lily didn't get the chance to comment on that as there was a sharp rap on the front door.

Maggie looked at her hopefully and mouthed, "Mark?"

Lily gave her an 'Oh, puh-lease' look, then stood and strode to the door, fervently hoping that it was, so that she could rip his ears off. Instead, when she wrenched the door open, face like thunder, she saw a tall, cute-looking guy, dark hair, good body, standing outside.

"Who the fuck are you?" she snarled, making an instant supposition that this was a mate that the lily-livered gobshite had sent over to collect a forgotten teaspoon.

Aiden took a step backwards. "Um . . . I'm from next door" He gave a vague gesture to the adjacent house. "How's Maggie? She was a bit under the weather last night."

"That's one way of putting it," Lily replied, not giving an inch.

On the second-bottom step of the stairs, Maggie, still mortified that this comparative stranger had seen her vomit and had put her to bed, cringed, her brain shouting a futile, no . . . no . . . don't let him in! but her legs lacked the strength to carry her upstairs so she had to sit tight where she was.

She heard Lily say, "She's got a mighty hangover, but she'll live, no thanks to that bastard."

Perhaps it was Lily's urban guerrilla outfit (combats, Docs, khaki T-shirt and army-surplus dog-tags) but Aiden, somewhat disconcerted by this five-foot-nothing ferocious-looking woman with wild red hair, standing guard in the doorway, said, "Well, eh . . . tell her I hope she's um . . . well . . . feeling better."

"Fine," Lily said, then shut the door in his face.

Relieved when Lily stepped back inside, Maggie exhaled. Her friend had a wide grin on her face. "Well, I wouldn't kick your new neighbour out of bed for eating crisps."

"What?"

"Yer man. He's a babe."

"'*She was a bit under the weather*,'" Maggie mimicked. "Patronising bastard."

Lily laughed. "Whatever." Then taking Maggie's arm, dragged her upright. "Come on. I'll run you a bath."

Maggie resisted. "No," she whined, "I want to be miserable. My boyfriend's just left me." She flopped down again.

"Fine," Lily said, yanking her up again (for a woman of her size she was frighteningly strong). "*Be* miserable, but you still need a bath . . . trust me on this."

Chapter 6

Sally wasn't much impressed by the three apartments she had viewed to date, but had been tempted to take the last one she had seen the night before – a rather pokey two-bedroomed affair with a balcony the size of a tea tray, in Ballsbridge – for fear of having to spend another night under the same roof as her mother. She was possessed by a very real fear that she'd be driven at some point, in a fit of weakness, to strangle her in order to stop the relentless criticism and her pathetic whingeing.

Thankfully when she'd phoned the agent he'd told her of a one-bedroomed loft on Great George's Street that had just come in, which sounded promising. She was astonished by how much rents had inflated since she'd last lived in Dublin, the only compensation being that the rental from her flat in Putney was at least covering her mortgage. She knew the sensible thing would be to sell up and buy in Dublin, but then she didn't want to burn her bridges. The only reason she had come back was to put some distance between herself and Charlie, certain that she would be unable to face bumping into him had she stayed around. Of course, the downside of that was that once off the scene in London she knew she'd soon be forgotten, which would narrow her options should she want to return. It was a kind of rock-and-hard-place scenario. Go for a new job in London, which with her present CV would be no problem, and risk bumping into Charlie all the time, or move to Dublin and possibly scupper further career opportunities. In the end it was no contest, and emotion, or rather cowardice, won over the shrewd option.

The loft was a sublet with nine months remaining on the lease. The décor was minimalist, mostly white, a further dividend (nothing worse than having to live with someone else's bad taste) and there was also access to the roof and secure car parking. Despite the exorbitant rent she decided that it would do very nicely, thank you, so went immediately to the agent's and paid a punitive deposit and a month's rent in advance.

She liked the thought of living in the middle of the city, only a short walk from Grafton Street and a ten-minute walk to work. That was one aspect of Dublin that was preferable to London: size. Most places were within walking distance or a reasonable taxi hop. But on the downside it was such a village. She wondered what was being said about her return. No doubt there'd be comment.

The loft had vacant possession which was an additional incentive, so Sally took the keys there and then and returned to check it out properly, with a view to making a list of any missing necessities. The living space was large and airy, about thirty feet by twenty, with wooden floors and three tall windows which let in plenty of light. There were two long cream sofas set at right angles in front of a cool-looking contemporary gas fire, and a beechwood dining-set with four chairs, a low coffee table and beech storage units made up the rest of the furnishings. A small galley kitchen, separated by a granite-topped unit from the main living area, had only the bare essentials – cooker, fridge, washer/dryer, microwave (which was of no consequence as Sally rarely ate in) – and the bedroom, quite small in comparison to the living area, had a compact, unremarkable en suite bathroom reminiscent of every hotel she'd ever stayed in.

Sitting down on the end of the king-size bed (a five foot would have been more practical taking into account the size of the room) Sally made a list. Bedding, colourful cushions, towels – might as well make it at least *feel* like home. She wandered through and checked out the kitchen cupboards: enough dishes for her needs, but short on glasses. She made a further note. The few bits and pieces that she hadn't left in situ in Putney, such as her trusty espresso machine, CD player, TV, DVD, her art collection and the rest of her clothes were due to arrive the following week. So, list completed, she set off for Habitat.

The weather was duller than the previous day, though not as chilly as normal for March. Cutting through the covered market to the Powerscourt Townhouse centre and then on through the lane adjacent to Bewley's, she made her way towards Grafton Street. There was a fair bit of activity around and a number of buskers were already in evidence competing for gratuities from the passing shoppers and the straggle of early Paddy's Day tourists.

As she reached South Anne Street the sun suddenly burst through a gap in the clouds so she decided to take advantage of it and sat at a table outside one of the many cafés, ordering herself a double espresso from the Spanish waitress.

Big mistake.

She was suddenly overtaken by a potent sense of déjà vu, of a sunny morning in Covent Garden, sitting with Charlie, sharing a breakfast of espresso and croissants like lovers do, before heading off, separately, to the office. She had an overwhelming urge to hear his voice, and dug her mobile out of her bag, hands shaking, as she found him in the phone book and pressed *call*. Her heart was thumping and she knew it was foolish but she couldn't help herself. She needed a fix. She needed to hear his voice.

She got his message-minder and was simultaneously relieved and disappointed. Listening to his instruction that he was unavailable to take her call, but to leave a message, she terminated the call before the tone. The rich baritone timbre of his voice tugged at her heartstrings and tears sprang to her eyes. She despised herself for being so pathetic but, as far as he was concerned, she knew she was not in control. Yet.

"You are OK?" The Spanish waitress back with her espresso, a frown of concern wrinkling her brow.

Sally wiped away a stray tear and gave her a brave smile. "Not really. But thanks for asking."

"Did you try pressing the redial button?" Lily suggested.

"Why?" Maggie asked.

They were sitting on top of the bed in the spare room,

it being the only comfortable place to sit now that her sofas had gone, discussing possibilities. After her crying jag, two more painkillers, the best part of a carton of cranberry juice and a soak in the bath that had been drawn for her, she felt a little more civilised and was able to talk about the situation without dissolving into tears.

"He could've called someone . . . *her*, I mean . . . after the removal men were finished. You know? To tell her he was on his way or something."

"Always assuming there *is* a her," Maggie said pointedly. She was having some difficulty accepting the possibility that there was someone else.

"Whatever," Lily said dismissively. She was having no such denial problem. To her it was obvious. If there wasn't a *her*, why hadn't he just come out with it? 'I'm sorry, Mags. I don't think this is working out,' or 'It's not you; it's me,' or whatever old shite men usually came out with when they wanted to break up. "He could have made a call though. It could give you a clue as to where he is."

Maggie couldn't argue with that; besides, she was anxious to talk to him. They couldn't leave it like this. She sighed, then slid off the bed. "Come on then."

"Spokes, Kennington, Cowdray," a cheery voice chirped. "How may I help yew?"

Maggie put her hand over the mouthpiece of the receiver. "His office," she whispered to Lily.

"Ask to speak to him!"

Maggie hesitated until she heard the receptionist repeat, "Spokes, Kennington, Cowdray, how may I help yew?"

"Um, could I speak to Mark Beyer, please?"

"I'm sorry, Mr Beyer isn't in the office. Can I take a message?"

"How, not in the office?" Maggie asked, surprised by the information. He hadn't said anything about being away.

"Um . . . away," came the reply. "On business."

"Where? What business?" Maggie snapped, not believing a word of it.

"I'm afraid I'm not at liberty to say," Miss Chirpy replied, adding helpfully, "but you could always try him on his mobile."

"I should be so lucky," she snarled and put the phone down. "He's not in the office. She said he's away on business, but he didn't say anything to me about a business trip."

Lily gave her a leery look. "Duh! Of course he didn't."

"Oh right. I see what you mean."

"How about the removal company? The cute guy next door might have noticed who he used." Lily Keane was nothing if not resourceful. "They could tell you where they took his stuff."

"I suppose we could always ask," Maggie said reluctantly, cringing at the memory of disgracing herself in front of said next-door neighbour. "Or maybe you could."

Lily took her arm. "Come on, kiddo. Best to get it over with and face him. I'm sure he's forgotten about your head spinning round and the projectile vomiting by now."

Lily, flanked by a sheepish-looking Maggie, stood at Aiden's open front door. They'd bumped into him on his way out, camera-bag over his shoulder. Maggie was still the worse for wear, the walking wounded, her face almost as pale as the clean white T-shirt that she was wearing over a pair of faded Levis, but she did look better than she had earlier.

"How's the head?" he asked giving her a knowing grin.

"I've felt better." She coloured slightly, which was probably an improvement in itself.

"I can see you're on your way out, but this won't take a tick," Lily said, grasping the initiative, "but we were wondering if you noticed the name of the removal company that Mark used?"

"They might be able to . . . um . . . to tell us where he went," Maggie said, flushing again, humiliated by how pathetic she felt.

"Still hasn't been in touch, then?"

Glowering and feeling distinctly patronised – *Poor loser! Her fella's done a runner* – she shook her head.

"Still not answering his mobile?" The grin was still in place, though he wasn't aware of it, too intent on trying to sound suitably sympathetic. Though disgusted by the brutal manner of Mark's exit, he was in no way sorry that he was off the scene.

Lily frowned. "No. And his office said he's away on business but wouldn't say where he –"

"So did you notice or not?" Maggie cut in abruptly.

Surprised by her sudden unaccountable hostility, Aiden cast his mind back, but at the time he'd thought nothing of it, so had paid little attention. "Um . . . it was green," he said, after a pause.. "Dark green with white lettering."

"Well, that narrows it down," Maggie muttered, heavy on the irony.

Lily gave her a dig in the ribs. "I don't suppose you noticed a phone number," she said to Aiden.

He hadn't seen that either so he shook his head. "If I'd realised it was important . . ."

Grabbing her friend's arm and yanking her back, Maggie snarled, "Come on. I told you it was a sodding waste of time."

They left Aiden standing on his doorstep, wondering what he'd done to merit Maggie's ire.

Lily had the same problem. "What was that about?" she asked, rubbing her arm to restore the circulation after Maggie had released her vice-like grip subsequent to slamming the door shut.

"Did you hear him?" she said, indignant. "'Hasn't been in touch, then?' – 'Still not answering his mobile?' Condescending, smug bastard!"

"He was only trying to be nice, Mags," Lily said reasonably, noting the beginnings of a bruise on her forearm.

"Nice? Nice? So what was that self-satisfied smirk on his gob, then? He thinks it's hilarious." She was angry again. "What is it with men?" she raged. "They're all the bloody same." Then sitting down on the second to bottom step of the stairs, tears spilling down her cheeks she said, "Why did he do it, Lil? Why did he leave me?"

Lily sat down next to her and, as she put a comforting arm across her shoulder, said, "I don't know, kiddo," at the same time making a silent promise to herself that the next time she saw bloody Mark Beyer, never mind his ears, she'd rip his sodding balls off.

"She's in bits."

"Good grief, I'm not surprised," Dom said. "And he really didn't say a word? Just upped and left?"

"Just upped and left," Lily confirmed. "And took most of the furniture with him too. Miserable git."

Maggie, overcome by sudden weariness, exhausted by the crying, was lying down again, so Lily had taken the opportunity to give Dom a call at the office to fill him in on what had transpired chez Fortune.

"Where is she now?" Dom asked.

"Sleeping. She got twisted last night, drowning her sorrows, so she's not the best today. I'd say she's still in shock too. I mean, you don't expect to come home from work to find that your fella's legged it with the furniture, do you?"

"Suppose not," Dom affirmed. "Poor Maggie. You'd better stay there with her. Don't bother coming back in this afternoon, but give me a call later and let me know how she is, OK?"

"Thanks, Dom. Will do," Lily said and hung up the phone.

Creeping to the top of the stairs she looked in on Maggie to check she was OK, found her sleeping and crept back down to the kitchen. She still couldn't get her head around the cowardice of Mark. It was one thing disliking confrontation, who doesn't, but to go without a word of explanation was not only spineless – it was cruel too. She contemplated calling his office and telling them there was some sort of family emergency, turned to go out to the hall, then remembered that his office number wouldn't be in redial now as she'd just called Dom.

"Bugger," she said and hunted round for the phone book. She couldn't find a directory, but came across Maggie's address book, so she flipped through that, hitting pay-dirt as soon as she turned to the *M* section. *Mark: Work.* A zero-one number – Dublin – obviously the office. Then, *Mark: Home.* A zero-two number –Cork. Never mind the office, she thought, I'll give his ma a call. Sitting in Maggie's favourite spot at the bottom of the stairs, she dialled the number. The phone rang for what seemed like an age before someone picked up and, in a breathless voice, repeated the number she had just dialled.

"Mrs Beyer?"

"Yes, yes. Speaking." She had a pleasant voice with a lovely Cork lilt.

"My name is Monica . . ." she groped for a surname, "Monica Ronayne from Spokes, Kennington, Cowdray. I need to contact Mark urgently but I seem to have mislaid his new number. I wonder if you could help me with that?"

"His *new* number?" she repeated. "I'm afraid I don't have that yet, Miss . . ."

"Ronayne," Lily repeated.

"I suppose you could always get him through the Melbourne office, but he's not due to arrive there till the day after tomorrow."

"Oh, right, right," Lily said a trace confused. "The Melbourne office. That would be Melbourne . . .?"

"Melbourne, Australia."

"Australia!?"

"Eh, yes," Mrs Beyer replied. "Eh . . . who did you say you were?"

Ignoring the question, Lily hung up after a perfunctory, "Thank you for your help, Mrs Beyer."

Australia! The bastard! The twenty-four-carat bastard had legged it to the other side of the world! That proved one thing to Lily. Mark Beyer must have known weeks ago that he intended to leave. You can't organise a transfer to the other side of the world in a couple of days. But why? What had he done? Why would he feel it necessary to relocate himself half a world away? It was a bit extreme. Then it occurred to her that maybe he hadn't relocated. Maybe it was just a business trip. Picking up the phone again, she dialled his office.

"Spokes, Kennington, Cowdray. How can I help yew?"

"Hello. My name is Monica Ronayne. I wonder could you tell me when Mark Beyer will be returning from the Melbourne office, please? I need to speak with him urgently, and seem to have mislaid his number."

"Mr Beyer? Oh, right, if you'd hold the line a moment, I'll check for yew."

She was entertained by a burst of Vivaldi's *Four Seasons* while she waited. Fair play to Spokes, Kennington, Cowdray, they played a better class of hold music. After twenty or so bars, she came back on the line.

"Mr Beyer's on a six-month secondment to Melbourne, Ms eh . . ."

"Ronayne," Lily repeated, not sure where she'd got the name from. "Well, thanks. I'll call Melbourne – would you have the number to hand?"

Paper rustled at the other end of the line then Miss Efficient reeled off the number.

"Thank you so much for your help," Lily gushed, then punched the air in triumph as she dropped the receiver back in its cradle.

At five thirty Lily climbed the stairs again. "I've found Mark," she said to a still half-asleep Maggie.

Maggie blinked and struggled into a sitting position, her back against the headboard. "You found him? Where?"

Lily sat down on the edge of the bed. "You're not going to believe this, kiddo."

Chapter 7

At the same time as Lily was revealing Mark's distant whereabouts to a stunned Maggie, Sally was moving into her new home. She'd suffered the usual guilt trip from her mother when she'd returned to the house to collect her suitcase, but got away without too much drama after promising to have Sunday lunch with her. She agreed to that only after she had discovered that James, Catherine and kids were also expected, confident that with her number-one son in attendance, Rhona would hardly even notice that her daughter was there.

The eight magenta silk cushions, purchased from an Indian interiors shop, added a touch of glamour to the monochrome living area, as did the lime-green rug she'd picked up in Habitat. In a fit of extravagance she'd also purchased a bold, colourful carborundum print she'd spied through the window when passing the Graphic Studio Gallery in Templebar, instantly recognising it as the work of Magda Mulligan, an up-and-coming artist she admired. She justified her recklessness on the grounds that it was an investment buy. With her new acquisitions in place, the loft felt almost like home. Next she made up her bed, struggling with the lilac, king-sized duvet cover, the way you do, and put fresh towels in the bathroom after unpacking her toiletries.

In the absence of her espresso machine she made a cafetière of coffee, then tore up some ciabatta to eat with a gorgeous lump of Brie she'd found in The Cheesemongers and, lighting the gas fire, she kicked off her shoes and curled up on the sofa. With the lack of a TV, or even a radio, the room was silent apart from a soft hiss of the fire, the double-glazed windows shutting out the traffic noise. She'd had a busy day with little time to dwell on thoughts of Charlie. Apart from the small lapse outside the café, that meant that he hadn't crossed her mind for a whole six hours, and she felt quite proud of herself.

"See! I can live without you," she said to the patch of bare white wall over the fireplace. "I don't need you, Charlie Penhaligan." This wasn't strictly true but she felt that if she told herself enough times it would become a fact. Speaking his name aloud was a mistake though. She was like a junkie fighting the need to shoot up, and her eye instantly shot to her mobile, though she resisted the urge to pick it up and dial his number.

One day at a time, she told herself, you can do this. Wondering why there was no Rejected Lovers Anonymous she could call for moral support.

Taking her mug and plate to the galley kitchen, she rinsed them under the tap and left them on the drainer. She tipped the coffee grounds down the sink and discovered a garbage-disposal unit which she played with for a couple of minutes, then washed out the cafetière, put the remaining cheese and bread away and wondered what to do with the rest of her evening. It was just past six thirty. Too early to go to bed. Charlie would be heading off to Soho House now for a few drinks before dinner. She wondered if he was alone.

No! Don't even think about Charlie. Find something to occupy your mind, she told herself. Be busy. That's the trick.

Dominic Heche had given her a pile of paperwork, to familiarise herself with the current state of play at Deadly Inc, so she spread it out on the coffee table, poured herself a glass of chilled wine from the fridge, thinking only briefly of Charlie as she took her first sip of the rather good Soave, then got down to work.

Maggie insisted that Lily go home that night.

"I'm fine, really," she'd protested and, after lots of are-you-sures Lily had reluctantly agreed.

She was worried by Maggie's complete change of humour. She seemed scarily calm and almost upbeat after the initial shock of discovering that the man she thought she might spend the rest of her life with had traipsed halfway around the world to get away from her.

In fact, being the pragmatist she was, it was just that detail that had brought Maggie to her senses. If he'd still been in town, or even in the country, there was still a possibility that he might come home, but with half a world between them, what was the point of even hoping? It gave the situation a sort of finality.

"You have to move on," she told her reflection in the bathroom mirror. "He doesn't want you." Then, in a fit of defiance, "You deserve better!"

It wasn't the first time Maggie had been dumped, though granted the last time it wasn't as serious a dumping; it was more a matter of principle. One does not expect a work colleague to steal your man, simply because she can, and that's exactly what Sally Gillespie had done to her: stolen Noel Percival out from under her nose. She'd been discreetly dating Noel for around six months when Sally had joined BBD&K as a copywriter. Noel, an art director, had been teamed up with Sally to work on a pitch to win the business of one of the major banks. It wouldn't have been so bad if he'd been straight with her, up front; it wasn't as though they were that serious. It was the underhandedness of it, of being the last one to find out, that had made her feel so stupid, so mortified

Noel had been completely smitten, but once Sally had tired of him, once the excitement had worn off, he was unceremoniously dumped too, which at the time had afforded Maggie a certain satisfaction. But she couldn't help but feel sorry for him. He was truly devastated. The episode didn't contribute to Sally's popularity at BBD&K and Sally didn't help herself either by virtue of the fact that she was totally career-orientated and enjoyed the company of men, eschewing camaraderie with her female colleagues. More galling was the fact that men were drawn to her like moths to a flame.

"Can you believe that he'd be so fucking gullible?" Maura Gill had commented to Maggie and Sarah when yet another poor sucker of their acquaintance had bitten the dust after succumbing to Sally's charms. "What's her bloody secret? She only has to toss her hair and they fall over themselves."

It was a mystery to Maggie too. She'd known only a few girls who had that X factor, whatever it was, that attracted men like a magnet, and some of them hadn't even been that special-looking either.

"Pheromones," Sarah said with authority . "It must be pheromones. I saw a programme on Channel 4 about it. Men are basically your primitive creatures, subconsciously searching for a mate to spread their seed, d'you see?"

"I'm with you so far," Maggie had said.

"Well, they get a whiff of these pheromones, and they're off. Can't help themselves, poor buggers."

"But don't we all secrete pheromones?" Maura had asked.

"Ah, that's the problem see. Some of these here pheromones are more potent than others, so yer one obviously has the industrial-strength ones."

"I think there's more to it than that," Maggie had replied, only half joking. "I think she's probably a witch and under that polished exterior, she has three breasts and 666 tattooed under her armpit."

"Well, there you are then," Sarah had said with an air of authority. "It's the three tits. You know what men are like with tits!"

And that was how Sally Gillespie had acquired her "Spawn of the Devil" tag.

Maggie was up bright and early the following morning –

showered, dressed and ready for work by eight-thirty. She'd lain awake staring at the ceiling in between bouts of fitful sleep throughout the night, probably due to the hours she'd already slept during the day, but it gave her time to think. She hated the concept of being a victim. Though by nature a sympathetic sort of person, it irritated her no end to listen to people whingeing on relentlessly about stuff, feeling a week was possibly the maximum time permissible to whine to your friends. If she were to avoid victimhood, she knew that she had to move on. For whatever reason, Mark had bailed out, that was a fact, but just because she had decided to move on, it didn't make it any easier to deal with. That established, she decided that she'd keep it to herself from here on in. As far as any of her friends were concerned (perhaps with the exception of Lily who knew her too well to swallow it) Mark had gone, so what, she'd live.

On the upside there was no one banging on the bathroom door urging her to hurry up. The loo seat was firmly down, and she didn't have to dry herself on a hand towel because Mark had used both bath towels and left them lying damp in a heap on the floor. But neither was there anyone to sidle up behind her, slide his arms around her waist and kiss her on the back of the neck as she stood at the dressing-table applying her make-up; no one to rub his morning erection against her and try and persuade her to come back to bed.

Bugger! This moving-on business was going to be harder than she thought.

It occurred to her that she should phone her mother. She and Mark had been due to drive down to the West for the Bank Holiday weekend, but now she wasn't sure she could face the post-mortem and the questions. Fond as her mother was of Mark, she was fiercely protective of her children and she knew that once Anna discovered the circumstances of his departure, to her Mark would become the kin of Osama Bin Laden. The Prince of Darkness.

I'll make up an excuse, she thought. I'll say Mark's got the flu and I have to stay and mind him. She dismissed that. It was only a short-term solution. Best to be up front. Tell her mother the truth. Tell her the truth but be resolute in her decision to cancel the weekend visit. "I'm not feeling great. Lily's looking after me." A brave I'll-be-fine kind of thing. She bit the bullet and picked up the phone.

When she walked into the office at twenty past nine with two takeaway lattes for herself and Tom, reception was empty, but through Dom's open office door she spied him, Lily, Leo and Tom talking quietly together. It didn't take Einstein to guess who was the subject of their confab, as the moment Tom caught sight of her, all conversation eased and they all looked very tense.

"It's OK," she said, standing in the doorway. "I'm not going to throw a wobbly or anything. He's gone. Big deal. I'm fine."

"Are you sure you wouldn't rather be at home today?" Leo asked. "Under the . . . em . . . the circumstances."

"No, Leo, I'd rather be here. Tom and I have a brief to work on, remember?"

"Ah, look," Tom started, "sure, that can wait."

"No, it can't. Come on, Tom. We've got work to do."

Tom gave the others a shrug, then ambled towards her

in his usual laid-back manner, hands dug deep into his pockets.

"Want me to sort him out for you?" he asked with a lopsided grin on his face, and Maggie laughed.

"Let's not go there," she said, grinning at the mental image of Tom, her gentle giant, sending Mark over the rooftops, Superman style, with one swat of his huge mitt.

The others visibly relaxed then, and Maggie and Tom wandered off to their office. Tom, being the gentleman that he was, didn't make any further reference to the Mark situation and they got straight down to work.

I-Sport was to be aimed at the eighteen to twenty-five market and the client wanted to convey a young sporty image. They wanted to use a young, up-and-coming soccer star or athlete to front the campaign, and wanted to put across the message that I-Sport was basically the best thing since sliced bread; to suggest that it prevents dehydration, keeps energy levels high, but above all, that it's cool to drink it. The campaign was to cover both print and broadcast media and had a substantial budget.

They discussed various ideas and came up with a few possible concepts, while agreeing that with the World Cup coming up in June, a soccer player would be more appropriate than an athlete, and definitely an *Irish* Soccer player. The question was, who? Although they had a decent budget, it still ruled out a lot of the obvious names who wouldn't get out of bed for less than a minor lotto win. Then Tom suggested Gavin O'Connor.

Maggie recognised the name, and had a vague notion that he played for one of the big UK Premiership clubs such as Man United or Liverpool, but that was about it.

"What's he like?" she asked. "Is he cute, as in photogenic?"

Tom shrugged. "My Jodie seems to think so. Has posters of him all over her bedroom walls," he said. Jodie was Tom's thirteen-year-old daughter. "He's a cracking player. Consistently kept his place on the first team this season. He's only twenty-one, but he's already got five caps so Mick's bound to select him for Japan."

"How do you reckon he'd be in front of a camera?" she asked.

Tom leaned back in his chair and laced his fingers behind his head. "I saw him on the *Soccer Show* a while back. He was good, relaxed, funny." He paused then wrinkled his brow. "What d'you think?"

"Great," Maggie said. "He could be a natural. Let's see if we can get hold of a tape of the show."

He laughed then. "*No problemo.* At this stage I'd nearly qualify as a feckin' sponsor. The lovely Jodie has the tape in her collection along with every poster printed, and every piece of merchandising with his gob on it."

They worked for the rest of the morning on various concepts, eliminating some, which left them with two fairly different approaches. Tom logged on to the Man U website and printed out a photo of Gavin O'Connor, and Maggie had to admit that he'd definitely appeal to their target market, both male and female, if for very different reasons.

After lunch Maggie had to go to the studio to record the holiday promo and a couple of other radio ads, so the afternoon flew by. She got back to the office just before five and found Lily shutting down her computer and getting ready to leave for the mandatory Friday night scoop in O'Neill's.

"So how are you, kiddo?" Lily asked, trying to sound casual.

Maggie stopped and thought about the question. Under the circumstances, it wasn't your usual "How are you?" meant as a greeting. It was a genuine, "How are you feeling?" question. She smiled at her friend. Basically she felt like shit, but on the upside her radio ads were all up to date and in the can, and the pitch for I-Sport was well on the way. It was all relative.

"Great," she said, lightly.

"No, I mean *really*," Lily persisted.

"On a scale of one to ten?" she asked.

"On a scale of one to ten."

Maggie made a calculation, the upside weighed against the downside of feeling rejected, worthless and emotionally spent. There was no point trying to kid Lily.

"On a scale of one to ten?" she repeated. "I'd say somewhere around a minus two."

Chapter 8

The usual Friday night crowd turned up at O'Neill's. It was a tradition that had started the week that Deadly Inc had opened, though on that particular Friday night there had been just Dom, Leo, Maggie and Tom to represent the creatives, along with Willy Dunning who *was* the accounts department; Neville Greene, finished art; Magnus Nutter, the production manager; Elaine Joyce, media; and Paul Brody the account director (though Dom and Leo also dealt with clients). Not forgetting Lily, PA, cum receptionist, cum general fixer extraordinaire, who Dom had brought with him from Dunne & Pointer. It was a whole other ball game now and, though still small by some standards, the staff at Deadly Inc had more than quadrupled, but as a company it still held onto Dom and Leo's original vision that it be a creatively led agency, an inspiring and innovative place to work.

As usual, some stayed for just the one while others made a night of it. Maggie was in a mood for drowning her sorrows. This acting as if she didn't give a toss was exhausting and she had, as her father would put it, the *goo* on her for drink, mainly to numb the pain. Being mindful however of how polluted she'd felt the previous day, she stayed away from the tequila, sticking to Budweiser, and pacing herself.

Unusually, by around seven-thirty, she seriously wanted to go home. It was obvious that everyone knew, and they were either studiously avoiding all contact or chattering like manic depressives on speed. Now and again the word "Australia" followed by an exclamation mark and panicky urges to *shush*, filtered to within her range of hearing. Lily was clinging to her side like a limpet and she felt that everyone was covertly watching and waiting for her to . . . what? Break down and weep? Do the hair-ripping and teeth-gnashing thing? Spontaneously combust? It was both gruesome and uncomfortable.

"I have to get out of here," she said to Lily. "I feel like the fecking cabaret. Everyone's expecting me to throw a fit or something."

Lily tried to laugh it off. "Piss off! You're just being paranoid."

"So you're telling me they don't know?"

She shrugged. "So what if they do?"

"Because it's humiliating!" Maggie hissed.

"Look, kiddo, it's bound to get round sooner or later. You know what the office is like. Best to get it over with, I say. It'll be old news after the weekend."

"You think?"

Lily gave her a positive nod. "Of course, it will. Anyway,

I never liked him. He was a tight-fisted bollox and you're better off without him."

That was news to Maggie. Not the tight-fisted part, she had no illusions about Mark's carefulness concerning money, it was legend, but the fact that Lily had just said that she'd never liked him.

Dom came over with a refill each then, so she didn't get the chance to pursue the matter. He and Lily started talking about the Paddy's Day fireworks for some reason but Maggie tuned out.

True, she and Mark had never socialised with her friends as a couple, and she rarely if ever mixed with his friends. They'd tried but he thought her mates were all smart-arsed, arty, dope-smoking morons (his words) and on the few occasions that she and Mark had gone out to dinner with his friends, she'd spent the evening bored witless as they made in-jokes about the firm and discussed property prices and matters fiscal. Did all accountants do that, she wondered? Did they, when in close social proximity, transmogrify into the most boring pompous group of individuals on the planet? It was perverse. Mark, on his own, was funny and sweet and romantic when the mood took him, and they had great sex. But on the other hand, neither liked the other's taste in music. He preferred foreign art-house cinema (though she sometimes suspected his enthusiasm was more to do with one-upmanship with his friends as to who could read the most obscure meaning into the story) while she enjoyed anything except slash films and sci-fi, having a particular passion for old black and white movies with Humphrey Bogart, Fred and Ginger, Gene Kelly or Judy

Garland. In fact, when she thought about it, other than sex, they had little in common, and even that had been on the scarce side since well before Christmas, only briefly reappearing during their ski trip to Andorra. She'd put it down to pressure of work, the end of the tax year etc, but now she wondered. Maybe he'd just gone off her? But then again, taking into account his appetite for matters carnal, it was more likely that he was having his fun with someone else. That realisation stung like vinegar in a paper-cut and rekindled her anger. Even though the subject had come up, until then she'd been in serious denial about the possibility. How dare he? How could he? She felt a stab of jealousy at the thought of Mark with someone else. Had they done it in her bed? Of course technically it wasn't her bed, it was his, but did that make it any the less despicable?

"So what do you think, Maggie?" Dom was looking at her waiting for an answer.

"Think?"

"About Saturday night?"

"The fireworks," Lily urged. "We'd get a great view from the roof of the office if you're interested. Dom and Leo are bringing their kids down."

"Oh, I don't know," Maggie said, desperately searching for an excuse. "I was going to go down home for the weekend." Only a white lie, but watching pyrotechnics, however spectacular, wasn't high on her list of must-do's right now. Putting on a brave face was taking it out of her and she was more into lying in bed, shutting out the world, and being miserable in her time off.

Dom nodded. "Well, if you change your mind, and you fancy the company, you know where we'll be."

"Thanks," Maggie said. "I'll bear that in mind."

Lily and a few others were all for making a night of it, but Maggie was no longer in the mood, so she took her leave of them and headed out to find a cab. The rain had set in as predicted and the evening air temperature had dropped to single figures. Digging her hands into her pockets, she set off towards O'Connell Bridge in the hope of catching an empty taxi on its way back to the rank, but the rain ruled out that possibility and there wasn't an empty cab to be had.

Great, she thought, on top of everything I'll get fecking pneumonia.

Standing in a taxi queue in the rain for half an hour didn't appeal, so she set off on foot towards home. The wind picked up as she passed Christchurch and the rain was blowing into her face now. She felt grim and miserable and regretted the fact that she was sober. Alcohol-induced oblivion seemed the more comfortable option by far, except for the resulting liver damage, that is. The rain suddenly increased in ferocity, a veritable monsoon downpour apart from the temperature, then a bus drove by, drenching her with spray. She let out a frustrated groan then, bizarrely, Gene Kelly came to mind and she laughed out loud.

"Sing-in' in the rain . . . I'm sing-in' in the rain!"

She skipped along the pavement, sloshing through the surface water, her feet soaked. Lamppost coming up, so she grabbed hold of it and attempted, not very skilfully, to swing around it.

Then one foot on, one foot off the pavement in the gutter. *Slosh, slosh, slosh . . .*

She stopped dead in her tracks. Unlike Gene Kelly, she couldn't say that the sun was in her heart, and she certainly wasn't ready for love . . .

The rain was running down her face and she was soaked to the skin. "Shit! I'm going mad!" she said aloud. "I'm going fucking mental." Any casual observer would have agreed in all probability, and a saying of her grandmother's came to mind. Something about a fool not having the sense to get in out of the rain. Her gran had a pathological aversion to getting rained on, blaming it for every illness and death in the town.

"Get a grip," she said aloud, and set off again, then about ten yards ahead of her she saw a taxi setting down a passenger, so she took off at a squelch and caught him before he drove away. He gave her dripping hair and soaking clothes the once-over, his eyes darting dubiously to the upholstery, then obviously felt sorry for her.

"Where to, love?"

"Gray Street, please," she said, gratefully sliding into the back seat.

"Terrible night," the cab driver said.

"Yes," she agreed, thinking, if you only knew the half of it!

It was only a short taxi-hop from High Street to Gray Street but, with her grandmother's words still in her mind, she was thankful to be in out of the rain.

"This is fine," she instructed, as the cab turned the corner of her street, and she handed him a five-euro note, indebted that he'd picked her up at all.

The rain had dwindled to a light patter as she clambered out of the cab, her wet clothes sticking to her –

isn't it always the way? – and as she rummaged in her sodden bag for her keys, Aiden's door flew open and her mother strode out.

"Maggie! Pet! You're soaked!" and despite the waterlogged clothes, she drew Maggie into a fierce bear hug.

Maggie groaned inwardly. It wasn't that she had any problem with her mother, in fact they had a really good relationship, but she couldn't face her right now. She wanted, like Garbo, to be alone. How could she wallow in misery and self-pity in front of her mother?

"Hello, Mum. What are you doing here?" was all she managed to bleat, before Anna set off on one, fussing about her catching cold and needing a hot whiskey to warm her through.

Aiden was leaning against the open doorway arms folded across his chest, observing the scene, a bemused look on his face.

As Anna hustled Maggie in her own front door she turned to him.

"Thanks a million, Aiden. You're *very* good."

"Any time, Anna," he said. "See you soon."

Anna?

Chapter 9

"So what *are* you doing here, Mum?" Maggie asked as she rubbed her hair with a dry towel.

"Do I need an excuse to come and see my own daughter?" Anna asked, hunting in the cupboards for whiskey.

"Top right," Maggie directed, adding, "It's lovely to see you, Mum, but there was no need for you to traipse all the way up here. I'm fine, *really*."

"I must get my case out of the car," she said, as if she hadn't heard. Then she picked out the bottle of ten-year-old single malt. "Haven't you anything else? It's a sin to use single malt for hot toddies."

"Sorry. That's it . . ." She was grateful that Mark hadn't taken it.

Anna raised an eyebrow, then gave a little, 'Oh well!' shrug and put the bottle on the worktop.

"But, Mum . . ."

"Better go up and have a hot shower and get out of

those wet clothes," Anna cut in. "You know your grandmother's feelings about getting wet in the rain."

Realising that argument was futile, Maggie gave in and did as she was told. When she returned to the kitchen fifteen minutes later, warmed and dry in her jammies and dressing-gown, Anna was sitting at the kitchen table sipping from a glass of hot whiskey, a large suitcase at her feet. She looked miles away, deep in thought, though as soon as she became aware of her daughter's presence, she got up and, after bringing the kettle back up to the boil, poured water over the whiskey and sugar which she had ready in a glass on the counter-top.

"He buggered off to Australia," Maggie said as she took the hot toddy from her mother. "With some Australian slut for all I know." She sat down at the table.

"Australia!" Anna pursed her lips. "I never liked him . . . he always struck me as the shifty type."

Maggie couldn't help but laugh, so Anna was forced to revise her last statement. "Oh all right. So I was taken in by him too, but it doesn't change the fact that you deserve better."

"Amen to that," Maggie agreed.

"Did you say he ran off with someone?" Anna asked, as if it had just registered.

Maggie shrugged. "I'm only surmising. Why else would the spineless git feel it necessary to split to the other side of the world, for God's sake?"

Anna sighed. "I don't know. Men continue to be a mystery to me." She stared into her drink again, as if searching for some inspiration. "So how are you *really*?" she asked after a pause.

Maggie shrugged. "Up and down. I only found out about two days ago, so I guess it's only just sinking in."

She nodded. "Understandable. You'll get over it though. Better you found out now rather than a couple of years down the line."

"I suppose so," Maggie agreed. "It was just the shock. I mean, I'd no idea. It makes me feel such an eejit."

Anna frowned. "Rubbish! He's the eejit. And believe me you're better off without him."

"Funny, Lily said that."

"And she's right. You young ones have it all sorted out," she said. "Not like in my day. You've got choices. You don't need a man to fulfil your expectations, the way my generation did. Back in the sixties all we expected out of life was to get a good husband who'd look after us, and as for going to college . . ." She made a loud '*phwah*' sound. "Your grandfather thought it was a waste of money to educate girls."

Maggie smiled. "But you did all right though."

Anna, who'd been staring into the bottom of her glass, looked up, then gave a shrug. "Depends what you mean by all right."

"Well, you've got a good marriage. You're well off. You have a nice life."

"Nice." Anna gave a rueful smile. "*Nice* . . . that about sums it up."

Maggie felt a stab of alarm. "But you got what you wanted out of life, didn't you?"

Anna drained her glass then placed it carefully back on the table. "I got what I *expected*. As for what I wanted, well, that's a whole other story."

"I don't understand."

Anna sighed. "Maggie, I'm fifty-four years old. My generation were the children of the sixties, for God's sake. People like Bob Dylan, Marianne Faithful, John Lennon, David Bowie, Mick Jagger." She counted out the names on her fingers. "My contemporaries were protesting against the Vietnam war, nuclear weapons. Experimenting with drugs and sex, taking the hippie trail to India, chilling out at Woodstock and Hyde Park, and what was I doing?" She didn't wait for a reply. "I was at home in Westport serving behind the counter of a chemist shop, and sneaking out to the Sunday night hop because your grandfather didn't approve of dances."

Maggie didn't know what to say. She'd never seen her mother like this, but it occurred to her that she'd never thought of her in the same breath as the likes of Mick Jagger, David Bowie, or Marianne Faithful either. Anna was . . . well, Anna was Mum.

"But you met Dad. You'd never have met Dad if you'd gone away," she said, making a desperate attempt to restore the status quo.

Anna leaned out of her chair and grabbed the whiskey bottle which was just within her reach on the worktop by the kettle. "Well, lucky me!" She said, making no attempt to conceal the irony, then poured a healthy dollop into her glass.

"But . . ."

"But nothing," Anna insisted. "I wanted to travel, Mags. I wanted to see the world. Maureen O'Connell and Deirdre Keogh were let go. They went to London. They were in the thick of it. Carnaby Street, the King's Road, the whole shebang. Deirdre's something big at the BBC now and Maureen's married to that chap with the beard who does the gardening on BBC2. And then Maddie McGreal and Davina Browne went out to San Francisco, met up with a hippie crowd there and they went off to India and Nepal . . . they asked me to go with them, you know?" She paused to take a sip of her drink. "I just feel like I've missed out, you see. I'm well over three quarters through my life and what have I done with it? Married at twenty, four kids by the time I was twenty-five. And who am I? All I am is Maggie Fortune's mother or Phoebe Carley's granny, or Dan Fortune's bloody wife."

Then seeing the shocked expression on Maggie's gob, quickly added, "Oh, I don't regret having you, Mags. I don't regret my kids, but Maureen O'Connell has a family, and Deirdre. Maddie doesn't because she's a lesbian, and Davina became a Buddhist nun, but that's beside the point. I *could* have gone. If I'd had the courage, I could have *done* something with my life. I could've gone, *despite* your grandfather."

Maggie reached for the whiskey bottle and topped up her glass. "So why didn't you?"

Anna sighed. "Because I was a coward. I was afraid of your grandfather. . ." She shook her head, "No. Let's call a spade a spade. I was just *afraid*."

"But you're happy with your life now?" Maggie said, the air of desperation still apparent.

"That depends on what you mean by *now*?" Anna said.

Maggie was at a loss. She thought the question quite straightforward. "You're happy with your life now." She was finding her mother's weird mood frustrating. *Jesus!*

She's supposed to be cheering me up, she thought. "Well . . . *now*. At the present time. As we speak." She bit back her irritation. "You're happy *now*."

Anna stared at her daughter for a long moment then smiled. "Well, as you ask, Margaret, no, I'm not happy with my life *now*. I haven't been happy for some time. That's why I've taken steps to remedy the situation."

"I don't understand."

"It's simple enough. If you'll excuse the cliché: '*Today is the first day of the rest of my life.*'"

Maggie stared at her mother, none the wiser, and Anna, equally frustrated by Maggie's apparent lack of understanding spelt it out.

"I've left your father, Maggie. I need to take time out for *me*. I need to *find* myself."

Maggie's jaw hit the floor.

Chapter 10

They shared Maggie's old pine bed in the spare bedroom that night, there being no other option. Anna, who never had trouble sleeping, dropped off almost as soon as her head hit the pillow, but Maggie lay awake for ages. In part, because her mother's snoring was epic, but mainly it was the bombshell that had plummeted down on her, temporarily removing any thoughts of Mark from her mind. She'd had no idea that her parents were having problems. But then she hadn't had a clue that her fella was about to decamp to another continent either.

She thought back to her last visit home. It was Christmas, and Mark had gone down to his mother's in Cork. (She'd never met his mother, and he rarely visited her, but he always made the trip at Christmas.) Things had seemed normal as far as she could remember. Lucy, her younger sister, was up from Kilkenny with her partner Jack Carley and their daughter Phoebe. Danny, her brother, was home from Boston, and Jonjo over from

London. She hadn't noticed any tensions, but then her father was hardly top of the class where communication skills were concerned, more used to dealing with large animals than he was people.

They'd all dutifully traipsed off to Midnight Mass then opened their presents as was their custom, then Anna had helped Lucy get Santa ready for three-year-old Phoebe. The following morning was taken up with preparing the Christmas dinner, including a turkey the size of a small goat, then they'd all slumped, comatose, around the TV afterwards, the way you do, nothing unusual there. Mary-Ann, her mother's sister, and her husband, Willie, had come round that evening in time for the turkey sandwiches, Christmas cake and Quality Street, and they'd all drunk too much and ended up having a sing-song, all encouraged to do their party pieces. It had been good old-fashioned craic, the kind you can only have without embarrassment amongst your own. On Saint Stephen's Day her father, Uncle Willie and the lads had gone off shooting, then the pub, not returning until supper time, and her mother and the girls had gone out for a long walk along the beach.

It struck her then that this was the norm, but the norm translated into her parents doing most things separately. Her father went shooting, fishing, racing and his poker school. Her mother liked cards too, her game being bridge, but Maggie wasn't sure if she still played. She was mixed up with the drama group, but it was at least five years since Maggie had been home to see a production, so she wasn't sure if she was still involved in that either. She baked cakes for the Country Market, a local cooperative of women who sold produce in the town hall every

Thursday morning, and as far as Maggie was aware, that was it. She felt a stab of guilt that she hadn't shown more interest in her mother's life; that she hadn't noticed that she was unhappy. She wondered what had triggered off her mother's decision to leave? Had they had an almighty row despite Anna's denials? In a funny way, that thought cheered her. People had blazing rows and stormed out from time to time; it didn't automatically mean they couldn't sort things out. Her parents had been married for thirty-four years. You don't walk out after thirty-four years . . . do you?

Her mother had resolutely refused to talk about it, firmly telling Maggie that she wanted to look forward not back, but when pressed did admit that she hadn't actually told Maggie's father yet – "at least not in so many words".

"How do you mean?" Maggie had asked, getting an uncomfortable feeling in her gut that Anna had behaved exactly as Mark had, and done a runner.

"I told him I was off up to see you for an extended stay," she said. "I filled the freezer full of frozen dinners from Tesco, and left him a list of bills he had to pay."

"And that was it?" Maggie asked. "You'd no row or anything? You didn't actually say you were *leaving* him?" She felt a surge of hope.

"I told him I was going," she said. "That I'd had enough. I told him what I told you, that I needed some space. That I need to find myself."

"And how did he react?"

"He said he was off to see Monty French's new bull."

"Are you sure he was listening to you? Are you sure he understood what you meant?"

Anna gave a shrug. "Who knows? He had his head stuck in the *Irish Times*."

She wouldn't discuss the matter further, changing the subject to what she intended to do with her future, which involved getting some sort of job, taking up new hobbies, such as yoga or kick-boxing, and . . . oh yes . . . *finding herself.*

"Um . . . what kind of job did you have in mind?" Maggie had asked.

Anna shrugged. "I don't mind. Anything to earn a crust."

Maggie was dubious. She couldn't ever remember her mother having a real job. She'd always stayed home to look after them. "But what kind of work would you be . . . I mean , what are you –"

Anna, sensing her daughter's scepticism, cut in. "You mean what skills do I have?"

Maggie nodded, uncomfortable with the implication. "Well, yes."

"Let's see." Anna counted off on her fingers. "I've got my European computer driving licence" – that was news to Maggie – "and I could do retailing – I've helped Monica Roland out in her second-hand clothes shop over Christmas, and I worked in the chemist. Or I could do reception work," she said, warming to the subject. "And I can knit. I could knit jumpers and sell them." She paused, and then added with a wicked gleam in her eye, "Oh yes, and I've run the business side of your father's veterinary practice for the last thirty years. Do you reckon that'd count as management skills?"

Chastened, Maggie had made them a cup of hot chocolate each before they retired to bed.

At four a.m., unable to cope with Anna's snoring any longer, Maggie got up and, in the absence of a sofa to curl up on, sought sanctuary in the mound of discarded bedding still lying on her bedroom floor. Even with both doors firmly shut she could still hear Anna snoring, but she managed to doze off nonetheless, though not before vowing to go out first thing to buy a new bed.

Sally was having a sleepless night too, lying awake thinking of Charlie Penhaligan.

She'd slept late on the Friday morning and had intended to eat a leisurely lunch then do some recreational retail therapy in the afternoon, but her plans had been scuppered when she'd bumped into her mother coming out of Laura Ashley on Grafton Street in the company of her sister-in-law. Catherine had invited her to join them for lunch and, unable to ignore the pleading look in her eyes, Sally had agreed. She liked Catherine and, after the previous endless evening of solitude, was glad of the company, the only downside being Rhona.

Sally didn't have any friends in Dublin. Acquaintances, yes, but friends, no. Particularly no female friends. Women, for some reason she couldn't fathom, didn't seem to like her, but then she wasn't all that partial to women herself, and she'd had never had a close girlfriend. Not even at school. She'd been the dumpy, spotty child with a squint and crooked teeth in primary school, whom the other kids had picked on. Early on she'd learned to be defensive and keep to herself, but the worm had turned when, at the age of fourteen, she'd suddenly blossomed. She'd lost the puppy fat, surgery had straightened the squint, orthodontics the teeth, the skin had cleared up, her hair had gone lusciously blonde and her figure had developed curvaceously. It was the ultimate revenge. While she metamorphosed into a beauty, the others had developed zits and greasy hair and, with her long blonde hair and air of haughtiness, the boys were falling over themselves to know her. And it had been the same ever since.

They had lunch at Eden, in Templebar, after which Rhona insisted that Sally show her the loft. Rhona liked the idea of a loft. Her friend Dorothy had a daughter in New York who was married to someone in Wall Street who lived in a loft in the East Village, so a loft was very acceptable. She was a little disappointed when she saw it however – no change there then – thinking Great George's Street not quite as up-market as say, Templebar, or the new Financial Services area on the river.

Sally had explained patiently that Great George's Street was all that was on offer, and way better than the shoebox she'd viewed in Ballsbridge. Then Rhona, true to form, started on about Ballsbridge being a much better area, until Catherine pointed out how close the loft was to Grafton Street, and that seemed to do the trick. Sally had made coffee then and Rhona criticised first the china then the décor, suggesting that a bit of fitted Wilton wouldn't go amiss, then pointedly looking at her watch told Catherine that it was time to leave. Too irritated to resurrect her plan for retail therapy, Sally had spent what remained of the day and the rest of the evening in the company of the demon drink and Dom's paperwork.

Lying awake, staring at the ceiling and thinking of

Charlie, she swore that she would never let it happen again. If love could make you feel this bad, what was the point?

"Never again," she repeated to herself, deep down aware that there was a flaw in the plan, knowing that if Charlie as much as crooked his finger, despite herself she'd be back to him like a shot. She'd dropped off to sleep eventually, but couldn't even escape him in her dreams.

Chapter 11

Maggie awoke to the smell of rashers grilling and the dull mumble of talk radio coming from downstairs. For a moment, disorientated, she thought it was Mark, then had a reality check as she rolled over and whacked her elbow off the varnished wood floorboards. She was stiff, sore and groggy from interrupted sleep, and had thoughts of crawling back to bed in the spare room, but the smell of bacon got the better of her so she padded downstairs instead.

Anna was fully dressed in jeans, runners and a white T-shirt, hair pinned up in a knot on top of her head. She looked as fresh as a daisy.

"Tea or coffee, pet?" she asked, as she popped two slices of bread into the toaster.

"Um . . . tea, please," Maggie replied, sliding a chair out and sitting at the table. "How long have you been up?"

"Oh, a good while. You'd nothing in for breakfast so I

went out to the shop. I must say the one round the corner's very handy. Aiden told me about it last night."

"Aiden?" Maggie was confused until she remembered that he'd sheltered Anna in his house while she was waiting.

"Nice fella. He's a photographer, you know. Just back from the States." The toast popped up, so Anna put in two more slices. "He's single, had a three-year relationship with a model in New York, but it ended last year." She pulled out the grill-pan and turned the rashers. "His folks come from Galway," she continued, "and – small world – his uncle Jarlath was in Galway University the same time as your father – they must have done pre-med together but then he went on to do dentistry. He has two sisters, one married with three kids . . ." Holding a piece of bacon, speared on the end of the fork, in mid-air, squinting at the ceiling in concentration, she paused. "The elder one I think, but I'm not sure. Anyway . . . where was I? Oh yes, his father's dead." She blessed herself with the impaled rasher. "God rest him, and his mother married again. He doesn't much like the stepfather but he keeps the fair side out for his mother's sake."

"How did you find all that out?" Maggie asked amazed. The only information she had gleaned since he'd moved in two months previously was that his name was Aiden, and she'd only gathered that the day before yesterday.

"Sure, didn't we have a long chat last night while I was waiting for you."

"Chat? Sounds more like an interrogation," Maggie muttered.

"So what happened to you last night?" Anna asked,

ignoring the remark, putting the rashers onto the plate while simultaneously pouring boiling water into the teapot.

"Umm . . . I couldn't sleep." She groped for a polite way to put it, then gave up. "Honestly, Mum, no offence, but you snore like a bloody Harley Davidson."

"That'll have been the whiskey. Whiskey always makes me snore." She put the plate of rashers and toast on the table along with the teapot and sat down. "So what are you going to do today?"

Maggie reached for a slice of toast. "I thought I'd buy a new bed and something to sit on," she said, "seeing as Mark took the sofas. What about you?"

"Well, I'm going to get my hair done, and maybe buy some new clothes," Anna said. "What do you think about colour?"

"Colour? As in . . .?"

Anna slipped the pins from her hair and it tumbled down onto her shoulders. "I thought some red highlights, and maybe have a few inches or so lopped off."

"Oh, your hair." For as long as Maggie could remember, Anna had worn her hair twisted up in a knot on top of her head. It was thick and, once upon a time, brown, but now it was flecked liberally with grey. "Um, yes, why not?"

"And I thought I'd go into Brown Thomas and get some advice on make-up too while I'm at it."

"Make-up!?" Maggie was stunned. Her mother only ever wore a scrape of lipstick, and maybe a flick of mascara if she was going out.

"And why not?" Anna asked. "You young ones don't have the monopoly on grooming, you know. Besides, if I'm to get a job, I'll need to look the part."

"A job?" Maggie was having difficulty stringing a sentence of more than two words together.

"I told you last night, pet. Anyway, I'll need a job if I'm to pay you rent."

"Rent?" She was at it again, but her average had just halved. She became aware that her mouth was agape too, adding to her complete-moron look.

Anna's rueful gaze confirmed her suspicion that her expression had that moronic edge to it. "I'll have to pay rent," her mother explained. "I mean, with Mark gone you'll need help with the mortgage. Don't worry, I'll pay my way."

"Don't be silly, Mum! I can't take rent from you."

Anna stared at her, chewing on her bacon. Maggie was getting panicky. All this talk of rent and jobs sounded very permanent.

"Look, Maggie. I know you're having difficulty with this, but whether I live with you or somewhere else, the fact is, I've left your father. From now on I'm an independent single woman, and the way I see it, better the devil you know. You wouldn't want to live with some stranger, would you?"

Maggie, still speechless, gawped at her.

"And if you're worried that I'll cramp your style," Anna went on, "forget it. Look on me as a housemate. You ceased being my responsibility the day you turned eighteen."

"But . . ."

Anna stood up and, taking a last gulp of tea, said, "I'm just popping next door. I need to have a quick word with Aiden. If you're ready for the off in –" she glanced at her watch, "say, fifteen minutes, I'll give you a lift into town."

With that, she gave her daughter a peck on the cheek, bustled out of the room and a moment later the front door slammed.

Maggie sat at the table in a state of shock, processing the information. Her mother was moving in. She intended to get a job and live in Dublin. She was serious when she said that she'd walked out on her marriage.

Leaping up from the table, Maggie ran to the phone in the hall, and dialled the home number. It rang for an age then voice-mail kicked in and she heard her mother's voice asking the caller to leave a name and number. Hanging up, she punched in her father's mobile. That too connected directly to voice-mail. She left a message asking him to call her urgently on her mobile, repeating the number in case he didn't have it to hand, which was perfectly possible seeing as he never phoned her anyway. Next she punched in Lucy's Kilkenny number, but her sister too was unavailable. She dithered for a moment about leaving a message, but demurred – hardly the information you want to hear on voice-mail. She hung up. Why was no one ever at the end of a phone when you needed them?

Calm down, she told herself, it's her mid-life crisis thing. It'll blow over. It has to. She wondered if her mother was taking HRT. She'd heard of women going a bit dotty during the menopause, but the hormone therapy was supposed to fix that. Then again maybe she *was* taking it, stuffing herself full of synthetic hormones – she'd also read in *Marie Claire* once that some women's libido went into overdrive when they took it. She shook her head to get rid of that thought. That was definitely more information than she needed and she had that sense of panic again. What if Anna started chasing after toy boys? How sad was that? She shook her head again. Don't be an eejit, she admonished herself, chill out. She's a mature adult. She knows what she's doing.

But that didn't help, even though Anna seemed perfectly together and not in the least bit manic.

It'll blow over, she repeated. Give her ten days and she'll get it out of her system . . . particularly when she can't find a job.

Still not convinced, but coming round to the idea, she headed upstairs for a shower.

By the time she was drying her hair and her mother had returned from her "quick word" with Aiden, she felt calmer, and fairly convinced that within a couple of weeks things would be back to normal. Just play along, she told herself, knowing that opposition would only bring out her mother's stubborn side.

With an agreement to hook up for a bite to eat at around two thirty at Café en Seine on Dawson Street, Anna dropped Maggie off on College Green. Maggie watched as she disappeared into the flow of traffic, mildly surprised that her mother appeared to have no problem with city driving.

As she wandered up Grafton Street, past the Brown Thomas department store, towards Saint Stephen's Green, she remembered the Saturday morning she and Mark had been in Brown Thomas's electrical department, looking at espresso machines. She felt a brief stab of sadness followed by a sharp surge of anger at the way he'd handled things.

If he was so afraid of confrontation, the least he could have done would have been to leave her a letter of explanation; feeble and cowardly, but better than nothing. But for Lily she wouldn't even have been aware that he was in Australia right now, and that made her feel foolish and her anger increased. *Hold on to the anger* she thought. *Hold on to the anger*. It was preferable to self-pity, to grief and, most of all, preferable to the empty feeling of missing him.

After visiting Habitat, FOKO and several other places across town, she finally settled on a smart-looking and (bearing in mind that she also needed a sofa) not too expensive bed in Argos. It had brushed steel ends and a comfy mattress, the only downside being that, because of the Paddy's Day bank holiday, they couldn't deliver until Tuesday. The girl in the store was very helpful however when Maggie explained her problem, suggesting that she buy an inflatable mattress which came complete with foot pump, to tide her over, adding that deflated it stored neatly under the bed and was very useful for those unexpected visitors. With memories of the hard bedroom floor fresh in her mind, mainly because of the sore spot just below her left shoulder-blade, Maggie purchased the inflatable mattress.

Her phone went off as she was leaving the Jervis Centre. It was Lily.

"How's it going, kiddo?"

"You don't want to know," Maggie replied.

A sharp intake of breath at the other end of the phone. "You didn't hear from that wanker?"

"No, but when I got home last night, my mother was

85

there. She's just walked out on my father after thirty-four years, in order to *find herself*."

"You're kidding!"

"'Fraid not."

It being close to two o'clock, they met up at Café en Seine and over a couple of lattes Maggie filled Lily in on her mother's plans.

"Well, fair play to her, I say," was Lily's comment which somewhat took the wind out of Maggie's sails.

"What do you mean by that?"

Lily took a sip of coffee. "Like she said, there's stuff she wants to do, stuff she missed out on, and she wants to do it while she's still young enough. I say she should go for it."

"What! Like going to gigs? Smoking dope? Following the hippie trail to fecking Kathmandu? She's fifty-four years old for God's sake!"

Lily shrugged. "Whatever. They're her dreams, not yours."

Maggie shook her head. "But what about Dad?"

Lily shrugged. "They must have discussed it. What does he think?"

She could well imagine but she prevaricated. "I haven't spoken to him yet. I left him a message to call me though." She paused. "I'm not sure he knows . . . . I mean, he might not have been listening when she told him, from what I can gather."

"Well, there you are then," Lily said. "He doesn't listen. How annoying is that?"

"Annoying, yes, but surely not reason enough to walk out?"

Lily leaned back in her chair and shook her head. "Mags, in fairness you don't know the full story . . . anyway, what are you more upset about? The fact that your ma's turned up on your doorstep with a master plan of her own, or the fact that she's left your da?"

Lily had her there. Maggie thought for a moment but couldn't come to a conclusion. "I don't know . . . both."

"Strictly speaking it's none of your business."

Maggie was incensed. "But they're my parents. Of course, it's my business!"

"Only in so far as they're your parents. You don't have a say in the state of their marriage. If it's not up to scratch any more, who are you to say that your ma should put up with it?"

If it were anyone else but her own mother, Maggie would have heartily agreed with Lily, but she had a vested interest here. She didn't want her parents to split up. Further discussion was halted however when Lily gave an enthusiastic, "Wow!" followed by, "She's certainly made a good start!"

Maggie followed Lily's gaze. Anna was walking down the long bar looking around as she went, then spying Maggie and Lily gave a wave and hurried over. The salt and pepper topknot had given way to a shiny jaw-length bob with fringe. All traces of grey now vanished, her hair was a nutty brown colour diffused with coppery highlights. It shone like glass.

Anna gave Lily a hug. "Lily! How are you?"

"Great, thanks, Anna. The hair's deadly."

Anna grinned with pleasure.

"It takes years off you," Lily enthused.

Anna glanced at Maggie for a verdict. "What d'you think?"

"It's gorgeous," Maggie agreed.

Anna, who was toting several carrier bags, settled herself down in a comfy chair, storing her bags underneath. "So have you two ordered?"

"No, we were waiting for you," Maggie said, eyeing up the half a dozen carrier bags including two from Marks & Spencer and one from Oasis.

"Did you get the bed?" Anna asked, picking up the menu. "I don't know about you two, but I'm starved!"

They ate a pleasant lunch with a bottle of Chardonnay over which the subject of Mark came up.

"So I thought it was a good opportunity," Anna explained. "I mean, I thought you could probably do with the company, now he's gone." She refilled their glasses. "I've been thinking about it for some time."

"Have you? How long?" Maggie asked.

Anna shrugged. "Since Jonjo left, I suppose."

Maggie was stunned. Her brother had left home six years before.

Staring into the bottom of her glass, Anna paused. "I thought, what's the point? Your father doesn't notice I'm there most of the time. We're like the proverbial ships that pass in the night. Sometimes we might only see each other for half an hour in a whole day." She took a sip of wine. "And as for sex, well –"

"Did you buy anything nice?" Maggie cut in, in desperation, a film of sweat swiftly forming on her upper lip.

Anna didn't appear to hear, "As long as his shirts are

ironed and his dinner in the oven, I might as well be invisible."

Maggie was relieved that her mother hadn't expanded on the sex part but was tempted to make the point that his shirts would now no longer be ironed, nor his dinner in the oven, and how would he manage? But she stopped herself when she realised that she sounded like some dinosaur out of a nineteen-fifties' home economics lecture.

"No," Anna continued, "let him pay a housekeeper and a secretary. I've done it for long enough. It's time I did something for *me*."

Maggie felt a stab of guilt at that. Like her father, in a lot of respects she'd always taken her mother for granted. Never really thought of her having dreams or of being unfulfilled, assuming she was content with her life. Though if she were honest, Maggie would have been horrified to think that her mother's lot was all there was on offer for herself.

"So what do you want to do?" Lily asked.

"Oh, lots of things," Anna said. "But first I want to get a job, if only to prove that I can."

Maggie knew better than to go into the 'but what can you do?' conversation, and was thankful when she saw Dom walking down the bar. She caught his eye and gave a wave, realising too late that he was in the company of Sally Gillespie.

Chapter 12

Sally was a trifle hung over when she awoke late on Saturday morning. She couldn't fathom why until she remembered that she'd opened a second bottle of wine with a view to having one more glass, then ended up finishing off the bottle. Rolling out of bed she hunted for painkillers and, after swallowing two with the best part of half a bottle of Volvic, she hit the shower.

She thought of calling Catherine to see if she'd like to meet up for coffee, but then remembered her saying something about James and her going to a wedding. How sad am I? she thought, Sally-no-mates.

She rubbed the condensation from the bathroom mirror and stared at her reflection. She'd never had this problem before. Before Charlie, that is. She'd always been self-sufficient, resourceful. When she'd gone over to London, at first she'd known nobody, but she'd still managed to organise a decent social life for herself within a month of arriving. What was so different about Dublin?

Nothing, she decided. You did it in London. You can do it here.

The reason she felt low was obvious. Charlie. She'd been so accustomed to being half of a couple. Albeit a clandestine couple, but because of their professional connection, there was never a problem being seen out together, and they were careful never to be touchy-feely in public, keeping a totally professional façade. Truth be told she'd enjoyed the secrecy at first, it had added an air of excitement, and she had thought she had things under control. She'd never expected to fall head over heels in love with him.

The mirror was steaming up again. Sally drew a moustache on the reflection of her upper lip. "Repeat after me," she said aloud. "Never again."

Dressing in black DKNY leather pants, white cotton shirt, wicked red Patrick Cox stiletto ankle boots and a John Rocha lambskin jacket, she took a last look at her reflection and headed out to resume her retail therapy, damned if she was going to let herself mope around because of some man. Even if that man had been, up until two weeks ago, the love of her life.

Compared to the previous day, it was bright and sunny if a little on the chilly side. She'd forgotten about the schizophrenic nature of the Irish weather, so was glad of the warmth of her jacket. Stopping off for a leisurely breakfast at the Espresso Bar, she read the *Irish Times* from cover to cover, then wandered down Grafton Street window-shopping. In a small shoe shop on Wexford Street she happened upon a rather gorgeous pair of Jaime Mascaro knee-length snakeskin boots, briefly dithered, but then bought them. This was retail therapy after all. Then she had a wander around the Irish Design Centre in Powerscourt Town House, and various antique shops therein, but saw nothing she really fancied, though she did stop off at French Connection on the way out to buy a mint-green cashmere top and yet another pair of black pants she saw in the window.

Outside, as she made her way towards the Stephen's Green Centre, she heard someone call her name. She stopped in her tracks and looked around, then saw Dom Heche walking toward her, a broad grin on his face. She smiled back and gave him a wave.

"Hi," he said. "How are you settling in?"

"Fine." Sally nodded. "I found an apartment on Great George's Street and moved in yesterday. The rest of my stuff's due over next week, so – yes – fine, thanks."

He sounded surprised. "You don't waste time, do you? Good for you."

Sally had first met Dom Heche ten years before when they'd briefly worked together at Madison & Prowler. They'd hit it off well, but then he'd moved to their London office and they'd temporarily lost touch. She remembered that she'd enjoyed his company and had been a bit miffed that he didn't appear to fancy her, but it hadn't bothered her greatly. Plenty of fish in the sea and all that. He'd contacted her, with a view to joining them, when he and Leo were setting up Deadly Inc, but at the time she'd had no notion of returning to Dublin, and had declined the offer. So it was with an air of confidence that she had called him up with the news that she wanted to come home, ostensibly to enquire if he'd heard of any suitable jobs on the grapevine, fairly confident that he'd offer her a job at Deadly Inc, which he had.

"Listen," Dom said, after a pause, "a few of us are going into the office tonight to watch the Paddy's Day fireworks from the roof if you'd like to come along? It's the same guy who designed the millennium show in Sydney, so it should be fairly spectacular," he elaborated, rightly assuming that perhaps watching a firework display wasn't Sally's idea of a fun way to spend a Saturday night.

He was right on that count, but after three stultifyingly solitary nights in a row, Sally was glad of the chance of some human contact. "Sounds great," she said, with what she hoped was enthusiasm. "What time's the kick-off?"

"Eight," he said.

Sally felt a sudden wave of sadness, remembering catching a fireworks display by default while having dinner on a barge on the Thames, with Charlie. Dom looked as if he was about to take his leave and she felt unexpectedly panicky. She couldn't face being alone again with thoughts of Charlie enveloping her like a suffocating parasite. "Fancy a coffee or something?" she asked, lifting her bags, in a form of explanation. "I could do with a pit stop."

"Um . . . yeah, fine," he said. "Could do with one myself," and they set off through the crowd of Saturday afternoon shoppers

"God! I haven't been here in years," Sally commented as Dom held open the door of Café en Seine for her.

She followed him down the bar, through the late lunch-time stragglers, then he suddenly stopped.

"Fancy meeting a couple of your new colleagues?" he

asked, over his shoulder, then led her over to a group at a table.

She vaguely recognised the tall dark-haired girl, but couldn't put a name to her. The other two, a small red-haired girl in hideous gaudy clothes, and an older woman in jeans and battered leather jacket, way past its sell-by date, she'd never seen before.

"I think you know Maggie," Dom said, and Sally had it then. Maggie Fortune, BBD&K.

"Of course! Hi," she said warmly, thrusting out her hand.

Maggie hesitated for a split second, then returned her smile, a tad less warmly, and shook hands. "Hi. How are you?"

"And this is Lily, without whom Deadly Inc would fall asunder," Dom said, grinning at his trusty PA.

The red-haired girl, Lily, shot a not very covert look at Maggie, then she too shook hands. "Howya?"

"This is my mother, Anna," Maggie said to Dom, and vaguely to Sally, then "Mum, this is Dom Heche, my boss, and Sally Gillespie," she hesitated, "also my boss."

Sally saw the older woman dart a questioning look at Maggie, and wondered what was going on. Then, Anna's face broke into a smile and she pumped Dom's hand. "Good to meet you at last, Dom. I've heard a lot about you." She glanced at Sally and gave her a cheesy smile. "You too, Sally."

"None of it's true," Dom joked. "Now, can I get anyone a drink?"

As soon as Dom had gone to the bar to order coffees of varying types, Sally excused herself and went in search of the ladies' loo.

Anna watched her go then said, "That's her, isn't it? The one you called SPOC,"

"SPOD," Lily corrected.

Maggie was taken aback that she'd remembered. "Good grief, Mum, you've a memory like an elephant."

"And why wouldn't I remember something like that?" she said, visibly miffed. "I take a keen interest in what happens to all my children." Then a thought struck her. "Did you say she's your boss?"

"As of next Tuesday," Maggie said.

"D'you reckon Dom's shag – d'you reckon they're an item?" Lily speculated.

Maggie shrugged. "Dunno. I doubt it. He wouldn't have given her a job if they were."

"Suppose you're right."

"Well," Anna said with a dismissive sniff, "I can't see what all the fuss is about. She doesn't look that special to me."

Maggie nodded. "I know what you mean. It must be a trial to have that perfect figure, porcelain skin and all that thick blonde hair."

"Huh! Handsome is as handsome does," was Anna's reaction to that.

"What does that *mean*?" Maggie asked. "I've often wondered."

"Haven't a clue," Anna said after a pause, and they all laughed.

"So, d'you fancy coming to the fireworks tonight, Anna?" Lily asked. "We'll have a deadly view from the roof of the office."

Anna's face lit up. "That sounds great. I love fireworks."

Maggie didn't mind, even though her plan for a quiet night in feeling sorry for herself was now scuppered. Still, she thought, feeling sorry for myself won't be an option now that Mum's around. Anna Fortune couldn't abide self-pity, and her efforts to jolly any unfortunate sufferer out of it were exhausting for all concerned. The easier option all round was to give in and postpone the self-pity for a quiet and solitary moment.

Dom returned from the bar then, and he and Anna got into conversation about the west of Ireland, Westport in particular. Maggie and Lily meanwhile were discussing Sally Gillespie.

"You reckon she'll get her claws into him?" Lily muttered, flicking a glance at Dom.

Maggie shrugged. "Who cares . . . More to the point what will she be like to work with?"

"Leo reckons she's fantastic at what she does."

Maggie gave Lily a leery look and said under her breath, "Didn't know he'd shagged her." To which Lily gave her a wallop in the ribs with her elbow, causing her to yelp and Dom and Anna to stop talking and look over.

"She's just being giddy," Maggie explained and laughed, at which point the Spawn of the Devil reappeared.

They went their separate ways a short time later with a view to meeting up at the office for the fireworks. Anna still had shopping to do, so she went off by herself, and as Maggie still hadn't bought a sofa, she and Lily went off to Habitat, where Maggie had seen one she fancied earlier.

"What I was saying before," Lily reminded her. "Leo reckons she's shit-hot at her job, so maybe it won't be so bad."

Maggie made a humphing sound. "Don't know why we needed a flaming creative director anyway," she muttered. "We were doing fine as we were."

"Dom reckons his workload's too heavy."

"Can't argue with that, I suppose," Maggie conceded, then after a pause, "Of course you know what's going to happen?"

"What?" Lily asked.

"She'll take all the interesting jobs for herself and dump the boring stuff on us. Watch it . . . I'll be doing fifteen-second radio ads and DIY superstore commercials from here on in."

"Well, there's one good thing," Lily said after a brief pause for thought.

"What's that?"

Lily gave a snigger, "There's no chance she can nick your boyfriend this time round."

It was Maggie's turn to inflict damage with her elbow.

Chapter 13

Maggie woke up late on Sunday morning, refreshed after a surprisingly good night's sleep on her inflatable mattress. She had been a mite sceptical when she'd taken it out of the nifty plastic storage case, expecting some class of grown-up beach lilo, but changed her mind after she'd inflated it. It was sturdy and bouncy and a good five inches thick.

There was no sound from downstairs nor, sadly, any waft of frying bacon, so she assumed that Anna was still asleep.

They'd had a good night and, true to Dom's word, the fireworks had been amazing, the river-based display going on for a good half hour. Leo had brought his ten-year-old twin girls along, and Dom his nine-year-old son, Jesse. Tom turned up with his wife Jill and their youngest, Marlon, who was six, so perhaps they were all infected by the children's wonder, all *oooohing* and *aaahing* with each explosion of colour and sound. Even super-cool, super-cynical Sally Gillespie had seemed impressed.

After the show they'd all gone down to the Crow's Nest, a child-friendly café bar in the dock basin, and enjoyed a bite to eat and a few drinks. Anna had got on famously with Jill, whom Maggie liked enormously and they, along with Lily, had huddled in a group, while Sally had kept company with the boys.

"No change there then," Maggie muttered, casting a clandestine glance in Sally's direction. They all looked over at Sally who was at her vivacious best, chatting and laughing with the men, even making an effort with Jesse and Marlon.

"No man too young," Maggie had hissed.

"So what's the story?" Jill asked, unable to miss the other woman's not so hidden animosity.

"She's a cow," Maggie said.

"Mags worked with her at BBD&Q and she nicked her boyfriend," Lily clarified. "She's a regular man-eater,"

"Is she after Dom, d'you think?" Jill asked, as she caught Sally laughing at some comment Dom had made while touching his arm and making big-time eye contact.

"Anything in a pair of trousers," Maggie had muttered.

At around ten thirty, Marlon having already crashed out on a sofa, there was a general move to leave.

"So what'll we play now?" Lily had asked.

"Well, I'm up for making a night of it," Jill said and, it being her turn, Tom had taken Marlon home and she, Maggie, Lily and Anna had said their goodbyes and headed off on foot towards town, eyes peeled for a taxi.

"D'you think we should have asked Sally?" Jill had said to Maggie when they were a few yards down the road. "The others are all going home."

Maggie stole a glance over her shoulder but Sally was nowhere in sight. "Too late. She's gone."

They'd rolled home, a smidgen the worse for wear, at around three.

When Maggie had showered and dressed, she peeked into her mother's room, expecting to find her still asleep, so was surprised to see the bed made and no sign of her. Perplexed she trotted downstairs to the kitchen, but she wasn't there either and, knowing that her mother wasn't a regular Mass goer, she doubted she was at the church. Then she spotted the note secured by a magnet to the fridge door.

It read: *"Gone off for the day with Aiden. See you later, Love Mum. xxx".*

Gone off? Where? And why Aiden?

Her mobile rang then. It was her father.

"Dad!"

"How are you, love?" he said. "You left a message."

"Yes . . . so what about Mum?"

"What about her?" He sounded surprised by the question.

"Dad!"

"What?"

"Look, Dad, surely you can sort this out. You're not going to give up without a fight, are you?"

There was a pause at the other end of the line, then he said, "Give up what without a fight?"

Maggie was stunned. "Your marriage! Dad, Mum's left you. She's up here looking for a job and talking about taking the fecking hippy trail to India, for God's sake!"

She heard him laugh at the other end of the line.

"Don't be an eejit! Sure who'd give your mother a job?"

Instantly, Maggie's hackles were up, forgetting that she'd had the very same initial reaction when Anna had first mentioned her plans. "Dad! Who's run your office for the last thirty years? And she's got her European Computer Driving Licence."

"What the feck's that when it's at home?"

He was getting on her nerves now. "It means she's computer literate, Dad. It's a qualification. She means it. She's left you."

There was another silence then he said in a pathetic voice, "But she can't do that . . . the VAT return's due."

If it weren't for the fact that there was a one-hundred-and-fifty-mile distance between them, Maggie could have shaken him, and her sympathies wavered in favour of her mother. "Is that all you're bothered about?"

"I want to talk to her," he said. He sounded annoyed.

"Well, you can't. She's gone out for the day."

"Then tell her to phone me when she gets in," he said. "There are things we need to talk about."

"You got that right," she snapped, frustrated by his attitude, but he didn't seem to notice.

"It's selfish, pure selfish when she knows the VAT's due," he grumbled. "And who's going to see to the Ministry forms?"

"I guess it's you now, Dad," she replied, barely holding on to her temper. "But if you want her back, then I suggest you eat a load of humble pie, because to tell you the truth, if I were her, I'd tell you to take a running jump." Then frustrated and unable to think of anything constructive to add, she terminated the call and switched off her phone.

"God!" she yelled at the wall. "Men! Who needs them?"

At the same time that Maggie was expressing her opinion of the male gender to the wall, Sally was expressing a similar notion to herself. "Women! Who needs them?"

The firework outing had been a mistake, she realised. She'd only gone because she hadn't wanted to spend another evening alone, but it had been grim and, on reflection, she wished that she'd taken in a movie or gone to the theatre instead. Dom, Leo and Tom had been friendly enough, but the others had been downright hostile, she couldn't figure out why; apart from Maggie Fortune, they barely knew her. And they hadn't even had the decency to ask her if she'd like to go on to wherever it was they were going. She'd slipped off to the loo, only to emerge to find that they'd left. How mean was that? Not that she'd wanted to go, but she'd have made the effort if they'd asked, even though a night out with the girls wasn't her sort of thing. Leo had called her a cab and he and Dom had waited with her until it arrived.

Towards the end of the evening it had been a real effort to appear interested and to make conversation. Her thoughts kept drifting relentlessly to Charlie and all she wanted to do was curl up in a ball and be on her own, yet at the same time she dreaded the idea of being alone.

She felt out of control and at one point became aware that she was bordering on manic, laughing too loudly and making a very obvious effort to be animated and lively. I'm losing it, she'd thought, and consciously calmed herself down.

It occurred to her later, as she slid between the sheets

of her very empty king-sized bed, that perhaps Maggie was jealous of her. Angry that Dom had brought her in as creative director. Maybe she'd had her eye on the job. Well, tough, she thought, the job's mine for as long as I want it. But that thought didn't make her feel any better. She knew without a doubt that it would be an uphill struggle if she didn't have the cooperation of the creatives.

God! Why did I come here? she wailed silently. Why couldn't I just leave things the way they were?

Chapter 14

When Anna arrived home at around eight o'clock that evening she only narrowly missed falling over a couple of bulging bin-liners in the hall, and the house reeked of chemical cleaning products.

"You've been busy," she commented as she entered the kitchen to find Maggie standing on a kitchen chair, replacing glasses in one of the high cupboards.

"Thought the place could do with a clear-out," she said. "Where were you?"

Anna detected a note of grumpiness, but didn't acknowledge it. "At a shoot," she said, shaking the kettle to check for water.

Maggie stopped what she was doing. "A shoot?"

"Yes. Aiden took me along to a fashion shoot he's doing for ICON magazine. We went down to Wicklow. It was all very interesting."

"A fashion shoot?" She was doing it again, but at least

the average word content of her sentences had increased by one third.

"Yes, pet. A fashion shoot. I was his assistant for the day."

"His assistant?" Oops, her average had just dropped again.

Clicking on the kettle, Anna sat down at the table. "Well – *honorary* assistant. It was great. There were three models, the stylist, a hairdresser, a make-up artist – honestly, I didn't realise there was so much to it. I have to say though, the clothes were awful, sort of . . . what's the word . . . grungy. I've seen better in a charity shop, but apparently they cost a fortune."

The kettle boiled so she got up from the table and made a pot of tea.

"And the models," she continued, "they didn't have a pick on them, looked as if they all had eating disorders, smoked all the time between shots and ate nothing, even though Gloria, the girl from the magazine, had a hamper full of delicious goodies along with her."

Anna's enthusiasm was infectious and Maggie's bad humour lifted.

"So you had a good day then?" she said, jumping down from her perch and snagging two mugs from the drainer.

Anna grinned. "As Lily would say – deadly!" and they both laughed.

Maggie had been in a sour humour all day which had started after she'd come across some of Mark's stuff that he'd forgotten: a couple of pairs of jeans in the bottom of the laundry basket, his favourite Munster rugby jersey, a pair of trainers. At first when she picked up the rugby jersey, the scent of him left her feeling sad, then she reminded herself what a bollox he'd been and dumped the lot in a bin-liner, commencing a military-style sweep of the house for any other remnants of his occupation: bits and bobs, papers, a Chelsea Football mug and his hair-dryer (yes, he owned his own hair-dryer) which she dumped in on top, tying the bag off ready for the wheelie bin.

The cleaning was cathartic in a way, and it was overdue after the winter. When moving out the bed, sofas etc, he hadn't even bothered to run a sweeping-brush over the floor, so the house looked remarkably well after she had finished. The bath taps sparkled, the shower and bath gleamed and she moved the small portable TV from her bedroom to the sitting-room, hooking it up, with some difficulty, to the video. All the past-their-sell-by-date jars and cartons were removed from the kitchen cupboards and the freezer, bundled into another bin-bag, and the cupboards scoured free of even the minutest microscopic speck of bacteria. After that she rearranged her wardrobes, taking stuff from the spare room and hanging it in Mark's vacated space, finding stuff she'd forgotten about, discarding stuff she knew she'd never wear again, the point of which was to leave space in the spare-room wardrobe for her mother's things, now that it was pretty clear that she was serious about staying, for the time being anyway.

At one point she found herself humming, "I'm Gonna Wash That Man Right Outta My Hair," and laughed out loud, though her sour humour returned when she found that he'd taken her two favourite Madonna CD's, whether by accident or out of meanness.

"So did you spend the whole day cleaning?" Anna asked.

Maggie nodded. "Pretty much . . . though Dad phoned."

"Did he?" She sounded uninterested, but it was obvious that she wasn't. Maggie let the sentence hang, until Anna prompted, "And?"

Maggie shrugged. "And he's worried about you."

Anna snorted, "More like he worried about the Vat return and the Ministry forms," which caused Maggie to blush.

"Well, he did mention that all right," she conceded.

"Of course, he did." She folded her arms and exhaled through her nose. "And I suppose he laughed when you told him I was going to get a job? You did tell him I'm looking for a job, I take it?"

"He didn't exactly laugh," Maggie squirmed. "Actually, his exact words were, 'Sure, who'd give your mother a job?'".

Although, after talking to her father that morning, Maggie could understand her mother's frustration, she still held out hope that it was a temporary thing, the way you do when it's your parents who are about to split.

"Is there no chance you can talk this through?" she said, breaking the silence that had ensued.

"Have you *tried* talking to your father lately?" Anna asked, in reply. "He's a selfish, miserable old bastard. Give him a month, the house will be a tip, the paperwork in chaos, and he still won't give me credit for anything."

"And is that what you want? Some appreciation?"

"Well, it wouldn't go amiss," her mother said, then shook her head. "But it's not just that, Mags. It's all the things I said the other night too. I want to spend some time on *me*. I want to be beholden to no one. *I* want to be selfish for a change. I think it's time."

Maggie sighed. In fairness she couldn't argue; Anna had spent her life looking after all of them, with little time for herself. Reaching out her hand, she placed it on top of Anna's, giving it a squeeze. "You're right, Mum. Go for it." and Anna's face lit up. Though secretly Maggie still harboured a tiny hope that once her mother got it out of her system, once her father had had to fend for himself for a while, they'd both come to their senses.

"Now," Anna said, jumping up from the table. "Would you like to see the clothes I bought yesterday?"

Sally's day was better than she had anticipated. As well as her mother, James, Catherine and the children at lunch, James had brought along David Heart, an old schoolfriend he had bumped into at the wedding. She remembered David because his sister, Tara, had been one of her chief tormentors at primary school and, as she remembered it, he'd fancied her along with most of his classmates when she was in her mid to late teens, but because of Tara she'd been particularly mean to him in payback. He'd reminded her of this over pre-luncheon drinks, and they'd laughed about it after she'd explained her motivation.

"And what's Tara doing now?" Rhona had interjected. "I always liked Tara, pretty girl. Intelligent. Didn't she go to Trinity?"

"She dropped out," David replied. "She's an ecowarrior now," and when Rhona stared at him blankly he explained. "Chains herself to trees to stop motorway development through beauty spots like the Glen of the Downs. I think she's involved in something to do with Orca whales for Greenpeace at the minute, out in the Atlantic."

"Oh," Rhona muttered, completely at a loss, "that's nice," and Sally couldn't help but give a smug little smile.

David was a journalist by profession, and had returned to Dublin on a six-months' sabbatical in order to write a novel.

"What's it about?" Sally asked, interested. She had, once upon a time, harboured ambitions to write but had never done anything about it, probably for fear of failure (though she would never admit that).

"Well, it won't be the great Irish novel," he'd qualified. "I thought I'd set it in contemporary Dublin. A sort of political satire. You know, corruption, ambition, a bit of sexual indiscretion thrown in."

Sally laughed, "God knows you've plenty of material over here!"

"So how do you earn a crust?" he asked.

"I'm in –" Sally started, but Rhona, earwigging as usual, cut in.

"Sally's a writer too, aren't you, Sally?" and virtually dived between them, grabbing David's arm. "Now . . . shall we go through for lunch?"

James caught Sally's eye and cast his skywards.

Later over pudding, when Rhona was occupied interrogating Catherine over rumours she'd heard about someone or other, Sally leaned over to David and said,

"As you've probably gathered, I'm a constant source of disappointment to my mother. She finds it especially embarrassing that I'm in advertising."

"Know the feeling. Mine thinks journalism's only one step above being a pimp."

"So how does she feel about Tara's vocation?"

"Delighted," he replied, heavy on the irony and Sally laughed.

"So what brought you home?" he asked. "I'd have thought you'd find Dublin a bit provincial after London."

Sally shrugged. "Ah, you know yourself. Provincial or not, I missed it." A monster lie, but candour about her disastrous love life wasn't the order of the day.

"Yes," he agreed. "There's something about home all right."

"So would you have come home if it wasn't for the book?"

"Probably, at some stage," he said, then gave a wicked grin. "Though the chance of a rent-free penthouse on the river while I was writing was a big incentive."

'Rent-free? Lucky you!"

"I'm house-sitting for a friend while he's in Australia," he clarified.

When James and Catherine made a move a while later, Sally quickly did the same, feeling mildly guilty that she couldn't hack spending another evening alone with her mother. David was without transport so she used the excuse of offering him a lift when she detected the first inklings of Rhona's industrial-strength martyrdom expression forming.

Liberal thanks and compliments about lunch were

piled on Rhona which cut her off at the pass, so to speak – she could hardly play the martyr card and be coy and self-deprecating in tandem. Then they all made good their escape.

As she pulled over to let him out of her car, he asked her for her phone number.

"Maybe you'd like to meet up for a drink sometime," he said.

She experienced a mild sense of panic, but then relaxed. "That would be nice."

Through the rear-view mirror, she saw him watch her as she drove away,

Chapter 15

A lack of courage in her youth was the colossal regret of Anna Fortune's life to date. She'd had opportunities but she'd been afraid. Afraid to go away to London the summer she'd left school. Afraid to go travelling with Davina McGreal and Maddie Browne. Her excuse to herself had been that her parents would veto any notion of her leaving, but in reality she knew that wasn't it. In reality she'd never brought the subject up, so she was aware that the problem lay with her deficiency in the backbone department.

Eventually suffocated by small-town life, she'd been seriously considering a move to Dublin, but then she had met Dan and fallen head over heels for him. He was new in town and she'd nabbed him in the face of fierce competition. He'd walked her home from the Sunday night hop at the tennis club and that had been that. She was in heaven.

Then she'd fallen pregnant with Maggie so the decent thing had to be done and a speedy quiet wedding arranged.

The fact that Dan was a vet soothed her mother's mortification at the disgrace of it, though as soon as the ring was on her daughter's finger she'd suffered an attack of selective amnesia.

Lying in bed beside him, she regularly tried to pinpoint the time when things had changed. Though never overtly demonstrative, in the early days Dan had held her hand or walked with an arm thrown across her shoulder. They'd fitted together perfectly, she nestling against his side, arm around his waist. He was tall, handsome-looking, with dark eyes that had a dangerous gleam, a gleam that had stopped her heart when he looked at her, and turned her legs to jelly. They'd make love, then lie together and talk into the small hours, cuddled up like spoons. When had that ceased? When had they stopped holding hands? When had the sex turned from exciting into a chore? There had been no incident. No major row. No infidelities. It was hard to nail it, it had been so gradual, but then didn't all relationships cool off in time, settle into a sort of comfortable familiarity? Ah, there was the rub! No comfort in it now, just an aching loneliness, an invisible barrier between them. Nothing left to say.

Although she'd been thinking about it for years in an abstract 'Next year in Jerusalem' kind of way, in the end it had been a spur-of-the-moment thing. Maggie's call had been the catalyst, her window of opportunity, and she'd jumped. Dan's utter lack of understanding that very morning had contributed, but it was definitely the fact that Maggie was now so abruptly on her own that had been the clincher. She'd packed a case, left a note for Dan and had driven away before her courage failed her.

Driving along the N4 towards Dublin she'd felt a weight lifting from her and a sense of excitement she hadn't felt in years. She was on an adventure, her adventure, and although a few butterflies of apprehension fluttered in her gut, she'd ignored them.

Now, in the space of three days, she had reinvented herself, met lots of new people, been on a photo shoot *and* had the offer of work. She wondered what Dan would think of that, and she felt a surge of annoyance at his negative reaction to the news that she was looking for a job. She briefly wondered how he was coping and if he'd managed the VAT return, if he'd remembered to feed the dogs, then thought, "Not my problem any more," and set off for her new job.

Maggie had made no alternative plans for her bank holiday Monday. Why would she? She'd been expecting to spend it at home in Westport with Mark. She loved bank holidays at home, which usually included bumping into old friends, walks on the beach and long sessions in the pub catching up. Strangely, out of Dublin, Mark seemed more relaxed with her friends and they always had good craic, generally eating and drinking too much, staying until late on the Monday evening to let the traffic jams clear, and avoid the mandatory crawl at twenty miles an hour from Enfield onwards.

Because of her lack of a plan, Maggie slept late, seeing no reason to get up, and only surfaced when she couldn't put off having a pee any longer. She showered, then threw on an old pair of sweat pants and a T-shirt and went in search of breakfast. Once again there was no sign of Anna, only a note secured to the fridge door by a magnet.

"See you later,
Gone to work.
Love Mum. xxx"

Work? What work? Only in the city three days and she'd found a job! Maggie was stunned; it was the first she'd heard of it. Picking up her mobile she speed-dialled Anna's number. It rang for a few rings then her mother answered.

"Hello, love."

Trying to keep her voice casual Maggie said, "Hi, Mum. Where are you?"

"At work, pet. Didn't you get my note?"

"Um . . . yes, but I didn't know you'd got a job."

She heard Anna laugh at the other end of the phone. "Sorry. It all happened rather quickly. You see I was talking to Aiden this morning and well, one word borrowed another and he offered me this job."

Exasperation was setting in. "What job?"

"Oh, didn't I say? I'm doing his paperwork for him."

"His paperwork?"

"You know, pet, you have an awful habit of repeating everything I say just lately, and to tell you the truth, it's a bit annoying."

"Annoy – sorry," Maggie said, genuinely contrite. It wasn't a lack of faith, it was the fact that her mother seemed so together, when she was feeling like hell. Whoever said that relationship break-up was more traumatic than bereavement obviously hadn't shared that pearl of wisdom with Anna.

"Look, pet. Why don't you come down here and we'll have lunch together?"

Stopping herself only in the nick of time from repeating the word 'lunch?'. Maggie said, "That sounds like a plan. Where's 'here'?"

The text message said: *"Miss you."*

Sally read it over and over. *"Miss you?"* What the hell did that mean? Accessing details, she re-checked the sender, though there was no need as she recognised the number. Charlie's number. Message sent: *"Today. 13.04."* He'd be in Gloucestershire for the weekend playing the dutiful family man. Probably entertaining friends with his horsy wife, Imogene, she of the twin-set and pearls. She of the old money. She who holds the purse-strings.

"Miss you."

"I bet you do," she said aloud, and viciously tossed the phone onto the sofa. She was angry with him for sending the message. What was the point? He was the one who had finished it. He was the one who, back-pedalling like crazy, had said that it was over. Why couldn't he just let it be?

The phone beeped to signal another text. She lunged at the sofa and scooped the phone up, angry enough to smash it against the wall, but she didn't.

"Fancy that drink?" it read. *"David."*

She hadn't expected to hear from him so soon, and on reflection wasn't that keen to take him up on his invitation, but what the hell. He was a nice enough guy, and it wasn't as if she was snowed under with offers right now. Accessing Messages, she typed: *OK.* And pressed send.

Then she replied to Charlie. The little animated winged envelope flew off the screen bearing the message, *"Go to hell."*

Chapter 16

The studio was in Sandymount, housed in the basement at garden level to the rear of an imposing Edwardian house near the seafront. Maggie knew the house well as it belonged to Mike Patterson, a photographer and director of commercials, with whom she'd often worked. The basement had been converted into a large studio which he shared with three other photographers and now, evidently, Aiden.

Maggie recognised Mike's vintage Jaguar parked in front of the house along with Anna's VW Polo and a battered and ancient Jeep she knew belonged to Luke Kenny, one of the other photographers. She was still slightly bemused that Anna had managed to get work so swiftly, even if it was of a temporary nature, and was quietly impressed that her mother wasn't letting the grass grow under her feet. At the same time though, her obvious resolve was a trifle unsettling.

She's just making a point, Maggie told herself to allay

her fears that this was indeed a permanent thing, and her parents had irrevocably broken up – conscious of the fact that her father didn't *do* subtle and the message needed to be hammered home with a mallet or he just wouldn't get it.

Making her way around the back of the house, through a wrought-iron gate set in a wall, Maggie reached the studio entrance and tapped on the door frame, then entered.

It was a large open space, bright because of its south-facing aspect. Anna was alone, sitting at a desk set against the wall, adding up a column of figures with the aid of a calculator. She looked around when she heard the footstep.

"On your own?" Maggie asked, casting a glance around the empty room.

"The lads have gone out to get the lunch," Anna said, swinging her chair around.

The lads?

She was wearing her new faux-leather pants (which had brought the words 'mutton' and 'lamb' to Maggie's mind when Anna had produced them the night before, but she'd said nothing) with a short-sleeved black and mauve cotton top and high-heeled ankle boots. She'd applied just a touch of make-up: a smudge of eye-liner, mascara and lipstick. Despite her reservations, Maggie had to admit that she looked great, more Tina Turner than Madonna, but not a bit mutton dressed as lamb.

"You look good," Maggie said, sitting on the edge of the paper-strewn desk. Beside her mother she felt suddenly dowdy, having thrown on an old pair of black

Levis, runners and a grey GAP sweatshirt over her T-shirt, with her hair dragged up in a pony-tail, devoid of make-up. "So how are you getting on?"

"Fine," Anna said. "It's pretty straightforward, just a case of organisation. Honestly, it never ceases to amaze me how useless men can be at organising simple paperwork."

Maggie laughed. "Don't knock it. Their ineptitude is your bread and butter right now!"

Anna nodded and gave a smug little grin. "Good point. Luke Kenny wants me to sort his VAT affairs out too, and he's *well* behind."

That was no surprise to Maggie. She'd known Luke for as long as she'd been in Dublin and he was 'laid-back' personified. Never put off till tomorrow things you can do maybe in a week or two, was his motto.

Anna's mobile rang then. She picked it up, looked at the display, then rejected the call. "Your father again," she said, chucking it into the bottom of her bag. "That's the third time today."

"Did you talk to him?"

Anna shook her head. "Don't be silly."

Maggie felt a stab of anxiety. "But maybe he wants to sort things out. Shouldn't you at least talk to him?"

"He wants to know where the Ministry of Agriculture forms are," she said. "He left a message – several messages, to that effect."

"Oh," Maggie said aloud, while thinking more along the lines of 'Oh bugger!'.

Anna pursed her lips. "I can read that man like a book."

"But –"

119

"But nothing, Mags. Your father and I are finished. It's over. Get used to it."

Maggie felt depressed. Her parents were splitting up . . . *had* split up. Mark had fled to the other side of the world to get away from her and Sally Gillespie was back, like a marauding cuckoo, to further disrupt the status quo. Only five days ago she'd felt secure in her world, now it was crumbling around her.

Anna had resumed punching numbers on the calculator, a grim look on her gob. After a moment she stopped and reached out for Maggie's hand.

"Look, pet. Things change. We move on. It's just one of those times. We *both* have to move on now. Mark's gone. So what? He obviously wasn't right for you. You deserve better and so do I."

Maggie sighed and gave her mother's hand a squeeze.

"I wish you and Dad weren't splitting up," she said.

"I know, sweetie," Anna crooned, "but it doesn't alter your relationship with him. He still loves you."

At that precise moment Maggie could have happily strangled her father for being an insensitive selfish gobshite, but on one level she felt sorry for him, well aware that Anna's absence would leave him floundering. The trouble was, Anna had made herself indispensable, but he obviously hadn't the wit to see that yet.

"But what if he changed? What if he . . . I don't know . . . what if he was less selfish?"

Anna shook her head, then darted a look over Maggie's shoulder. "Is that a flying pig I see out there?" she said, cracking a grin.

Involuntarily Maggie cast a glance over her shoulder, than laughed. "OK. It was just a thought."

The crunch of footfalls on gravel announced *the lads'* return, and a moment later Luke and Aiden walked in bearing a carrier bag of food .

"Oh, excellent, here's lunch," Anna said, getting up and clearing a space on the desk.

"Thought we could eat outside," Luke said, then spotted Maggie. "Howya, Mags?"

"Fine thanks, Luke. How's yourself?" Then she caught Aiden's eye. "Hi." It irritated her that she still felt sheepish in his company, embarrassed about barfing in front of him – but he seemed oblivious.

"Hello again," he said, giving her a smile.

"Is it warm enough outside?" Anna asked.

"Ah yes, there's heat in the sun out of the breeze," Aiden commented and, after collecting paper plates and glasses, they all trooped outside, making their way across the lawn to a table and chairs set at the far side of the garden.

Lunch was from the local Indian takeaway and the lads had selected a vegetarian curry, chicken korma, chicken tikka masala, lamb koftas with lime pickle and boiled rice and naan bread, to be shared. They all helped themselves, a little of this, a little of that, style. Very *al fresco*. Lager (what else?) was the liquid accompaniment.

"So how come you're all working on the bank holiday?" Maggie asked, for want of something better to say.

Aiden's mouth was full so Anna enlightened her. "Aiden had to process the prints for ICON. I'm dying to see them."

"I'm just hanging out," Luke said, adding, "The food's mighty, isn't it?"

Anna took another kofta on to her plate. "I always regret I didn't get to India, when I was young,"

"I was in India," Luke volunteered. "Man, the drugs are something else. Weed like you've never smoked." He closed his eyes and inhaled. "And the Nepalese Temple Balls . . . man! "

"I've never smoked cannabis," Anna said. "What's it like exactly?"

There followed a split second of complete silence, then Luke said, "Uh . . . deadly."

"Have you got some? Can I try it?" Anna asked earnestly.

Maggie didn't know how to react, mainly because she wasn't sure if her mother was serious or just winding him up. It appeared she was serious.

"I'm conducting a sort of experiment, you see," Anna said, making the point by waving her fork like a baton. "I missed out on a lot of stuff when I was younger so I thought I'd like to experience as many of those things as I can before I'm too decrepit."

Sex, drugs and rock 'n' roll came to Maggie's mind. The rock 'n' roll she could live with but didn't want to think about the rest in the context of her own mother.

Luke and Aiden stared at Anna for a moment, then a wide grin spread over Luke's face. "Mighty!"

Maggie groaned inwardly, knowing the last thing her mother needed was encouragement. She was about to raise an objection, but thought better of it. What was the point? Anna had a bee in her bonnet and there was no talking to her. Anyway, what was the harm if she smoked a little dope? There was hardly a danger she'd become an addict or want to try class A drugs . . . hopefully. She quickly changed the subject.

"So have you done much work for ICON, Aiden?"

"In the past. This is the first job I've done for them since I came home though."

"And what brought you home? Didn't you like New York?"

He shrugged. "Ah, it was grand, but I'd had enough of the States. I prefer the pace of life here."

Maggie wondered if his broken relationship had also been a factor. Then she became aware that Luke was enlightening Anna on the merits of the various types of cannabis, and cocked an ear, but had to tune out because Aiden touched her arm and said in a soft voice,

"So how have you been, since?"

Maggie stiffened. "Since?"

"Since yer man went AWOL."

Deadpan, she said, "I'm fine," while thinking, don't beat about the bush.

He nodded. "Good."

She felt patronised so had the need to expand. "It was just a bit of a shock, that's all. People normally mention it over breakfast if they're about to leg it to the other side of the world."

"Yes. I suppose they do," he said. "So did you talk to him at all?"

She shook her head. "What's the point? He obviously doesn't want to be with me. It's time to move on."

He nodded again. "Good for you." Then, after a pause. "But it's not always that easy, is it?"

He'd got that right.

"My mother doesn't seem to be having a problem," Maggie replied, eyeing Anna across the table, regretting the words as soon as they were out of her mouth.

"Your mother?"

Maggie shook her head. "Forget I said that. By the way, I don't usually make a habit of puking in front of strangers, and thanks for putting me to bed."

He grinned. "Don't mention it." He too looked across the table to where Luke and Anna were deep in discussion. "Your mother's a great woman," he said. "We had a long chat while she was waiting for you the other night."

Maggie relaxed and laughed. "Chat? It sounded more like an interrogation to me."

He held his hands up and grinned. "Well, she does have a certain way about her that makes you open up,"

"You'd better believe it, buddy. Stronger men have withered under my mother's grilling."

They laughed together, then he made full-on eye contact for the first time and she saw that his were deep and blue, the kind of eyes a girl could drown in. Sharp intake of breath. Take a step back, she thought. Quick.

"Well, there's your hash and your weed," Luke said. "Weed, or grass, is the leaves or the buds of the plant and gets you high, but hash is the whole plant, processed into a resin, and it gets you stoned."

"What's the difference?"

Luke frowned. "I'm not with you?"

"Well, between high and stoned?"

Luke organised his thoughts. "OK. High is . . . well,

high, you know, up there, and stoned is a more mellow, spaced-out kind of thing."

"Right," Anna said. "And which do you prefer?"

Luke ran his hands through his long curly hair while considering the question. "Well, that depends. In the daytime I'd be more likely to smoke weed. Skunk's a good one, a lovely bit of bud, but if I wanted to get stoned I'd go for the resin – hash. Moroccan, sometimes called rocky or soap, is your most commonly available. It's low grade but you still get a good buzz. Personally my favourite smoke's a bit of polm. It's high-grade, the extra-virgin olive oil of the cannabis resin world, not unlike the buzz you get from Nepalese Temple Balls."

"Nepalese Temple Balls? You mentioned them before," Anna observed, storing the information for future reference. She'd heard some of the terms years before. Davina was always going on about getting stoned in her letters from India, but it was good to have it all explained properly.

"Yeah. The hash is laced with opiates in the Nepalese. It's a slightly different buzz. More intense. But it's quite hard to get hold of."

"Right," Anna said. "So grass makes me high and hash gets me stoned."

"That's about it," Luke agreed. "Mind you, Thai sticks are grass and they get you stoned rather than high, very intense, but as a general rule that's it . . . I'd go for the skunk for your first smoke."

"So you reckon I should go for high before I go for stoned?"

Luke nodded. "Yeah. Definitely."

125

"And can you get me some skunk?"

Luke grinned at her. "Sure. I'll see what I can do."

Anna was delighted with herself. It was all very interesting and she'd no idea there was so much to it.

Maggie, on the other hand, who had heard the tail-end of her conversation, was horrified. Start with high? Just how detailed was this research going to be? It was time for a quick change of subject.

"Um – I'm recording a couple of radio ads tomorrow afternoon, Mum. Would you like to come along?"

Luke drove Maggie into town after lunch. Anna still had Aiden's VAT return to finish off and Aiden the ICON prints so, after calling Lily and arranging to pop over to her apartment, she left them to it.

"Yer ma's a great woman," Luke said as soon as the Jeep was in motion.

Echoes of Aiden's opinion – Aiden, and all of her schoolfriends, whom Anna used to let hang out in their house after school, never complaining about the noise and feeding them a never-ending supply of frozen chips and tomato ketchup.

Her mother's talk with Luke over lunch had rung alarm bells in Maggie's head, however. "You're not really going to get dope for her, are you?"

"Why not?" he said.

"Ah come on, Luke. This is my mother we're talking about."

"Will you chill out, Mags? Yer ma's a grown up, or hadn't you noticed? She's just after a few new experiences. What's the harm? She just wants to try it the once?"

"Not the way I heard it," Maggie said stiff-lipped.

"Jesus! Mags, listen to yourself. You sounds like an aul' one."

He had a point. She'd smoked dope the odd time herself in her student days so perhaps it was time to give her mother some credit for being an intelligent adult with a fixed agenda. An agenda with a definite mid-life-crisis slant, but nonetheless, a personal agenda to experience the things she felt she'd missed out on in her youth. What was the harm? She didn't comment on her father's forty-Marlborough-a-day habit which was far more injurious to his health than a couple of spliffs were going to be to Anna's.

"You're right," she said, suddenly feeling foolish. "I'm just being over-protective."

He dropped her off on Leeson Street and Maggie stopped off at the local bakery to pick up a couple of Pecan Danish to have with their coffee. Lily answered the door still in her pyjamas, a rumpled duvet on the couch, and a couple of rental videos on the floor, evidence that it was obviously veg-out day. While she went off to make coffee, Maggie phoned her father. He picked up on the first ring.

"Anna?"

"No, Dad. It's me."

"Oh," he said. "I was expecting your mother to call. I left her messages. Where is she?"

Maggie couldn't believe her ears. Was he so insensitive that it had escaped his notice that his wife of thirty-four years had upped and left him?

"Mum's at work," she replied with the aim of shocking him into some kind of action.

"Work? What are you talking about? Isn't she up there for a break with you?" He sounded genuinely mystified.

It was exasperating. "Dad, haven't you been listening to a word I've said over the past couple of days? Mum's left you."

A silence ensued at the other end of the phone, then after what seemed like an age he said, "Don't be an eejit. Why would she do that?"

He was obviously in big-time denial so it was time to be brutal. "Dad, Mum came here Friday night with her suitcase and told me she'd left you. As far as she's concerned she's a single independent woman now, and she wants to live a little before she's too decrepit. Her words, not mine."

"Live a little?" he said, as if the concept was totally alien to him.

"She means it, Dad. She's got a job already, doing book-keeping, and she's had her hair cut and bought a rake of new clothes. Leather jeans and stuff."

"You're not serious? Why would – ? I mean, what about – ? Left me?"

"Yes, Dad. Left you. And if you want her back I suggest you get your ass in gear."

"But what can I do? She won't answer her phone?" His voice had a whiny edge.

Maggie thought about it, then came up with a brain wave. "Woo her," she said.

"What!?"

"Woo her. Give her a reason to come home."

He gave a nervous chuckle. "Don't be daft. We're too long in the tooth for that class of shenanigans."

"You're never too old for a bit of romance, Dad," Maggie said. "Trust me on this. That's what she wants."

He laughed nervously. "You're jokin' me." Then he was silent again, obviously thinking over the suggestion, before asking, "Mags, would you do me a favour?"

"Anything, Dad. Name it," she said, full of hope that at last he'd seen the light. Her hope was dashed a moment later.

"Would you ever ask your mother where she put the shagging Ministry forms?"

Chapter 17

Sally was up bright and early on Tuesday morning, choosing her outfit carefully: a black trouser suit worn with the mint-green cashmere top she'd purchased the previous Saturday. Businesslike but not too formal.

There'd been no further texts from Charlie, a fact that both relieved and disappointed her. Her drink with David had been a pleasant if unexciting affair. They'd gone to Sam Sara, a trendy watering hole on Dawson Street, but by the end of the evening she realised that although she liked him and they had a reasonable amount in common, and he was good-looking in a quirky sort of way, she wasn't in the least bit attracted to him. He was good company though, and if relationships were definitely off the agenda for the foreseeable future, what was the harm in seeing him again on a casual basis? She was relieved therefore, that after he'd walked her home, before they'd parted company, he hadn't make a move on her.

It was with unaccustomed anxiety that she entered the

portals of the Deadly Inc offices just before nine-fifteen. Anxious because it was imperative that if she were to avoid bridge-burning, she had to make a spectacular success of this job, or she could kiss goodbye to any chance of a triumphant return to London; and that was plan A. She didn't have a plan B.

She was greeted by Lily who, in her opinion, needed serious guidance in the style department. She was wearing a truly gruesome lime-green tunic top over shiny black cropped pants, and black high-top Docs with fishnets visible in the gap betwixt.

"Howya," was Lily's greeting. "If you'd like to follow me, I'll show you your office."

Sally smiled engagingly. "Love to," she said, with a view to getting off on a positive note after the disaster of Saturday night.

Lily led her upstairs to a bright and fairly spacious corner office with a river view.

"This used to be the small conference room," Lily explained. "When you're settled, if you come down, I'll give you the guided tour."

Sally gave her the full 400KW smile. "Great."

"Your personal email address is in the office directory on your I Mac, and I've emailed you a sort of orientation memo thingy I put together."

Orientation memo thingy?

"Thanks."

"Oh, and if you've any queries for accounts," Lily added, "be warned. They don't answer calls before lunch."

"You're kidding?"

Lily cast her eyes skywards and shook her head. "If

only. And they'll hassle you for your time sheets, but it's wise to photocopy them because it's not unknown for them to lose the odd one, then you're in the shit at the end of the billing month, because who remembers?"

"OK. Anything else I should know?"

"Well, if your I Mac starts playing up, don't bother to call the engineer, call Neville. He's one of the MAC monkeys in Finished Art and if he can drag himself away from whatever nerdy computer game he's playing, he'll fix it."

Sally was relieved that Lily didn't appear to be hostile towards her, which led her to assume, correctly, that it was Maggie who was the instigating begrudger in the woodpile.

"Oh," Lily added, "the normal Monday creative meeting's in the big conference room at ten, and if you fancy a coffee you're better to get it takeaway from Macari's on the corner of Lime Street. The stuff that spews out of the coffee machine in the kitchen's shite."

"I'll bear that in mind," Sally said, stifling a smile.

As soon as Lily left her alone, she moved her desk so that it was diagonally across the corner, giving her views of both her office door and the river, then checked the drawers for stationery and unpacked her Rolodex from her briefcase. An orange I Mac hooked up to a printer sat on the desktop so she booted it up, then checked her personal email which had no messages, then her office address which, as promised, held Lily's mail with the "orientation memo thingy". As it turned out it was concise and informative, listing the various personnel in the different departments, along with their internal extensions, details about office practice such as the ritual Friday night get-together at O'Neill's and the weekly Monday morning creative conference.

Sally relaxed a little. So far so good.

In going over the material Dom had supplied she'd noted the I-Sport pitch which he'd given to Maggie Fortune and Tom Mulligan. Ordinarily she'd have taken that account for herself but, mindful of Maggie's attitude, she decided to play the diplomatic card and see what concepts she and Tom would come up with first. No point in getting a reputation for cherry-picking at this early stage, and judging by Deadly Inc's client list, there'd be plenty of interesting high-profile campaigns to get stuck into.

Maybe this is going to work out after all, she thought.

Lily had poked her head around Maggie's office door. "SPOD alert. She's in."

Maggie, who was on the phone to Argos to confirm that they were delivering her bed that morning, gave a heavy sign in reply and, putting her hand over the mouthpiece, said to Tom. "Bet she snatches I-Sport."

So she was surprised when no such action was mooted at the creative meeting. Straightaway she thought, what's the catch? But Tom, reasonable as ever, said she was just being paranoid, and suggested that she give Sally a fair chance.

Fair chance? Fat chance, she thought. Why should I?

She then spent what remained of the morning working with Tom on the two final concepts that they had settled on.

Anna phoned just before one to let her know that the bed had been delivered, which was good news. Everything being relative, her enthusiasm for the comfort factor of her inflatable mattress, in comparison to the floor, was on the wane and she looked forward to sleeping in a real bed again. They arranged to meet at two thirty at the recording studio, to which Maggie gave her directions.

She'd only invited Anna along in a desperate attempt to divert her attention away from talk of hash and grass and skunk, but now she was glad of the opportunity to show her mother some small part of how she earned a crust. She also thought Anna, being of a thespian bent, would enjoy seeing how voice-overs were done.

Anna was waiting for her outside the Real to Reel sound studio when she arrived, talking on her mobile phone. She was wearing a smart charcoal trouser suit today with a magenta top (another of her new acquisitions) and looked the quintessential businesswoman. She finished the call before Maggie reached her.

"That's another job," Anna said, full of excitement. "A friend of Luke's wants me to take a look at his accounts too. Isn't that great?"

"Terrific," Maggie agreed. "I hope you're charging them through the nose."

"Oh, you bet! Excellent! Can my day get any better?"

Stephanie Valentine was waiting in reception. Maggie often used Steph, an accomplished stage and TV actress, for voice-overs as her range was very versatile. Today Maggie needed her middle-class housewife voice for three twenty-second supermarket promotional ads, and Anna's day just got better as she was introduced to Steph.

"It's soooo exciting to meet you," she said, completely losing her cool. "I always watch you in *Liffey Town*, and I loved that cameo you did as the psychotic social worker with the fixation on Ken Barlow in *Coronation Street*."

Steph, who was bundled up in a heavy overcoat with a Doctor Who-length scarf wrapped half a dozen times round her neck, smiled and, finally managing to release her hand from Anna's, said, "Thanks,"– thrilled to her knickers with the positive review of her soap career.

"Look, we'd better go in. We have a good bit to get through," Maggie said, amused by her mother's obvious excitement.

Harvey Halliday, the sound engineer, was an odd bod with a dour way about him. Five foot four and thin, with round wire spectacles and a penchant for wearing Fairisle home-knitted tank tops over stay-pressed pants, he had the look of someone who might keep dismembered body parts in the freezer, but Maggie had booked him specifically because, despite all the above, she liked working with him and he was best sound engineer she knew. She introduced him to Anna, and Steph settled herself behind the booth mike, removing her coat and unravelling her scarf. Harvey gave Anna a curt nod, then poured six sugar sachets into his coffee and stirred vigorously.

"OK, Steph," Maggie said, "we're middle-class housewife today. It's for Super Savings so it's a bit wordy. But nothing you can't handle."

Behind the glass Steph nodded, gave her the thumbs up, then took a sip of her latte while reading over the script.

"Stephanie Valentine! Wait till I tell Barbara Malone," Anna hissed to Maggie giving her an energetic nudge in the ribs, then eyed up Harvey's sound board and the computer screens. "It all looks very complicated," she said.

Harvey ignored her as was his way, but Anna was too interested in everything to notice.

"Give me something to get levels, will you, Steph?" Harvey said and Maggie groaned inwardly as the actress read the first couple of lines of copy from the script. She sounded more like Lily Savage with an adenoidal problem and a hundred-a-day habit than middle-class housewife, and the reason for the scarf became immediately apparent.

"Sorry, Mags," which came out as "Sorry, Bags". She gave Maggie an anguished look. "It only came on this morning. I thought I'd be OK," she croaked.

This left Maggie with something of a problem, to put it mildly. The first ad was due for airing in three days' time, and while there was every possibility that she'd get a substitute voice-over, studio time would be the problem.

As if reading her mind, Harvey said, "Don't even ask. We're chock-a-block till the middle of next week."

"Is there a problem?" Anna asked.

Harvey sniffed, looked at Mags, then pushed his wire-framed glasses up the bridge of his nose, indicating Anna with a chuck of his head. "She's got a good voice."

With Harvey and Maggie both staring at her, Anna pointed to herself.

"Me?"

"Oh, I don't know . . ." Maggie said, uncertain. They'd only had the Super Savings account for three months and their marketing executive was apt to throw tantrums if everything wasn't perfect.

"Well, the way I see it, it's either her," he indicated Anna again, "Harvey Fierstein in there," a nod at the booth, "or *nada*." Leaning back in his chair he steepled his long thin fingers. "So what's it to be? The clock's ticking."

"Oh I couldn't," Anna protested but, knowing her mother like she did, Maggie could tell that she was raring to give it a lash.

Harvey looked over his glasses and rocked his head from side to side. "Tick-tock, tick-tock . . ."

Maggie sighed. "It's worth a go, I suppose."

A contrite and embarrassed Stephanie went home to bed with a box of Lemsip while Anna took over the booth. Maggie was a tad trepidacious, and had there been any other alternative wouldn't have gone for it, but as it turned out Anna played a blinder, her theatre training, albeit at an amateur level, standing her in good stead. As Maggie had previously pointed out, the script was wordy for a twenty-second ad, but it only took five takes to get the first one right and Anna enunciated every word perfectly while giving it the exactly right tone. They broke for a quick coffee then, after which Anna, well into her stride now, did the other two in one take each with recording time to spare. Maggie was impressed, Even Harvey, his Royal Weirdness, was impressed.

"Well, I've done amateur work over the years," Maggie heard her coyly telling him before they wrapped it up.

"How much?" Anna asked, astounded, as they stood on the pavement outside Real to Reel.

Maggie repeated the figure. "And then there's the studio fee on top of that, that's another ninety-eight euro per ad."

"Good grief! What's a studio fee for?"

"Basically for turning up," Maggie explained before they parted company, Maggie to return to the office, the day saved, and Anna to the more mundane task of Luke's VAT statement.

Chapter 18

When Sally arrived back from lunch she found an exotic and humungously expensive bouquet sitting on her desk, the kind that have a big spiky thing like a pigmy pineapple at the core and leaves and fronds and the odd curly twig, with a few totally unrecognisable blooms thrown in. She felt that little jerk of excitement every woman does on having flowers delivered and searched for a card, but it was taped to the cellophane and her shaking fingers had difficulty liberating it. Slipping it out of the envelope she read: *"Still miss you."*

She felt a brief surge of happiness before the reality check. What's he after? she thought. Why is he doing this?

Her obsession kicked in then and she had a overwhelming need to talk to him, if only to hear his voice again, but she pulled herself together. What was the point? Nothing would change. Give him a month and he'll have a new bit on the side, she thought, trying to be hard, but even the abstract concept of him with someone else was like a stab in the heart. She was tempted to make a grand gesture and stuff the bouquet in the bin (it wouldn't have been the first time) but she couldn't. Instead she dumped them on the floor beside the filing cabinet out of her immediate view either to slowly die of thirst or to be thrown out by the contract cleaners, then collected her notes for the strategy meeting with Dom, Leo and Paul Brody, the account director.

When she returned to her office just before five, she found that some busybody had rescued Charlie's bouquet and placed it a galvanised bucket full of water.

"This is a fucking conspiracy!" she said aloud, then jumped sky high as Lily spoke from the doorway.

"Just because you're paranoid, it doesn't mean they're not out to get you."

Sally spun around. "What!"

Lily gave her a leery look then said, "Joke," and when Sally continued to stare at her blankly, added, "Paranoid? The talk of conspiracy? It was a joke."

Sally felt foolish then. "Oh, right, yes. A joke . . . I see." And gave a feeble laugh. After the emotional rollercoaster of the past couple of weeks her nerves were in tatters. "Um . . . who put the flowers in water?"

"I did," Lily said. "Shame to let them die for want of a drink," while thinking that however shit-hot Sally Gillespie might be at her job, she was sadly lacking in the sense-of-humour department.

"Can you put them somewhere else, please?" Sally asked. "I . . . um . . . I get hay fever."

Lily shrugged. "Sure, no problem. I'll put them in

reception." Then picking up the water-filled bucket added, "Good touch, the bucket, what? A stylish juxtaposition is what the poncy lifestyle magazines would call it, but to me it's just a bunch of flowers in a fecking galvanised bucket. But then what do I know? I'm only from Finglas."

"Whatever," Sally snapped, already tired of this conversation. "Just get them out of here."

Lily was tempted to ask her what her last servant had died of but picked up a 'Don't mess with me when I'm in this mood' vibe, so discretion being the better part of valour, just snapped back, "Whatever," and stomped out.

Sally cringed, noting Lily's disgruntlement, but the flowers had temporarily knocked her off kilter again. Basically she felt like screaming. It was like the Chinese water torture; just when she thought she'd got him out of her head, splat, there he was again, attempting to sidle his way back into her life. It had to stop.

Picking up her phone she dialled his number, expecting to get his voice-mail, so was shocked to the core when he answered.

"Charlie Penhaligan."

She gave an involuntary gasp, then recovering, said, "Leave me alone, Charlie."

"You got the flowers."

His mellow treacly voice sent a ripple down her spine and it took her a moment to unscramble her brain.

"Why are you doing this?"

"Because I miss you, cherub."

She hadn't bargained on the sheer killer sexiness of his voice getting to her so easily and went suddenly weak at the knees, supporting herself against the edge of the filing cabinet. Don't let him do this, the voice of reason screamed inside her brain. Don't let him do this!

"Leave me alone," she said.

"How can I?" A pause. "I love you." He sounded soft and enticing, full of sincerity.

She closed her eyes tight to contain the tears but they seeped through the lashes and a huge lump of longing lodged in her throat. She swallowed. "You have to leave me alone, Charlie," she begged. "It's over. You ended it."

"The biggest mistake of my life," he said simply, sincere regret in every syllable.

Don't let him do this! the voice in her head repeated.

Summoning all her strength she took a deep breath, exhaled, then said, "I'm going to hang up now. Charlie. Don't phone, email, text or send me flowers again. It's over."

Quickly terminating the call, she switched off her phone, her hands shaking, but already the doubts had started. Maybe he was sorry. Maybe he'd come to his senses and realised he couldn't live without her. She stared at the blank screen, knowing that he'd be trying to call her back, but that irritating voice of reason was at it again.

"He's using you. He doesn't love you or he wouldn't have let you leave," it said, and how could she argue? She'd given him a choice and she'd come second . . . or third or fourth.

"Are you OK?"

Startled, Sally fumbled and dropped her phone. Maggie Fortune was standing in the open doorway, a sheaf of papers in her hand.

"Are you OK?" she repeated.

Sally coughed and bent to pick up her phone, giving her damp cheeks a surreptitious swipe. "Um . . . I'm fine. Fine. Did you want something?"

"I was wondering when you'd be free to discuss the outline concepts for I-Sport?"

Sally's brain was on overload. She understood all the individual words but had no comprehension. She stared at Maggie. "What?"

"The concepts," Maggie repeated. "For I-Sport."

"Oh . . . right. I-Sport." Then reached for her Filofax, her shaking fingers finally negotiating the pages of the diary. "How about tomorrow afternoon? I've a window at two."

Maggie stared at her as she fumbled with the pages. "Are you sure you're all right?"

Putting the Filofax and her phone on the desk-top, Sally ran her hands through her hair then gave her a stiff smile. "I'm perfectly fine, thanks." Then, because Maggie was still standing there staring at her, added pointedly, "Tomorrow at two then."

Maggie didn't move for a further split second, then shrugged and walked away.

The interruption had been good though. It had stopped her powering up her phone and calling Charlie back to ask him if he meant it when he'd said "I love you". How pathetic would that be? She heaved a sigh of both relief and weariness, determined that she wasn't going to be one of those sorry emotionally used and abused women who put up with all kinds of shit to hold on to their men, though she was beginning to get an insight into how easy it would be to get sucked in. Circling her head to ease the tightness in her shoulders and neck she closed her eyes and inhaled deeply, holding on to the breath for five seconds then emptying her lungs the way she had learned in her yoga class. Deep cleansing breaths. "You don't need him," she told herself. "You'll get through it."

This emotional stuff was exhausting.

"What's up with SPOD?" Maggie asked Lily, who was packing up for the day.

Lily shut down her computer and clicked off the monitor. "As in?"

"If I didn't suspect that she's probably incapable of it, I'd say she'd been crying," Maggie said. "Not that it would take Miss Marple. She had black panda-rings under her eyes."

"Did you tell her?"

"Didn't like to," Maggie said. "I was embarrassed."

Lily gestured towards the bouquet, now languishing in a tall elegant glass vase on the floor by the corner of the reception desk. "I think it's something to do with those," she said. "I found them dumped on her office floor and I got the impression she wasn't best pleased that I put them in water."

"Who were they from?"

"Don't know," Lily said, "but it looks like he wasted his money."

Maggie nodded. "No change there then, but the crying's new. What's that about?"

"Maybe she was the one who was dumped?" Lily suggested. "Maybe she had her heart broken."

"What heart?" Maggie commented and Lily gave her an old-fashioned look. "So what are the flowers about, then?"

Lily thought about that. "Guilt. Maybe your man's feeling guilty about dumping her and sent the flowers to make himself feel better."

As a possible explanation it had a feasible ring to it.

"Wouldn't you know it?" Maggie said. "I get dumped and he takes the sodding furniture. She gets dumped and she gets sent flowers. Is there no justice?"

Lily laughed, then caught sight of Sally descending the stairs. "Shhh!" she said lowering her voice. "Incoming SPOD at nine o'clock."

Maggie glanced over her shoulder. Sally had reached reception now. She looked composed and normal, the panda-eyes no longer in evidence.

She gave a crisp "Goodnight," as she strode past them and didn't look back or wait for any acknowledgement.

"Well," Maggie commented, "she seems to have got over it pretty well."

Lily smiled wryly. "Like you, you mean?"

"What d'you mean by that?" Maggie asked, irate.

"Time you moved on, kiddo. Personally I reckon you should go after the lovely Aiden before someone else snaps him up. He of the tanned six-pack and kissable lips. He of the cute arse and boyish charm."

"Cute arse? Smart-arse, more like," Maggie said dismissively.

So why did she feel a sudden flash of panic when Lily said,

"Whatever. You won't mind if I take a crack so?"

145

Chapter 19

Aiden Dempsey was biding his time because he didn't want to risk blowing it. Not a good idea to go steaming in when someone's just been dumped. Whatever about hell having no fury, in his experience a woman scorned was apt to use the scattergun approach where the male gender was concerned and he didn't want to get caught in the crossfire. No. Keep a safe distance, he thought, on the periphery, around, sympathetic, but not threatening or obviously interested, that was the plan. Let her relax in his company, look on him as a mate, and when things calmed down, maybe then he'd ask her out without risk of bodily harm.

"You need to sign this before you send it off with the cheque, pet."

He looked up. Anna was proffering the VAT return form for signature. He liked Anna. She was easy company, good craic and had a way about her that made him feel he'd known her for ever.

She'd knocked on his front door and, after explaining who she was, asked if he had a spare key to Maggie's. He hadn't, of course, but he'd asked her in to wait, and they'd got to talking. He'd laughed afterwards, amused by the way she'd wheedled his history out of him without appearing to be nosey. She reminded him of his mother in some respects – maybe it was because she too was from the West, but he couldn't imagine his own mother, who would be around the same age as Anna, wanting to smoke dope, or discussing the difference between high and being stoned, and the relative merits of polm and rock as opposed to skunk.

He had no idea why he had asked her along to the photo shoot either. It had just happened sometime between her telling him how she liked Tom Waits' music and his account of seeing Waits sing live in a New York Lower East Side club. Then on the Monday morning he'd bumped into her on his way out to the corner shop and they'd stopped to chat, and she'd asked him where he was going, and he'd moaned about paperwork, and before he knew it she'd offered to sort it out for him and he'd agreed.

Fortuitous, as it turned out, because Maggie had joined them for lunch and he'd had the chance to talk to her. She'd seemed a bit defensive at first, a bit prickly, but generally, after she'd loosened up a bit, he felt they'd got on OK.

"Oh! The ICON photos!" Anna said, leaning over his shoulder to get a proper look at the black and white prints he was examining for flaws. "You know, that was such good craic. I can't believe I've done so many new things in such a short space of time. It was so nice of you to ask me along, and everyone was so sweet. I hope I didn't get in the way."

"Don't be daft," he assured her.

It was her enthusiasm that was so infectious. She seemed hungry for life.

"Well, must get on," she said. "I'm going to check out a yoga class this evening."

"Yoga?" he said. "You do yoga?"

"Not yet. But I've always wanted to try it."

"I'd say you'd enjoy it," he offered.

"Really? Do you do it?"

"Did," he explained. "Briefly, in New York,"

"And did you like it?"

"Yeah, the bit I did. You should get Maggie to go. It's great for de-stressing."

"You know, that's not a bad idea. I might just do that."

Maggie's thoughts were far from yoga just then. She was on the phone to her sister Lucy in Kilkenny.

"So when did all this happen?" Lucy asked.

"Last Friday night when I got home from work," Maggie said. "I thought she'd come up because of Mark, but later she just came out with it. 'I've left your father,' she said. 'From now on I'm a single independent woman and I'm getting a job.'"

"A job? She'll never get a job. What experience has she?"

Maggie gave a groan. "Don't you start. She ate the face off me for asking that. Anyway it's irrelevant. She's already doing VAT returns for some people I know and, would you believe, a voice-over on a radio ad for Super Savings."

"What! How come?"

"Don't ask. The thing is, I'm really worried. Dad's useless, and the longer he leaves it to grovel, the more she's enjoying being single. We've got to do something before it's too late."

"But what?" Lucy moaned.

"You have to talk to Dad. He listens to you."

It was a fact that Lucy was Daddy's girl, the apple of his eye, so if anyone could talk sense into him, Maggie felt sure it was Lucy. "Tell him to woo her. Send her flowers, make romantic gestures, anything to get them talking. I think Mum has some sort of serious mid-life crisis thing going on."

"Right," Lucy said, ever the practical one. "Maybe I'll drive up there with Phoebe at the weekend. See if I can't talk him round."

"You'll need to do a lot of talking," Maggie assured her sister. "He's in big-time denial about it."

"And how about you?" she asked. "About Mark, I mean. How are you coping with that?"

Funnily enough, her concern about the state of her parents' marriage had sidelined her feelings about Mark, to a certain extent. She was still stung by it, but it felt somehow unreal. Did that mean that she hadn't really loved him? Or maybe just not enough? Surely if she had, she'd still be in a state of abject misery, being as it was barely a week since he'd flown the coop?

"Up and down," she said. "The official line is that I don't give a damn, but you know yourself. This business with Mum's kind of taken my mind off it."

"I never liked him. And he was so bloody tight-fisted. You know he asked me for petrol money when he gave me a lift down to Westport that time?"

Maggie was enraged. "What? Why didn't you tell me?" Her face burned with anger and embarrassment.

Lucy let the question pass. "Well, I'm glad you're feeling OK. And don't worry, I'll talk to Dad. Between us we'll sort this out, Mags. Don't worry."

Maggie heard her mother's key in the lock then. "Got to go," she whispered. "Mum's back." She put the phone down as the front door swung open.

Anna swept in like a tornado and after she'd dumped a paper carrier-bag full of receipts on the kitchen table said, "So what do you think about yoga?"

"In what context?" Maggie asked warily.

"Classes," Anna replied, kicking off her shoes and slumping down on the kitchen chair.

Maggie shrugged. "Not top of my list of must-do's."

"Well, I'm starting a class tonight. Why don't you come along and give it a try? It's only in Christchurch."

"Oh, I don't know," Maggie said. "Yoga's never really appealed to me. It all sounds a bit brown-rice and sandals-with-socks."

"Nonsense! Anyway it'll do you good. You need to get out more."

Going to a yoga class wasn't Maggie's idea of getting out more, nevertheless she found herself an hour or so later reluctantly signing up for ten weeks in a stuffy room above a pub.

They were a disparate group. Six in all including the instructor. Anna, Maggie, a tall hippy-dippy girl with long thin dishwater hair, who said 'amazing' a lot, whose name turned out to be Skye and who'd brought her own mat (obviously an expert, if she had her very own mat), a girl called Dani, petite, pretty, blonde, in her early twenties who looked pregnant and who was with a slim, camp young man whose name Maggie didn't catch. She didn't catch their instructor's name either. It sounded something like Shrumm, but after asking twice and not getting it, she felt embarrassed to ask again. Anna didn't catch it either.

"Her real name's Ursula," Dani confided. "She's very good but quite strict, isn't she, Conor?"

The slim guy nodded and rolled his eyes. "You better believe it," he agreed.

"You've had her before then?" Anna asked.

"Twice," Conor confirmed.

Ursula was German, thin but wiry with not an ounce of excess fat and a well-toned body, if a little deficient in the boob department. Her hair was sun-bleached and cropped short, her skin very tanned, and she took no prisoners. Moments later the class was called to order with a sharp crack of her hands and a command to: "Take a mat und make a circle."

They were instructed to lie down on the mat and close their eyes, then Shrumm, aka Ursula, took them through relaxation and breathing exercises with their eyes shut.

Vee haff vays of making you relax, Maggie thought, regretting that she hadn't stayed downstairs in the bar.

After breathing, it was stretching; neck and shoulders; lying down; on their hands and knees, then standing. The stretches had names like The Cat, The Hare and The

Cobra and Ursula told them about a ritual called Salutation to the Sun, a series of movements she did every morning which apparently stretched every muscle in the body; but she went on to say, that as there vere beginners in the class they'd be doing it in two veeks' time. (Maggie thought she detected a note of disdain in her voice when she said the word "beginners" but it was hard to tell because she had that kind of voice anyway.)

For the last portion of the class they were on their backs again and it was at that point that Maggie dropped off to sleep and, because she was lying on her back, started to snore quite robustly. The falling asleep was apparently quite acceptable but later, downstairs in the bar when Anna had gleefully told her about the snoring, she'd felt mortified.

"Don't worry about it, it's better than farting," Dani had commented. "And since I've been pregnant I can't stop, particularly when she makes us draw our knees up to our chests and rock from side to side. Didn't you hear me? I was like a fecking motor bike."

Nobody around the table admitted hearing her, but that was either due to good manners or to the racket Maggie had been making.

Shrumm had declined the invitation to join them in the pub afterwards.

"Her body's obviously a temple not to be sullied by alcohol," Maggie muttered to Anna as they were making their way down the narrow staircase. She'd found the whole experience a tad too earnest for her liking, but she had to admit, if only to herself, that she felt very relaxed after it.

"It's not that," Dani said, overhearing the remark. "She has a drink problem. She's an alcoholic."

"You're not serious," Maggie said aghast.

Dani nodded. "She'll tell you herself, I expect. She's been sober for five years now and she puts it down to a vegan diet and embracing yoga as a lifestyle." ·

"It just goes to show," Anna said. "Isn't she great?"

"What exactly is her name," Maggie asked then. "It sounded like Shrumm, or something."

"Siram's the name she adopted since she qualified as an instructor. Yoga teachers often take a yogic name," Conor explained. "I was thinking of taking that road once upon a time."

Dani gave him a dig in the ribs. "You were not! Don't listen to him. He likes junk food and alcohol way too much."

"Well, I could've," he muttered defensively.

Skye was a trainee yoga teacher, a student of Ursula's, and was soon to head off to Northern India for an advanced course with some renowned yoga teacher.

The mention of India got Anna going again.

"Oh, lucky you! I so envy you!" Then she and Skye got into a conversation about the various disciplines and levels of yoga, so Maggie tuned out and turned to Dani and Conor.

"So when's your baby due?" she asked Dani, eyeing the girl's neat basketball bump.

Dani placed a protective hand on her belly. "June first. But my mother reckons I'll probably go over."

"And d'you want a boy or a girl?"

Dani shrugged. "Don't mind as long as it's healthy.

They asked me if I wanted to know at the scan, and I was tempted, but I said, no, I'd wait and see." While she was talking she rummaged in her bag, eventually drawing out a curly photo which she held out to Maggie.

"Would you like to see?"

Maggie took it, rather awkwardly, not sure what was expected of her. All she could make out was a blur of swirly lines with a lumpy bit to one side.

"Wow," she said.

Dani pointed to the lumpy bit. "That's the head," she said, then tracing a milky swirl with her finger said, "and that's the spine."

Maggie peered at the photo but however hard she stared it still looked like a blur of swirly lines with a lumpy bit to one side. "Wow," she repeated.

"I couldn't make it out either," Conor said, deadpan, and they all laughed.

Dani and Conor were friends and shared a flat on Francis Street. Both were fashion students at NCAD and both had part-time jobs waiting tables in the Elephant & Castle, a café in the heart of Templebar. Conor imparted this information without any prompting and went on to confide how Dani's boyfriend had recently buggered off .

"The rotten bastard," Maggie sympathised, adding, "Was it a shock?"

"You could say that." Dani took a sip of her medicinal Guinness. "I mean, he was so thrilled when I told him I was pregnant."

"And it wasn't as if she tried to trap him or anything," Conor cut in. "She was thinking about . . ." he glanced in Anna's direction then lowered his voice, "you know . . . a trip across the water, what with the diploma show coming up next year . . . but it was he who persuaded her to go ahead and have it."

"So what made him change his mind?" Maggie asked.

Dani shrugged. "I've no idea. Mind you, at the end of the day, I'm glad he talked me into keeping the baby. That's one good thing he did . . . well, two," she qualified, unconsciously placing a hand back on her belly.

"But didn't he give you a reason?"

Dani shook her head. "Didn't even say he was going . . . well, not to my face."

Conor pursed his lips in disgust. "He sent her a text. A fecking text. Can you believe that?"

After her own recent experience, Maggie could, without difficulty. Then, probably because she could empathise, she said, "My fella went off without warning too, a week ago. I came home from work and he'd taken most of the furniture and didn't even leave a note. And I'd brought Thai curry home for dinner because I know he prefers it to Indian."

"No shit!" Dani said, obviously stunned by the concept. "How could he like Thai over Indian?"

"He took the feckin' furniture?" Conor gasped, more to the point in Maggie's opinion.

"Yes. The bed, TV, sofas, microwave, and he took my two favourite Madonna CDs," she said with venom. "I felt such an eejit. I hadn't a clue. It just goes to show."

Dani and Conor nodded agreement.

"Just goes to show," Dani repeated.

Then they lapsed into silence for a few moments, each with their own thoughts.

"Is there no chance he'll come back when he's had time to get used to the idea? Or at least help you support the baby?" Maggie said after a pause.

Dani shook her head, then looked down at her stomach and patted it gently. "He'd plenty of time to get used to the idea, didn't he? Anyway, we'll manage. Who needs him?" She smiled at Maggie. "You've just got to get on with it, haven't you?" It was said bravely but it must have been a daunting prospect. She stood up. "Excuse me, I have to pee again. My bladder only seems to hold an eggcupful these days."

After she'd gone, Conor said. "Don't let her talk fool you. She's in bits really."

Somehow, hearing Dani's story brought things into perspective for Maggie. There she was feeling sorry for herself because Mark had gone off and left her and taken a couple of sticks of furniture. She still had her own home and a good job, while Dani had to contend with bringing up a baby by herself, probably on Social Welfare, while at the same time trying to finish her course, all because the father had refused to take responsibility after encouraging her to have it in the first place. She briefly wondered what Mark's reaction would have been if she'd fallen pregnant, then decided there was no point even wondering.

"So will Dani's family help her?" she asked Conor.

He sighed. "Well, her family lives down the country in Longford, and her ma's on her own too, so she can't help her out much with money. And going home's not an option if she wants to finish her diploma, but I'll help out all I can."

"She's lucky to have such a good friend," Maggie said, but Conor just brushed the compliment aside.

"It's what friends do," he said.

Dani came back then.

"Can I get you guys another drink?" Maggie asked.

Dani shook her head. "Not for me, thanks all the same. If I've more than the one I'll be murdered with heartburn all night." She started to gather her things.

Then Anna, who had caught the last remark, said, "Your baby'll have a head full of hair then. I had fierce heartburn with all of mine and they all came out with hair."

"That's what Gran said." Dani rubbed her midriff. "I should have shares in Rennies by now! I'm eating them like they're going out of fashion."

They all made a move to leave then, and outside the pub said goodbye-and-see-you-next-week.

"So do you think you'll go again?" Anna asked Maggie as they walked up Church Street towards home.

Strangely, despite her preconceptions and the earnestness of it all, she realised that she probably would.

Chapter 20

Sally was depressed. Depressed, angry and confused. Hearing Charlie's voice, actually talking to him in person, had been hard to deal with, but she didn't regret hanging up on him and was determined to reject all further calls and contacts.

At least she had been when she'd left the office. Now, two hours later, she was dithering between calling him back and dumping her mobile down the garbage-disposal unit. She'd even thought of changing her number until it occurred to her that it was futile because he knew where she worked; with the contacts he had in the advertising industry it was hardly surprising that he'd tracked her down.

What did he want? Did he expect to pick up where they had left off, the same ground rules, regardless of the fact that he had rejected commitment, rejected her? She felt as if he was playing with her like a cat plays a goldfish, claws out, one paw in the bowl, and that angered her further, but she couldn't help herself. He was like a drug and she was in serious withdrawal.

Her phone was in her hand and she was half willing it to ring or to beep with a text-message notification and that made her feel even more powerless. Chucking it on to the sofa she went in search of drink. The remainder of the bottle of Soave she'd opened the previous night was sitting forlornly in the empty fridge door, so she pulled it out, but the condensation on the glass bottle caused it to slide from her grasp and it shattered on the floor, drenching her bare feet. She hadn't even the emotional energy left to swear. Instead she stood there looking down at the mess, shook her head and sighed, then carefully picked up the shards of broken glass and mopped up the spilled wine.

I need company, she thought wearily. I need something to take my mind off Charlie. Then realised with startling certainty that what she really needed was some totally meaningless sex.

Of course, bar picking a stranger up in a pub, a perilous exercise, her options were severely limited, so on impulse she scooped up her phone and dialled David's number. He answered on the second ring.

"Sally! How are you?" He sounded happy to hear from her.

"I'm fine," she said, all upbeat. "So what are you doing with yourself this evening?"

"Not a lot," he replied. "Just hanging out in front of the TV, to be honest."

"Lucky you. Mine's still in transit."

He laughed. "Trust me, you're not missing much."

Time to take the bull by the horns. "Fancy some company?"

The call left her feeling in control again, which was a welcome relief. Taking a lightning shower, she changed her clothes, choosing a sleeveless DKNY red jersey dress with her sexiest La Perla underneath, neutral lace-topped hold-ups and red Manolo mules.

"Right," she said to her reflection in the full-length bedroom mirror. "Time for seduction."

As she parked her car near the entrance to David's (borrowed) penthouse apartment, she felt a sudden wave of anxiety. It was over three years since she had last been single and she'd almost forgotten the rules. The anxiety was a new phenomenon though, born of Charlie's rejection, and it unsettled her. What's up with me? she thought. He's only a man, for God's sake. Get a grip.

Checking her make-up in the sun-visor mirror, she rubbed her lips together to freshen up her lipstick. "How could he resist you?" she asked her reflection. "He'll be putty in your hands."

The penthouse had its own private lift which required either a key or the occupant to send it down. David came down with it and they travelled up together. She had stopped off at the off-licence on the way over and bought a bottle of very good Cabernet Sauvignon which she proffered as the lift came to a halt.

"My favourite," he said. "Thanks. We starving writers have to forgo such luxuries as we freeze in our garrets, you know."

"Hardly a freezing garret!" she said as the elevator door hissed open and she caught the breathtaking view for the first time through the wall of glass. It was a large open living space, not unlike the loft, but scaled up. There the similarity ended however, mainly because of a huge central fireplace around which there were three long sofas which afforded both the comfort of the fire and the view from the roof garden. On a raised mezzanine level was the dining area which led into a high-tech kitchen. The glass-topped dining-table, fuzzy with finger-marks and mug circles, held an open laptop, several dirty coffee mugs, notebooks, a printer and a jumble of printed-out sheets.

"How's the book coming on?" she asked as she wandered around, picking things up and putting them down again, while David opened the wine.

"Slowly," he replied, standing in the kitchen doorway. "It takes a while to get this tortured creativity thing going, you know."

"Tortured creativity? I thought you were writing a political bonkbuster."

Slapping his hand over his heart in feigned hurt he said, "I'm wounded. All creativity's supposed to be tortured. It's the nature of the beast."

"Yeah, yeah," she said then smiled provocatively; best to cut to the chase. She made eye contact and held his gaze until he suddenly looked away – a trifle flustered, she thought – then poured the wine.

They moved back to the sofas, sitting close together facing the wall of glass. It was dusk and the clouds were tinged with pink and gold. "Stunning view," she said after a while, leaning back against the soft cushions.

"Yes," he replied, and she realised he was looking at her. She leaned over and kissed him on the lips, her hand resting on his cheek. The kiss was brief but sensuous and she stayed close gazing deep into his eyes. A microsecond passed before he reacted which caused a moment of anxiety, but then he kissed her back, not unsexily, a brief brush of tongues – then she ran hers, light as a feather, along his top lip. He pulled back, his face a couple of inches from hers, and brushed a stray wisp of hair from her cheek, then his arms enveloped her and his lips met hers again, ravenously, and she felt his evening beard grazing her chin but she didn't care.. He eased her onto her back and she was aware of his stiffening erection against her thigh. Then they were pulling off each other's clothes.

"No," he said, "leave the stockings," and she did.

She wasn't in the mood for lengthy foreplay, for getting to know him. This was pure lust. She wanted it hard and intense and she wanted it now, so she pushed him back roughly and took him in her mouth, feeling him harden even more, caressing him, arousing him. He moaned and after a few minutes of increasing intensity, fingers in her hair, he pulled her off and tried to roll her onto her back but she resisted, she knew what she wanted, and on her knees, her back to him, her torso resting on the sofa cushions, she invited him in.

It was energetic, powerful, primal, exactly what she needed.

"Harder," she ordered and he thrust deeper, faster and harder and she came quickly and with frightening intensity. He was only moments after her. When it was over he wrapped his arms around her waist and lifted her to the floor where they lay locked together, until she released herself and rested her head on his flat belly, until their breathing was back to normal.

"Stunning view," he said, brushing his thumb across her nipple, then cupping her breast in his hand.

She raised her head and watched as his eyes took in her body, lying there, unselfconscious, aware that she was beautiful. She felt good. She glanced down at his watch: less than half an hour since she had stepped out of the lift. How soon would it be decent to leave, she wondered. She might need him again so she didn't want to hurt his feelings or leave him feeling used. Men had such fragile egos.

God! I hope he doesn't want to talk, she thought. She wasn't in the mood. Sated and satisfied for now, she just wanted to go home.

The phone rang then and he had to get up to answer it, solving that awkward hiatus. She threw on her clothes and was fully dressed by the time he returned. He looked surprised, but she ignored it, sliding her arms around his neck, kissing him long and languorously. Something stirred against her leg so she drew away, refusing to notice.

"Sorry, have to go, lover," she whispered.

"But . . ." he started to say, and she silenced him again with her lips, all the time making progress towards the lift, and he capitulated.

"When will I see you again?" he asked.

"I'll call you," she said as the lift doors closed.

Chapter 21

Maggie was in the office bright and early the following morning after the best night's sleep she'd had in a week due either to her new bed or her yoga class, she wasn't sure which. She stopped on her way through reception to chat to Lily.

"You'll never guess what I did last night," she said.

Lily, who was sitting at her desk, sipping from a take-away carton of hot chocolate, leaned back in her chair and regarded her, unaware of the foam moustache clinging to her upper lip.

"Hmmmm," she said, thoughtfully. "Discovered the meaning of life? Shagged the gorgeous Aiden? Won the Lotto?"

Maggie shook her head. "None of the above. I went to a yoga class."

Lily's eyebrows shot up her forehead. "Yoga! Isn't that a bit . . ." She frowned. "What's the word I'm looking for? Boring, maybe?"

"Could be," Maggie agreed. "The yoga teacher was scary, and while I was doing it I didn't enjoy it that much, but I felt great afterwards."

"ESS," Lily said with an air of authority.

"ESS?"

"Exercise-Sandal Syndrome."

Maggie stared at her blankly.

"It's like those wooden clog exercise-sandals," Lily explained. "I reckon your feet only feel good because it's so bloody uncomfortable clunking around in them all day, it's bliss when you take the sodding things off."

Before Maggie could make further comment, Sally breezed in, a wide grin on her chops, fresh as a daisy. "Morning, ladies," she chirped. "What a wunnn-derful day!"

Taken by surprise by her sunny disposition they only managed a perfunctory "hello" in return before she virtually danced up the stairs to the upper floor.

"Someone got laid last night," Lily said in a low voice, her eyes following Sally Gillespie, Ray of Sunshine.

"Wouldn't you bloody know it!" her friend muttered, swallowing an irritating twinge of jealousy.

Maggie and Tom worked all morning on the I-Sport concepts in advance of their meeting with Sally and Paul Brody. The campaign itself was to consist of a series of three teaser posters followed by a two-week run of the full fifty-second TV ad, then fifteen-second cut-downs thereafter, plus radio, press, cinema and outdoor.

Tom tidied up his rough storyboards and Maggie worked on the script so the morning flew by. Half an hour before lunch her phone rang.

"Aiden on line two for you," Lily announced.

"Aiden? As in, next-door-neighbour-Aiden?"

"The very same."

"What does he want?"

"You, kiddo," Lily replied, then put him straight through.

"Uh . . . hi," Maggie said. "How are you?"

"Hi, yourself," he replied. "How did you enjoy the yoga last night?"

"Actually it was OK," she said. He'd obviously been talking to Anna. "Despite the fact that the teacher frightened the life out of me."

He laughed. "So your mother said. Anyway, the reason I'm calling. I'm after a favour."

"Such as?" Maggie asked, aware that she owed him one for being so nice to Anna.

"I was wondering if you could set up a couple of appointments at the agency for me to show my book. Seeing as I'm the new kid on the block, I'd really appreciate it."

"Sure," she said, relieved that it was something she could deliver on. "No problem. I'll get back to you on that."

"Great!" he said, then paused. "Um, listen, I'll be in O'Neill's at one. Do you fancy a bite to eat? My shout."

"Anything for a free lunch," she quipped.

After she put the phone down she couldn't help a smug little smile, realising that it was over two years since she'd been asked out to lunch as a single and unattached woman. Was he interested, she wondered, or was it just a thank-you in advance for helping him out? Notwithstanding her protests to Lily, she hoped it was the former. After being so humiliatingly dumped, her ego needed a boost, and Lily was right, Aiden Dempsey was distinctly fanciable, so why not? Anyway, if Sally bloody Gillespie could do it, so could she. Maybe it was time to put aside the "all men are bastards" generalisation and poke a toe back in the water.

As it was a bright and pleasant day, Aiden bagged a table by the window overlooking the river. He had his portfolio with him for a meeting later in the afternoon with Barry Penrose, the creative director of BBD&K and, apart from activating phase one of his plan to win Maggie's confidence by having a friendly lunch with her, he hoped to pick her brains, having learnt from Anna that she'd worked with Penrose at BBD&K before joining Deadly Inc

It was tough getting a foot in the door again after so long away and he was relieved that Gloria Fitzsimon, the fashion editor of ICON, had been so pleased with the results of the shoot. She'd had very definite ideas about what she wanted and he knew that he'd delivered; but he was also aware that he couldn't just rely on word of mouth – he needed to be proactive if he was to get the work.

He was thinking over his options, staring into what remained of his pint when he felt a hand on his shoulder. He looked up.

"Hi, sugar."

She looked as gorgeous as ever and was aware that all eyes in the room, both male and female, were appraising her slender shapely body, shown off to perfection in hipster pants and GUCCI leather jacket over a white top, short enough to show a tantalising glimpse of firm coffee-coloured skin.

"Jesus!" he said, completely taken by surprise. "What are you doing here?"

She pulled out a chair, spun it around and sat astride it, her back straight, her arms resting on the back, in a pose he'd shot her in many times.

"Now what kind of a welcome is that?" she asked, flicking her jet-black hair and affecting a pout with bee-stung lips. "I fly across an ocean and all he can say is 'What are you doing here?'"

Recovering, he gave a strained laugh. "Sorry, but you're the last person I expected to see, that's all."

She smiled at him and proffered her cheek for him to kiss. "That's me, sugar. Always the unexpected."

He gave the peach soft cheek an obligatory peck. "So what are you doing here?"

"Here, as in the Emerald Isle, or here, as in O'Neill's?" she asked.

"Here in general," he said, still bemused by her sudden appearance.

"Work, of course," she said, giving him a playful bat on the arm. "You didn't think I came to see you, did you?"

She didn't see him at first, and her eye was only drawn in his direction when she spotted the girl. She was sitting astride a chair, her arms resting on the back, impossibly beautiful and fully aware of the fact. Obviously a model. She had his full attention and the attention of every other man in the crowded room and suddenly Maggie felt invisible. As she made her way over, her confidence plummeting with every step, the girl laughed, throwing her head back and flicking her hair, then leaning forward again she touched his arm and said something which caused him to smile.

Maggie was right on top of the table before he noticed her, but as soon as she caught his eye, he jumped up, smiling a welcome.

"Maggie. Hi!"

"Hi yourself," she said, her eyes landing on the girl. It was impossible not to stare. There was a moment's silence, then the girl held out a limp hand.

"Sinita," she said. "Aiden and I are old friends." The accent was transatlantic with a hint of Southern Belle laced with honey. Maggie shook her hand, then in a lithe and languorous movement Sinita stood up. In her three-inch heels she had at least seven inches on Maggie who for the first time since primary school felt short and dumpy.

"Nice to meet you," Maggie said politely, looking up at her and managing a smile.

"You too," she purred.

There was another silence, then Aiden pecked Sinita on the cheek and said pointedly, "Don't you have to be somewhere?"

Silence for a further beat, then she looked at Maggie and mouthed a silent 'Oh', then nodded, and touched his wrist.

"Call me," she said. "I'm staying at the Morrison."

All eyes followed her and the crowd parted like the Red Sea as she glided across the room towards the exit.

"Wow," Maggie said, her eyes too drawn like a magnet to the retreating figure.

169

"My ex," Aiden said as he pulled out a chair for Maggie. "Now, what would you like to drink?"

In spite of the shaky start, lunch was enjoyable, the food was very good, and he was such easy company. Unable to resist, she'd asked him about Sinita and he'd explained that they'd broken up almost a year ago, that it was amicable, that they were still friends but had both moved on and weren't involved any more, which pleased her, and that Sinita was in Ireland for her first acting role in a Jackie Chan action movie. Then the subject of Mark had come up and it was weird, but she felt as if she was talking about a stranger, she felt so removed from the situation. It was as if the whole thing had happened a lifetime ago rather than just over a week. There was a good bit of banter and a definite light-hearted flirting vibe going on over the course of the hour, which had positively flown, then he walked her back to the office.

"So how did it go?" Lily asked, recognising a cat-who-got-the-cream grin if ever she saw one.

"Early days yet," Maggie said. "But it was nice."

Never one to beat about the bush Lily said, "So did he ask you out, or what?"

"No," Maggie said, smiling over her shoulder as she hurried towards her office. "But he will."

Chapter 22

Maggie wasn't looking forward to the meeting with Sally and Paul Brody, anticipating opposition for no good reason, so despite her flying humour after her lunch with Aiden, she felt herself tensing up at the prospect.

She made the presentation with Tom flipping the storyboards, starting with their least-favoured option, the one which stuck to the letter of the client's brief.

"The first concept is 'A Legend in the Making,'" she said. "Opening with the throbbing guitar riff from the beginning of the Irish Olé Olé soccer anthem over a montage of great Irish sporting legends of all disciplines – athletics, swimming, Gaelic, rugby, equestrian, rowing, soccer etc – through the years in chronological order from the nineteen fifties through to the present day."

"Colourful speedy cuts to loud music," Tom interjected. "Ending with Gavin O'Connor scoring goals for both Ireland and Manchester United."

"Final shot," Maggie continued, "has Gavin against a

background of Landsdowne Road full of Ireland soccer fans, cheering and roaring. Cut to close up. He takes a long drink from a bottle of I-Sport, wipes his mouth, then thrusting the product out to camera he says 'I-Sport – It's Isotonic.' Zoom in for the pack shot. Male voice-over: 'I-Sport – A Legend in the making.'"

Sally looked unimpressed.

"Yeeee-es," Paul said thoughtfully after a silence. "I can see where you're coming from. A legend in the making. The client should go for that." He looked at Sally.

"So what's the other concept?" she asked without enthusiasm, the subtext of the question leaning towards, I hope you can come up with something more original than that.

Maggie shot a glance at Tom, who was shuffling his storyboards ready for the second presentation.

She took a deep breath and lashed into it. "The second concept is 'The Extra Man'. I-Sport is 'The Extra Man'," she explained.

"We start the same guitar riff and the Ireland Olé Olé anthem with subtitle, Euro 88, over the famous Ray Houghton goal against England, then cut to special effect of Gavin O'Connor scoring a second. Cut to cheering fans. Cut to the score board: Ireland 2 England 0. Cut to subtitle, Italia 90 over the Schillachi killer goal that put us out of the quarter finals. He shoots. Special effect, Gavin O'Connor heads it past the post. Cut to shot of Ireland fans cheering wildly. Cut to subtitle, USA 94 over the Mexico match. Gavin kills the second Mexico goal. Gavin scores at the other end. Cut to the score board: Ireland 2 Mexico 1. Cut to cheering Ireland fans. Cut to The Holland Match. Gavin saves the Holland goal. Cut to cheering Ireland fans. Cut to Gavin. He slides towards the camera on his knees, a bottle of I-Sport in his hand. He drinks thirstily from the bottle, head back, then wipes his mouth, looks to camera, grinning, holding the product to camera."

Maggie paused a beat for effect.

"Zoom in to close-up. Gavin's voice-over: 'It's Isotonic.' A pause. 'I-Sport! It's The Extra Man.'" Extreme close-up pack shot."

An ominous silence hung over the room. Maggie gave Tom a questioning look, but he just shrugged his caterpillar eyebrow in reply.

Then to Maggie's surprise Sally said, "I think it's great. Well done."

"I don't know," Paul said, obviously the only man in Ireland who wasn't a soccer fan. "Our target market's 18 to 25's. They wouldn't get it. It's all ancient history to them."

Sally shook her head. "I don't agree with the words 'ancient' and 'history', Paul. With apologies to concept number one, I think we're talking Legend here. I remember it for God's sake and I'm not even a fan. The whole country was sucked in."

The whole country with the exception of Paul Brody, Maggie thought.

Paul shook his head. "But don't you think it's a very negative message. I mean we didn't win, did we? We lost. And Gavin O'Connor wasn't even playing."

"But that the whole point, mate," Tom cut in. "It's the dream. It's what could have been if we'd had the extra man. Ireland beating Italy twice. Ireland beating Italy in the quarter finals. Scoring two against the old foe, England.

We're off to the world cup again in June. It's about the dream, mate. Don't you get it?"

He didn't, but by the time the meeting broke up an hour later, he did.

They discussed the teaser poster campaign: black background with just the words, "Who's the Extra Man?" in I-Sport Orange, then Sally questioned which production companies had the expertise to handle the blue-screen special effects. That talked through, the meeting ended on a positive note with Paul almost as enthusiastic as Sally. In fact, the way he was talking, a casual observer would have been under the impression that the whole concept had been his idea.

"Well, that went surprisingly well," Maggie said as she and Tom returned to their office. "I was sure she'd go for the boring option if she went for anything."

"Why?" Tom asked.

He sounded surprised and Maggie realised she didn't know why. It was just a knee-jerk reaction.

Even without client approval there was still stuff to do. Tom commenced work on the final storyboards for the client presentation, and Maggie called up Herbie McFly at "Fly On The Wall Productions", explained the concept and asked him for a for a ballpark figure for the project, to quote to the client. After that she called Gavin O'Connor's agent again for a fee quotation, and to enquire about the footballer's availability for a two to three day shoot, subject to him being agreeable.

"Are you up for a jar?" Tom asked as the small hand reached five and the big hand six on the clock.

Instead of O'Neill's they went off to Tom's usual evening-scoop venue, the Palace, on Fleet Street. The teatime crowd was thinning out as they arrived and they got seats at the bar. Maggie ordered a Bud and Tom a pint of the black stuff. It had been a satisfying day all round, the biggest surprise of which had been Sally Gillespie's enthusiasm for 'The Extra Man' concept.

"I was thinking, I'd like Mike Patterson to direct," Maggie said to Tom.

He nodded. "Good choice." Then after taking a swallow of Guinness added, "Though what about Mossie Hunt? He did a great job on Kiddie-Vite."

"Mossie's good too," she said, then after a pause, "but he's not the easiest to work with, is he? He can be a bit of a prima donna sometimes, don't you think?"

"Only when he's on the gargle," Tom said, "but he's been on the wagon this last three months."

"Are you serious?" Maggie was unaware that Mossie had forsaken the demon drink.

"Speaking of the devil," Tom said, looking past her. "How's the form, Mossie?"

Maggie turned her head to see Mossie limping towards them with the aid of crutches, his right foot in plaster.

"What happened to you?" she asked, eyeing up the grubby cast.

"Fell off the sodding treadmill at the fecking gym, didn't I," he said and both Tom and Maggie burst out laughing. "Bloody gyms," he continued, leaning the crutches against the bar and hiking himself up, with difficulty, on to a bar stool. "This healthy lifestyle business can be seriously fecking dangerous."

"So what caused you to go on the quest for the body beautiful in the first place?" she asked.

"Doctor's orders," he replied, without elaboration, then Tom asked him what he was drinking and Maggie was half relieved when he ordered an orange juice. He looked quite well, off the drink – the whites of his eyes had lost that drinker's yellow tinge. Maybe that was it, she surmised. Maybe it was to do with his liver. Whatever the reason it must be serious, she thought, or there's no way he'd have taken any notice. In fairness to Mossie, even when he was on the sauce, he never drank during the day on a job, and despite being difficult to work with, he always got the job done to a very high standard. It was just the stress levels he induced in everyone else that was such a bummer. It did make her wonder briefly if the drink was the catalyst for his creativity, and if he'd be as inspired a director on the wagon.

"Did I hear it right that you've got the lovely Sally Gillespie at Deadly now?" he asked, addressing the question to Tom.

Tom nodded. "Yeah. D'you know her?"

Mossie took a drink of his orange juice, giving an involuntary shudder as the citrus tang hit his tastebuds. "Do I know her?" he repeated. "On a number of levels, my friend." It was one of those nudge-nudge, wink-wink, lad moments.

"Are you serious!" Maggie said. "You and Sally Gillespie?"

"We had a brief liaison," he said, the laddish, smug grin still on his gob.

It wasn't that hard to believe. He was the type Sally used to go for. Tallish, slim (though he'd developed a small beer-pot in the interim), creative – she always seemed to go for creative types.

"So how brief was brief?" she asked out of interest.

He gave a little shrug. "Ah, a couple of months, on and off."

That was par for the course. Sally usually lost interest after a month, two at the most. "So why did you split up?" she asked for pure devilment.

"Irreconcilable differences," he said after a moment's thought.

Tom gave him a knowing look. "She dumped you, then."

There was a brief hiatus, then Mossie sighed and nodded his head. "That's about the size of it."

He was unable to disguise his sad regret, causing Maggie to wonder, yet again, how she did it. Then the words 'Treat 'em mean to keep 'em keen', popped into her mind and she realised that that must be it. It was true, and there was the evidence sitting up at the bar beside her. Whatever weird pathology men possessed, Sally obviously had it well and truly sussed.

Until now, it occurred to her, remembering Lily's theory regarding the flowers and the tears of the previous day. But then again, she'd been in brilliant form that very morning, so obviously if she had been dumped it was only a minor blip in her firmament, so the theory clearly didn't work the other way round.

I really must get this man-stuff sorted, she thought to herself as Tom and Mossie waffled on about the football.

If only.

Although it was utterly untrue to say that Charlie's treachery was but a blip in her firmament, Sally was in a happy frame of mind as she made her way home at four thirty to receive the remainder of her in-transit belongings which were due for delivery. The episode the previous night with David had soothed her battered ego and, in truth, the sex itself had been very satisfying if brief, but that had been her choice, not his. She been pleasantly surprised too, by Maggie and Tom's 'Extra Man' concept after their awful initial, 'Legend in the Making' attempt.

It was with an air of excitement therefore that she set off for home, looking forward to having her familiar things around her again; although comfortable and quite stylish in an anonymous sort of way, the loft still didn't feel like home.

Since the earlier sudden heavy shower had cleared up, she decided to walk rather than call a cab, and outside the office had to step around a large hairy mongrel dog which was standing in the doorway, its coarse coat still wet from the rain. It looked up at her appealingly, wagging its tail, but she sidestepped it in disgust, being disinclined towards animals in general, then she strode off towards home, taking a short cut up Lime Street, a narrow thoroughfare leading on to Pearse Street. As she looked behind her to check for traffic before crossing the road, she saw the dog again. It appeared to be following her at a steady amble. She ignored it in the hope that it would go away, but as she crossed over Hanover Street into Erne Street, it was still there. She stopped but so did the dog, about ten yards behind her.

"Go home, dog!" she said in an authoritative voice, but the dog stood stock-still. She stood for a further moment, then when the dog made no attempt to move, shrugged her shoulders and hurried on.

He must have been hiding in a doorway on the quiet side street waiting for a likely mark, because she didn't see him, only felt the power of his grip on her arm, and the rancid smell of his body odour as he grabbed her from behind. She screamed and tried to pull away, hanging onto the strap of her bag as he tried to wrestle it from her grasp. It was an automatic reaction on her part as, apart from her (easily cancellable) credit cards and a few euro in cash, there was nothing of value in it. Then suddenly her attacker was thrown against her with force, knocking both of them off balance, and she was aware of a high-pitched scream of pain, and the unmistakable sound of a dog snarling and growling. Her attacker let go of her, too intent on releasing the strong set of canine teeth gripping his upper arm, and she staggered, almost falling against the wall, her heart pounding. Then she caught her breath and, infuriated by the effrontery of the gurrier, now admittedly at the mercy of the dog, started to beat him about the head and shoulders with her umbrella.

"Gerroff!" he yelled, trying to duck away from her assault, while attempting to ward off the dog who, having lost interest in his upper arm, was now doing its level best to castrate him. He kicked out, catching the canine a lucky but hefty blow on the side. The dog yelped and then, as his grip loosened, the gurrier made his escape, hands clutched to his groin, bellowing like a wounded rhino.

Sally's heart was still pounding, her ears ringing, and she felt momentarily weak from the shock of the sudden attack. Her bag was lying on the pavement, the strap broken, and her umbrella didn't look the best either, bent and battered from the vigour of contact with the gurrier's upper body. The dog was standing a couple of feet away, panting, his eyes following the limping assailant as he hobbled away.

"Um . . . thanks . . . er . . . dog," she said, feeling both grateful and a touch stupid that she was actually thanking a dumb animal, nonetheless conscious that she did owe it for coming to her rescue. Uncertainly she reached out her hand and, taking a quick look around to make sure no one was watching, gave him a tentative pat on the head. "Good boy."

The dog wagged its tail enthusiastically, still panting, looking up at her, and she had a sudden sense of déjà vu, remembering her dilemma of the previous night, wondering how soon it would be decent to leave.

"Well, must get on," she said, still self-conscious that she was explaining herself to an animal. "Got to get home for . . . well . . . got to go . . . OK?"

My God, I'm asking it if it's all right to go now, she thought as she stooped to pick up her bag. They stood there for another beat, the dog looking up at her, tail wagging, she itching to get away, then she abruptly turned and walked off up the street, still shaken by the attack, but with a sense of adrenaline euphoria that an unexpected escape can produce.

Now and then, as she made progress across town towards Great George's Street, she stole a glance over her shoulder and was relieved that by the time she reached College Green the dog was nowhere in sight.

She stopped off at Marks & Spencer's food hall for a few groceries and a couple of bottles of wine and, as she emerged back onto Grafton Street, saw the dog sitting patiently by the exit. She thought she'd lost it as she made her way past Powerscourt Townhouse, but caught sight of it again as she arrived at her building. It was definitely following her. Creepy. She felt a little uncomfortable considering the animal had saved her, not sure what it expected of her, but then it sat down about five yards down the street and started to wash its paw, apparently uninterested.

Her belongings arrived at five fifteen and she spent some time unpacking them, holding her art up against the wall to see what looked best where and so forth. The delivery men, Arthur and Gary, insisted on tuning in her TV and hooking up the DVD player, so she let them, taking for granted the fact that they should go to the trouble which was above and beyond their remit. Giving them a twenty euro each as she invited them to leave, they were perhaps a bit disappointed that they hadn't pulled (possibly having put money on it) but the tip apparently made up for it.

Then, as Arthur was going through the door, he shouted over his shoulder,

"Will I let the dog in?"

So taken up with delight at seeing her familiar stuff again it took a moment for his words to register and by that time it was too late. Her hairy rescuer was standing inside the door, panting and wagging his tail, steam rising from his shaggy damp coat.

"No!" she said. "You can't come in," but the dog lay down by the door, oblivious to her protest, put its head on its outstretched paws and closed his eyes. "No," she repeated firmly, but the dog was having none of it.

"All right," she said after a brief moment of silence, then purposefully walked into the kitchen and rummaged in her shopping for some food to give it, not inclined to attempt to remove it by force having witnessed what the animal was capable of. Anyway it probably weighed twice as much as she did.

It's most likely hungry, she thought. She wasn't even sure what dogs ate except that you weren't supposed to give them chicken bones, or was that cats? She wasn't sure. With her limited larder, she unpacked the two M&S boneless cooked chicken fillets she'd intended to eat with a ready-prepared mixed salad, then made her way to the door and opened it.

"Look, doggy," she said, wafting the scent of chicken in the snoozing dog's direction. "Din-dins!"

The dog opened one eye, then closed it again, emitting a huge sigh.

"Din-dins," she repeated. "Yum-yum!"

The dog sighed again, then lifted his head and looked in the direction of the proffered food. Sally edged towards the door. After a brief face-off, the dog stood up and stretched, then took a few steps towards her, eyes on the chicken, while she backed away through the open front door into the hallway. The aroma of the chicken obviously got to him then because he followed her as she backed down the stairs all the way to the street. Once outside, she placed the cooked chicken fillets on the ground about four feet from the door, and as soon as the dog was well out of the doorway in pursuit of dinner, she bounded inside again, slamming the door after her, strangely uncomfortable, but at the same time pleased with herself that, in her view, she had paid a debt.

Chapter 23

The following morning at around eleven, Maggie's mobile rang and the caller ID told her that it was her father.

"Hello, Dad," she said.

"Your mother's on the radio! I heard your mother on the radio telling people to go to Super Savings!" he said without preamble.

It had slipped Maggie's mind that the first of Anna's Super Savings promos was due for transmission that morning.

"That's right, Dad. She did a voice-over for me when the actress I'd booked was sick."

"Oh," he said, then there was a silence.

"Dad? Are you still there?"

"I am. What's your mother up to, Mags?" He sounded despondent.

"I told you already, Dad. She wants to spend some time on herself. In fairness you can't blame her. You hardly pay her any attention."

She heard him sigh at the other end of the phone.

"But what can I do? She won't answer her phone." He sounded pathetic, whiny, and Maggie's hackles were up.

"I already told you what to do, Dad. Court her, send her flowers, let her know you care about her. I think she feels . . ." she floundered for the right words but could only come up with, "old . . . neglected and old."

"Sure none of us is getting any younger. That's daft."

"Maybe to you, Dad. But have you ever asked her how she feels?"

It was clear that the question had flown straight over his head. "How do you mean? Is she sick?" He sounded fearful.

Maggie closed her eyes and swallowed her annoyance. "Dad. Do you want Mum home?"

"Of course, I do. What kind of a question is that?"

"But why, Dad?" she asked. "Why do you want her home?"

She heard him breathing deeply at the other end of the phone, obviously thinking.

"Because it's where she belongs," he finally said. "Here with me."

"But why, Dad?" she persisted. "What's in it for her?"

That concept too went way over his head. "How do you mean?" he asked, genuinely flummoxed. "Are you sure she's not sick?"

"No, Dad, she's not sick, at least not in the way you mean. Heartsick maybe."

"I don't know what to do," he said helplessly. "I'm no good at the romantic stuff. Your mother knows I love her." Even that admission was hard for him.

"But that's just it, Dad. She doesn't," Maggie pleaded.

"Tell her. Send her the biggest bouquet you can, and tell her. Come up here and tell her in person even if you think it's daft."

"How can I when she won't talk to me?"

"I said come up here. She'll hardly turn you away if you make a grand romantic gesture. Women are suckers for a grand romantic gesture."

Particularly when it's so out of character, she thought.

A further silence, then he said, his voice a tad more positive. "Are you sure?"

"I'm a woman too, Dad. Trust me, I know what I'm talking about. Come up tonight."

"But Lucy and young Phoebe are coming up this weekend," he moaned.

"So put them off. You can see them another weekend. This is way more important." She didn't bother to fill him in on the true reason for their visit.

He sighed again. A long heartfelt sigh full of regret and sadness. "I suppose I could," he said. "I need her, Mags And I miss her auld nagging."

"Tell her, not me," Maggie said. "And promise me you won't mention the nagging. It would kind of spoil the moment."

After he had promised to think carefully about what he would say to her and assured Maggie that he would not mention nagging, VAT or Ministry forms, she said goodbye, a much happier bunny.

Just before eleven twenty-five, when she and Tom were walking through reception to head up to the conference room for a meeting with Paul Brody and Gerry Starling, the marketing manager of Super Savings, Anna breezed in beaming like a Cheshire cat who'd just snaffled the last Rolo.

"Did you hear it?" she asked. "Did you hear it?"

"The ad?" Maggie said. "No, but Dad did. He called me."

"Never mind about that," she said full of excitement. "I had the radio on all morning waiting for it, then I went to the loo and nearly missed it. Isn't that gas! And it didn't sound a bit like me. You know how it is when you hear your voice recorded, it sounds completely different to the way you hear it in your head."

Lily gave her hug. "I heard it up in the kitchen when I was getting Dom's coffee and you sounded great."

"Do you really think so?" Anna asked. "You don't think I sounded boring?"

As Lily was assuring Anna that she'd given a performance worthy of an Oscar, the front door opened then Gerry Starling walked in, shoulders set, wearing a thunderous expression. Maggie wasn't sure what to make of him. He had a blunt manner and, in the three months she'd been dealing with him, she had found him unpredictable – one day nit-picking, the next enthusiastic about everything. So she was a trifle worried about how he'd react to her substituting the Super Savings voice without consultation, and judging by his body language she expected the worst.

As he approached her however, he did a double take, then he stopped dead in his tracks behind Anna, who was still discussing her performance with Lily and stared at her, his jaw slack.

"Gerry," Tom said, slapping him on the back, "how are you?"

Gerry seemed mesmerised as he stood there watching and listening to Anna who was oblivious to the fact that she had so rapt an audience. He was a short man, about five seven, with rusty hair and fair freckled skin. Tom towered over him. After a few beats he got his act together again and turned to Tom.

"Who's that?" he asked, under his breath, indicating Anna with a sly tilt of his head. She was wearing her leather pants and high ankle boots and it was obvious that he was enjoying the view, so Maggie jumped in.

"Gerry, let me introduce you to Anna Fortune, the voice-over who generously offered to fill the breach and save the day after Steph fell so unexpectedly ill." She grabbed Anna's arm.

"Anna, I'd like you to meet Gerry Starling, from Super Savings."

Anna stopped in mid-sentence and turned to Gerry (in her heels they were about the same height). She instantly turned on the charm.

"Mister Starling! How wonderful to meet you," she gushed, surprising even Maggie.

He was instantly smitten. "Please," he said, visibly shaken, "call me Gerry." He took her hand in both of his and held on to it. "I'm delighted to meet you." Then, as if a light had gone on in his brain added, "Fortune?" He glanced at Maggie. "Any relation?"

"Well, as a matter of fact Anna's my mother," Maggie admitted.

"Your mother? Good grief, I thought she was your sister!"

Out of Gerry's eye-line, Lily mimed pushing her finger

down her throat but Anna went all coy, and gave him a shove on the arm.

"Oh, don't be silly," she said.

"No, really," he protested. "And you have a wonderful voice. I was just about to tell Maggie and Tom here how pleased I am with the new promos."

Considering his body language as he'd walked in, added to the smarmy compliment, Maggie was expecting his nose to grow like Pinocchio's, but nothing happened. Gerry, who was still hanging onto Anna's hand, was beaming like a moron, unable to take his eyes off her.

"I hope you'll be able to work for us again," he added.

Anna's face lit up. "I'd love to," she said.

Tom glanced over at Maggie, the corner of his mouth twitching into a smile. "Will we go up to the conference room, Gerry? I think Paul's up there already," he said.

Reluctantly Gerry released Anna's hand, with another "Wonderful to meet you".

Anna smiled coyly. "Nice to meet you too," she agreed, making big-time eye contact, which Maggie thought a touch over the top.

The meeting went like a dream. Gerry was in raptures about Anna's voice and Anna in general, which caused Maggie an inward sigh of relief, but then he dropped the bombshell.

"And I'd like you to rethink the whole TV campaign," he said. "I want Anna Fortune to be the new face of Super Savings, instead of me, and I'd like an ongoing theme, like BBD&K did for us last year, only better, of course."

Paul who was nodding in agreement while throwing

comments like, "Great, great," now and again, was mentally rubbing his hands at the notion of a larger budget.

"Um . . . the thing is," Maggie said tentatively, "I'm not sure Anna will be available."

Gerry's facial muscles tensed. "Not available?"

"You see, she may not . . ." Maggie started but Paul cut her off at the pass.

"Don't worry about that, Gerry," he assured his client. "I'm sure we can come to some arrangement."

After the meeting concluded and Paul walked a chirpy Gerry out, Tom said, "What's the problem with your ma? Sure wouldn't she only love to do it?"

Maggie shook her head. "That's the problem. If she gets her feet under the table and starts earning good money, there's a chance she and Dad will never get back together."

"Ah, will you get real!" Tom said. "The fact that she's earning a few bob of her own won't stop her if that's what she really wants."

"But I'm not sure it is," Maggie said.

"Then you've no right to try and manipulate the situation," Tom said. "Your ma's a grown-up, or hadn't you noticed, and she'll make her own decisions." He paused then, smiling to take the harm out of it. "Anyway, it's better than having our friend Gerry in front of the camera, for God's sake. Did you see those BBD&K ads?"

Although it wasn't what she wanted to hear, she couldn't fault Tom's logic. The fact was, it was now all down to her father's efforts to win his wife back and that was a very scary thought. She could only hope that he'd put some wellie into it.

She was therefore delighted when Lily waltzed into her office at five o'clock bearing a huge bouquet of lilies with lots of ferns and greenery, for one Anna Fortune.

Sally left the office at five thirty after being excused from the mandatory Friday night drink in O'Neill's on the grounds that she was expecting delivery of the rest of her belongings. She wasn't wild about that particular custom and felt the following week was soon enough to start socialising with the troops.

She didn't see him through the glass doors as he was sitting out of view, to one side of the entrance, either by chance or stealth, she didn't know which, so was taken completely by surprise when she spied him sitting there, his tail wrapped neatly around his feet, to all intents and purposes waiting for her. Her astonishment meant that she had no time to think of a strategy. She hesitated, then without making eye contact or acknowledging his presence in any way, turned to her right and hurried off up the Quays. After her experience with the mugger the previous day she took the scenic route home which gave her the opportunity to check out shop-window reflections to see if he was following her again, but by the time she reached Westmoreland Street there was no sign.

Stopping off again in M&S she bought a couple more cooked chicken breasts and some pasta sauce and fresh penne, some ciabatta, croissants and other snacky bits and bobs, it being Friday, then headed for home.

Her first week had been surprisingly OK work-wise and she was coming round to the fact that perhaps joining Deadly was a good career move after all. Leo had invited her to work on two of the company's larger accounts with him, and she was reviewing the work of the creative team as a whole. Mulling this over as she walked through the arcade to Great George's Street, her mind elsewhere, it was only at the last moment that she observed him again. He was sitting beside her front door like a large garden ornament.

"What do you want?" she asked, irritated, then felt silly as a passer-by gave her a wry look.

The dog turned his head and looked up at her, then stood as if waiting for her to open the door to let him in.

"No!" she said. "You can't come in. I don't do animals!"

She could have sworn he looked hurt at that, and felt a flash of guilt until she reminded herself that she was talking to a dumb animal who didn't understand a word she was saying. Taking her key from her purse she opened the door a crack, taking care to exclude any chance that the dog could squeeze past, closing it firmly after her.

Halfway up the stairs she became aware of the scent of roses and when she turned the corner of the landing was greeted by the sight of a large bouquet of long-stemmed red roses, at least twenty, lying on the floor outside her front door. Her first thought was David and she felt both smug and pleased that she hadn't blown it by her quick exit, but thought red roses a bit over the top after such a brief encounter. Still, she thought, better to keep them hungry for more – any doubts she'd had about herself evaporating. Things were finally getting back to normal.

Unlocking the door, she picked up the roses and carried them inside, clicking on the lights and dumping the bouquet on the granite counter along with her groceries. It was good to come home and have familiar things around her again. She lit the gas fire, zapped on the CD player and hunted around for a vase. A sudden heavy shower of rain with the wind behind it lashed against the window making the place seem even cosier. Under the sink she came across an unremarkable glass vase which she filled with water humming along to Sting, then tore the cellophane off the bouquet and placed the flowers in water, absently tearing open the envelope to read the card.

Her good humour evaporated instantaneously. The card read simply: *"I love you. C."*

She felt the colour drain from her face and was overcome by a sudden strong weakness, which caused her to grip the counter-top for balance. How did he get my address? was the first thing to cross her mind. Followed by, why can't he leave me alone?

Her first instinct was to phone him and call him all the foul names under the sun that she could think of; to demand that he leave her alone, even threaten to call the horse-faced Imogene and blow the whistle, but something stopped her. Perhaps it was a deep-seated desire that things could still be the way they were, a reluctance to finally shut the door on that part of her life, or perhaps it was the words "I love you". She didn't know, or at any rate didn't want to think about it, disgusted as she was by her spinelessness. But the feeling passed after a few moments, and she sighed. This was hard, but maybe it was for the best. If he kept this up she'd grow to hate him. At that moment she felt miserable, angry and used. Charlie had used her. Used her, lied to her, then discarded her when it suited him. Now he wouldn't leave her alone, even though he had given her no indication that the rules would be anything other than what they had previously been. How cruel was that?

What kind of pathetic idiot does he think I am? she asked herself. He doesn't love me or he wouldn't have let me go.

Then the needy voice in her head urged: maybe he does love you, maybe he's sorry and really does want you back.

But the irritating voice of reason was having none of it. Don't be a fool. Of course he doesn't love you. He's using you, manipulating you again and you're falling for it, you idiot! He might want you back, but on his terms.

Bastard!

Her anger turned to fury then and she abruptly pulled open a drawer, thrashing through the contents until she found the kitchen scissors. Then deliberately she took each rose in turn, cutting off its ruby velvet head into the sink (all twenty) then switched on the tap and fed them down the garbage-disposal unit.

It was a very satisfying experience which left her ravenously hungry so, with Sting still warbling in the background, she cooked the pasta, nuked the sauce in the microwave, opened a bottle of wine and sat down to eat.

The last Sting track faded as she took her first mouth full of pasta, leaving the room silent except for the gentle hiss of the gas fire. The shower had turned to a steady downpour and intermittent gusts of wind lashed it against the window. Suddenly she felt very alone.

Chapter 24

Maggie left O'Neill's early and got home at around seven bearing her father's peace-offering. She met Anna, who was on her way downstairs, in the hall.

"Gorgeous flowers!" her mother said. "Who are they from?"

Maggie thrust the bouquet into her arms, a coy grin in her gob. "Why don't you read the card. They're for you."

Anna's newly reshaped eyebrows elevated. "For me?" Then she giggled. "How exciting!" and hurried into the kitchen with her arm full of lilies. "Who do you think they're from?"

"Haven't a notion," Maggie lied.

Anna tore off the envelope and slid the card out. Maggie filled the kettle, smiling to herself as she heard her mother exclaim, "Oh, how sweet! What a charmer!"

"So who are they from?" Maggie asked innocently.

Anna went all coy again. "An admirer," she said, clutching the card to her chest.

Maggie played the game, not wanting to spoil her mother's moment, she too grinning like an eejit. "So who is this admirer? Anyone I know?"

"Yes," Anna said, "and a very charming man."

A tad over the top perhaps. Charming wouldn't be one of the chosen adjectives that Maggie would have applied to her father; nevertheless, it was good to see that the gesture appeared to have had the desired effect.

"So don't keep me in suspense," Maggie urged. "Who is it?" Still playing the game.

Anna was positively glowing as she glanced down at the card. "He thinks I'm amazing!"

"Mu-uum!"

Anna grinned, enjoying the moment. "Gerry, of course!"

A moment's stunned silence, then, "Gerry! Gerry who?"

"Gerry Starling. Who else would it be?"

"But I thought they were from Dad!" If she'd had the first notion that they were from bloody, smarmy, creepy Gerry Starling she'd have binned them.

"Your father?" Anna gave a disdainful, "Pwah!" than glanced over Maggie's shoulder towards the dresser. "That is from your father."

Sitting on the dresser top was a pot plant. Admittedly a fairly decent-sized succulent with a single salmon pink flower at its centre and a pink bow tied around the plastic pot, but in the battle of the romantic gestures a cactus, albeit an aristocratic cactus, was no match for an armful of lilies with ferns and fronds.

"But what did the card say?" Maggie asked clinging to the last straw of hope.

Anna pursed her lips. "See for yourself." She pointed

at the card, which had been skewered into the compost. Maggie picked it out.

"Come home. Dan."

Come home? Was that the best he could do? Maggie put on her enthusiastic face. "See. He misses you. He loves you, needs you and he wants you to come home."

Anna gave her a leery look. "All it says is 'Come home', Maggie – where did you get the other rubbish from?"

"But he loves you!" Maggie wailed. "You know he loves you."

Anna sighed, then shook her head. "Maybe in his own way, pet. But it's not enough any more. Don't you understand?"

"But he's trying, Mum. Can't you at least meet him halfway?"

"In Longford, you mean?" Anna said giving a wicked smirk.. "He's over a hundred and fifty miles away, Mags. If he was that bothered he'd be up here now, not propping up Matt Molloy's bar."

"But maybe he's on his way," Maggie bleated, desperate to turn the situation around.

"Well, that's a pity," Anna said as she filled Maggie's only vase with water, "because I'm going out."

"Out? Out where?" This wasn't part of the plan.

"Out to dinner if you must know, with Gerry."

"But you can't!" Maggie protested.

Anna, busy arranging her lilies in the glass vase, stopped and looked up. "Excuse me?" The look on her face could have stripped paint.

Maggie backed off. "But what about Dad?" she said feebly, for the first time noticing that Anna was dressed to kill in a new black dress and high court shoes. "And you know nothing about Gerry Starling. He could be married for all you know. Probably is, in fact. Married with half a dozen kids."

Satisfied with the floral arrangement, Anna placed it on the kitchen table and stood back to admire her handiwork. "There," she said, as if she hadn't heard. "Isn't that magnificent?"

Maggie didn't know what to do. She made a final plea. "Mum?"

Anna sighed. "I'm not going to discuss this with you, Mags. It's just dinner, for God's sake." And picking up her coat and bag walked past Maggie towards the hall. "Don't wait up," were her parting words.

The front door banged.

"Only because the weather's so shit," she said. "And don't think I'll make a habit of this because I won't."

I'm doing it again, she thought, I'm talking to a bloody animal – but found herself continuing, "It's just for tonight, then we're even, OK?"

Shit! I'm asking it for an opinion now. What have I come down to that the only company I can find to talk to is a sodding dog?

It was loneliness that had driven her to let the dog in. It was too soon to call David and anyway it wasn't sex she needed, it was company, but she didn't feel like making conversation. She also had an uneasy feeling of obligation towards the dog knowing it was probably sitting out there in the lashing rain.

Once inside it had shaken itself, soaking her legs, then

it trotted ahead of her up the stairs and into the loft, without a by your leave.

She came across an old towel in the back of the airing cupboard and used it to rub the hound dry. He stood there quietly allowing her to minister to him, now and then wagging his long thin tail in approval, then when he figured he was dry enough, padded over to the fireplace, stretched out on the rug and closed his eyes.

"Well, great company you turned out to be," she said aloud, but he ignored her.

Sally settled herself on the sofa and switched on the TV. The nine o'clock news was on, full of old guff about the forthcoming general election, so she muted the sound and watched the pictures.

He was a big dog, probably some part wolfhound because of his general shape and the coarse coat, with a bit of Irish setter thrown in as the coat was rusty-coloured and he had floppy setter ears. Bigger than a setter but smaller than a wolfhound. A wolfter or a sethound? A wolfter, she decided as she watched the steam rising from his damp coat. He was a truly ugly brute, and the joke about a giraffe being a horse designed by committee came to mind.

"I should give you a name. I can't keep calling you 'dog'," she said, then added quickly, just in case he got any ideas, "Not that this is in any way a permanent arrangement, you understand. It's just a case of manners."

The hound opened one eye and stared at her.

"How about Wolfie?" she enquired. No, too naff. "Or Gnasher, after Denis the Menace's dog?"

He closed his eye and gave a deep sigh, possibly of contempt.

"OK," she said, suddenly inspired, "I have it! I'll call you Hero because you came to my rescue."

Although still, to all intents and purposes, uninterested, the dog's tail thumped a couple of times against the floor; a gesture, Sally decided, of tacit approval.

"Fine," she said. "That's settled then. I'll call you Hero."

Half an hour later, as she switched to Channel 4 to watch a Father Ted rerun, the dog got up, stretched himself and sauntered over to the fridge where he stood staring at the door. It took her a moment to cop on that he was probably hungry.

"You want dinner?" she asked, then felt foolish again when she realised that she was waiting for a reply. I'm bloody losing it, she thought as she peeled the plastic off the chicken breasts and placed them on the floor by the sink, and suddenly an image of her Auntie Pauline came to mind and she shuddered. Auntie Pauline was a blue-rinsed spinster in her sixties, her mother's sister and a retired librarian who kept a snotty little white poodle with a pink bum and watery eyes whom she called Precious, and fed shredded cooked chicken breast and frozen prawns.

God! I'm turning into Auntie Pauline, she thought, so swiftly informed the dog, "Don't think I'm going to buy Marks and Sparks chicken breasts for you all the time. This is an emergency." Adding, "And you're not my Precious!"

The dog, who had polished off the chicken in a couple of gulps licked his lips and gave her a jaundiced look, then reared up on his hind legs with his front paws on the sink.

"Oh, you want a drink." Taking a Pyrex bowl from

under the sink, she filled it with water and placed it on the floor. The dog drank thirstily, licked his lips again, burped, then padded back to the fire to resume his snooze.

Sally watched him settle himself and wondered what the hell she was doing inviting a stray dog the size of a small pony into her home, then sighed in resignation. He was the best that was on offer at the moment – besides, she thought smiling to herself, at least what I see is what I get. No mind games and fragile egos here.

She'd never experienced the phenomenon of mind games until she'd got involved with Charlie. She'd played mind games herself with men all the time, blissfully unaware that she was doing so, but had never been on the receiving end until she'd fallen in love. It took her a long time to recognise what an expert manipulator he was, in fact it was only in the last couple of weeks that she had realised the extent of his mind-game playing, and it filled her with contempt for herself as much as for him. She had always been a strong person, self-sufficient, independent, but he'd turned her into a needy idiot, the kind of woman who invoked in her a strong urge to shake by the shoulders and say, "Why don't you cop on, for God's sake!"

Easy to say. Part of her still wanted Charlie. He was the first man with whom she'd really connected. She felt he was her equal and he was fun and interesting and intellectually stimulating and amazing in bed. She still loved him and she knew beyond doubt that if he came to her door, professed his love and promised to leave Imogene she'd be gone with him like a shot but, being a realist, she knew that was not going to happen. Charlie

Penhaligan had too much to lose and he certainly wasn't going to throw it away for love, if indeed he had ever truly loved her in the way that she loved him – all-consuming, bordering on the obsessive. He had his own agenda to which she wasn't party but she did wonder what he was at. What were the flowers and messages about? Did he really expect her to pick up where they had left off, regardless of his refusal to commit?

"I'm not going to think about this," she said aloud, causing the dog to lift its head and look at her. "Nothing," she said to him. "Go back to sleep."

Tears of hopelessness stung her eyes and a rogue sob escaped. She brushed the tears away angrily before weepiness could set in. Angry that he still had the power to make her cry, angry at herself for being so weak.

The dog was on his feet then, standing in front of her, one giant paw resting on her knee. The physical contact was comforting. She stroked his head and snivelled.

Giving a shuddering sigh, he lumbered onto the sofa beside her, lay down and rested his head in her lap, closing his eyes. She sat there, one arm resting across the animal's shoulder, stroking his flanks, still miserable but glad of the heat of another body next to her, determined that she would survive Charlie Penhaligan and move on.

As soon as Anna had left the house, Maggie dialled her father's number. After a few rings he answered, though his voice was barely audible due to the general hubbub of conversation in the background, prompting Maggie to deduce that Anna was right and he was without a doubt holding up the bar in Matt Molloy's pub.

"Where are you?" she asked, unable to keep the irritation out of her voice.

"Who's that?" he asked.

"It's Maggie, who do you think it is?"

"Oh, Mags, how are you?"

"Why aren't you up here?" she demanded. "You should be up here!"

"Did your mother get the flowers?" he asked. He sounded pleased with himself, as if a cactus was all it would take.

"You mean the pot plant?" she said. "Yes, she got it, but you were supposed to deliver it in person. That was the whole bloody point."

"You said send her flowers."

"I said court her. I said come up here and tell her you love her, not send her an Interflora bloody cactus. How Freudian is that?"

"What?"

She despaired. He just didn't get it. Her mother was out on a date with another man and her father was in the pub oblivious, thinking that a succulent in a plastic pot could fix his ailing marriage. It was time for decisive action.

"Dad. First thing in the morning you're to drive up here and talk to Mum. Beg her to come home. Tell her you love her. Buy her the biggest bouquet of roses you can find in Westport and there's a slim chance that she might, just might, listen to you."

He was silent at the other end of the phone; all Maggie could hear was the general hum of conversation in the pub, the clink of glasses and the odd peal of laughter.

"I don't know what to do," he said helplessly. "I'm no good at talking about . . . that stuff."

The desperation in his voice tugged at Maggie's heartstrings but at the same time if she'd been standing beside him she could have thumped him. She sighed.

"Look, Dad. This is serious. If you want Mum back then you'd better get your butt up here and fast."

"What's the panic?" he said in an attempt to put off the inevitable. "Sure she knows the story. She got the flowers, didn't she?"

"The story?" Maggie repeated, stunned.

"The story," he said. "You know? About her and me. About how I . . ." he lowered his voice, ". . . about how I feel."

Maggie snapped. "That's just the point, Dad. She doesn't know how you feel and the panic is, that as we speak, your wife is having dinner with an admirer."

"An admirer?" he repeated. "Your mother has an admirer?" He sounded incredulous. "You mean she has a gentleman friend?"

Maggie almost laughed despite the seriousness of the situation, the term 'gentleman friend' was such an oddly archaic way of putting it. "Well, not exactly. Just an admirer at the moment, but he's very charming and she's very vulnerable right now, so I'd get up here if I were you to nip it in the bud."

At last she seemed to have hit the mark. "You're right," he said, at once all businesslike. "I'll drive up first thing in the morning."

Chapter 25

The following morning Maggie was up, showered and dressed by nine. Anna had come home at around midnight, full of the joys of spring, but gave her daughter little detail about her date other than that she'd had a very nice time thank you, and Gerry Starling had been a perfect gentleman.

"So what did you find out about him," Maggie had persisted. "Is he married?"

"Separated," Anna had replied, "much like myself," which caused Maggie to inwardly cringe. It was the first time the word 'separated' had been uttered aloud in relation to her parents. Anna had forestalled any further questions by claiming that she was tired and was going to bed.

Maggie brought up a tray of tea and toast at nine fifteen, deciding that she couldn't wait around to grill bacon, instead she'd grill her mother. Anna was awake, lying there listening to Saturday morning radio when she brought the tray in.

"So how did you sleep?" Maggie asked for openers.

Anna sat up and stretched languidly. "I had a great sleep," she said as Maggie set down the tray. "What's this? Brekkie in bed. To what do I owe the privilege?"

Maggie shrugged, "Why not? It's Saturday," then sat down on the side of the bed. "So, how did you really get on last night?" she asked, keeping one eye on the clock, anticipating that her father would arrive at around ten thirty.

"I told you, I had a lovely time and Gerry was a perfect –"

"I know," Maggie cut in. "A perfect gentleman. But what did he want?"

Anna's cup stopped midway to her mouth. "Want?" She paused. "Is it so hard to believe that two mature adults could enjoy good food and wine and a few hours of good conversation without there being some hidden agenda?" Her tone was frosty and Maggie realised that she was treading on thin ice.

"No, no, not at all," she said hastily, wondering at her mother's naiveté . "So are you seeing him again?"

"Possibly," Anna said. "He wants me to be the face of Super Savings, you know . . . me!"

"Yes, it came up at the meeting," Maggie admitted. "Are you going to do it?"

Anna gave her a disbelieving look as if it could actually be an issue. "And why wouldn't I? I'd be mad not to. You never know what it could lead to."

"That's what I'm afraid of," Maggie muttered under her breath, though Anna didn't appear to hear.

A loud rap on the door echoed up the stairs.

"Who's that?" Anna said.

"God knows," Maggie replied getting up from the bed, hoping against hope that it wasn't Gerry bloody Starling.

When she opened the door she was greeted by a wall of flowers. Surprised, she stepped back as the delivery boy, a short, terminally spotty youth of about eighteen, turned sideways and thrust the arrangement into her hands.

"Anna Fortune?" he asked and Maggie nodded. The card was in a sealed envelope but as her mother was now halfway down the stairs, obviously having heard her name mentioned, she could hardly check it out surreptitiously .

"Are those for me?" she asked like an excited schoolgirl. Not surprising considering that, apart from the previous day, the only other times Anna had received flowers was on the birth of her four children, the youngest of which was pushing twenty-seven. "I could get used to this." She almost snatched the delivery from Maggie's arms.

Too much to hope that they were from her father, so Maggie looked on forlornly as Anna ripped off the envelope and slid out the card. Her face flushed and her smile grew even wider.

"Oh, how sweet," she chirped, then read from the card: *To the new face of Super Savings. A beautiful and talented woman.*

"He must have shares in a bloody florist's," Maggie muttered as she clomped down the hall to the kitchen; in the battle of the flowers this definitely qualified as overkill. Anna was one step behind her.

"Now that's not a very nice attitude to have," she said. "It was very kind and generous of Gerry to take the trouble."

"Whatever," Maggie said through gritted teeth.

Luckily for the flowers, there being no other vase in the house, they were wrapped in that nifty way where the wrapping itself is filled with water. Anna placed it on the kitchen table next to the lilies then went back upstairs to shower and dress.

Maggie took the opportunity to phone her father then, but was put straight through to his voice-mail, leaving two possibilities. One: he was driving up and was out of coverage. Or, two: he was still in Westport and his phone was switched off.

The cactus sitting forlornly on the dresser seemed an ever more paltry offering next to the two large bouquets jeering at it from the kitchen table. Maggie thought them ostentatious, but was somewhat prejudiced by the identity of the sender.

Lighting the grill she chucked a few rashers on to cook and, with a view to creating some space to eat, or perhaps just to get them well out of sight, she moved the flowers into the sitting-room, replacing them with the potted cactus, which was of more reasonable proportions.

As she was lifting the bacon from the grill Anna came in, dressed in jeans and another new top. She looked relaxed and happy so Maggie didn't have the heart to nag her about Gerry Starling and his intentions. Instead she asked, "One egg or two?"

"Oh just the one," Anna replied, taking her place at the table.

As Maggie served up there was another rap on the front door. She cast a glance at the clock – nine forty-five – anxious that it was too early for her father to put in an appearance, if indeed he was coming at all, concerned that it could be the awful Gerry.

"I'll get it!" she said, closing the kitchen door after her – why, she wasn't sure; it was hardly likely, even with the door shut, she'd be able to successfully get rid of Gerry without her mother hearing.

To her surprise, when she opened the door her father was standing on the doorstep, unshaven, red-eyed and rumpled-looking.

"Dad!"

"I left at seven," he said. "Is she here?" He must have driven as if the hounds of hell were after him. He was also empty-handed.

"She's in the kitchen," Maggie said, standing back, and her father headed resolutely down the hall.

Anna was chewing on a piece of bacon as he walked in and, without a hello or how are you, he said, "I want you home where you belong, Anna."

Anna turned her head, stopping in mid-chew, appraising him from head to toe. She swallowed. "Jesus, Dan, you look awful," was her reply, before she picked up her cup and took a drink of her tea.

"I'm not going back without you," he said, and Maggie cringed. Had he listened to one word she'd said?

"Mum, what Dad's trying to say is he loves you and he'd be really pleased if you'd consider coming home." She glanced at her father, a pleading look on her face. "Isn't that right, Dad?"

"Don't put words into his mouth," Anna snapped. "He's a grown man. He can speak for himself."

If only.

"Please, Anna," he said. "I'm no good with words, you know that, but Mags is right. Come home." He sat down at the table opposite her, a sad and desperate man. Anna continued to eat her breakfast, apparently uninterested in the fact that her husband of over thirty years had driven at warp speed from coast to coast, to plead his case, however inadequately.

Maggie stood by helplessly, then frustration mounting, she ignited.

"You're like a couple of five-year-olds," she snarled, angrily. "I'm leaving the two of you to sort it out between you. Don't even think of leaving this room until you've reached an agreement."

Both of her parents turned and stared at her in amazement, gobs gaping. She stood there for a moment longer staring back, then realised that she should do as she had stated and leave them alone.

"Right," she said, feeling particularly awkward. "I'll be back in one hour. Just . . . deal with this."

She stomped from the room, down the hall, slamming doors in her wake before she realised that she was outside on the pavement with no coat, no money with her and nowhere to go. To add insult to injury she was also starving with hunger and regretted that she hadn't had the presence of mind to grab a piece of bacon and a slice of bread to wrap around it, on her way out. Standing there, she wondered what to do next. Then the fickle finger of fate took a hand, and Aiden's front door opened.

"Are you OK?" he asked. "You look a bit lost?" He was

in Levis and a T-shirt, his feet were bare, and he had a half-eaten piece of toast in his hand.

"Have you got breakfast on the go?" she asked, her stomach rumbling. "I can't get mine because my parents are making a feeble attempt to sort out their marriage."

He stood for a beat, then stepped back to let her past.

"Rasher and egg OK? I've no sausages."

"Rasher and egg's fine," she said, then strode down the hall towards the kitchen, following the taste-bud-teasing waft of bacon and fresh coffee. She was livid with her parents for behaving like spoiled children.

"What's so hard?" she snapped. "Why can't he just say the words?"

Aiden, who was at the cooker putting on a few more rashers said, "Sorry. You've lost me."

"My father!" she snapped, as if he should know. "Why can't he just tell my mother he loves her? Why hasn't he the sense to ask her to come back instead of doing his bloody caveman routine?" She paused, reprising her father's entrance. "'I want you home where you belong, Anna.' Can you believe he said that? Bloody Neanderthal!" She mimicked her father again, trying the words out for size. "'I want you home where you belong.'" Aiden opened his mouth to comment but Maggie thrashed on. "I can't believe that he'd be so bloody ham-fisted after all I said to him." She had built up a head of steam, totally frustrated by her father and his lack of any semblance of charm or romance. "And the cactus. What was that about?"

She'd totally lost him now. Bemused, he picked up a couple of eggs. "Fried or scrambled?"

"A bloody cactus!" she repeated then added, "Scrambled please . . . I mean how Freudian is that? A bloody cactus in a plastic pot? What's wrong with red roses, or at least lilies like sodding Gerry Starling?"

"Who's Gerry Starling?"

The interjection brought her to a halt and she felt foolish all of a sudden. "Sorry," she said, then shook her head and sat down at the table. "It's my parents. They're driving me daft."

"Anna's not too keen to go home then?" he said as he beat up the eggs with a fork.

"You could say that," Maggie replied, picking up a piece of dry toast and smearing butter on it. "She's got this bee in her bonnet that she's missed out on life. I suppose I can't blame her really. I mean, judging by Dad's performance I don't think I'd rush back in her place. It's just . . . I don't know, I hate to think of them splitting up."

Aiden poured the beaten-up eggs into a small saucepan and stirred vigorously. "Not much more you can do though, is there? It's up to them now."

That was the problem. It was up to them, and on the present showing it didn't look too promising.

He served up the bacon and scrambled eggs, then found her a cup and she poured herself coffee.

They ate in silence for a few moments, then he said, "You know even if they do split up, it's not such a bad thing. I mean you're all reared, and if she's unhappy with her life why shouldn't she change it?"

"But what about Dad? He's useless on his own."

Aiden grinned. "How do you know? He managed all right before he met your mother, didn't he? And necessity's the mother of invention. He'll manage if he has to. Give him a break."

Put that way it didn't sound so bad. "I suppose you're right," she conceded, but wasn't all that convinced, since she'd never seen her father so much as boil water. On the upside however at least Westport had an abundance of cafés and restaurants so he wouldn't starve to death.

"So who's this Gerry Starling?" Aiden asked after a further silence.

"A client," Maggie said. "Super Savings, the supermarket chain. My mother stood in for the regular Super Savings voice-over who went sick the other day, and Gerry was smitten. Wants her to be the new face of the Super Savings TV ads now."

Aiden looked impressed. "Good for her! A week in town and she has a new career. Not bad going by anyone's standards."

True again. She hadn't given her mother proper credit for that, but then Anna was the proactive one in this. She wasn't the one who'd been unceremoniously dumped and judging by the way she'd felt when Mark had done his vanishing act she could empathise with her father. It wasn't just the fact that Anna had gone, it was the shock of it all, the rejection, the unanswered questions; and she knew beyond doubt that her father hadn't the first clue why her mother had bolted. Despite her efforts to enlighten him it was beyond his comprehension.

Aiden refilled their cups. "He sent her flowers then, this Gerry Starling character?"

Maggie nodded. "In abundance and she went out to dinner with him too." She poured milk into her coffee and took a swig. "I can't believe she's so naïve. She thinks all he's after is her company."

"So cynical for one so young," he mocked but the way he said it, she couldn't take offence, and just laughed.

"I suppose I feel bad for Dad because he's the dumpee," she said after a pause. "And I know what that's like."

Aiden nodded. "But you're coping all right. You seem to have moved on."

Maggie shrugged then took a sip of coffee. "I don't know about coping," she replied. "I haven't had time to think about it what with my mother turning up, and then trying to get across to my dad the seriousness of the situation."

"Do you miss him?" he asked out of the blue. "Mark, I mean?"

"Like I said, I haven't had the chance."

He wasn't buying it. "I mean when you're on your own. Late at night, in bed, d'you miss him then?"

"Before Mum showed up," she admitted. "But I'm not sure if I still do. I'm more mad with him for being such a bollox."

Another silence followed.

"That's why Sinita and I split."

"Sorry?"

"Sinita and I," he said. "She was away for over a month in Europe at the runway shows and I realised I didn't miss her. Not even slightly. I felt bad about it at the time. I didn't want to hurt her, but I couldn't see me staying with her after that."

"So what did you do?" Maggie asked.

He gave a reflective smile. "Well, after she came home I was pussyfooting around it until she announced that we had to talk. It turned out she'd come to the same conclusion, so it was relief all round. I moved out and the rest, as they say, is history."

"And you're still friends," Maggie said. It was a statement not a question.

"Still friends," he affirmed.

"How very mature." She had an ironic grin on her face.

He laughed. "Oh, very mature, that's me."

"I can't say I've stayed friends with any ex-boyfriends. By the time the relationships ended I was usually sick of the sight of them."

"Do you think you'd have stayed with yer man if he hadn't legged it?" he asked. "I mean, I assume you were happy enough, in so much as you weren't planning on dumping him or anything."

Maggie shrugged. "Suppose so. We were kind of coasting. But as you say, I was happy enough. I can't say I had any yen to get married though, so I guess I wasn't thinking in terms of permanent."

"See, that's what I mean," Aiden said. "There has to be more or what's the point of carrying on with it?"

"I suppose that's what he thought," Maggie said, feeling suddenly sad. "He wanted something more and I just wasn't it."

"He could have handled it better though," Aiden said.

Maggie laughed. "Can't argue with that. The least he could have done was to leave one of the sodding sofas!"

A juddering thud caused them both to stop and look towards the hall.

"That's my front door!" Maggie said, leaping up from the table and rushing for the hall, but by the time she made it outside to the street all she saw was the brake-lights of her father's Land Rover as he screeched around the corner and disappeared from view.

Anna was angry. Angry that Dan hadn't made more of an effort. Angry with Maggie for interfering. It was obvious that she'd had a hand in Dan turning up out of the blue like that – he'd never have taken the initiative himself, let alone think of sending flowers – well, a cactus. Who ever heard of sending someone a cactus as a peace offering? Even a moron could see the irony. And it was obvious that he hadn't the slightest notion why she'd refused to go home with him, fixating on the fact that she had (as he insisted on calling Gerry) a gentlemen friend. How ridiculous was that? She'd only been out to dinner with him, for God's sake. It was obvious to a blind man that the only reason he'd bothered to come all the way up to Dublin was out of jealousy, and nothing to do with understanding how dissatisfied and disappointed she was with her life. Someone had had the cheek to trespass on his property. It was such a man thing. So petty. He didn't get it when she tried to explain how she felt, just kept harping back to Gerry and she'd seen red.

"Well, at least he noticed me," she'd snapped. "At least he recognised that I'm a woman, an individual, and he recognises that I have talents."

"Oh, I'll bet he does," Dan had snarled back, the statement full of innuendo.

She'd slapped him for that. A crack across his left

cheek with her open palm which left him reeling and she as shocked as he. Neither had ever lifted a hand to the other in the thirty-four years of their marriage and she realised then that it was terminal. With his hand held to his burning cheek, humiliated, he'd stared at her in disbelief for a split second, then turned on his heel without uttering another word, and stormed out of the house, slamming the front door almost off its hinges.

Shock and fury turned to a niggling anxiety as she realised that the slap had killed any chance of quenching her burning bridges, knowing now that she was committed, but hastily rationalising that this was a good thing. At least she knew where she stood with Dan now. The fact was, he didn't care enough to fight for her.

It was a profound disappointment to her.

A small part of her had hoped that her leaving would provoke a more positive reaction, but it was not to be. Instead of her knight in shining armour, charging up on a silver steed to win her back, he'd stormed in, indignant and overbearing, making demands and insulting insinuations, treating her like a chattel.

With a deep sigh she sat down at the kitchen table. Her breakfast had gone cold, the egg lying congealed and unappetising. She prodded it with her fork, then reached out and put her hand on the teapot. It too was past its best. Bit like me, she thought, her bravado and upbeat optimism of the previous days merely a case of whistling in the dark.

Maggie's banging on the front door brought her out to the hall and, anticipating the inevitable interrogation, she forestalled her.

"Before you ask, I did try, but he wasn't prepared to listen," she said. "All he wanted to talk about was Gerry. He wasn't in the least bit interested about why I left in the first place, or how I felt, just demanded I go home, and kept going on about Gerry, making nasty insinuations." She paused. "I suppose you told him, did you?"

Maggie felt herself flush, the accusation causing her to feel disloyal. "Only to shake him up . . . I thought it would make him see sense." Even to her it sounded lame. "I'm sorry."

"It doesn't matter," Anna said, getting up from the table and clicking on the kettle to boil. "At least I know where I stand now. Your father couldn't care less about me."

"But that's not true!" Maggie protested. "He came up for you. He loves you really. He's just crap at putting it onto words."

Anna turned to face her, the teapot in her hand. "Don't kid yourself, Maggie. He came up because he didn't like the idea of some other man sniffing around, that's why, no other reason, apart from the fact that he's short of an unpaid housekeeper and secretary maybe."

The kettle clicked off, so she popped two tea bags into the pot and poured the boiling water on top. "I know it may not seem like it right now, but this is for the best, Mags. For the best all round."

Maggie made more toast then and they'd sat together, though both of them had lost their appetites.

"I can't believe he'd make such a bloody pig's ear of it," Maggie commented after a while. "Despite what you think, I know he loves you. He told me."

Anna gave up the pretence and pushed her plate away. "I don't doubt it, in his own way, but it isn't enough, pet. I'm not prepared to settle for that any more."

Maggie nodded and looking across the table at her mother saw a sadness in her eyes, no doubt disappointment too, and she suddenly felt proud of her courage. She doubted that in Anna's position, at her age, she would have the courage to start over, so decided the least she could do was give her moral support. She reached her hand across the table and gave Anna's a squeeze. "It'll be OK," she said and Anna returned the squeeze and smiled back, nodding in agreement.

Then suddenly she was confident proactive Anna again. "Right," she said, pushing her chair back. "How about a bit of retail therapy? I saw a lovely top in Oasis that would suit you down to the ground."

Chapter 26

He was nowhere around when she returned to the loft late on Saturday night. She'd been half expecting to see him and was all prepared to sternly send him away with his tail between his legs (no point in giving him ideas) but when push came to shove she found that she was disappointed by his absence. Or maybe it was more a case of feeling rejected again. Get a grip, she reproached herself when that thought crossed her mind. He's a only a dog for heaven's sake!

She'd had a surprisingly pleasant day. Catherine had called in the morning and they'd taken the children to the zoo. Under normal circumstances Sally wouldn't have entertained the notion of the zoo, let alone the kids, but aware that beggars can't be choosers, she'd gone along for want of something better to fill her empty Saturday.

As things turned out she'd enjoyed it enormously, even enjoyed the kids, who'd had a ball and were full of questions about the animals. Especially an exceptionally lusty boy baboon who was intent on repeatedly having his wicked way with a harlot of a lady baboon, which had caused both Catherine and her to giggle like adolescents.

It was years since she'd been to the zoological gardens, remembering only the psychotic polar bears pacing backwards and forwards in their tiny pit, so she was impressed by the improvements – in particular, the African plains enclosure with freely roaming herds of beasts. It was all so much more civilised. The polar bears had a roomy new enclosure too, but sadly it was all too late to save their sanity and they still paced aimlessly back and forth albeit in greater comfort.

They had fed the kids lunch in the cafeteria, then after a spot of shopping for fluffy animals in the zoo shop, had taken them home.

While Michael watched a Bob the Builder video and Melissa had her nap, they'd sat around in the warm sunny conservatory drinking chilled white wine and, after the mandatory twenty minutes spent bitching about Rhona, Catherine asked her if David had been in touch, and to her surprise Sally had found herself blushing.

"We went out for a drink," she said, choosing to be economical with the truth.

"I like David," Catherine offered. She seemed to have missed Sally's blushing incident. "You two hit it off quite well, I think."

"Yes," Sally agreed. "He's nice."

"So have you seen much of him?" her sister-in-law asked.

"More than you might think," Sally said, a wicked sparkle in her eye. She'd surprised herself as she didn't normally do sharing, particularly not with women, and afterwards put it down to the wine.

"Are you serious!" Catherine glanced over her shoulder and lowered her voice. "So what was he like?"

"Catherine!"

"Come on," her sister-in-law urged, giving her a nudge. "You can't make a statement like that, then go all coy on me. It's not fair."

So Sally thought, what the hell. "As you ask, he was all right."

"All right? Just all right?"

"Well, maybe more than all right," she conceded, sniggering as a picture of the rampant baboons sprang to mind.

"On a scale of one to ten then?" Catherine persisted.

"What, on a scale of one to ten?" James asked, making them both jump. They hadn't heard him come in.

"None of your business," Catherine said, giving Sally a wink.

Later on, after the kids were in bed, James went out for Chinese take-away and a video and they'd all veged out in front of the TV.

It was only as she locked the loft door behind her that she realised that she hadn't thought of Charlie all day.

Chapter 27

On Sunday afternoon Maggie and Anna met up with Lily for a late brunch at the Elephant & Castle. Maggie had been keeping a close eye on her mother since the previous day, conscious that her determined cheerfulness and positive attitude was partly a sham but playing along with it anyway.

She'd tried to call her father when Anna went for a soak in the bath, but he wasn't answering his phone which annoyed, but didn't surprise her. She did however manage to get hold of Lucy. She was disappointed but philosophical when Maggie filled her in on the debacle that was her father's attempt to win their mother back, reminding her sister that he had never been good with words – as if Maggie wasn't all too aware of that. She attempted to cheer her up with the notion that it would all blow over in time, a notion that Maggie, after hearing her mother's tale, didn't have much faith in.

Lily was waiting for them at a table by the window

when they arrived. They shared a couple of baskets of buffalo wings with side orders of fries and salad and ordered a bottle of house white to go with it. As the waitress was clearing the debris away, Anna spotted Dani, the girl from yoga, and waved to her. She gave a smile of recognition and came over, sliding into the seat next to Maggie.

"How's it going?" she said, a grin lighting up her elfin face.

Anna introduced her to Lily, explaining that they knew her from yoga.

"Where's your friend today?" Maggie asked.

"Conor?" She looked over Anna's shoulder to the other end of the restaurant. "Over there. He's just finishing his shift." They all followed her gaze.

"Will you join us for a glass of wine?" Anna asked.

"Sure, why not," was Dani's reply.

Two bottles of house white later, with Conor now also at the table, they agreed to the plan.

So it was that at eleven thirty Anna and Maggie found themselves on a chilly March night outside the Olympia waiting for Dani, Conor and Lily while Maggie (now cold stone sober, and feeling slightly grumpy the way you do sometimes after drink in the afternoon) wondered what had possessed her to come to see a Welsh ABBA tribute band called ABBA-RYSTWYTH.

Her brief attack of sourness was short-circuited however when she spied, first Conor, then Dani approaching. They had totally bought into the whole spirit of the gig. Conor was dressed as the dark one, Freda, complete with wig, make-up, in shiny satin and silver platform boots, and Dani as the pregnant version of the blondie one, her eyelids heavy with blue eye-shadow which matched the baby-blue satin jumpsuit perfectly. Anna was disappointed that she hadn't realised it was fancy dress, claiming that she'd have dressed up if she'd known, prompting Maggie's relief that they hadn't gone to the *Rocky Horror Show*. Then Lily put in an appearance. She too had dressed for the occasion, or at least appeared to have, in her Boho skirt and blouse worn with fringed suede boots, but with Lily you could never really be sure.

By midnight when the gig got under way there was a full house and soon Maggie, Anna and the rest of them were unashamedly singing along to 'Waterloo' and 'Dancing Queen'. Anna knew all the words which surprised Maggie, forgetting that her mother remembered the Swedish band the first time round. ABBA-RYSTWYTH, apart from being very good look-alikes were also musically terrific, just like the real thing. Dani was having a ball and her enthusiasm was infectious. She and Lily got on like a house on fire, kindred spirits, bopping away, Dani like a satin Teletubby. Anna and Conor mimed a duet to 'Money, Money, Money', using Conor's Budweiser bottle as a microphone and, not to be outdone, and probably spurred on by her fourth bottle of Heineken, Maggie duetted with Lily to 'Fernando', from time to time forgetting the words but substituting a good few de-dum-de-dums and lah-lah-lahs.

They were high as kites when it ended and Conor suggested that they stop off at their flat for coffee as it was on the way home, Lily having decided to stay the night at Maggie's.

Dani and Conor's flat was situated on the first floor

I'm Sorry

above an ironmonger's shop on Francis Street and was reminiscent of many of Maggie's student lodgings, small and tatty, but they'd added their own unique touches to the décor to brighten it up. The garage-sale easy chairs were covered in faux leopard throws, and fifties kitsch bits and pieces were dotted around.

As Maggie helped Dani with the coffee in the tiny kitchen she noticed a blue and white Chelsea mug on the drainer. She picked it up.

"Who's the Chelsea fan?" she asked.

Dani, who was spooning instant granules into mugs, glanced sideways at her.

"Not me that's for sure," she said, then took the mug from Maggie and dropped it on the bin. "Bastard!" she muttered, with venom.

Maggie got her drift immediately. "Your ex?" she said, adding, "Mine was a Chelsea fan too."

"Are you serious?" Dani asked. "You reckon it's a character flaw?".

Maggie grinned, though in truth the thought of Mark had dampened her good humour. "What? Being a Chelsea supporter or just a spineless git?"

Dani gave her a leery look. "Take your prick."

"You haven't heard from him since, then?" Maggie said and Dani shook her head.

"No. Don't suppose I will now."

She looked sad and suddenly very young and Maggie felt sorry for her again, suspecting that her sadness wasn't just about being abandoned – she felt that, despite Dani's show of dumping the mug in the bin, she missed him.

"And have you any idea where he is?"

The girl said nothing, apparently concentrating on her coffee-making.

"I mean, even if he doesn't want to be involved with the baby, he has a responsibility to help you out financially," Maggie persisted. It annoyed her that after actively encouraging her to have the child, he'd baled out leaving her to carry the can, so to speak.

Suddenly the mask was up again and Dani tossed her hair. "Sod him," she said defiantly, then after a pause, "How about your fella? Did you hear any word?"

Maggie shrugged. "Only that he's in Australia."

Dani burst out laughing at that. "Are you serious? Mine too."

"In Australia? Really?"

Dani nodded her head. "Not that he told me. I had to find that out for myself. He wouldn't answer his mobile you see, so I tried his office but they wouldn't give me any information either until Conor told me to say that I was his sister. "On a six-month secondment" the snotty receptionist said. So he must have known for a good while."

Déjà vu.

"A six-month secondment?" Maggie repeated, bemused. "Um . . . what does he do, your fella?"

The kettle had boiled so Dani poured water into the mugs. "He's an accountant," she said and instantly Maggie felt nauseous.

"What's his name?" she asked though she already had a scary gut feeling. It was too much of a coincidence.

"Mark," Dani replied, stirring the coffee vigorously to dissolve the granules. "Why?"

She'd have been less flabbergasted if Dani had produced

a wet halibut and walloped her across the head with it, so it took a brief moment for her to catch her breath. "His second name wouldn't be Beyer by any chance, would it?" It came out as a squeak.

Dani's head spun around. "Do you know him?"

Maggie swallowed then pulled out a chair from under the shelf that served as a breakfast bar. "I think you'd better sit down," she said, her voice now but a croak.

Dani stared at her, concern flooding her face. "Nothing's happened, has it? He hasn't had an accident or anything – oh God! I knew it had to be something like that – I knew he wouldn't just–"

"He hasn't had an accident," Maggie cut in, taking Dani's arm and guiding her towards the chair. "He's OK. At least as far as I know he is – more's the pity."

At that precise moment she'd gladly have forced his scrotum through an electric mincer while it was still attached to his body. "Dani, there's something you should know," she started, her brain screaming for a sensitive way to say it, but finding none. Conscious that the girl was over six months pregnant and that it was probably inadvisable to be blunt. "The thing is," she went on, "the fact is, your Mark, Mark Beyer is . . . well, um . . ."

Dani was staring at her, concern turning to puzzlement as Maggie, unaware she had turned a whiter shade of pale and that her body language was distinctly manic, fidgeted with a tea towel, still searching for a way to break the news to Dani that the father of her baby hadn't exactly been up front with her.

"The thing is, your fella and mine are one and the same. Your Mark Beyer's my Mark Beyer."

There. It was said.

Dani's mouth dropped open.

"He and I have lived together for the past two years . . . until he did a runner to Australia last week, that is," Maggie said, making an effort to bring her voice down the three octaves it had risen in the course of the past half minute.

Dani visibly relaxed then shook her head. "No. No, you're wrong. My Mark lives – used to live with Tony. Tony Holland. They worked together. They shared an apartment. You're wrong."

It was Maggie's turn to do the head-shaking. Tony bloody Holland. She'd never liked the little runt.

"I know Tony too. Short guy, frizzy black hair and sallow skin, wears tweed a lot?"

Dani nodded, her brows furrowed. She was having a huge problem taking it all in.

"Works with Mark, has an apartment in Haddington Road?" Maggie went on. "He and Mark were at college together."

Dani stopped nodding, then whispered, "You and Mark?"

"For the last two years. I met him at my cousin's wedding." She didn't know why she'd added that particular piece of information.

Dani inhaled deeply, then exhaled slowly. "Let me get this straight. You're saying that you've been living with Mark for the past two years in your house on, where is it? Gray Street?"

Maggie nodded.

"And he hasn't been living in Haddington Road?"

"That's right," Maggie confirmed. Then a thought struck her. "Do you have a photo of him?"

"A photo? Yes –"

The hanging plastic strips that formed a barrier between the narrow kitchen and the sitting-room parted and Conor waltzed in, still resplendent in his ABBA gear.

"Where's the coffee? A girl could die of the thirst for want of a drink in this place," he said, then seeing the faces of both women stopped dead in his tracks. "What's up? What's happened?"

"Maggie knows Mark," Dani said, a tad economically.

Conor made a snorting sound like a racehorse in the starting stalls. "I wouldn't say that's anything to brag about."

"No . . . I mean Maggie knows Mark," Dani emphasised. "They were, you know . . . together."

"Together?" Conor said. "How do you mean?"

"Together. A couple," Maggie said. "At least we were until he legged it to Australia. He was seeing the two of us. Or more accurately, living with me and seeing Dani at the same time."

"No – he lives over on Haddington –"

Dani grabbed Conor's floppy satin cuff. "No, he doesn't, Conor. That was a lie. He lied to me."

"But you were there." Conor was now the one having difficulty with the concept of Mark Beyer, Two-Timing Rat. "You were in his flat."

"Maggie knows Tony too," she said, as if that explained everything.

"But are you sure it's the same guy?"

Dani gave him a sceptical look. "How many Mark

Beyers do you know who are accountants and have just buggered off to Australia for six months?"

"The bastard!" Conor said, then turned to Maggie. "Did you know about this?" It was in the order of an accusation.

"Only in the last five minutes," she said, somewhat defensively, though technically she was the wronged woman, the one who was being cheated on. "I'm as shocked as Dani."

Lily poked her head through the curtain. "Shocked about what?"

There wasn't any hysteria, or wailing or crying, at least not then. For both of them, on a scale of one to ten, discovering that Mark had been seeing the other was less of a shock than finding out that he'd legged it to the Antipodes, proving that everything is relative.

Dani dug out a couple of photos of her with Mark, one taken in Herbert Park, the other with her sitting on his knee beside a Christmas tree.

"Where was this taken?" Maggie asked.

"At home," Dani said taking the photo back and staring at it. "He came up to Longford the day after Christmas. He was down visiting –"

"I know, visiting his mother in Cork," Maggie finished, bile rising in her throat. "So how long were you actually seeing him?"

"Since this time last year. He came into the Elephant a lot when I was working the lunch-time shift during the college vacation and we got talking, the way you do. Then he asked me out for a drink." She paused, her mind lingering on the memory. "He was so sweet, so funny. Different from most of the guys that hit on me there."

"You were seeing him a whole year?" Maggie's gast was once again flabbered. "A year?"

Lily was equally stunned. "Jesus! James Bond has nothing on him. How the feck did he manage that without either of you finding out?"

Maggie gave an ironic laugh. "Logistics was one of Mark's subjects at college."

"My mum loved him to bits," Dani said, "spoiled him rotten. I haven't had the heart to tell her yet. She'll be devastated."

"I have to admit, I was taken in by him too," Anna said, happy that she wasn't the only one. "I even knitted him a beautiful sweater, didn't I, Maggie?"

Maggie nodded, remembering the chunky Aran jumper that Mark had never put on his back.

"If it comes to that," Conor admitted, "I liked him too."

"Well, I fecking didn't!" Lily snapped. "He was a mean lying bollox!"

Dani was suddenly weepy. "But he was my mean lying bollox," she said, regret in every syllable, and the echo caused Lily and Maggie's eyes to meet.

"What a mess," Anna murmured, as she put her arms around Dani and gave her a hug. "Men! Who needs them?" Then she cast a glance in Connor's direction. "Saving your presence, Conor."

Lily passed peacefully out as soon as her head hit the pillow when they finally got to bed at around three-thirty, but Maggie hardly slept all night, her mind racing as it was. It was the sheer audacity of it. Mark had been living a double life. She'd read about men like that and wondered at the stupidity of the women involved for not suspecting anything; but she hadn't had a clue, not the slightest suspicion. She racked her brains trying to remember anything suspicious in Mark's behaviour, but came up blank. That Tony Holland was complicit in the whole business didn't surprise her one jot, and the more she thought about it the angrier she got. It was obviously with Tony's consent that Mark had been able to use his apartment as a shagging-pad. She wondered if Mark had dressed the room with a few of his possessions to make it more believable, and decided that he probably had, being such a stickler for detail. The fact that he had been instrumental in Dani's decision to keep the baby seemed out of character though. The subject of kids had never come up between them, and as far as she knew he didn't have any strong feelings one way or the other about abortion – so why encourage Dani to keep the baby if he'd no intention of hanging around? It was with this thought niggling that she finally dozed off into a restless dream-filled sleep.

Chapter 28

When Sally arrived home on Monday evening she was greeted once again by the scent of roses, fifty this time. She knew because she counted them as she set about decapitating each one individually into the sink. As she got to number twenty-seven there was a tap on the front door. Her first thought was Charlie, maybe subliminal wishful thinking, but when she opened the door it was David Heart who was standing in the hallway.

"Hi. The street door was open," he said by way of explanation. "I was just passing."

She stared at him for a moment, nonplussed by his presence as he was the last person she expected to see, then gathered herself together.

"Hi . . . come in." She stood back to let him past. "I'm just in from work. Would you like a drink – tea, coffee?"

"Coffee would be good," he said.

She stepped over to the kitchen and switched on the espresso machine, checking for water first.

"Lovely place," he said, hands in pockets, looking around.

"Not as cool as yours," she countered. "How's the book coming on?" She was groping for something to say, still reeling a little from Charlie's persistence.

"Slow," he said, a half smile on his lips. "I'm too far away from a deadline to have any sense of urgency so I guess I'm not as disciplined as I should be."

As he spoke Sally resumed her task of decapitating the roses, mentally continuing the count.

Thirty-five, thirty-six . . .

"A task fills the time available," she said. "You'll get your ass in gear when you've only a couple of months left."

Forty-one, forty-two . . .

"I hope so," he said, then after a pause, "Remind me never to send you flowers."

She had counted forty-seven and there were only three roses left intact. "OK," she said, not offering any explanation. "Espresso or cappuccino?"

"Espresso's fine."

He stood watching her, somewhat bemused as she hacked the heads off the last three blooms. Judging by the discarded stalks there must have been at least four dozen. What was that about?

He picked up one of the mutilated stems. "You're not mad about roses, then?"

"Depends who sends them," she said, giving him a smile that didn't reach her eyes.

"Ah," he said, getting the picture.

It was hard to get a handle on Sally Gillespie. She was

a stunning-looking woman and he had been surprised by her warmth and sense of humour, vividly remembering her acid tongue from his teenage years. He also recalled how she had been his adolescent fantasy and that of all his mates. He hadn't thought about her in years and had been pleasantly surprised to bump into her at the lunch party. It was James who had urged him to ask her out, pointing out that as they were both new in town and at a loose end etc (a statement that would have incensed Sally had she known).

They'd met up for a drink and it had been enjoyable enough but he'd figured that it would be the last he'd see of her – amazing how the inadequacies of youth can subconsciously linger – and he was surprised when she'd called him that night asking if he'd like company.

Company?

It had been a strange encounter, the stuff of his youthful fantasies, erotic, urgent, primal, but afterwards, when she'd left so abruptly, he wondered what it had been about. Brief to say the least; a wham, bam, thank-you-sir encounter. Not that he was complaining – it wasn't every day that a gorgeous woman waltzes into your life and blatantly seduces you.

The espresso machine was hissing ready for the off and Sally went about making two cups of espresso, leaving the sink full of scarlet debris. As the cups slowly filled with the dark brown dribble she turned on the sink tap and switched on the garbage-disposal unit, but it wasn't equal to the task of processing the copious dross and protested noisily. Sally stood back, staring at the sink, doing nothing, so David reached over and clicked it off.

"I think the bin's your best bet unless you want to burn out the motor," he said. Sally nodded and opened the cupboard under the sink, pulling out the bin, then proceeded to scoop the now soggy rose-heads into it. David assisted by breaking the stalks into a suitable size and depositing them in the bin along with the rest.

"It managed twenty the other day," she said out of the blue and it took him a moment to get back on track.

"You minced twenty rose-heads in the garbage disposal?" he said, grinning at the mental image. "From the same guy, I suppose?"

Sally, her face now grim, nodded, then seeing his expression smiled too and gave a mock curtsey.

He laughed. "I like your style, but as I said, remind me never to send you flowers."

She handed him his coffee. "Never send me flowers."

As Sally finished cleaning up the last of the mess on the granite counter-top, David watched her. She seemed tense and he suspected the flowers had a lot to do with it. Obviously from someone she had a problem with. "They're not from a stalker, are they?" he asked, half serious.

"In a manner of speaking. They're from my ex. He keeps hassling me and to tell you the truth it's wearing a bit thin."

"I can imagine," he said, though actually he had no idea.

Having cleaned up all the wreckage, Sally picked up her coffee and took it over to the sofa, leaving it down on the coffee table and lighting the gas fire. As she did there was a thud on the front door, as if someone had thrown their whole weight against it. Both froze for a second before there was another thud, then a dog barked, a deep baritone bark suggesting a large animal. David, being wary of dogs, stood still staring at the door, briefly wondering if it could be Sally's stalker and attack-dog, but she, to his surprise, strode to the door and opened it before he could register a protest. He tensed, then to his further astonishment saw a huge dog standing in the open doorway panting and heard Sally say:

"Hero! Where were you? I thought you'd deserted me, you monster!"

With that she was down on her knees, her arms around its neck, petting it and cooing to it. The dog, obviously delighted, stood still wagging its stringy tail, enjoying the attention as if by right.

"Nice dog," David said somewhat warily.

"Not mine," she said. "He sort of adopted me. I'm not an animal person at all."

"You could've fooled me," he said as Sally and dog advanced on the fireplace.

"Allow me to introduce you to Hero," she said, then turning to the dog, "Hero, this is my friend David."

My friend?

"Good to meet you, Hero," David said, tentatively stroking the brute's ears. The dog, obviously revelling in the attention, pushed his head against David's hand, encouraging him to continue.

"I'm not really an animal person," Sally repeated, "but Hero saved me from a mugger the other day, then sort of followed me home."

"Are you serious? You were mugged?"

She nodded. "Would have been but for this guy," she said, then as if embarrassed by her show of spontaneous affection for the animal, stepped back. The dog stretched and then lay down on the mat in front of the fire. "Anyway," she continued, "I felt sort of under an obligation to it then so I let it sleep here because it was raining."

"So he's a stray?"

"Looks like it," she said.

"I didn't have you down as the 'taking in waifs and strays' type," he said, smiling at her.

"I'm not," she said, defensively. "Hero's the exception, and I haven't taken him in. He just stays here occasionally."

She put on some music then and she and David sat opposite each other on the sofas and sipped their espressos. The conversation was relaxed and neither made any reference to their last encounter, then a while later David left with a vague mention of meeting up sometime for a drink or dinner to which Sally agreed in a non-specific way. Nonetheless, David left with a spring in his step.

She was relieved that he'd made no reference to their last meeting. Seeing him again had caused her unaccustomed embarrassment, but then considering that she'd practically raped him, with hindsight she found that an understandable reaction. He must think I'm stark staring mad, a bloody bunny-boiler, she thought. First I fling myself at him without a hello-how-are-you, then he sees me ripping the heads off fifty roses and attempting to stuff them down the garbage disposal, not to mention slobbering over a stray dog. She felt that he couldn't get away fast enough so wasn't surprised that he hadn't made a specific date to meet up again. Probably afraid I'll do a Lorena Bobbit if he looks crooked at me, she thought, then laughed out loud, which relieved the tension.

"I figure I scared the life out of him," she said to the dog. "I doubt we'll be seeing him again."

Pity, she thought, not sharing that sentiment with the dog – she didn't want to give it the impression that she was soft. Though she wasn't overly attracted to David, he was quite good-looking in a quirky kind of way, easy company and the sex had been good, but she'd blown it.

"What of it?" she said aloud to Hero, causing him to open one eye. "Plenty more fish in the sea."

The dog didn't look convinced. "Well, maybe not plenty," she qualified, realising that since meeting Charlie every other man that had shown an interest had fallen short on some score. The truth was, since Charlie she hadn't been even vaguely attracted to any other man, until David perhaps, in a fuzzy kind of way. How scary was that? The thought that she could spend the rest of her life alone suddenly loomed large. What if I end up like Auntie Pauline? she thought.

Reaching for her phone, she looked up David's number, then dithered. Charlie's rejection was bad enough – what if David made some feeble excuse?

Nothing ventured, the voice of reason goaded, adding: remember Auntie Pauline.

A text. I'll send him a text, she thought. At least I won't have to listen to him waffling on trying to think up an excuse to put off the ball-breaking mad woman. But what to say? Dinner was too suggestive of things to follow and that could put him off. Lunch, she decided. Lunch was an non-threatening meal, and there was a valid and unembarrassing excuse to leave.

What's the matter with you? her alter ego roared in her ear. Has that bastard Charlie Penhaligan completely addled your brain? You're still the same sexy gorgeous woman that men fall over themselves to be with. He'll jump at the chance to see you again, you eejit!

Even while she was with Charlie she was always being hit on, but maybe that was the thing. She had a different agenda now. She wasn't just looking for excitement, she was ready to settle down but Charlie didn't want to play. What if no one wanted to play, ever again? She was all too conscious that the clock was ticking, she was thirty-five and most of her contemporaries were either married with kids or determinedly single career women. What if she ended up a sad blousy middle-aged joke, running after toy boys? Or worse, a blue-rinsed matron with a watery-eyed, pink-bummed poodle?

Pulling herself together she decided it was time to be proactive.

She texted: *Lunch, tomorrow, O'Neill's. One o'clock?* And after hesitating a beat, hit the 'send' button.

Chapter 29

On Tuesday morning Aiden came into Deadly Inc with his portfolio to show Maggie, Tom and the other creatives. Maggie hadn't seen him since her hasty exit the previous Saturday morning, so was glad that she bumped into him in reception so that she could thank him for giving her both sanctuary and scrambled eggs and bacon.

"I gather it didn't go too well," he said. "Anna was still spitting feathers when I ran into her on my way out."

Maggie gave an ironic snort. "I don't blame her. It was a total disaster."

"Hey, you haven't heard the half of it," Lily said, earwigging from the vantage point behind her desk. "It turns out Mark was having it off with a young one behind Maggie's back and now she's six months pregnant."

Dom, who was on his way to his office through reception, stopped dead in his tracks and stared at Maggie. "You're six months pregnant!"

"Not her," Lily said. "This young one Maggie's fella was having his end away with."

"Mark was having it off with a young one?" Tom was in on the act now.

"For a whole year!" Lily elaborated. "A fecking year and she didn't have a clue."

"Oh, for pity sake!" Maggie railed at Lily. "Why don't you just put it out over the sodding PA?"

"Put what out over the PA?" Leo asked from halfway down the stairs.

"Ask Miss Motor Mouth over there," Maggie snapped.

"Well, pardon me for breathing," a miffed Lily uttered as Maggie stomped to her office.

It became evident that the whole office had a typically cock-eyed version by lunch-time as Naomi from accounts, whom Maggie bumped into in the ladies' loo, asked her when she'd be starting her maternity leave.

"Do I look six months pregnant!" she snapped, to which Naomi, not known for her diplomacy, looked her up and down and just shrugged. And on her way out to lunch with a sheepish Lily, Paul Brody, casually eyeing up her stomach, asked if she'd still be around to work on the I-Sport account.

"You're buying," Maggie snarled as they headed for O'Neill's, to which Lily made no objection. Neither did she object when they bumped into Aiden on the way into the pub and he offered to stand them lunch but Maggie declined, invited him to join them and insisted that Lily was buying.

"Thanks again for the introductions," Aiden said after they had settled themselves at a table.

Maggie shrugged off his thanks, "No problem. How did you get on with Sally Gillespie?"

"Grand," he said. "I worked with her before, years ago."

Maggie was surprised. "Really?" she said, with an air of casualness, while wondering if he was amongst the sad fellowship of her discarded victims.

Lily smirked. "She's a bit of a barracuda, you know," and fearing that her friend was in sharing mode again, Maggie butted in, giving Lily a fierce look which shut her up sharpish.

"So have you picked up much work since you've been back, Aiden?"

"Steady. I had the shoot for ICON and they want me to do more, and I've done a bit for Mike Patterson, and I'm doing a job for Barry Penrose at BBD&K. It's going fine, thanks."

"Great."

As they chatted, Magnus Nutter, the production manager, strolled past with a plate of shepherd's pie and a pint of rock shandy. Seeing Maggie he did a double take and headed over.

"I believe congratulations are in order, Mags," he beamed.

At a loss, Maggie stared at him, then it clicked. "Thanks all the same, Magnus, but you've got the wrong end of the stick."

"It's a young one –" Lily started, but a kick on the shin from Aiden shut her up.

"What Lily's means is, my ex, who as you know, after nicking most of the furniture, has since decamped to the other side of the world, was having it off with a young one behind my back and it is she who is six months pregnant, not I. So perhaps you could put that on the bulletin board, or do an internal email memo maybe, or better still, drop a note to Campaign Magazine just in case there's someone out there who hasn't heard."

Magnus blinked at her from behind his milk-bottle specs, then gathering himself together, gave her a stiff smile, muttered, "Oh, right you are then," and scuttled off.

"That was a bit strong," Lily said. "He was only being polite."

"Well, I'm fed up of everyone knowing my business," Maggie whined. "It's bad enough that he buggered off to Oz without the rest. It's so – so humiliating."

"I wouldn't worry your head about it," Aiden commented. "Mark Beyer is obviously completely, certifiably, stark, staring bonkers."

Maggie didn't know what to say to that. The remark could have come across as blatantly patronising, but the genuine warm-hearted smile that was on Aiden's face radiated out towards her and warmed the bruised cockles of her heart.

At the other end of the bar, Sally was having lunch with David Heart. He had replied to her text almost immediately which she thought sweet, and was there waiting for her when she arrived at a little after five past one, a half-finished pint of Guinness in front of him.

"The benefit of being on your own time," he said. "You get to beat the lunch-time rush and get a good table."

"So did you write much today?" she asked after they had got their food.

He grinned at her. "Actually, yes. I got a fair bit done this morning, which makes a change. I was beginning to worry that I had writer's block, and seeing as I'm only on chapter two that would have been a bit serious."

Sally grinned back. "Or a very short novel."

They ate in silence for a few moments, then David said, "So have you heard from your stalker since? Any further floral tributes to mutilate?"

"Not yet, but the day is yet a pup."

"Speaking of which, if he puts in an appearance you could always set that monster dog on him."

Charlie putting in an appearance wasn't something Sally had given any thought to other than in the abstract, and the mention of the possibility pulled her up short. "You think he could come here? To Dublin?"

Seeing the horrified look on her face and realising that he'd put his foot in it, he tried to backtrack. "Er . . . no. Hardly . . . I mean . . ." Then gave up. "I don't know. Would that worry you?"

Sally shrugged. In truth she didn't know. Half of her wanted desperately to see him. Hoped that he'd come running with a declaration of undying love and a commitment to divorce Imogene, but she knew that wasn't going to happen; the other half of her wanted to inflict as much pain on him as he had on her.

"I don't know," she said honestly, leaving David to wonder who had actually ended it, but suspecting that it wasn't Sally.

"So how long were you together?"

Sally didn't want to go there. Charlie was her business and her business alone and she certainly didn't want to discuss him with David Heart.

"I don't want to talk about it," she said sharply. Suddenly she'd lost her appetite. She glanced across the table at David. He'd taken the hint and was concentrating on his food, waiting for the awkwardness to pass. This was a mistake, she thought. What am I doing here? Why aren't you Charlie?

After finishing lunch on a high, feeling flattered by Aiden's attention, Maggie's day deteriorated thereafter when she and Tom had to attend a briefing with both Paul Brody and Gerry Starling about the Super Savings TV campaign. Gerry had very definite ideas which, surprise, surprise, centred on the new face of Super Savings. He was also adamant that Anna replace Steph as the voice of Super Savings too, claiming that market research had confirmed that the public at large responded better to Anna's voice than to Steph's; though how he could have gleaned that information after less than six days was beyond her.

She sat quietly listening to Gerry rattle on, and to Paul agreeing with everything he said, while Tom made some pertinent suggestions, but her heart wasn't in it. Not that she begrudged Anna her moment of glory, and had the client been anyone other than Gerry Starling she'd have been all for it, but she was afraid that her mother was going to get hurt as Starling obviously had his own sleazy agenda going on, about which Anna was apparently ignorant.

Tom tackled her when they got back to their office.

"What was that about?" he asked.

"What?"

"You and Gerry Starling. You may as well not have been there for all the input came from your direction."

"I don't like him, that's all. And he's trying to get off with my mother."

Tom laughed. "So? She's an attractive woman"

Maggie sighed. "And he's a lounge lizard, Tom. I just don't want her to get hurt."

Tom put his arm around her shoulder and gave her a squeeze. "Your mother's old enough to look after herself, Mags. Anyway, this'll be good for her. And it's not as if she isn't equal to the job either. She played a blinder on the voice-overs. You said so yourself. "

She couldn't argue with that, but that wasn't the point. What if she and Gerry got together? What if Gerry stayed as smitten as he obviously was? Where would that leave her father?

Nonetheless, there was work to be done, so despite her reservations she and Tom spent what remained of the afternoon working out a storyline for the short series of ads.

She felt better about it by the end of the day, convincing herself that Tom was right and she wasn't giving Anna enough credit. The storyline they had created was funny and light-hearted and Maggie was sure Anna would be brilliant, having seen her play comedy with perfect timing on many an occasion. Aiden's comment about her mother having a right to change her life had registered also, and it struck her that his subtext hinted at begrudgery on her part. She felt guilty about that, realising that he could be right. Maybe she was feeling a tad resentful that Anna seemed so together while she was still more or less in whingeing self-pity mode.

It was to be a day of ups and downs. As she was packing up for the day she heard Tom stifle a guffaw and mutter, "Oh shit!"

She looked over at his desk where he was staring at the screen.

"What's up?"

"I think you'd better check your email," he said.

There was only the one. An internal office memo originating from Magnus Nutter.

Maggie read it then gave herself a mental swipe across the head for forgetting that Magnus had no sense of irony and, putting up her hand to the fact that it was her own fault, sighed. "Oh well," she said to Tom, "at least everyone has the right story now."

Arriving home that evening after a quick scoop with Tom at the Palace, she found a note on the fridge door.

"Don't wait up. Out to dinner with Gerry."

Chapter 30

Maggie didn't see Anna until Wednesday evening as she was still asleep when she left for work that morning. She hadn't heard her come in, despite having had an ear out, so was relieved that she had come home at all. It had briefly crossed her mind that she should have a little chat with Anna about safe sex, not sure if her mother was aware of the present-day perils, but dismissed the notion as far too embarrassing, recalling Anna's belated and excruciating facts-of-life talk when she was twelve. Anna's abundant use of euphemisms would have left her totally confused were it not for the fact that Joanna Meany, whose mother was a midwife, had given her chapter and verse when she was ten years old, calling a penis a penis, a vagina a vagina and a period a period (as opposed to a 'winkle', a 'nu-nu', and 'my visitor').

A large bouquet was once again sitting on the kitchen table when she got home, irises this time.

"I suppose those are from Gerry," she said, unable to muster up any enthusiasm.

"Actually they're from your father," Anna replied and Maggie's spirits lifted. At least he was making an effort.

"Gerry sent me ten beautiful white roses," Anna continued, "but I put them in the sitting-room."

"I love irises," Maggie enthused. "Wasn't that sweet of Dad?"

As if she hadn't heard, Anna remarked. "You'd better get a move on or you'll be late for yoga."

Skye was doing ballet stretches when they got there, barefooted and dressed in baggy sweat pants and a thin vest, her hair tied up in a pony-tail, but there was no sign of Ursula or Conor and Dani. She gave them a languid "Hiii," and continued with her stretches, while they rolled up their coats and chose a mat each. The room was stuffy so Anna attempted to open a window but it was stuck fast with multiple layers of old gloss paint so she had no joy. Then they heard footsteps on the stairs and Ursula bustled in, her usual basic self.

"Ve should get started. Vare are Dani and Conor?"

More footsteps on the stairs answered the question and a moment later the other two hurried in.

"Sorry we're late," Dani said, then gave Maggie and Anna a little wave hello.

"Ve start now, ya?"

Skye unrolled her mat and the others quickly grabbed one each and placed them in the circle, then Ursula commenced with breathing exercises.

Despite her resistance to most things overtly healthy, Maggie found she was enjoying it after the first fifteen minutes, subsequent to the light-headedness wearing off, remembering bits and pieces from her first class and even managed to stay awake until about five minutes before the end. The ninety minutes positively flew by.

Ursula seemed to be happy with their progress in as much as you could tell by her comment of: "Ve are not so stiff this veek, I think." But she once again declined Anna's invitation to join them in the bar afterwards with an economical "No".

"Well, I felt I should ask," Anna said as she brought over a round of drinks on a tray. "It seemed rude not to." Then she and Skye resumed their conversation about India of the previous week, with Conor taking a close interest.

"So how have you been?" Maggie asked Dani.

The girl shrugged. "Ah, you know yourself. One minute I'm grand, then the next I'm all weepy, but my hormones are all over the place at the moment, so I'm not sure if it's that, or . . . well, you know. How about you? I felt really bad after the other night, but honestly, I'd no idea."

Maggie put a reassuring hand on her arm. "Hey, I know. Don't worry about it. It wasn't your fault. He was cheating on the two of us."

"Not really. He was living with you," Dani said, but Maggie waved her objection away.

"I was thinking," she said after a pause, "if you could find out exactly where he's living, you could go after him for some financial help." Dani didn't look enthusiastic, so Maggie went on. "At least until you've finished your course. It doesn't seem fair that you'll have to deal with all that by yourself."

"I know where he is. He's in fecking Australia."

"But I bet if you could talk to him, if you could get his phone number – you know how he hates confrontation. I'm sure he'd help out."

She wasn't totally sure about the helping out, considering that it involved money, but she had a hunch, sure as hell, about the confrontation part. Mark couldn't stand confrontation and on several occasions, once she'd copped on to that, she'd taken advantage of the fact. It was self-evident that it was the fear of conflict that had prevented him from facing either of them.

"Er, the thing is, Maggie, I've met a young one and she's pregnant," or "Sorry, Dani, I can't take responsibility for the baby because you see I'm in a long-term relationship already and Maggie wouldn't like it," was hardly going to result in a sweet, "That's OK, Mark, I fully understand".

Dani too had obviously copped on to the confrontation thing because her expression changed and she said, "I wouldn't mind if he wanted to help out. But once I've finished my course, I'll be fine. I can get a decent job, then I won't need any help."

"Exactly," Maggie agreed, adding, "But if he offered to support the baby after that you shouldn't cut off your nose to spite your face. I mean you have to think about childcare and stuff like that . . ." She didn't see why he should get away with it. He had a responsibility to both Dani and the baby.

"Whatever," Dani said, then shrugged. "Anyway, it's all academic, I don't have his address or his phone number and sodding Spokes Kennington Cowdray aren't going to give it to me."

Then a thought struck Maggie. "How about his mother? Your baby's her grandchild, after all. I'm sure of she knew . . ."

"She's old," Dani said. "Not that well according to Mark. I wouldn't want to upset her. Anyway, I don't have her number either."

Not that well? Mark had never said anything to Maggie about his mother not being well. As far as she could remember she, the Merry Widow, travelled a lot to long-haul destinations such as Hong Kong and Egypt. That didn't sound like the pastime of a sick woman.

"Not well? How not well?"

Dani shrugged. "I dunno, just delicate, a bit helpless from what he said."

Maggie put that option to one side for the moment. "OK, then, how about Tony Holland? Maybe if you went to see him?"

Dani didn't seem at all sure about that either. "Oh, I don't know," then added pertinently, "He must have known well about you, so he's hardly going to give me Mark's address, is he?"

"Why not?" Maggie said. "You could shame him into it. Better still, why not confront him in his office. Go to Spokes Kennington Cowdray and make a scene there."

The thought of Tony Holland cringing with shame and embarrassment in the middle of his work colleagues held a certain satisfaction for Maggie.

Dani cast her eyes downwards and fiddled with the strap of her bag, then puffed out her cheeks and expelled the air. "I don't think I'd have the bottle. I probably wouldn't even get past security."

Good point.

"OK," Maggie said. "Go to his apartment on Haddington Road. Confront him there. I'm sure if he saw your situation . . . For all you know he might not know his pal Mark got you pregnant. Or does he?"

Dani shrugged. "I don't know. The last time I saw Tony I wasn't showing. I don't know if Mark told him or not."

"There you are then."

Dani nodded, once again fiddling with the strap of her bag, her eyes on her lap. Then she looked up. "Would you come with me? He knows you. He knows Mark was living with you, so he'd know that we know that he knew, if you know what I mean."

It took her a moment to unscramble all the we-knows and he-knows, but once she had, Maggie could see the sense of it.

"You're on!" she said, and they high-fived and grinned at each other.

"What do you two look so smug about?" Anna asked, distracted from her conversation with Skye and Conor.

"We have a cunning plan," Maggie said.

Much later when they got home, Maggie filled Anna in on the details of said cunning plan. Anna thought it a terrific idea, like Maggie, if only to see Tony Holland squirm after the way he'd helped Mark in his duplicity.

"So when do you plan to go?" she asked.

"The weekend. Probably Saturday morning so we'll be sure of catching him in. Can we borrow your car?"

Anna nodded earnestly. "Absolutely, but you'll have

to drop me over to Skye's place on the way. I'm thinking I might go travelling to India with her, you see, so we've a lot to talk about."

Maggie, who was way past being shocked by anything Anna said any more, just agreed, confident that by not objecting in any way, the plan would be more likely to die a death.

"India? Good for you," she said. "When did you decide this?"

A look of surprise flickered fleetingly across Anna's face, obviously due to the lack of any opposition. "Well, it's not actually decided yet," she qualified, "but it's a definite possibility."

"So do you plan to do the yoga course too?" Maggie continued, warming to the game, and Anna shrugged noncommittally.

"I might. I haven't decided yet. It depends whether Gerry joins me or not."

"Gerry!?"

"Oh," Anna said, a smug smirk on her gob, "didn't I say? It turns out Gerry's always wanted to take a trip to India too, so we might just meet up there. Isn't that great?"

Great wasn't the word Maggie would have chosen.

Chapter 31

As is always the case with client presentations, both Tom and Maggie were trepidacious on Thursday morning as they waited to go up to the conference room. There was always the possibility that the client just wouldn't get it, and taking into account the original brief, there was still the chance that he'd go for the safe boring option, namely the 'Legends in the Making' concept – or worse, neither. They were both therefore relieved that Sally Gillespie had decided to sit in on the meeting. Conscious that she was so completely behind the Extra Man treatment, collective enthusiasm would hopefully win out in the end if the client had any doubts.

In the event the presentation went flawlessly and the Legends theme didn't even come up. It turned out that Denis Morgan, ex-Shamrock Rovers left-winger and chief executive of I-Sport, one-man band and self-made millionaire was not only a rabid soccer fan, but a lifelong supporter of Man United and the Ireland team, so therefore was delighted with both the concept and their choice of Gavin O'Connor to front the campaign. His only caveat was that Shona, his twelve-year-old daughter, be allowed on set to meet Gavin.

"She can keep Jodie, my thirteen-year-old, company," Tom joked and that was that. Twenty-five minutes more outlining the details of the campaign and they were done.

"If only it were always that easy," Maggie murmured to Sally as Paul was walking Denis Morgan out.

"In your dreams," the creative director replied.

It was all systems go for the rest of the day. They solicited two further quotes from production companies, though in all probability Fly on the Wall, the most experienced with the blue-screen special effects required, was top of the list to get the job. Then Maggie contacted Gavin O'Connor's agent to firm up possible dates that he would be available for the shoot, and Tom gave Mike Patterson a call to see if he was available to direct, and to arrange a meeting to discuss the project.

Just before five-thirty Sally swung by the office and poked her head in the door.

"Celebration drinks on me in fifteen minutes at O'Neill's?" she asked.

Maggie was stunned speechless by the invitation, but Tom spoke up for both of them.

"Great. See you there," he said.

It was over half an hour before they made it to O'Neill's as Gavin O'Connor's agent called back with possible dates, and Maggie had to get on to Herbie McFly at Fly on the Wall to fill him in on that. Then she'd called her father.

He was much heartened by Maggie's embellished account of Anna's reaction to his bouquet of irises.

"Honestly, Dad. She was thrilled. Thrilled to bits."

"Really? So has she seen that Gerry character since?" he said, making the word 'Gerry' sound like something unpleasant he'd found on the sole of his shoe.

"Not since," Maggie said crossing her fingers, not stating since when, and definitely omitting any talk of India. "You should call her and have a talk. You both got a bit hot under the collar last time."

"Maybe I will," he said. "I miss her, you know, Mags. The place isn't the same without her."

"You should be telling her that, not me," Maggie said fondly, and hung up feeling hopeful that her father had at least seen the light.

Sally had a bottle of champagne sitting in an ice-bucket when they arrived. At first, as they walked across the pub to where she was sitting alone at a table in the alcove, Maggie thought she looked a tad pissed off.

"We're only fifteen sodding minutes late," she muttered to Tom. "What's her problem?" but as they approached her face lit up in a smile and she waved.

"No, Mags. What's your problem?" Tom muttered back. "Give the woman a break, will you? Don't be such a fecking party-pooper."

Tom and Maggie pulled chairs over, while Sally made a production out of opening the bubbly.

"Right, guys," she said, as they sat with their glasses filled. "I don't normally do this kind of thing. It's just that I-Sport is a big account and, credit where credit's due, you both did a great job."

If Maggie hadn't known better she would have sworn that the real Sally Gillespie had been abducted by aliens and the person sitting there, sipping from a champagne flute, thanking them for their hard work, was a replicant.

"I have to admit," Sally continued, "when I decided to come home to Dublin to join Deadly, I was a bit concerned that it was a backwards step, but on the evidence so far I know now that I made the right choice. Particularly as far as the calibre of the work put out by the agency is concerned."

Maggie couldn't question her sincerity and felt a bit disorientated by it. It's hard to re-evaluate someone you've had such fixed ideas about, but as Sally raised her glass to them, she thought, sod it, and smiled back, for once taking the gesture on face value.

"Cheers, Sally. It's nice to be appreciated."

"Well, credit where credit's due."

Tom raised his glass, giving Maggie a furtive nod of approval. "Cheers!"

On the way home from the pub, Sally stopped off at a Spar and bought milk, a few oranges, then paused at the dog-food section. It occurred to her that perhaps M&S boneless cooked chicken breasts weren't a substantial enough meal for an animal the size of Hero, but it was all rather confusing. There were tins of common or garden dog-meat with names she recognised like Pedigree Chum and Pal, then there were big bags of stuff called mixer that according to the packaging illustration looked like giant hamster droppings, and was supposed to be mixed with the tinned meat. There were also bags of stuff called Complete, and on top of that there were the biscuits and chews. Bone-shaped, round, square, different colours and some mint-flavoured, presumably to help the animal's oral hygiene. True enough, Hero's breath left something to be desired so she picked up a box of those, then dumped three tins of Chum and a bag of mixer into her basket, along with two large stainless-steel dog bowls. Her hand hovered briefly over a dog-grooming kit – a brush and vicious-looking steel comb – but she resisted as a vision of Auntie Pauline combing Precious flashed across her consciousness. She gave an involuntary shudder and almost put the lot back, but then calmed herself and proceeded to the check-out.

There was no dog around when she reached home, which caused her a moment of disappointment, but thankfully there were no roses either. Neither had she received any voice or text messages from Charlie, causing a sigh of relief that hopefully he'd finally got the message.

Just as this thought was passing through her mind her phone rang and her heart juddered, afraid that she'd spoken too soon, but the caller identification read: mother.

Dealing with Charlie would have been preferable to her mind, conscious that she hadn't called her mother in over a week, so she braced herself for the inevitable guilt trip, but to her amazement Rhona was all sweetness and light.

"Hello, darling. How are you?"

"I'm fine thanks, Mother. How are you?" Big mistake to ask, but the words had slipped out before she could stop them.

However, instead of the usual whinge of ailments, Rhona said: "Wonderful, darling. Just wonderful."

"Oh . . . um . . . that's good."

"So, darling, I was wondering. What have you planned for the weekend, it being Easter, I mean?"

"Easter, right," Sally said, aware that an invitation was in the offing, and groping for a plausible excuse, but Rhona had caught her on the hop. "I was um . . ." Her mind was a complete blank. "Actually I'd nothing planned, as such," she admitted, inwardly cringing at the prospect of a weekend at home. "Why?"

"Excellent!" Rhona said. "Auntie Pauline and I are going for the weekend to the K Club, for Jack and Rita Power's thirty-fifth wedding anniversary party." Her voice was simpering, so Sally suspected that somewhere along the line something was required of her to facilitate the trip.

"That's nice," she said. Jack was her late father's practice partner.

"So we were wondering . . ."

Here it comes, Sally thought.

". . . if you'd take Precious for Pauline, just until Monday evening."

Precious! Yeuk!

"Are you serious?" Sally's brain once again refused to come up with a valid excuse.

"Serious? Why wouldn't I be serious?" Still simpering but on status orange, ready to attack.

"No reason," Sally winced. "You see, the thing is, I'm not sure my lease allows for animals."

"Oh, for heaven's sake," Rhona snapped, the mask of reasonableness slipping away. "It's only from Saturday to Monday. Who's going to know?" Then martyred, a sigh and, "Of course, if it's too much trouble . . ."

"No. No, of course not," Sally said wearily. "When are you leaving."

Friday evening apparently, and not only was she lumbered with the care of Precious for the weekend, she also had to pick the wretched critter up from Auntie Pauline's house.

Still, when she'd had time to simmer down, on balance, a couple of days caring for a small dog was less onerous than a weekend in the company of her mother. Anyway, how hard could it be?

So it was that on Friday evening she left work early, the usual Friday night Deadly Inc get-together in O'Neill's not an option due to the pubs being closed on Good Friday (yet another unexpected bonus) and, after picking up her car, drove over to Auntie Pauline's house in Sandymount.

It was years since she'd visited her aunt's house, probably in the region of twenty, so she was momentarily disorientated by how small and tatty it looked. The front was in need of a paint-job and the garden looked neglected, weeds strangling the few daffodil bulbs that had been vigorous enough to fight their way through the tangle.

She rang the door bell and waited as Precious went bananas in the hall. After a brief pause, Auntie Pauline opened the door, Precious now held under her armpit, still yapping. On seeing Sally, however, the dog bared her teeth and growled.

"Come in. Come in," Pauline said, standing back to let Sally past. "I've put all her luggage together in the kitchen."

Luggage?

Luggage was not too strong a word. Apart from a dog-bed, a pink circular moulded plastic effort with its own foam mattress and matching pink baby-blanket, there was her twin ceramic doggy bowl, also pink, for both wet and dry food and a glass water bowl – because Precious couldn't bear to use the plastic kind. Sally gave a shudder as Pauline handed her the very same dog-grooming kit she had almost bought for Hero, and had trouble keeping her lunch down when her aunt handed her a pink toothbrush and a tube of doggy (yes, doggy) toothpaste, instructing her that Precious was to have her teeth cleaned morning and night, giving her further cause to heave by pointing out that this was because of her gingivitis – a galloping gum disorder apparently.

The words "In your dreams, Sunshine" were close to popping out, but Sally bit them back and smiled agreement, confident that Precious's teeth wouldn't fall out between Friday evening and Monday night for want of a brushing, and if they did, well, tough.

As Sally loaded the bed and other accoutrements into the Beetle, Pauline went back in, emerging moments later with a cardboard carton containing the critter's food – small foil sachets of meaty grommets in gravy, and a box of the hamster droppings, only in miniature, a bottle of vitamin tablets, and prescription medicine for Precious's dickey ticker, along with a trowel and a roll of plastic bags. Sally stared blankly at the trowel, until Pauline enlightened her that it was a pooper-scooper. Instantly the thought of a weekend with Rhona didn't seem so bad compared to shovelling up dog-shit and putting it into plastic bags – whatever about accidentally omitting to clean the animal's teeth, she could hardly leave piles of steaming dog-turds littering the city streets – but it was too late, she was committed. With a sigh of resignation she took the trowel from Pauline's hand and chucked it in the boot with the Barbie bed, after which Pauline produced a neatly handwritten list of instructions which took up two sides of an A4 sheet covering virtually every moment of the dog's waking hours.

Precious spent the journey yapping incessantly and occasionally snarling from her travelling basket on the front passenger seat, causing Sally to consider stopping by the canal, tying a couple of bricks around the dog's neck and dropping her in. She resisted the temptation – in part for fear of appearing on the nine o'clock news, but mainly to avoid the inevitable repercussions should she fail to return the precious Precious to her doting mistress – certain in the knowledge that this was going to be a very long weekend indeed.

Chapter 32

Maggie was up bright and early on Easter Saturday morning, fighting fit and mentally ready for the confrontation with Tony Holland. Anna was due over at Skye's place at ten, so they left just before nine fifteen, taking into account that they had to call for Dani on the way.

Dropping Anna off at the Bleeding Horse junction on Camden Street which was but a spit from Skye's flat, they took the left-hand fork and headed off towards Haddington Road.

"Are you nervous?" Dani asked as they sat in traffic at the lights.

Nervousness hadn't crossed Maggie's mind. "Not at all," she replied. "Why should we be nervous?"

Out of the corner of her eye, she saw Dani giving a shrug. "Dunno really, but I am. What if he won't tell us?"

"He'll tell us," Maggie said with confidence. Tony Holland, on the few occasions she had met him, hadn't struck her as being particularly tough so she felt getting the information they wanted out of him would be a piece of cake, particularly if they laid a heavy guilt trip on him.

"Stick your bump out," Maggie instructed. "Try to look as pregnant as you can. And vulnerable, look vulnerable."

"I'm better at hysteria," Dani replied.

Maggie thought about that. "Make a stab at vulnerable, and if that doesn't work go for the edge of hysteria. Most men can't handle hysteria, especially when coupled with pregnancy," adding after a beat, "but don't upset yourself for real. It's bad for the baby."

As luck would have it, Maggie got a parking spot right outside Holland's apartment and before Dani had a chance to get out of the car, Maggie laid a hand on her arm.

"Hang on a sec," she said, groping in her bag for her mobile. "Let's just check to make sure he's in."

Accessing his number which was already on her phone's memory, she hit speed-dial and waited. A mistake perhaps, because Dani started to have second thoughts. Squirming in her seat she looked at Maggie.

"Maybe this isn't such a good idea."

Maggie held up her hand for silence, then gave a smug smirk as she terminated the call. "Don't be silly. We're here now, and he's in there." Then without giving Dani the chance to chicken out, she got out of the car and stood waiting for her.

With little enthusiasm Dani struggled out of the car and joined Maggie at the foot of the steps to Tony Holland's building; the steps which Dani had climbed many a time, under the impression that this was Mark's apartment. Maggie had only been there the once for a drinks party, the first Christmas she and Mark had been together.

"Wait here," Maggie instructed, ran the few yards to the pay-and-display ticket machine, fed in a few euro, then hurried back and stuck the ticket on the inside of the windscreen. "No point risking being clamped," she said, then taking Dani's hand and giving it a squeeze she led her up the familiar steps.

It had occurred to Maggie that the brave Tony might not let them in, so she was relieved when, as they reached the top of the steps, a neighbour – who obviously knew Dani as he gave her a smile of recognition – was on his way out, and he held the door open for them. Dani returned the squeeze to give herself courage and they hurried to the lift.

He hadn't changed at all except for the fact that he was without his glasses, which caused him to blink a lot. Maggie couldn't be sure if this was due to his short-sightedness or to the shock of seeing the two of them standing together, still holding hands, at his front door.

"Hello, Tony," Maggie said, pushing past him into the apartment, dragging Dani after her. "Long time no see."

As entrances go, she felt it was on the corny side, more suited to an episode of The Bill perhaps than to real life, but her options were limited, and what was the point of going into a long explanation? The two of them on his doorstep, one of them in the family way was, to her mind, self-explanatory.

Shock had obviously rendered Tony temporarily speechless, because they were all in the living-room before he uttered a sound.

"Maggie, isn't it? And Dani. I didn't know you two knew each other." He gave a nervous laugh and blinked rapidly and at that moment he reminded Maggie of Mole from *The Wind in the Willows* which made her laugh.

"What's funny?" he asked.

"Absolutely nothing," Maggie said, at once serious. "We want to know Mark's address. There are certain things we want to talk to him about."

She saw him glance at Dani's swollen belly, accentuated by her pregnant-woman stance, hand in the small of the back, bump thrust forward, and she could see his mind racing.

"Oh shit!" he said, which under the circumstance was pretty eloquent. It was obvious that he'd had no idea, about the pregnancy that is, but Maggie hadn't forgotten his part in the rest of it.

"Yes, Tony, I'm pregnant," Dani said. "And it's Mark's. And before you ask, he knows, so don't go giving me any old guff!"

His top lip had broken out in a thin film of sweat as his eyes swivelled from Dani to Maggie. "So what are you doing here?"

"Call it moral support," Maggie said. "Whatever about dumping me without a word, leaving Dani in this predicament just isn't on."

He shook his head and averted his eyes. "I know. You're right. I'm sorry, but I honestly didn't know."

"Didn't know I was pregnant, or didn't know he was shagging me behind Maggie's back?" Dani said, as if it was in doubt.

Tony blushed, which gave his sallow countenance a

weird hue similar to a pink grapefruit, but what could he say, he was caught bang to rights, as they'd say in The Bill.

"I didn't know you were pregnant, I swear. Mark just said he had to get away. That the whole situation . . ." – he made a vague gesture encompassing both women – "was getting too much for him."

"And you didn't have a problem with that?" Maggie snapped.

He shrugged. "None of my business. Mark's a mate."

Maggie was disgusted. She cast a glance at Dani then riveted Tony Holland with laser-strength eye contact. "That's bullshit, Tony, but we'll let your feeble excuse pass. Just give us Mark's address and phone number and we'll go."

He shook his head. "I don't have it."

It was the bout of rapid blinking that alerted Maggie to the fact that he was lying.

"Bollox! Of course, you have it. You're mates, remember?"

"I don't have any authority to give you that information," he mumbled, averting his eyes. "Now I'd like you to leave." He walked towards the living-room door and held it open.

Maggie and Dani stood their ground.

"Not until you give me his address," Dani said, her voice rising, and her face crumpling. "He's the father of my baby and I need his address."

She hadn't made much of a go of vulnerable, but the edge of hysteria was shaping up well.

"I told you," Tony said, with less conviction. "I'm not authorised to give you that information."

"For fuck sake, Tony. It's not the Revenue

Commissioners you're talking to. All Dani wants is the
address of the man whose child she's carrying. How hard
is that?"

"I neeeeed that address!" Dani wailed. *"I'm carrying his
baaaa-by for God's sake!"* Tears were positively spurting from
her eyes and her voice was rising by the syllable. She
clutched her bump and sank down on the sofa. *"Give it to
meeee! Give it to meeeeee!"*

Tony hesitated, staring at Dani as she lay back against
the cushions screaming at the top of her voice. Maggie
could see the look of indecision coupled with panic
developing as his eyes darted between the sofa and the
door.

"For God's sake, Tony," Maggie raged as she leaned
over Dani, trying to comfort her. "Hush," she cooed. "It's
bad for the baby to get yourself into a state, pet." Then she
shot a toxic look at Tony. "For pity's sake!"

Tony threw up his hands. "OK, OK. Just stop crying,
please. I only have his email address." Maggie glared at
him again and he caved. "All right, so I have his phone
number, but don't tell him you got it from me." Digging
his hand in his pocket he drew out an electronic organiser.

"Well, that went well," Maggie said as she slammed the
car door shut. "I have to compliment you on your edge of
hysteria. It was really convincing."

Dani sniffed as she rummaged inside her bag for a
tissue. "That's because it was real," she said, then gave a
half smile. "Blame it on my sodding hormones."

So this is what stoned is like, Anna thought as she exhaled

after holding the smoke in her lungs for what seemed like an eternity, unaware of the soppy grin on her gob as she lolled against the cushions of the sofa. Luke had called her just as she was leaving Skye's flat to tell her that he'd managed to get hold of the gear for her experiment. It had been a good ten days since they had talked about it and she thought he'd either forgotten or had been just playing along out of politeness, so she was pleasantly surprised that he'd gone to the trouble. They'd arranged to meet up at Maggie's house half an hour hence.

"Right," Luke said, as soon as Anna had closed the front door. "I know the plan was for you to try grass first, but I managed to get hold of some wicked polm."

"Polm? That's the resin, right? The one that gets me stoned as opposed to high? Like the Nepalese Temple Balls."

Anna's down-to-business earnestness amused Luke. He grinned. "Right. Well remembered."

"OK," Anna said, leading him into the sitting-room, butterflies of anticipation in her gut. "Let's do it."

Parking in Fleet Street carpark, Maggie and Dani wandered over to the Elephant to get a bite to eat and to discuss what to do next.

"I think you should phone him," Maggie said as soon as they'd settled themselves at a table. "An email gives him time to think and he could well ignore it, whereas if you call him up out of the blue, the element of surprise should be to your advantage."

"What's to stop him just hanging up on me?" Dani observed.

Maggie shook her head. "No, he won't. Mark likes to be Mister Nice Guy. It would go against the grain for him to do that. He hasn't the guts."

"You reckon?"

"Trust me," Maggie assured her. "He might waffle on a bit, but he won't hang up on you. But you'll need to figure out what you're going to say to him beforehand, what approach you're going to take."

Dani nodded. "I thought about that. No point in being antagonistic. When he realises it's me he'll be afraid of a row and he'll feel guilty, so if I'm reasonable it'll take him off guard and hopefully he'll be so relieved he'll agree to help me out. I mean it's not as if I'm asking him to be involved. I only want a bit of help until I get on my feet."

It sounded like a plan. Not a plan that Maggie would have been content with, but nevertheless a plan. She was certain in Dani's position she'd be unable to be reasonable and admired her for being so apparently adult about it. At that precise moment she knew that if she saw Mark she'd hardly manage civil, let alone reasonable. It was bad enough that he'd upped and dumped her without a word of warning, taking his precious furniture, but what really hurt was the whole ego-denting, self-esteem destroying, younger prettier woman aspect of it; the unpalatable fact that he'd turned her in for a newer, younger model. It wasn't even as if it was a one-off mistake, he'd been seeing Dani for a year, a whole year. But worse than that, he'd convinced her to keep a baby he had no intention of taking responsibility for. How had he intended to get away with that?

It was hard for her to come to terms with the fact that

the Mark she thought she knew, loved even, was a stranger to her in the light of his actions. Never in a million years would it have crossed her mind that he'd cheat on her, lie to her. OK so he was a bit on the careful side with money, but aside from that and the fact that neither got on with the other's friends, they'd had a good two years together, each prepared to make the compromises that an adult relationship requires. At least she thought that they had. But obviously that wasn't true if he'd felt the need to be with Dani for half of it. She wondered, but for the pregnancy would he have just carried on seeing both of them? Had he not been backed into a corner would he have had the courage to be straight and make a choice?

True she had never thought of marriage, as such, but despite what she had said to Aiden, neither had she been actively looking for someone else, maybe taking for granted that they'd drift along, then when the time was right and talk of babies inevitably came up, they'd get married. A wave of emotion overtook her, the first since the day her mother had arrived and dropped her own bombshell, and she had to concentrate hard to stop herself from being consumed by it.

I'm in serious denial, she thought. I know he's gone, I know he doesn't love me any more, but I'm not really dealing with it. I'm avoiding it, taking on other people's issues so I don't have to deal with it.

It would have been easier if she'd had someone to take it out on, someone to rage at, but she hadn't. She genuinely liked Dani and believed her when she said that she'd had no idea that Mark was already in a relationship.

In a tiny corner of her heart she knew she still had feelings for him, at least the Mark she thought she knew, the kind, funny, sexy, sometimes unexpectedly romantic man, but equally she was aware that it was a sham, because on the evidence to hand that person didn't really exist. If you don't have trust in a relationship, you have nothing.

She looked across the table to where Dani was concentrating on her pasta. "Do you love him?" she asked.

Dani glanced up, her fork halfway to her mouth. She looked so young and vulnerable it tugged at Maggie's heart-strings. After a beat, she gave a tiny nod.

"Yeah. Bummer, isn't it?"

It certainly was. "It might be easier if you tried to stop loving him," Maggie said after a silence.

Dani nodded. "I know, but I've tried hating him and I can't. I'm angry with him, I feel let down, but most of the time I feel empty without him." She paused looking down at her plate, then looked up again and sighed. "I'm all cried out, if you know what I mean."

She did. "The hard part for me was the frustration of wondering why," Maggie said. "I mean all his email said was 'I'm sorry' and I hadn't a clue what it was about because 'sorry' was so . . . so . . ."

"General?" Dani prompted. "Inadequate?"

Maggie laughed "You could say that. Pathetic was the word I had in mind. I mean, 'sorry'. Puh-lease."

Dani pushed her plate away. "He's such a fecking ostrich."

They sat in silence for a few moments, each immersed in her own thoughts, then Maggie asked, "If he walked through that door right now and begged your forgiveness, would you take him back?"

Without hesitation Dani replied, "Like a shot."

After dropping Dani off, Maggie drove home, then sat in the car outside the house, running the situation over in her mind. Admitting to herself that she hadn't been dealing with it left her depressed. On finding out about Dani, she'd been so incensed by the way Mark had upped and abandoned her, well aware that she was pregnant with his child, she had focussed her anger on that rather than the detail that he'd been having an affair with a pretty young blonde more than ten years her junior for the past twelve months. Acknowledgement of that fact had plummeted her self-esteem to an all-time low along with making her feel a complete and utter eejit.

She wondered if Mark had any concept of the emotional havoc he had wreaked, but came to the conclusion that he too was in denial, and the words pot and kettle came to mind.

She wondered again how long he'd been planning his flight. He must have been thinking about it for a number of weeks, at least long enough to organise the transfer to the Australian office, and then there was the small matter of the furniture. But for that she could almost have convinced herself that it was a classic case of blind panic on his part; even the secondment could have been in the pipeline for all she knew, but the calculated way that he'd arranged to have his stuff carted away and put into storage stank of big-time premeditation. And what about their plans to spend the Paddy's weekend in the West? It had been at his suggestion. What was that about? To lull her into a false sense of security? But what was the point of that? She'd felt perfectly secure, thank you very much.

More fool me, she thought. The main thing she couldn't come to terms with on any level was the way he'd said nothing. They hadn't fought, fallen out or even bickered. He'd given not the slightest hint that he was unhappy with her, or that he had grown tired of her, apart from the sex being less frequent, that is. But she'd put that down to the stress caused by the end of the financial year which, in the light of what she knew now, made her feel all the more foolish. She inwardly cringed at her stupidity and hit her forehead with the heel of her hand.

"Duh!"

After two years together, she felt he could have had the decency to pick a fight so that at least she'd have had some inkling.

"Sod you and your fecking fear of confrontation, you lying spineless gobshite!" she said to the steering wheel. "You don't deserve either of us."

It was at that point that she heard her front door opening. Her head shot around and she saw her father storming out, his face incandescent with rage as he made for his Land Rover which she now realised was parked just in front of her. She leapt from the car but he was oblivious of her proximity, fumbling with his keys as he muttered incoherently.

"Dad!" She reached out and put a restraining hand on his arm, casting a glance back at the open front door. "Dad! What's up?"

Angrily he shoved her hand aside. "She's in there with

her fancy-man," he snarled, eyes wild, face almost puce. "In there off her head on drugs with that fecking Gerry, her fancy-man."

"Dad, Dad, calm down," Maggie urged, afraid that he was heading for a stroke. "What's going on?"

"Ask your mother," he snapped, then heaved himself up into the Land Rover. "Ask your bloody mother! Her and her – her toy boy."

Maggie put her hand on the open door to prevent him driving off. "Dad. Wait. Gerry? Her toy boy?" In the wildest stretches of the imagination Gerry couldn't be described as a toy boy.

He grabbed the door and looked down at her, hurt and anger in his eyes as if she herself had betrayed him. "Court her, you said. Send her flowers. Is it some kind of gubbaun you think I am?" He pulled at the door. "Move away."

Maggie stood her ground. "No, Dad. Not until you tell me what's happening."

"What's happening is, I'm sick of being taken for a sucker," he said, yanking the door so hard Maggie had to jump out of the way. Without another word, he fired up the engine and accelerated away leaving the stench of burnt rubber in his wake.

Maggie stood gobsmacked, staring after him, then made a run towards the house.

The smell of hash hit her as soon as she took her first step into the hall, and through the open sitting-room door she saw Anna lolling back on the couch, laughing hysterically, while Luke lay in a heap on the floor, equally mirthful, holding a huge wad of tissues to his bloodied nose.

Chapter 33

Sally sat back on the sofa and drank in the silence. Bliss. Perfect bliss. Only another thirty-eight hours and twenty-five minutes to go she thought, checking her watch, and I can take the pesky critter home. She had grossly underestimated how difficult looking after a small bad-tempered dog was going to be, the only other animal she'd had close contact with up until then being Hero. Even as a child she hadn't wanted a pet and it was she who had talked her parents out of buying her a King Charles Spaniel, reminding them sternly that a puppy wasn't just for Christmas.

By nine o'clock the previous evening she had despaired of getting through the weekend with her sanity intact due to the constant yapping and snarling of precious bloody Precious. It was perhaps proof that animals have a sixth sense where human's feelings are concerned, because Sally certainly didn't hold her Auntie Pauline's companion in any kind of regard. In fact she actively disliked the animal, but she hadn't been unkind to it, had even made a half-hearted attempt to pat its woolly head at one point, an action which prompted more frenzied yapping, teeth baring and growling. So after that she hadn't bothered with shows of friendliness, just did the minimum required to see to its needs as per Pauline's list, mentally crossing off the unnecessarily disgusting stuff such as teeth-cleaning, bum-wiping and such.

At nine-thirty, according to said list, she was required to take Precious out for her night-time pee so, risking mutilation by the canine's canines, she clipped the natty extendable lead to her (pink) bejewelled collar and dragged her towards the door. The dragging was necessary because Precious steadfastly refused to cooperate, but Sally had no intention of mopping up doggy urine from her rented maple floors; shovelling shit into a plastic bag was bad enough. Thankfully the dog couldn't get any purchase on the shiny wooden floors so it was a simple enough matter to drag her out to the hall. The stairs were another matter however, but after bumping it down a couple the animal slithered down the rest and out into the street. Luckily it was only one flight.

She didn't need to bring Pauline's trusty trowel – according to the list, pooping was a morning activity (ten o'clock sharp) – so turned left and headed down Great George's Street dragging the poodle, still yapping and snarling, in her wake. Down to the corner of Dame Street and back should be far enough, she reckoned, seriously considering shoving a pillow over its head and sitting on it if it didn't shut up, or alternatively slipping a couple of Valium into its food.

Suddenly she felt a rush of pleasure as she spied Hero about ten yards down the street, standing in a doorway taking in the evening air. He turned his head and saw her, then ambled over, wagging his tail and panting.

"Hello," she said rubbing his head, surprised by how pleased she felt. "I've got food for you at home. Meaty stuff and hamster-droppings, but according to the bag nine out of ten breeders recommend it."

He pushed his head into her hand, angling it, inviting her to scratch his ears, and it was then that she realised that the yapping had ceased. Glancing round she saw Precious lying down submissively on the pavement, looking up in awe at Hero.

"You have to stay the weekend," she pleaded with Hero. "Pleeeease stay the weekend!"

As soon as the poodle obliged by peeing (in terror, Sally suspected) they'd headed home. Getting Precious back to the loft still involved a certain amount of dragging, but at least she was quiet so Sally chatted to Hero as they walked along, telling him how much she'd missed him, and how pissed off she was about being trapped into looking after Precious, but what could she do, etc. Strangely she felt in no way stupid talking to the dog, certain now that he understood her every word and was sympathetic to her plight.

Once inside Precious had kept her distance, curling up in her doggy bed, keeping a weather eye on Hero as he gobbled up his dinner from his shiny new bowl, took a drink, burped, then settled himself on the mat in front of the fire and went to sleep. Sally remembered reading somewhere once that dogs could sleep for up to twenty hours a day, so considered the possibility that maybe lack of sleep was Precious's problem.

On Saturday morning Catherine phoned to ask what she was doing for the weekend, having heard that she was minding Auntie Pauline's Precious, and between them they decided on a picnic in Herbert Park, weather permitting.

So it was that Catherine called at around one and they loaded Precious, in her travelling basket, into the boot compartment of Catherine's Cherokee Jeep along with the picnic basket and the cooler bag which Sally had brought. Precious was a bit on the dopey side due to the Valium that Sally had, out of desperation, ground up into her food bowl to shut her up, as Hero had taken his languid leave when she had brought the poodle out (with trowel and plastic bag) just before ten that morning. She was pissed off with him for abandoning her, especially after Precious had started yapping again, no doubt emboldened by Hero's exit.

That's the male gender for you, she thought. Unreliable to the last. They take what they want from you then bugger off without a by-your-leave.

It was a bright sunny day, if a little on the cool side, and, after parking the Jeep and clipping the lead to Precious's collar, Catherine carrying the picnic basket, Sally the cooler bag, and Michael the travel rug, they set up camp near the playground. Sally stood outside the fence with a subdued Precious and looked on as Michael and Melissa played on the swings and the slides. Catherine was having as much fun as the kids were and, watching her, Sally marvelled at what an amazing mother she was, the way she played with the children. She had no memories of her own mother playing with her as a child. Sometimes she wondered if there was something wrong with her, in as much as she possessed no maternal instincts whatsoever. Maybe it's genetic, she thought, mildly uncomfortable with the notion that she must take after her mother. But there it was. Even when she had fantasised about settling down with Charlie, a baby was just an abstract concept. She had never thought seriously about it, had never been one to gaze into prams or coo at infants the way other women seemed to, let alone be even remotely tempted to play with them. In her opinion children were an alien species.

Across the playground, by the climbing frame, a woman who looked to be in her forties was lifting what looked to be a four-year-old up to the monkey bars. There were several fathers around too, all involved in the play, or keeping an eye from the picnic table as they read their papers. She idly speculated as to whether Charlie had ever played with his kids when they were young. Hard to imagine.

After half an hour Sally walked back to base camp and set up the picnic, tying Precious's extendable lead to a tree in case she absconded out of spite, which was unlikely in her sedated state.

Opening a bottle of wine Sally poured herself a glass and sat on the rug. Then her mobile rang. She checked the caller ID and seeing that it was David, dumped the call, not sure if she wanted to see him again, uncomfortable with the notion that he must think her either a nymphomaniac or unbalanced bordering on psychotic due to her weird behaviour on their last three brief meetings. The feeling of not being in control left her ill at ease, and in the past few weeks, her emotions had been erratic to say the least.

Shortly afterwards Catherine and the kids joined her and they ate a tasty lunch of cold chicken and salad, while Michael and Melissa feasted on cold sausages in finger rolls, plastered with ketchup, washed down with juice.

Three young boys of around ten or so were playing with a Frisbee close by and Precious, now coming out of her tranquillised stupor, started to yap at them, excited by the activity. One of the boys missed his catch, the Frisbee flying over his head, but Precious launched herself off the ground and caught it in her mouth. The boys and the kids all cheered, then one of them retrieved the Frisbee petting the poodle who, lapping up the attention, licked his hand and wagged her stumpy tail.

"Bloody hypocrite," Sally muttered to Catherine. "The little varmint's been a total Antichrist since I picked it up last night. Look at it! You'd think butter wouldn't melt."

Catherine laughed. "Just like your Auntie Pauline."

"Not a bit like Auntie Pauline," Sally corrected. "She's equally rude to everyone."

The boys started to throw the Frisbee for Precious then and Sally let her off the lead in case she strangled herself. Michael and Melissa roared and screamed encouragement and Sally was hopeful that the dog would exhaust itself and sleep for what remained of the weekend.

Catherine refilled her glass. "So have you seen David lately?" she asked, a mischievous smile on her face.

"No," Sally said, unconsciously glancing at her phone. "We parted on bad terms the last time I saw him."

A slight simplification. After his glib questions about Charlie, she'd clammed up and turned frosty, the resulting atmosphere killing any chance of conversation. In the end she couldn't get away fast enough, and invented an excuse to leave, her lunch only half eaten.

"That's a shame," Catherine said, but knew better than to pursue the matter.

Sally pointedly turned her attention to the boys playing with the Frisbee, not wanting to talk about David, but neither wishing to be rude to Catherine. Then a cheery hello from behind her caused her to turn around and she saw Aiden Dempsey walking towards them, grinning broadly at Catherine.

"Aiden! Hi," Catherine said, jumping up and giving him a hug and a peck on the cheek. "I thought you were in New York!"

"Back a couple of months. How are you? You look great." He noticed Sally then, his eyebrows shooting up in surprise. "Oh, Sally. Hi."

Sally smiled and raised a hand in reply.

"You two know each other?" Catherine asked.

"Yes. We worked together way back," Sally explained adding, for Aiden's benefit, "Catherine's my sister-in-law."

"Are you serious?" There were murmurs of small world all round as Catherine explained that Aiden and her brother, Clive, had been at school together as teenagers.

As Catherine invited him to join them for a glass of wine, suddenly Precious, who was still playing Frisbee with the boys, launched herself off terra firma to make the catch and seemed to stop at the apex of her leap, then gave a yelp and dropped to the ground like a sack of sand, twitched a couple of times and lay stone stock-still.

Sally and Catherine didn't react for a split second, waiting for the dog to get up, then, when she still didn't move, glanced at each other and made a run over to where the poodle lay, mouth open, tongue lolling.

The boys ran over too, followed by Michael, Melissa and Aiden, and the small group stood together looking down at the inert body of Precious waiting for her to wake up.

Aiden knelt down and put his ear to the animal's chest. "It's not breathing."

"You could give it the kiss of life," one of the boys suggested. "I seen it on Pet Rescue where they give this dog the kiss of life."

Sally shuddered at the thought of putting her face anywhere near Precious, but the ever-practical Catherine had matters in hand. "Heart massage's a better idea," she said, glancing in Sally and Aiden's direction. It was clear that it was a lost cause and that Precious was as dead as a Dodo, most probably due to a heart attack, so she suspected that it was for the benefit of the kids as Catherine rolled Precious onto her back and commenced thumping her chest with the heel of her hand, counting as she did so. Meanwhile Michael and Melissa were looking on, interested in what was going on but apparently unaffected by Precious's demise, obviously unaware that the dog was dead, or possibly unaware of the concept of death in general, Sally wasn't sure. How soon do kids learn about death she wondered, concerned that they could be traumatised by it, but she needn't have worried – the older boys seemed cool enough about it, so Michael and Melissa followed suit and just looked on while Catherine gave the unfortunate animal's chest a couple more thumps, then called it a day. "I think Precious has gone to see Grandpa in heaven," she said to her children.

"You mean it's dead?" one of the ten-year-olds said matter of factly, then a discussion started amongst the older kids as to whether animals went to heaven or not..

Sally groaned. "Oh God! How am I going to tell Auntie Pauline? She'll go bananas."

Catherine winced. "Rather you than me."

"It's not yours then?" Aiden said.

Sally shook her head. "I was minding it for my aunt for the weekend."

"Were you fond of it?" he asked, looking down at the inert Precious, still lying on her back, spread-eagled.

"Couldn't stand the yappy little beast," she muttered under her breath, in deference to small ears in the vicinity.

Aiden suppressed a grin. "You didn't strike me as the poodle type."

Sally grinned back, having a hard time trying to quell a sensation of imminent nervous hysteria. "What am I going to say to Auntie Pauline? She'll kill me." Then a thought occurred to her. "The dog has a heart problem."

"Not any more," Aiden commented, stating the obvious.

Catherine cocked her head to one side trying out suitable phrases in her mind, then gave up. "No easy way to put it really, is there?"

"Maybe you shouldn't mention the Frisbee incident. How about 'died peacefully in her sleep'," Aiden offered.

"That's usually what the death notices say in the paper."

"Do you reckon I should call her up and tell her?" Sally asked Catherine.

Her sister-in-law shook her head "No point spoiling her party. Tomorrow's soon enough."

Sally was horrified. "But it's dead! What am I going to do with it until tomorrow, for God's sake? Won't it . . . well, go off?"

Aiden glanced over to the remains of the picnic. "You could always put it in the cooler bag."

"That's an appalling idea!" Sally said, not sure if he was joking.

As the three adults stood in a huddle staring down at the deceased dog, the kids having lost interest resumed their game with Michael and Melissa spectating.

"Have you got a better idea?" Catherine asked.

Sally groaned as a thought struck her. "Oh fuck! Do you think it could have been the Valium?"

Catherine stared at her confused. "What Valium?"

Squirming Sally explained. "I sort of crushed a couple of Valium into her food. It was the incessant yapping, you see. It was driving me up the wall."

Catherine and Aiden's eyes met, then they both sniggered

"It's not funny, guys," an irate Sally hissed. "I could have killed Auntie Pauline's Precious, for fuck sake. It's not funny!"

"You're quite right," Catherine said. "Poor Auntie Pauline."

"More to the point, poor Precious," Aiden muttered, then looked at Sally. "Valium's a sedative, isn't it?"

Sally nodded.

"Then, ten to one, it was the exercise that saw her off."

"Aiden's right," Catherine confirmed. "It was probably the exercise,"

"Oh God! I'll never live it down," Sally moaned. "Rhona will harp on about it for ever."

"No one can blame you," Aiden said. " The dog had a heart condition." He paused. "It looks pretty old." He had a point.

After a further pause, Sally looked at Aiden and inclined her head in the direction of the cooler bag, and Aiden, getting the message, bent down, lifted up the lifeless dog, carried it over to the picnic rug and, when Sally had removed the remaining contents, placed it carefully in the bottom of the cooler bag, arranging the body so that Precious appeared to be asleep, her head resting on her front paws. Sally and Catherine watched, offering suggestions. Then when they were all satisfied, Sally zipped the lid closed. The three adults stood once again in a circle, looking down at the cooler bag. Sally sighed. "God! How am I going to tell Auntie Pauline? That dog was her life."

"Rather you than me," Catherine said.

Maggie couldn't get any sense out of Anna and Luke, though it was hardly surprising seeing as they were both completely stoned and thought the situation absolutely hilarious. Maggie's irate finger-wagging lecture on irresponsibility only caused further hilarity, and Anna to flap her hands and tell her to "Chill out," while Luke concentrated on rolling them another joint. Frustrated, and angry that Anna had so little regard for her father's feelings, Maggie got back up on her high horse, clopped out of the house into the street and sat on the bonnet of her mother's car, quietly fuming.

The world's gone mad, she thought. I've been cheated on, lied to and dumped on. My mother's going gaga and regressing to her lost youth, and my father's about to have a stroke.

"Who rained on your parade?"

She looked up. Aiden was just getting out of his car.

"Don't ask," Maggie replied.

He strolled over and sat next to her on the bonnet, his arms folded. "Why not?" then nudged her. "So who did rain on your parade?"

Maggie inclined her head towards the house. "My mother's in there with Luke, both stoned off their heads."

"So?"

"So my dad just left, after blowing his top and decking Luke."

Aiden's eyebrows shot up. "He decked Luke?"

"He thought he was Gerry Starling," Maggie said as if that explained everything. "He drew blood. I thought he was going to spontaneously combust. He was livid."

Aiden nodded. "Understandable, I guess."

Maggie sighed and shook her head. "I don't know what to do. I can't deal with this."

Aiden put a comforting arm around her shoulder. "Not much you can do," he said. "It's up to Anna and your dad. Anyway, it's not that bad. She told you she was going to smoke dope. It's not as if it's a surprise. It's just unfortunate that your dad chose to call today, of all days."

Maggie cringed. "I sort of encouraged him to."

"There you are then," Aiden said. "You should leave them to sort it out themselves."

She couldn't argue with that, but resented the implication that she was interfering. "But . . ."

"Never mind 'but'," he said. "You need to clear your head. Fancy a drive?"

"A drive?"

Aiden nodded. "Yeah. A drive to Dún Laoghaire."

"A drive though? I haven't been on a drive since I was a kid and Dad used to insist on driving us all out to Old Head on a Sunday afternoon after lunch, except he used to call it a spin."

"A much-neglected pastime," Aiden commented, then stood up and grabbed Maggie's hand. "Come on. If a walk on Dún Laoghaire pier doesn't blow away the cobwebs and cheer you up, I'll buy you a drink to drown your sorrows."

Maggie sighed. "Oh, all right," she said, grudgingly, mildly irritated that she wasn't being allowed to fester all by herself. "But if it's raining when we get out there, it's straight to the pub, OK?"

"Deal," he said.

Chapter 34

When Sally awoke on Sunday morning her first thought was that she should take Precious out, until she remembered that said poodle was way beyond wanting a pee or anything else come to that. She looked at her watch. Nine-thirty. Auntie Pauline was an early riser as far as she remembered so maybe it was best to get it over with. Then her courage failed her and she decided to shower and have a double espresso first. After all, what was the rush? Precious was going nowhere.

After cleaning her teeth, she padded out to the kitchen and cranked up the espresso machine, and while she waited her eyes alighted on the cooler bag sitting on the floor by the fridge. The espresso machine hissed in readiness, so she deferred the decision to call to Auntie Pauline until after her morning kick of caffeine.

By eleven she was showered, dressed, buzzing after three double espressos and, unable to put it off any longer, picked up her mobile and called her mother. It rang half a dozen times then Rhona answered. "Sally. What do you want?"

Hello to you too, Sally thought. "Hello, Mother. Did you enjoy the party?"

"It was wonderful," Rhona started, "The food was spec –"

Sensing that she was setting off on a long rigmarole, Sally cut her off at the pass. "The thing is, I'm afraid I have some bad news," she said.

A gasp at the other end of the line, then, "Oh my God! Nothing's happened to James or the children?"

Perish the thought that Rhona would worry about her. "No, Mother. I'm afraid it's Precious."

"Precious?"

Sally gave a little sniff for effect. "I'm afraid I found her this morning. And you know how she has this heart condition, well, the thing is, she . . . um."

"Get on with it," Rhona snapped. "What's happened? I hope you gave her her medication."

Sally winced. "Of course I did, but the thing is, well, despite that, Precious died peacefully in her sleep last night."

She heard her mother gasp again. "Oh poor Pauline! She'll be devastated. That dog was her life."

Guilt landed with a leaden thud square on Sally's slender shoulders.

"But Precious had a good life, and she was quite old," she said. "Could you break the news to Auntie Pauline? I don't think it's something she should hear over the phone."

Rhona agreed to break the news to Pauline, promising

to call back in a while to let her know their plans. It occurred to her that her mother wouldn't be best pleased that her weekend away was being curtailed due to a dead pet, however beloved it was by her eldest sister, but Sally gave a silent sigh of relief that at least she wouldn't have to break the sad news to her aunt.

It hadn't rained but it was blustery which was a good thing because the walk against the sea breeze to the end of the pier literally blew Maggie's cobwebs away and she felt miles better. After that they went to a pub and had a few drinks and a long chat about anything and everything (except Mark), then Aiden suggested something to eat. The sea air and the couple of scoops had rendered them both ravenous, so they repaired to a seafood establishment and ate oysters and lobster and Maggie forgot her troubles. Relaxed by the drink and the company and the sexy food they had flirted outrageously with each other, then afterwards had taken another turn on the pier, where Aiden had kissed her. It was a lovely kiss, tender but sexy, a sensuous mixture of lips and tongues, and Maggie had responded in kind. Then, with the superficial excuse that they'd had too much to drink to risk driving, they booked into a hotel and spent the night together.

"So what was it like?" Lily asked as she plonked mug of coffee on the table in front of her. It was Sunday afternoon and, as Maggie had a prearranged brunch date with Lily, Aiden had dropped her off at Leeson Park after a lingering farewell kiss.

"He's a great kisser," Maggie said.

"And?"

"And what?"

Lily gave her a shove. "Oh come on! You can't spend a night with the delectable Aiden then just say he's a great kisser. I want the gory details."

Maggie grinned. In fact she'd been grinning since she had woken up that morning next to him in the big double bed at the Marine Hotel. There had been no morning-after awkwardness, and they had enjoyed each other all over again after the room-service breakfast.

The I-got-laid grin was a dead giveaway to Lily who, the moment she saw her, declared, "You had sex. Tell me all."

"It was nice," Maggie said.

"Nice? Just nice."

Maggie gave in. "Oh, all right. It was terrific. Different. Very different from Mark. You know what it's like with someone new, but we found our way around, and it was really . . ." she searched for the right word, "really erotic."

"Erotic? Wow!" she sighed. "Lucky you. I haven't been even close to erotic in the last year. Come to think of it, I'm not sure I ever have. Larry wasn't what you'd call the erotic type."

Lily had been free and single for the past six months since splitting up with boyfriend Larry whom she'd been dating on and off for five years.

"So do you reckon you'll be seeing him again?" Lily asked.

"He's my next-door neighbour. I can hardly miss seeing him."

"You know what I mean," Lily said testily. "Are you an item, or what?"

Maggie shrugged. "I don't know. You know what men are like."

It was a glib reply, but in reality an honest one. Her recent experience with Mark had left her insecure to say the least. "I hope he doesn't start playing those stupid mind games," she said, thinking aloud. "You know, where he doesn't call in case I think he's too keen and all that old guff. I'd sooner he was up front."

Lily shook her head. "Doesn't strike me as the type to play mind games."

"I know but –"

"Shut up," Lily said. "Stop making problems. He's not Mark bloody Beyer. Just enjoy it for as long as it lasts. You're young . . . well, maybe not so young," she qualified, "but you're free and single. Go with the flow."

Go with the flow? It sounded like a plan.

Chapter 35

Arriving home at around six, she found Anna in a state.

"Where were you?" she demanded. "I was worried sick when you didn't come home last night."

Maggie was unimpressed. "It's a wonder you noticed. The last time I saw you, you were stoned out of your head." There was still a strong sickly smell of hash hanging in the air, so Maggie, irritated by her mother's attitude, pointedly sniffed the air then slid open the top sash window.

"A phone call wouldn't have gone amiss."

"That wasn't in the ground rules," Maggie pointed out. "Just housemates, you said."

"I'm still your mother and I worry about you."

"But I'm not allowed to worry about you," Maggie countered. "You can smoke dope, go out with sleazy lounge lizards, turn Dad's life upside down and I'm not allowed to worry."

Anna made her humphing sound. "That's different. I told you what I'm doing and why. And Gerry's not a lounge lizard. He's a very sweet man."

"That's a matter of opinion," Maggie snapped.

They stood there each glaring at the other, then Anna sighed. "I just worry about you, that's all. And I'm sorry to fuss. I'll get used to the ground rules in time."

In time? That sounded ominous.

"So where were you, out of interest?" Anna persisted after a silence.

"None of your business," Maggie replied, then changed the subject. "So how's Luke? Is his nose broken?"

Anna shook her head. "Only superficial injuries. Honestly, that's just like your father. Act first, think later."

"He was hurt. He came up to apologise and he thought Luke was Gerry Starling, so naturally he got a bit upset. He cares about you."

"He thought Luke was Gerry?" Anna burst out laughing. "That's a hoot."

"A hoot? He nearly had a bloody stroke he was so angry," Maggie raged. "Have you no idea what he's going through?"

Anna pursed her lips. "Not my problem any more. Now if you'll excuse me, I have to get ready. I'm going out for the evening with Gerry." With that she flounced out of the room and up the stairs without a backward glance.

Maggie flopped down on the sofa, her elation flattened like road-kill under a juggernaut's wheels. It was clear that Anna was determined to continue seeing Gerry Starling and it frustrated her that there was nothing she could do about it.

Then Lily's words came back to her. Go with the flow.

Right you are, she thought, mentally aiming the remark at her mother. I'll go with the flow. But don't come crying to me when Gerry Lounge Lizard Starling starts messing you around.

A tap on the front door made her rise from the sofa. If it's the Lizard I'll be cool, she thought, but it wasn't, it was Aiden.

"Hello, gorgeous," he said, reaching out for her and pulling her into a hug. "Fancy a Chinese takeaway and a boring night in front of a wide-screen TV watching a couple of videos?"

Maggie looked over her shoulder, up the stairs. "Right now I couldn't think of anything I'd like better," she said, a warm glow settling over her like a cloak.

In the middle of the afternoon Sally went to Stephen's Green for a walk to clear her head and bumped into David. She was glad of the company.

"So how was your weekend?" he asked as they walked back down Grafton Street.

She winced. "Not great. I was looking after my Aunt's poodle and it went and died on me."

"Died!"

"Dickey ticker," she explained. "Dropped dead. Auntie Pauline's going to kill me. They're due back in half an hour."

"Oh dear. Would you like me to stick around?"

His offer came as a huge relief on the grounds that Rhona's sense of propriety would prevent her from making her usual scene with an outsider present.

"So has Hero been around?" he asked as they turned into Great George's Street.

"Briefly," she said. "He baled out on me yesterday morning, but at least his being there on Friday night stopped Precious's incessant yapping. She has to have been the most bad-tempered creature I've ever come across . . . with the exception of Auntie Pauline and my mother, maybe," she added and David laughed.

Rhona and Pauline arrived at half past three, Pauline weepy and Rhona stoic. The blanket was reverently drawn back and they viewed the body, whereby Pauline broke down, and even Sally felt sorry for her, she was so obviously grief-stricken. She stuck to her story about finding Precious that morning and was suitably sympathetic as was David. Tea was made and biscuits produced and Pauline and Rhona reminisced about poor Precious as if she'd been a human being; though in fairness, as far as Pauline was concerned, she had been her surrogate child. After an hour, Rhona tired of it and suggested that they make a move, so David offered to carry Precious to the car, at which point Pauline broke down again.

Rhona fussed over her sister, trotting out the usual platitudes that people do to the bereaved, then said out of the blue, "I think it would be better if Precious stayed here tonight. You can bring her over to Sandymount tomorrow for the burial."

"The burial?"

Rhona nodded, her brow furrowed with annoyance. "You can't expect Pauline to cope with . . ." she glanced at her distraught sister and lowered her voice, "with Precious lying dead in the house, can you? I'll get that gardener fellow to dig a hole near the apple-tree in Pauline's garden and we can have a suitable service tomorrow afternoon."

Then with a comforting arm around Pauline's shoulder and without further discussion, they left.

Sally, too stunned by the swiftness of their departure, sans dead body, just stared open-mouthed after them. Rhona had surpassed herself.

"I can't believe she just did that," she said, shaking her head in disbelief. "What the hell does she expect me to do with Precious until tomorrow. It's not as if I've got bloody mortuary facilities!"

"Don't worry –" David began.

"Don't worry? There's a dead dog in my kitchen!" Then recognising how surreal the situation was, she laughed.

"We can cover the basket – got any large shopping-bag, preferably plastic?"

"Bin-liners?"

"Good thinking, Batman."

Sally got a large heavy-duty bin-liner, and between them they slid the doggy bed inside and tied the top securely.

Afterwards they decided to go to the pub for a well-deserved drink and as they walked down Great George's Street David said, "Well, as dates go, that was pretty unusual."

"Dates?" Sally repeated, grinning. "Are we on a date?"

"Well, we would have been, had events not overtaken us. I came round with the intention of asking you out, despite your psychotic tendencies."

"My psychotic tendencies?" as if she had no idea.

"Well, the flower-decapitating incident, for one, the very brief lunch and the way you left so abruptly after . . ." he hesitated.

"After I lasciviously seduced you last week?" she said.

David grinned. "Not that I'm complaining. It was brief but wonderful. The point is, I like you. I think you're cool."

"Cool?"

"Yeah. Weird, but cool."

They walked on in silence for a few steps, then he said. "So are we on a date?"

She decided there and then that she did like David, particularly the way he seemed so unfazed and unintimidated by her . "If you play your cards right," she said, smiling to herself.

Chapter 36

On Wednesday evening when she got home from work, Maggie saw Anna for the first time since Saturday evening. It wasn't that they'd been actively avoiding each other, but between one thing and another their schedules had left them like ships that pass in the night; Anna having gone off somewhere all day Sunday and Easter Monday, presumably with the Lizard, and Maggie leaving for work on Tuesday and Wednesday morning before she was up. Anna had, however, pointedly left notes on the fridge door to say she'd be home late. It made little difference to Maggie though as she'd spent the whole weekend with Aiden, following Lily's sage advice about going with the flow.

Anna was dressed in her loose yoga gear and was fussing over something at the kitchen sink. "I made tea," she said when Maggie walked into the kitchen. "Are you going to yoga?"

Yoga had slipped Maggie's mind, but it was a good

opportunity to see Dani; also if she didn't go she knew it would be like slapping Anna across the face with her olive branch.

"Yes. And a cuppa would be great, thanks," she said. "I'll just go up and change first."

That was the thing about Maggie's relationship with her mother. They could fall seriously out, but neither was apt to make a meal of it, and had an unspoken understanding that they would agree to differ on matters that left no room for compromise, and would heal the rift after a reasonable length of time by one of them making a gesture (usually tea and Jaffa Cakes).

When she came back downstairs Anna was sitting at the table with a cup of tea in front of her and the open packet of (peace-offering) chocolate-covered, orange-jelly-and-sponge biscuits. She poured a cup for Maggie.

"You got Jaffa Cakes," Maggie said, forcing a couple out of the packet. "My favourite."

Anna glanced at her over the rim of her raised teacup. "Tell me if it's none of my business, but are you and Aiden . . . er . . . seeing each other."

Maggie nodded. "Sort of."

"I like Aiden," Anna said, not pushing for details. "He's a nice fellow. Way nicer than Mark."

Maggie wondered if that was an invitation for her to say how much she liked Gerry Starling, but she couldn't bring herself to pretend, even in the spirit of reconciliation.

"Yes," she said. "Aiden's a babe."

And that was as far as their conversation went, having served its purpose of breaking the ice.

Dani, Conor and Skye were at yoga ahead of them,

Skye doing her usual ballet stretches. Anna went over to her, but Maggie made a beeline for Dani.

"Did you talk to him?" she asked.

"Not yet," Dani said. "I can't seem to work out the time difference properly to catch him in."

"Are you sure that bollox Tony Holland gave you the right number?" Conor asked.

Maggie was pretty sure he'd be afraid to lie about it and said as much, adding, "Melbourne's eight or nine hours ahead of us."

Dani frowned. "Ahead? Shit! I thought it was behind."

Maggie studied her face. "You're not chickening out, are you?"

Dani shook her head. "No way, but I keep forgetting to get phone cards, or I don't have one with enough credit left on it."

It hadn't occurred to Maggie that Dani hadn't a home phone, or the fact that calling Australia on a mobile would be prohibitively expensive for her. She felt terrible, then made a quick mental calculation. "Look, why don't you come back to my place after class and we can call him at around eleven? That's around seven a.m. Melbourne time. We should catch him before he goes off to work. Also he'll probably be just up, so he won't be properly awake and you're more likely to get your point across."

"Would you mind?"

"No sweat. I don't know why it didn't occur to me before," Maggie said.

Skye and Anna walked over to them then, both looking worried.

"What's up?" Maggie asked.

Skye said. "It's Ursula. I'm worried about her. It's not like her to be late. "

Maggie glanced at her watch. True enough, Ursula was close to fifteen minutes late.

"She's probably been held up."

Skye shook her head. "No, she's an obsessive compulsive. She might get here right on the button for a class, but she's never late."

"Skye thinks she could be ill," Anna said. "She's had problems lately."

"Problems?" Maggie repeated.

Skye shrugged. "She's been depressed."

"Do you know where she lives?" Maggie asked.

Skye nodded. "Do you think I should go round there to make sure she's OK?"

Collectively they decided that they should all go, so set off for Ursula's bed-sit which was only a short distance away.

"I hope she isn't drinking," Skye commented. "She said the doctor warned her that her liver could pack up if she took alcohol again. That's why she never comes down to the pub after class.

Anna glanced at Maggie. "I didn't realise her drinking had been that serious."

"Oh yes. She was a bottle of vodka before tea-time girl until she joined AA," Skye said. "She told me all about it, and how yoga and AA helped her to kick the habit."

"So do you really think she'd go back on the booze?" Maggie asked.

"I don't know," Skye said. "I'm just worried about her. She's had some really shitty luck lately what with her ex getting custody of her kid and taking him out of the country and stuff. I'm just afraid for her, that's all."

"Oh the poor girl," Anna said. "As if she didn't have enough to deal with!"

"I know," Skye, said. "And she's been trying so hard to get her life back together. It's not fair."

Maggie caught Anna's eye again, wondering if she too felt as badly for whingeing about the minor ripples that had lapped against their relatively untroubled lives.

Skye rang Ursula's door bell and they all waited. After while she rang it again, then stood back in the road and looked up at the first-floor window.

"Her light's on," she said.

Maggie stepped up to the door and rang all the bells. Suddenly she had a very bad feeling in her gut. After a short interval the door-release buzzed, so she pushed it open. "First floor?" she asked over her shoulder.

"Yes. First floor front," Skye called back as they all trooped up the narrow steep staircase. Skye stepped forward then, and knocked on the door, calling Ursula's name, but there was no response. Through the door they could hear music playing. Wagner. Very loud.

Music to top yourself by, Maggie thought. Skye rapped on the door again, once more calling Ursula's name.

"Do you know if she leaves a spare key anywhere, with a neighbour or anything?" Anna asked and Skye shook her head. Conor, who was way ahead of all of them, reached up and felt along the top of the door frame, and when he found nothing there, lifted the edge of the worn carpet and revealed a key which he handed to Skye.

She'd taken pills, lots of pills by the evidence of the empty brown-plastic pill bottles lying on the floor by the bed, but no drink, probably because she had none in the house. Her breathing was shallow, but there was evidence that she'd been sick which was one good thing. The other, that she'd been lying on her side so hadn't choked on the vomit.

There was no note.

The ambulance arrived within ten minutes and whisked her off to hospital, still clinging to life by a thread, accompanied by Skye, while the others followed in Anna's car.

They all sat in Accident and Emergency waiting, then after several hours and numerous cups of hospital tea, at just after two am. the doctor came out and told them that it had been a close call, but that Ursula would be OK. It was sighs of relief all round, followed by the usual 'what ifs'.

"Let's just be grateful," Anna said. "And we must all try and support her as much as we can when she comes out."

"She can stay with me," Skye said. "I've a bed settee in my living-room. And I'll take the yoga classes for her if that's all right with all of you? I know she'll be worried about that."

"They'll probably keep her in for a few days," Anna continued. "She'll have to see the psychiatrist. I'll visit her tomorrow afternoon."

"Do you think she'll want visitors?" Dani said.

"Probably not," Anna replied. "But she must have felt very alone if she tried to take her own life. She needs to know that there are people out there who care what happens to her."

Dani nodded. "You're right. Maybe we could work out some sort of visiting schedule or something."

As a group it was agreed, and there being no purpose in staying any longer, Anna drove them all home.

Dropping Dani off, Maggie proposed that she come round to Grey Street the following evening so they could have another go at catching Mark before he left for work.

Back home neither Maggie nor Anna felt like sleep, so sat together at the kitchen table drinking hot whiskeys in the hope that it would help. Suicide was something outside their collective experience, at least on a personal level.

"I can't even imagine how hopeless she must have felt," Anna said as they sat there sipping their hot toddies. "That poor girl."

Maggie nodded. Although she hardly knew Ursula, she still felt affected by it, and like her mother couldn't conceive of feeling so low that she'd want to die. She shared this thought with Anna.

"I don't think it's about wanting to die," Anna said wisely. "I think it's more a case of not wanting to live any more."

Aiden tapped on Maggie's door the following morning at eight, and they ate breakfast together while Maggie filled him in on the previous night's drama, then Anna came in and joined them, having given up on sleep.

"Couldn't close an eye all night," she said. "I kept thinking about the hopelessness of that poor girl."

I'm Sorry

"Kind of puts things into proportion, an incident like that," Aiden said and both women agreed.

He was heading away on a three-day photo shoot to Cork for ICON so Maggie walked him to the door shortly afterwards.

"I'll call you later," he promised, miming the call with his little finger and thumb splayed at his ear.

Maggie waved him off, feeling a touch guilty that she felt so happy.

Chapter 37

Maggie stopped to have a chat with Lily on the way in, or more accurately, Lily collared her for interrogation as to the state of play with Aiden, not having had the chance to get an update earlier in the week. From past experience Maggie knew better than to attempt to pull the wool over her friend's eyes, but in any case, she saw no reason. She was happy, that elated happy you only get at the start of a new relationship when battered self-esteem is restored due to the fact that someone you fancy the Calvins off thinks you're the best thing since sliced bread and has difficulty keeping his hands off you. The kind of happy which induces that wonderful state of amnesia concerning the experience of past relationships or the possibility that this one might not last for one reason or another.

Not content with generalities, Lily insisted they discuss it at length in O'Neill's at lunch-time. As the arrangement was being made, Tom walked into reception with two takeaway lattes in his hand and he and Maggie went off to their office together where they made final preparations for a script-approval meeting with Gerry Starling.

As the format for the ads was to be the same, in as much as they were to be shot in a local Super Savings branch, the only difference being the actual script and the fact that Anna would be delivering the lines instead of Gerry Starling, the changes didn't involve much reorganisation. The shoot for the first commercial was scheduled for the following week with Mossie Hunt directing.

The meeting went well, considering that Maggie spent most of the duration quelling a strong urge to excise Gerry Starling's heart with a blunt teaspoon, but being the professional that she was she desisted, mainly on the grounds that she knew she'd get fired if she killed a client who spent as much money with Deadly Inc as Gerry Starling did. Contributing little to the meeting, she let Tom take the reins and it went without a hitch. Starling was delighted with the new scripts, complimented them both on their work and insisted on shaking Maggie's hand at the end of the meeting, holding it between both of his for longer than necessary.

After he had gone Maggie gave an exaggerated shudder and, sticking her hands out in front of her, said, "God! I feel like immersing my hands in boiling water for twenty minutes. That man's such a sleazebag."

"I can see you're going to be a bundle of laughs at next week's shoot," Tom muttered, half to himself.

Before lunch she gave her father a call with a view to setting the record straight.

"About last Saturday, Dad," she said after the formalities,

"that wasn't Gerry Starling you hit. It was Luke, a friend of mine."

"I knew it," he said. "So she's after young fellas now. She's only making a fool of herself, so she is."

"No, she is not!" Maggie snapped, though in truth she agreed with him if for different reasons. "Will you shut up and listen for a minute!"

"Don't you raise your voice to me –" he started, but Maggie cut him off.

"Just listen, will you? Mum isn't going out with Luke. He's a friend of mine. And all he did was to do her a favour. I told you about her wanting to try out stuff she felt she missed when she was young – well, one of those things was smoking dope, and Luke was kind enough to get some for her. You shouldn't have hit him."

"A favour? A favour is it? Giving her drugs? The next thing she'll be injecting heroin."

"Oh, for God's sake, Dad! You know that's not true. You're overreacting."

It must have occurred to him that she was right about that because after a pause he said, "Well, maybe." A further pause, then, "What's got into her, Mags? I don't know what do. I tried the things you said, but . . . well, you saw for yourself."

"I know. And I'm sorry. The thing is, she's all at sixes and sevens at the minute. You used to be her knight in shining armour and now you hardly look at her. And don't give me that guff about being too old for the romantic stuff."

She heard him give a heavy sigh at the other end of the line. "Knight in shining armour?"

"That's about the size of it," she said. "She doesn't feel wanted, Dad. She needs to feel wanted. Do you know what I mean?"

He was silent for a long time, and Maggie only knew he was still there because she could hear him breathing. Eventually he said. "I think I do. I'll see if I can come up with a plan." Another pause, then, "I love your mother, you know, Mags. I always have. It's just over the years I took it for granted that she knew."

Thinking of her own experience, and resolving to learn from it, she said. "It's never a good idea to take anything for granted, Dad."

Anna visited Ursula that afternoon, and true to prediction she wasn't best pleased to have a visitor, and lay on her side with her back to Anna feigning sleep. Anna was up to her however and prattled on as if she was awake, the way people are advised to talk to coma patients, reassuring her as she arranged the flowers she had brought, that Skye was going to take her classes until she was better. Eventually, when she realised that Anna wasn't going to give up, Ursula rolled onto her back and opened her eyes.

"Vy did you interfere?" she asked accusingly. "Vy did you not mind your business?"

Anna sighed. "In case you changed your mind," she said simply. "Sometimes in desperation we do things that we regret later, so we thought it was best to be on the safe side."

"I vish you did not do this," she said, a touch less bitterly.

Anna placed the flowers where Ursula could see them

on the bedside locker. "Life's precious, you know. And it seemed a shame for you to go when you've fought so hard to get yours back."

Ursula was unimpressed and just shook her head. "It is kind of you to take this trouble. But you know nothing about me." Then she closed her eyes again and sighed. "I am tired. You will go now, please."

On the way out, Anna bumped into Conor on his way in, carrying a couple of magazines and a small cactus in a plastic pot. What is it with men and cacti? she thought.

"She's not in the best of humour," she said to him, perhaps understating the situation. "But go in anyway, even if you only stay a minute. Just so she knows she's not alone."

He held up his prickly offering. "I got her this for her. Thought it had a better chance of survival in the dry hospital atmosphere," he explained.

"That was very thoughtful of you," Anna said. "Take no notice if she's bad-tempered. I think part of that's because she's embarrassed."

"Stands to reason I suppose," he commented, then with a cheery "See you later," he turned and walked off down the corridor towards Ursula's ward, humming "Always look on the bright side of life".

Anna watched him go thinking it sad the only people Ursula had to worry about her was a motley group of comparative strangers. Thank God I have my family, she thought. Thank God I'm not alone. Her thoughts shifted to Dan then and she felt doubly sad. What had happened to the dashing, passionate, impulsive man she'd married over thirty years ago, she wondered. She'd seen a tiny spark of that passion the previous Saturday when he'd hit out at Luke, but figured, rather than love, the green-eyed monster had been his motivation. Poor Luke. He'd been so sweet about it. Of course, that could have been something to do with the fact that he was stoned senseless.

It all was such a disappointment. Not just Dan's reaction, but the whole thing. Getting stoned wasn't all that great, at least it was a bit of a let-down after all the stories about being stoned that she'd heard in her youth from Devina. In fact it felt little different from being drunk and sleepy. She wondered what all the fuss was about. Never mind, she thought. At least I've tried it now, and mentally crossed it off her list. Next stop, a travel agent's to check on the price of an air ticket to India.

Hero was waiting for Sally when she left the office that evening. "Where were you?" she asked. "And why did you bale out on me?" She stood for a moment staring at the monster who was panting and wagging his tail, then felt silly as she realised that she was waiting for a reply. "Never mind," she said, "come on," then walked off towards Lime Street, feeling the short cut was safe now that Hero was around. He trotted after her, caught up and then kept pace as they headed across the city.

"I still have food for you. Good job it's tinned or it would have gone off by now," she said, feeling a bit miffed that it was almost a week since he'd put in an appearance. She wondered where he spent his time when he wasn't with her. Did some other person have the same kind of relationship with him as she did? Or indeed, several people? Did he drop in on them when he fancied a change? This notion aggravated her somewhat, until she rationalised that she was talking about a dog, not a lover, which caused her to laugh out loud.

"OK, so you're a free spirit," she said to the dog. "I accept that." Somehow the fact that he had chosen to be with her at all left her feeling privileged.

When she reached home, Hero trotted up the stairs ahead of her and, by the time she'd picked up her post from her mail box, was standing by her front door, sniffing at a large bouquet of red roses. She let out a groan. Not again, she thought, surprised to note that she felt irritated this time, rather than angry and sad. Standing over the flowers (fifty again) she contemplated what action she should take. Decapitation was a passionate act born out of anger and seemed like too much trouble now that her anger had waned. It was strange. Time and distance had lessened her sense of loss until she hardly felt it any more. Charlie was becoming an abstract concept. An annoyance. She could think of him without a lump of longing filling her throat. Stooping, she ripped the card off the cellophane and slid it out of the envelope. It read, "I'm sorry," and was signed, "C."

"I'll bet you are, Sunshine," she said aloud, then, picking up the flowers, walked over to the garbage chute and tried to stuff the bouquet in, but it was too bulky.

"What the hell am I supposed to do with fifty long-stemmed red roses?" she said to Hero. "Should I hack them to pieces again, or just leave them here to wither?" He didn't offer any opinion one way or the other, of course, and Sally made a mental note to stop asking the dog questions, particularly ones which required an either-or reply.

Then she had a brain-wave. Hurrying inside the loft, she found a sheet of paper and wrote a sympathetic note, attached it to the bouquet, then called a taxi and had them delivered to Auntie Pauline. There, she thought, satisfied with herself. That should make her feel better.

As if.

The burial of Precious had been a surprisingly emotional affair. Auntie Pauline was weepy and Rhona sympathetic, which was a surprise to Sally who thought that her mother would have lost interest. David had offered to help her take Precious over to Sandymount, which wasn't that much of an imposition considering he'd spent the night at the loft, but Sally thought it sweet of him anyway. Pauline insisted on kneeling down and laying her Precious to rest in the grave that the gardener had dug under the apple-tree, wrapped in her pink doggy blanket, the doggy bed being too large to fit in the hole. The sight of the barrel-shaped wrinkly pensioner, kneeling in the dirt of her suburban garden with tears making channels in her pancake make-up was an oddly surreal sight, a bit like Yoda in a polyester two-piece, but watching it unfold, seeing Pauline's genuine grief, Sally felt really guilty. She didn't dwell on the dose of Valium. Then remembering how distraught she had felt after Charlie, and him not even dead, felt instantly worse.

If only there was some way I could make it up to her, she thought, more out of a need to assuage her guilt than out of affection for her aunt.

"What do you think, Hero?" she asked as she emptied a tin of Chum into his bowl on top of the hamster droppings. "What would fill the void for her?"

317

Then all at once, in a Eureka moment, it came to her.

"I know. I'll buy Auntie Pauline a new dog."

"Here's your script," Maggie said, dropping the stapled sheets of A4 on Anna's lap. Her mother was sitting on the sofa painting her nails a dark plum colour. It was the first time Maggie had ever seen her apply nail varnish. Anna held up her hands, allowing the wet varnish time to dry.

"Oh, how exciting!" she chirped, scrunching up her eyes in delight and flapping her fingers to help along the drying process.

"Whatever," Maggie said ungraciously, unable to muster enthusiasm for anything that involved her mother being in the same room as Gerry Starling. "Did you visit Ursula?"

Anna nodded. "I did. She's still depressed, and I think she's a bit embarrassed . . . you know, about the whole thing. There must be nothing worse that trying to kill yourself only to have some busybody spoil it all by saving you." Then seeing her daughter's stunned expression she clarified. "Oh, I'm not saying we shouldn't have. I'm just looking at it from her point of view right now, in the aftermath."

Put that way, Maggie could see what she meant. "Skye said she's going tonight, so I'll call in tomorrow. What should I bring? Does she need anything, do you know?"

"A reason to live," Anna suggested without a trace of irony.

At ten thirty, Dani arrived in the company of Conor and, while Maggie made coffee, they discussed Ursula. Conor reported that she'd been in shitty humour when he'd seen her and how he'd stuck it out for half an hour before she told him, less politely that she had Anna, to go away. Anna made her point again about how pissed off she must have been waking up in hospital when she'd had the hereafter in mind.

"She's seeing the shrink tomorrow. I heard the Ward Sister telling one of the nurses," Conor said. "Maybe he'll give her something for the depression."

"You know, often a suicide attempt's a cry for help," Anna said. "That's why we must do all we can to support her."

There was a general murmur of agreement, then Maggie, conscious that the hands of the clock (or in this case the knife and fork that constituted the hands of her kitchen clock) were climbing towards eleven pm, caught Dani's eye. "Might be a good time now," she said. "Will I come with you, or would you rather be by yourself?"

"By myself," Dani said, standing up. "I'll be better by myself."

Disappointed, Maggie closed the kitchen door to give her some privacy, hoping that the girl wouldn't lose courage.

"So what do you think he'll say," Anna whispered. "Do you think he'll try and get out of it?"

"I don't know," Maggie said. It was an honest answer. At that moment, for all her talk to Dani about Mark wanting to be Mr Nice Guy, and being more likely to listen to her because she was catching him off guard and such, in truth she realised that the man she'd lived with for the past two years was a total stranger to her. He'd done things she would never in her wildest dreams have thought him capable of. Carrying on a secret affair for one thing, along with all the associated logistical problems, and behaving as if nothing had changed at home. Well, almost. Not differently enough for her to have any suspicion that he was hiding stuff anyway.

Am I a total moron? she asked herself. Were there signs I just didn't pick up on? OK, so the sex had slowed down a bit, but she'd dealt with that, and put it down to pressure of work, but that was the only difference. Did that mean that all their relationship was based on, as far as Mark was concerned, was sex? She dismissed that notion. In the early days they done lots of stuff together . . . hadn't they? Well, maybe not lots of stuff, but they used to go to the pub and to restaurants and parties and sometimes to movies, though on second thoughts they had totally opposing taste in films. Then her thoughts turned to Aiden and what they had in common. They'd talked a lot over the weekend and she learned all about his childhood and he hers. They'd discussed movies and books and holidays and hopes and dreams, the same stuff she'd talked about with Mark, but it occurred to her then, that with Mark it was she who had done most of the talking and she really knew very little about his life before they met, only superficial stuff.

Anna was talking but she hadn't been listening. "Sorry?"

"I said there must be some legal way Dani can get Mark to help her if he won't cooperate," she said.

"I'm sure there is," Maggie replied, "but with him being out of the country it would be a long-drawn-out affair, and lawyers cost. I doubt Dani has the cash to spare."

They heard her walking down the hall then so all looked expectantly towards the kitchen door as it opened, studying her expression for any hint of an outcome, but her face gave little away. Then she smiled and they all relaxed.

"He's going to help me," she said. "He was very sweet about it, and promised to help me out."

Anna made her humphing sound. "Pity but he wouldn't," she said. "It takes two to tango."

Maggie too was annoyed by Dani's apparent gratitude to the man who had abandoned her after promising to stand by her. "Mum's right," she said. "It's the least he should do."

"Oh don't be like that," Dani said. "He was so sweet. And he said he was sorry."

Where have I heard that before? Maggie thought.

Chapter 38

Friday evening and Maggie was greeted by an excited Anna as she stepped through the front door.

"I'm definitely going to India," she said. "I've priced a ticket and I can well afford it out of the money I'll make from the Super Savings ads. What do you think?"

Now there was a loaded question.

"India? Really? With Skye?"

"More or less," Anna said. "We won't be on the same flight, but we'll meet up there at some point."

At some point?

Rummaging in her bag, Anna produced a *Rough Guide*. "There's loads of useful information in this book. Skye has it so I went to Eason's and got one for myself. It's really good. It has –"

"I've seen a *Rough Guide* before. I know what it is," Maggie cut in, a touch sharply, which caused Anna to look hurt and Maggie to feel guilty. "I'm sorry," she said. "I didn't mean to snap, but I've had a shitty day."

Anna gave a smug smile. "And you're probably missing a certain person."

It took Maggie a moment to realise what she meant and she inwardly cringed. It was like being a teenager again, like the first time she'd ever brought a boyfriend home and her mother had been so thrilled that Maggie had nabbed a fella she'd positively vibrated with glee.

"No," Maggie said in a measured tone. "I've just had a shitty day."

"You and Aiden haven't had a row or anything?" Anna asked, her voice anxious.

Maggie was having a hard time holding on to her temper. "No," she said, again keeping her tone measured. "But we're not joined at the hip."

It was true Maggie had had a shitty day, but not shitty enough to put her in bad humour. It was also true that she wasn't missing Aiden mainly because she had just got off the phone after talking to him for fifteen minutes, it wasn't even the fact that it looked like Anna's plan to go to India was coming together, it was the implication that her mother might be sitting on Diana's seat in front of the Taj Mahal with Gerry bloody Starling rather than her father that had raised her hackles.

"I was only asking," Anna said, sounding hurt. "I worry about you."

"You're doing it again," Maggie said. "Housemates. Ground rules. Remember?"

Anna pursed her lips. "Well, I'm sorry, but after forty-six hours in labour, no pain relief and fifteen stitches it's hard to forget that I'm your mother."

"Well, please try," Maggie said. "This isn't going to work if you don't."

Anna's eyes sparked with anger. "So let me get this straight. Your ground rules dictate that I mustn't pass any comment on who you see or what you do, but you have licence to freely criticise my friends, what I choose to do and where I choose to go?"

That was about the size of it, but Maggie wasn't about to admit to it.

"Now you're being childish," she said defensively.

"Childish? I think if anyone's being childish here, it's you. I'm fifty-four years of age, Maggie, and I think I can just about handle my life on a day-to-day basis. I'm capable of choosing my friends and deciding how to spend my time without your approval, thank you very much. So do me a favour and just butt out!"

She pushed past Maggie then and, picking up her coat and her bag, strode towards the hall, anger oozing out of every pore. "Don't wait up."

After the front door slammed, Maggie slumped down on the sofa. She felt guilty about her double standards, but at the same time, angry and frustrated that there was nothing she could do about the Gerry situation. "Fuck!" she said to the wall. "Fuck you, Gerry Starling! Fuck! Fuck! Fuck!"

The *Evening Herald* had ads for kennels but nothing particularly local and, even though Sally was anxious to placate her conscience by finding a new companion for Auntie Pauline, she didn't fancy a schlep out to Kildare or even out of the city if she could help it.

"What do you think, Hero?" she asked. "Know any stray poodles looking for a home?"

The dog opened one eye, then yawned, wafting an invisible mist of halitosis in her direction. So much for the mint-flavoured dog biscuits.

It was Friday evening and Sally was sitting by the fire in the loft sifting through the classifieds in the evening paper, having made good her escape from the O'Neill's Friday-night Deadly Inc get-together after a single G&T, as she was going to a photographic exhibition at the Templebar Gallery later with David. They hadn't met up since the burial of Precious though they had spoken on the phone a couple of times.

Having David around made her wonder if her grief after Charlie was really grief or just a panic reaction to rejection, a very real fear of being alone. She dismissed that notion as psychobabble, feeling embarrassed by her pop-psychology spin on the situation. Her grief had been genuine all right, frighteningly so, but she prided herself on being a realist. What was the point in pining for something you can't have? Charlie wasn't looking for a new wife, he'd made that patently clear, so that was that. Nevertheless, having David around had helped. That he was so different from Charlie was a bonus too. She'd read about women who repeated their mistakes by always going for the same kind of man, time after time, never learning the lesson. Well, she was smarter than that. Way smarter, and she had far more dignity.

That's me through with getting emotionally dependent, she thought. Never again. Never again will I let a man get under my skin the way I let Charlie Penhaligan.

The exhibition wasn't great, mostly misty sepia prints of bog land which Sally found neither aesthetically pleasing nor original, so after fifteen minutes or so they left and went in search of dinner, finally settling for Thai.

"So any word from the stalker lately?" he asked after a lull in the conversation.

"Another bouquet," she said, spearing a stray tiger prawn on the edge of her plate. "Fifty roses. I recycled them. Sent them to Auntie Pauline to cheer her up."

"I bet the garbage disposal breathed a sigh of relief," he said.

Sally smiled. "Probably. I'd say it's the first time Pauline ever got roses delivered, poor devil, and it had to be after losing Precious."

"Losing? That's one way of putting it." He had a crooked grin on his chops.

She kicked him under the table. "Stop it. I feel bad enough about that. I'm going to get her another dog, to make up for it."

"Does she want another one?" he asked.

Sally hadn't taken that into consideration, but surely she would. Surely she didn't want to be on her own. "Of course she does. She's always had a dog."

"How long were you two involved?" he asked suddenly. "You and your stalker."

The question knocked Sally off kilter; she wasn't sure she wanted to discuss Charlie, and David's interest was unsettling.

She shrugged. "Three and a half years . . . ish."

"That's a long time," he said. "My longest relationship was three. Well, close on."

"So what happened," she asked, in an attempt to deflect the conversation.

"The usual," he said. "We started fighting, the way you do, when you're looking for an excuse." He paused. "I suppose we wanted different things in the end, you know how it goes. You start off going down the same road, then one of you changes direction."

"Only too well," she replied, before she could stop herself.

"Is that what happened to you?" he persisted.

Sally nodded. "Yes, but I'd rather not talk about it." She felt raw again. Not the grief-stricken raw she had suffered immediately after the event, but nonetheless raw, and uncomfortable. "I think I'd like to go home now," she said, rooting in her purse and dropping a twenty onto the table. "I have to find a dog for Auntie Pauline tomorrow." She pushed her chair back and grabbed her bag.

David was startled by her abruptness. "Hey. What's the matter?" He stood also, touching her arm. "I'm sorry. I didn't mean to upset you."

"You didn't," she said, averting her eyes. "I just want to go."

He counted out some cash and left it on the table, indicating it to their waiter, then followed Sally out of the restaurant, kicking himself for being so insensitive and for having the memory-span of a goldfish not to recall that the same subject had caused her to leave equally abruptly halfway through their lunch date.

She stood on the pavement looking out for a taxi, avoiding his eyes. Reaching out, he took her arm. "Sally. Listen to me." She turned to him, her jaw set, anger in her eyes. "I'm sorry. That was crass and insensitive. I promise that subject's taboo from here on . . . deal?"

She stared at him, her body language yelling that she didn't want to be touched, but he held on to her arm for fear that she might run away. After a good five seconds she closed her eyes and exhaled, relaxing her shoulders, then nodded.

"OK. Deal."

Linking arms, they walked together. "I'm sorry," he repeated. "Put it down to the fact that in another life I'm a journalist and therefore a naturally nosy person."

She gave a weak smile. "Just this once," she said. He did most of the talking on the way back to the loft, trying to salvage the situation, not wanting to part on bad terms, and by the time they turned into Great George's Street she seemed to be in better spirits. Then she suddenly laughed out loud and quickened her pace.

"Look. There's Hero."

Ten yards up the street, he saw the dog sitting patiently by the door of the building. "He's been with me since yesterday; I didn't think he'd come tonight." The excitement in her voice was genuine and touching.

As they reached the door, Hero stood up, his tail wagging, and it was then David noticed he'd brought a friend. He nudged Sally. "Look."

He had the gangly legs and floppy ears of a puppy. Short coat, black with a white bib, about eighteen inches to the shoulder, obviously a mongrel. The pup was standing back cowering against the wall, tail between its legs. Sally cast a glance at David then addressed the question to Hero. "Who's this?" She reached out a hand to the pup. The pup looked scared and flinched until she gingerly touched his head and gave him a pat. Then, deciding that he liked that, he took one step forward so that she could do it again.

"Is this a friend of yours, Hero?" she asked, but the dog stayed shtum. The pup by this time was wagging its thin tail. He had the look of a greyhound crossed with a sheepdog – lean body, potentially long legs, soft floppy ears "Did you tell him you were looking for a dog for Auntie Pauline?" David said in jest. Then to his surprise, Sally gave a yelp, leaned over and hugged Hero's neck.

"Hero! You clever old thing, you!" she said.

David shook his head. "No . . . I was only joking. You can't . . ."

"But don't you see," Sally said. "You're right. I did mention it to Hero and he obviously decided to sort it out for me."

It was at that point that David began to have serious reservations about Sally's sanity.

Despite said reservations, however, he found himself driving with Sally over to Sandymount the following morning, with the pup in the boot and Hero stuffed into the back seat of the Beetle.

"Are you sure this is a good idea?" he asked.

"But, oh course!" Sally said. "Why wouldn't it be?" Having so recently discovered the joys of pet ownership, loosely speaking, it didn't occur to her that her aunt could possibly object, particularly as she was a dedicated dog-owner herself.

She had phoned her mother's sister before leaving to

check that she would be in but hadn't mentioned the pup. Pauline had been surprised by the phone call, it being the first ever, but had thanked her tearfully for the floral tribute which, she informed her niece, she had placed on Precious's grave. Not quite what Sally had had in mind, but if that made her happy . . .

Parking outside, they left the dogs in the Beetle and, as they walked up the path, Pauline opened the front door.

"I've something to show you?" Sally said. "A surprise."

"What?" her aunt asked, a cautious look on her face. Auntie Pauline wasn't famed for her love of spontaneity.

"Come and see." Sally turned and led her back down the path to the car. Everything being relative, it was a possibly a good thing that the first beast that the elderly librarian laid eyes on was Hero, because she gave a stifled scream and flinched back.

"Good grief! What's that?"

"Oh that? That's my dog, Hero."

"I wasn't aware that you had a dog," Pauline said, then her hand shot to her mouth. "Oh my God! Did you have that monstrous creature in your flat when my Precious was there?"

"Um . . . well, yes," Sally replied, not sure where this line of questioning was leading, but having an uncomfortable feeling about it anyway.

A horrified look spread across the spinster's face. "Oh my God! Oh my God! It must have frightened the life out of my poor Precious. No wonder she had a heart attack. She was very sensitive."

Her voice was rising, causing David to fear that she was close to cardiac trauma herself.

"No. No. Quite the opposite, I assure you," he soothed. "They got on like a house on fire. In fact I can truthfully say that I've never seen two dogs get on better."

Pauline, brows furrowed. "Really?" Surprise, surprise, she sounded sceptical.

"Absolutely," David affirmed emphatically, and Sally stood there amazed but grateful for his bullshitting skills, but then he went a bridge too far. "In fact, I think our Hero was, well, a bit sweet on her." Appalled by the implications, Pauline's pencilled-in eyebrows shot up her forehead, but alert to his faux pas, David hastily added, "But he was a perfect gentleman at all times, of course," and Pauline relaxed, relieved that her late companion's virtue hadn't been compromised.

"So anyway," Sally said, moving to the back of the Beetle, "we knew how lonely you'd be now so . . . it was fate really."

Pauline was staring at her, waiting for her to get to the point, while David wondered where the pronoun 'we' had come from. Opening the boot, Sally stood back triumphant, then the startled pup jumped out of the boot and David had to make a grab for it as, terrified, it lurched into the road towards an oncoming speeding car. There was a screech of brakes, a line of burnt rubber on the road and some choice language from the apoplectic driver, but thankfully both the pup and David were left unscathed.

Pauline was all of a dither again, but once David had assured her that he was fine she calmed down. She didn't seem to associate the pup with Sally's surprise though, and when her niece asked her what she thought she went into a rant about cars driving too fast along Park Avenue and how the council had refused to put in speed bumps.

"No," Sally said. "I mean about the pup? We brought you a new companion."

For probably the only time in her life, Pauline was rendered speechless. She stared at the pup, whom David was holding by the brand-new red collar that Sally had bought that very morning, her mouth agape.

The pup had calmed down somewhat after its brush with death, as had David, but it was still jumpy and he had to hold fast to the collar in case it bolted again.

"It's the unfamiliar surroundings," he explained. "He'll be fine in a bit."

"But it's a boy dog," Pauline said. "And a mongrel." As she said the word 'mongrel' her lip curled in distaste. "And it's . . . big."

Sally couldn't argue with that, but couldn't see her aunt's problem. "Well, yes, he's all of those things, but mongrels are really faithful. And he'd be a good guard dog too," she said, wondering why Pauline wasn't jumping for joy.

Then the pup did an extraordinary thing. Prompted by eons of evolution towards domestication, nudged in the right direction by generations of genetic memory, the distant recollection of wild dogs approaching the fires of hunter gatherers in the realisation that a scrap thrown from the circle was an altogether easier way to get food than the hit-and-miss affair of hunting for one's self, the pup pulled free of David's grasp and sat at Auntie Pauline's feet, looking up at her appealingly. Pauline flinched away, but the pup rubbed his head against her skirt, then lay down on his back inviting her to rub his tummy.

"I think he wants you to stroke him," Sally offered, still somewhat surprised by Pauline's negative reaction to the pup.

"He's submitting. He's telling you you're the boss," David said, casting a covert glance in Sally's direction.

"Really?" Pauline said, bending down and giving the pup's smooth black belly a tentative stroke. "Submitting, you say?"

It occurred to Sally that the concept of submission had most likely been alien to the cantankerous Precious.

"Oh yes," Sally said as the dog rolled over again and sat up, panting, a cutsie look on its face as he lifted his paw for Pauline to take. She was all of a dither again at that, and giggled like a schoolgirl as she shook the pup's paw.

"Oh look!" she burbled. "Isn't that sweet?"

"Gosh. He never did that for me," Sally said with exaggerated regret and David nudged a warning not to overdo it.

"What's his name?" asked Pauline, positively enchanted.

"We don't know," David said. "He's homeless."

Pauline gasped. "Homeless! But how awful!"

"That's why we thought of you," Sally said. "What with you having such empathy with animals."

"Empathy? You think so?"

David shrugged and indicated the pup, who was now rolling on his back, trying out various expressions for Pauline, each more engaging than the last. "Well, it speaks for itself. Look at the way he's taken to you."

"He has rather, hasn't he?" she said.

"So what do you think?" Sally asked.

Pauline looked down at the pup. "I'd have to give him

a name, and take him to obedience classes, and get the vet to give him shots and give him the once-over."

"So you're going to keep him then?"

The pup by this time was sitting up on its hind legs, both front paws a-begging, utterly irresistible by anyone's standards. Pauline's too, apparently.

"Well, you've given me no choice really, have you?" she said to Sally. "He'll be heartbroken if you take him away now, and that would be too cruel."

So the deed was done. They took the pup inside and he immediately settled himself beside Pauline's chair and, after the obligatory cup of Earl Grey, they left Auntie Pauline and her new companion, for whom she had yet to choose a name.

"Well, that went surprisingly well," David said as they took Hero for a walk along Sandymount strand.

"I could tell she wasn't against the idea in principle," Sally said, "but you have to admit the mutt made a pretty good case for himself. What a slut!"

They walked on in silence enjoying the fresh sea air, then Sally gave him a thump on the arm and laughed. "Never seen two dogs get on better?"

Chapter 39

Maggie had another shitty day on Wednesday, but then she hardly expected it to be anything else as it was the day of the Super Savings shoot, but she had no idea how monumental the shittiness was going to get.

As shoots go it was pretty trouble free with only the usual minor hitches, but it was the proximity of Gerry Starling and his solicitous attention to Anna and her playing up to him, that ruined it for her.

"Chill out, will you," Tom urged, weary of her whingeing and under-her-breath sniping. "Gerry's the client and he wants your ma to do the ad. Get used to it."

He had a point, of course, but matters between Maggie and her mother hadn't improved by dint of the fact that neither had made the gesture and bought Jaffa Cakes. While Mossie Hunt was snarling instructions at his assistant as they prepared for the closing shot, she cast a bitter glance at her mother, who was chatting to Gerry between takes, and muttered, "I'm ready for my close-up,

Mr de Mille," which solicited a rumbling guffaw from Tom.

At the end of the day, as Maggie was preparing to leave, Anna came up to her. "Do you want a lift? It's yoga tonight." Her tone was neutral.

Maggie had considered giving yoga a miss because the state of affairs between herself and her mother was so tense and she didn't relish spending social time with her. But what was the point of cutting off her nose to spite her face?

"I'm meeting Aiden for a drink after work," she said, "but I'll be going to yoga."

Anna smiled, seeing it as a gesture, she too finding the atmosphere at home uncomfortable. She hated arguing with Maggie but in this case she was being so unreasonable, Anna didn't see why she should give in and be the one to buy the Jaffa Cakes.

"Right you are. I'll wait for you at home then," she said.

Aiden was in the Palace ahead of Maggie, sitting at a table reading the *Evening Herald* and her stomach churned deliciously at the sight of him.

"How did the shoot go?" he asked putting the paper aside, and giving her a kiss of hello.

"Fine," she said. "Mossie's his usual ray-of-sunshine self, but things are still a trifle tense with Mum."

"Maybe you should make the first move. It's daft to let this Gerry Starling cause a rift between you." He stood up. "What would you like to drink?"

Maggie ordered a glass of Guinness and when he returned with it she said, "I know you're right, but I can't help it. She's going off to India and he's going to meet up with her there and she'll be sitting on Diana's seat with him instead of Dad."

"You've lost me," he said, and Maggie explained about the Taj Mahal and the celebrated shot of Princess Diana sitting alone in front of the famous mausoleum.

"And are you sure she's going with Starling? That's definite, is it?"

Put that way, she wasn't sure. "Well, not all the time. Not with him exactly, but she said they might meet up."

"And are they an item? I mean, you know, are they actually sleeping together?"

In truth Maggie didn't know, or particularly want to go there. She shrugged.

Putting his arm around her, Aiden gave her a squeeze and kissed the side of her head. "I wouldn't worry about it. Your ma's a smart lady. If you ask me, getting involved, I mean properly involved with the likes of Gerry Starling is far from the top of her list of things she wants to do."

"But –"

"She said she wants to do the stuff she didn't get a chance to do because she got married young, right? She needs to be single to do that. That's the whole point."

"But what about the Lounge Lizard?" she said.

"What about him? She's just enjoying the attention right now. I bet he never goes to India. I bet Anna's just winding you up about that. And him too," he added.

She sighed. "You reckon?"

"Knowing Anna, it wouldn't surprise me. She did the hash thing, right? And the yoga?"

Maggie nodded.

"So that leaves India," he concluded.

"And kick boxing. Don't forget the kick boxing," Maggie said, laughing. Then her phone rang. She didn't recognise the Caller ID number and when she picked up the call heard Skye's voice.

"Maggie?"

"Is that you, Skye?"

It was noisy in the pub and the signal was breaking up, so she had to put her finger to her other ear to hear what the girl was saying.

"You have to come." She sounded frantic.

"What's wrong. What's happened?" said Maggie, Skye's anxiety infecting her.

"I tried to get hold of Anna, but her mobile's switched off. Please come. I'm at home. Please come. It's Ursula."

The call dropped. Maggie repeated Skye's name several times and tried to redial, but couldn't get her on the network.

"What's up?" Aiden asked, concern in his voice.

"Have you got your car with you?"

On the way she tried Anna's mobile but it was switched off as Skye had said, and Maggie assumed that she'd just forgotten to switch it back on again after the shoot.

"Do you reckon she's taken pills again?" Aiden said, as he manoeuvred the traffic around Stephen's Green.

It was a strong possibility, given Skye's frantic call. "I hope not. But she sounded pretty worried."

She gave him directions and fifteen minutes later they pulled up outside Skye's flat behind an ambulance and a Garda car. It didn't look good.

Skye met them at the door, her face white as a sheet,

visibly shaking. A cop was standing, his back to them, blocking the doorway of the bathroom.

"I found her," she said. "She's dead. I meant to be home earlier but I was delayed – shit, no – I went for a drink with a friend – I should have been here."

Maggie put her arms around the girl and she burst into tears, her head buried in Maggie's shoulder.

"Hush," Maggie soothed. "It probably wouldn't have made any difference." Maggie had no idea whether this was the case or not, but what else could she say?

As it turned out, she heard the cop telling a colleague over his radio that Ursula had been dead for some time, so that was some cause of comfort to Skye, who had taken the guilt of her friend and mentor's death upon herself.

At that point Maggie and Aiden, and Dani and Conor who had arrived just as Skye burst into tears, had no idea how Ursula had chosen to end it all this time, but later, after the ambulance had taken the body away to Saint James's Hospital mortuary, and Anna had arrived breathless and pale, Skye told them what had happened.

She had come home to find Ursula lying in the bath, the water stained red from the blood that had drained from her now lifeless body through two vertical slashes in her left and right wrist. On the kitchen table she found a note that read simply: "I'm sorry."

After the ambulance and the cops had all gone, they went to the pub for a drink. Needless to say the atmosphere around the table was subdued.

"I can't believe she's dead," Skye said, voicing the thoughts of the rest of the party. "She was doing so well."

Conor shook his head. "No, she wasn't. She was still

depressed. And the medication was doing sod-all for her."

"She wouldn't take it," Skye said. "She flushed it down the toilet. She was scared she'd get hooked on it, so she went for meditation and chanting instead. Two hours morning and night."

"Fat lot of good that did her," Aiden commented.

They sat in silence, sipping their drinks.

After Ursula had come out of hospital to Skye's flat the previous Saturday, only Conor had bothered to visit her on a daily basis, and despite their best intentions, both Anna and Maggie had only managed one visit each. The problem was, it was such hard going. Ursula didn't want them to be there and refused to initiate any conversation, replying to questions in monosyllables and staring off into space most of the time.

Dani sighed. "I didn't go to see her at all after she came home. Do you think if we'd visited her more, she might not have done it?"

"I doubt it would have made any difference," Aiden said, able to view the situation from a distance. "She was determined. Seems to me she set it up so there'd be no danger of anyone stopping her this time."

Anna took hold of Dani's hand. "It was out of our control. Aiden's right. Ursula wasn't crying for help when she took the pills. She meant business and we only spoiled it for her the last time."

"But imagine wanting to die," Conor said. It was a concept he couldn't get a handle on.

Maggie glanced at Anna. "It's like Mum said, Conor. Ursula didn't want to die; she just didn't want to be alive any more. It was her choice."

"Poor Ursula," Dani said, then gave a long sigh, and raised her glass. "To Ursula wherever you are. I hope you're at peace now."

The others raised their glasses and mumbled, "To Ursula."

Thinking of her caused them all to ponder on their own troubles and reminded Maggie how inconsequential hers were. Even Dani's plight seemed pretty manageable compared with losing the will to live.

They dispersed after another drink as no one was in the mood for making conversation, and Anna offered Dani and Conor a lift home. As Skye was saying her goodbyes to everyone, Maggie touched her mother's arm.

"See you at home," she said. "I'll bring the Jaffa Cakes."

Nothing like a sudden death to make a person realise that life's too short.

Chapter 40

The following week was a very busy one for Sally as the account that she and Leo were working on was coming together, and she hardly managed to leave the office before eight any night, ten on one occasion. The campaign was for a new brand of fruit-flavoured bottled tequila-based cocktails called ShockFX aimed at the eighteen to twenty-five market, and had a substantial budget to cover all media – print, broadcast, cinema and outdoor. Also they had, in the face of fierce competition, snatched the account from a large well-established agency, which was a feather in their collective cap.

Consequently she'd seen nothing of David, but had had the pleasure of Hero's company almost every night. He'd taken to waiting outside the office for her and, after Lily had commented on the monster dog sitting outside on the first evening, Sally had brought him inside and up to her office letting him lie on the floor by the radiator. After the first couple of days Lily became quite chummy with him, and took to bringing him up herself, whereupon people stopped passing comment – whatever about Sally, no one at Deadly would dare to mutter about the redoubtable Lily behind her back.

On Friday afternoon Sally picked up a message to say that Auntie Pauline had called. Circumstances dictated against her being able to return the call until she was about to leave the office that evening at seven thirty, early by the week's standards.

The call went something like this.

"Hello, Auntie Pauline. It's Sally. You left a message."

"It's about Humphrey Bogart."

"Um . . . yes. What about him?" She's losing it, Sally thought.

"How old would you say he is?"

Humour her. "Well, hard to say. Around the ninety mark, I suppose, if he were still alive."

"No. No. Not that Humphrey Bogart. My Humphrey Bogart."

Then it dawned on her. "Oh. You called the pup Humphrey Bogart. Good choice." When leaving the pup she had felt a certain culpability at the prospect that the poor critter might be saddled with some totally inappropriate name such as Cuddles or, heaven forbid, Precious Mk. II.

"Yes. I always had a soft spot for Humphrey Bogart when I was a girl."

The thought of her prim, bad-tempered, spinster aunt having a soft spot for anyone was a revelation.

"The thing is," Pauline continued, "I was wondering how old he is."

"Sorry. I don't know. He's a stray, but by the look of

him I wouldn't say he's a year old yet. Why?" Having no experience with animals this was a wild guess on Sally's part.

"Oh. Just wondering," her aunt replied which led Sally to wonder what was the real purpose of the call. There was a pause.

"Well, I suppose I should get to the point," Pauline said. "You see . . . well, I'm not very good at this, but I have to admit, I never really liked you that much, Sally. You're too much like your father, not that I ever speak ill of the dead, God rest his soul, but I always thought you were a selfish sort of girl."

Thanks a bunch, Sally thought.

Her aunt continued. "However, I feel it's only right to tell you that I've changed my mind about you. You were so sweet after my poor, poor Precious so tragically passed away, and so sympathetic, it was obvious that you were as griefstricken as I was. And then to find me a wonderful companion like Humphrey . . ."

Sally wanted the floor to open up and swallow her. OK so she'd found her aunt a new companion but only because she'd virtually murdered the last one. She flushed with embarrassment as Pauline went on. "And it was such a comfort to me to know that my Precious, when I couldn't be with her myself, passed away in the company of a person who really cared about her."

Sally stayed silent, mainly because she didn't have the first idea what to say.

"Anyway," Pauline said after a pause. "I just thought I should call to thank you for bringing Humphrey and me together. He's sitting here at my feet as we speak."

I'm Sorry

"I'm . . . er . . . glad it's all worked out so well," Sally said.

"You must come round for tea sometime," her aunt continued. "And bring that nice young man with you. What's his name? Donald, is it?"

"David," Sally corrected, still perplexed by her aunt's apparent personality transplant. "Er . . . thanks. I'll get back to you about that."

After Pauline had gone, Sally looked over at Hero who was snoozing by the radiator.

"You'll never guess who that was."

"No, who was it?"

Sally stared at Hero, her jaw slack, then heard a sound behind her and turned to see David standing at her open office door. Noticing her stunned expression he said, "Sorry, didn't mean to startle you, but I was passing and saw your light on, so I thought you might like to go for a drink or something." Then he looked over at Hero. "Hello, boy!"

Hero got up, stretched himself and, padding over to David, offering his head for a stroke.

"Actually no," Sally said, causing a flash of disappointment for him. "I'm whacked, but I'd love to share a bottle of Chablis with you at home, if that's OK?"

His face lit up in a smile. "Chablis it is then."

As they walked through reception, past the contract cleaning lady who was hoovering, she said to David, "Auntie Pauline sends her love."

"You were talking to her?"

"She phoned to say she never really liked me."

David stopped by the door. "That was a bit harsh."

345

"Not really," Sally continued. "It seems Humphrey Bogart has caused her to have a complete personality makeover."

"I think you'd better explain," he said, taking her arm.

"I used to go out with his brother," Lily said.

There were sitting together in O'Neill's. It was past eight and most of the Friday night get-together crowd had gone but, as circumstances had contrived to keep them apart, Maggie and Lily were enjoying the opportunity to catch up on things.

"Really?" Maggie said.

Lily nodded. "Yes, he lived around the corner from us in Finglas. Aaron still does as far as I know."

"Aaron's the brother?"

"That's right. There's Aaron, who's my age, then Clint, then Gavin and Wayne, they're twins, and Iggy the baby."

"Wow. So you went out with Gavin O'Connor's brother. Is he as cute as Gavin?"

"Last time I saw Gavin he was skinny and spotty and had a serious problem in the personal hygiene department," Lily clarified. "And I only went out with Aaron for about six months, but we'd knocked round together in a group all the time I was in school."

"So Gavin's a twin. What's he like?" Maggie asked.

Lily wagged her head from side to side. "Dunno really. The family's dead on, but he and Wayne used to wind Aaron up something rotten by trailing round after him. You know what it's like when your kid brother or sister tags along like a fecking bad smell and won't go away. Well, he had two of them."

Maggie did, only too well, remembering the way Lucy used to make a nuisance of herself, latching onto her when she was trying to talk to her friends about fellas. Four years' age difference is huge when you're only fifteen.

"Well, I hope he hasn't turned into some gobshite-prima-donna now he's rich and famous," Maggie commented. She had worked with some in her time and it was a pain. Strangely it was the actors and celebrities who had an excuse to be uppity that generally turned out to be nice and professional and undemanding, compared to the nouveau famous, who graced the covers of *Hello* and *VIP*, the Irish equivalent – sometimes referred to by the pub wags as 'Howya Magazine' – who were inclined to think themselves legends in their own lunch-time, that caused problems.

"Shouldn't think so," Lily commented. "Anyway, if he is, I can always get Aaron to give him a clip around the ear."

"Well, look him up," Maggie said. "The shoot starts on Tuesday so we might need to employ his clipping-around-the-ear skills."

Lily laughed. "I'll see what I can do."

Sally had David in peals of laughter as they walked along, regaling him with an exaggerated interpretation of Auntie Pauline's phone call.

"Anyway," she said, as they reached the front door, "she invited me around for tea along with that nice boy Donald."

"Donald? Well, I'm glad to see I made such a lasting impression on your venerable aunt."

Then, as she put the key in the lock she heard a familiar voice.

"Sally."

Momentarily paralysed, she caught her breath and spun around.

Charlie Penhaligan was standing on the broad pavement about ten feet away.

He looked tired and drawn, and slightly travel-rumpled which was unlike him. Unable to make either her brain or her vocal chords work she stared at him as he stood there, so out of context. Finally she managed to say his name.

"Charlie!"

He smiled and walked towards her, but she stepped back, stumbling against David, who put out a hand to catch her.

"We need to talk," said Charlie. Then his eyes turned to David. "Alone."

Rooted to the spot, Sally became aware of a low rumble which grew in intensity. Hero stepped forward and stood four-square in front of Charlie, his lips drawn back to reveal his sharp canines, growling menacingly. Charlie took a hasty step back, several steps in fact, then glared at David.

"Does your dog bite?" he asked, trying to appear nonchalant and unafraid.

David, reminded of the Pink Panther joke, was tempted to take on Clouseau's voice and deliver the "Thet is nut mai doge" line but realising that it was totally inappropriate, instead looked at Sally and asked, "Are you all right?"

Sally had gathered herself together by this time, and

she placed a restraining hand lightly on Hero's back, whereby the growling diminished in intensity, but was nevertheless still apparent.

"I'm fine thanks, David," she said. Then addressing herself to her former lover, asked, "What are you doing here, Charlie?"

"We need to talk," he repeated. "Please. Just hear me out."

He looked defeated and sad and despite herself, Sally's heart went out to him.

"Just hear what I have to say, then I'll go," he said.

Putting two and two together David said, "I take it this is your stalker," and Charlie glared at him again, whereby David added, "You don't have to do anything you don't want to."

"This is between Sally and me," Charlie said. "It's no concern of yours. Nothing to do with you."

David took a step forward. "Sally's a friend, and I think you're upsetting her."

"I'm fine, David," she said. "But there are things Charlie and I have to talk about. Would you mind?"

The 'would you mind' wasn't so much an enquiry, more an invitation to leave. He was reluctant, his motives not entirely consisting of concern for Sally. Without doubt he was worried about her, but he also had an intensely selfish, deep-down, gut-based worry that she might be persuaded to go back to stalker-man given half a chance.

"Are you sure?" he asked and when she nodded said, "Well, you have my mobile number if you need me."

"Thanks, David." She touched his arm. "I'll call you later."

Anna O'Malley

He hesitated, not happy about leaving. Then, recognising that there was no alternative, casting a glance in Charlie's direction, he said, "OK. Talk to you later," and walked away down Great George's Street.

Sally watched him go, then looked at Charlie, who was still standing some feet away due to Hero's quietly rumbling proximity, a wary eye on the oversized hound.

"I've missed you," he said.

I've missed you too, Sally screamed inside her head, but said aloud, "Have you?"

"More than you'll ever know," he said, then ventured a fairy step forward which prompted Hero's growling to increase in volume.

He stepped back again. "That dog doesn't like me."

"Like doesn't come into it. He doesn't trust you. He's a good judge of character." Then she stroked Hero's head. "It's OK, boy. He's not going to hurt me." Her own choice of words caused her to smile at the irony. "Well, not any more than he already has," she added, and Charlie winced.

Hero, still not happy with the vibe of the situation, continued to stand between Sally and Charlie, though he ceased growling.

"Good boy," she cooed, then glanced at her former lover. "That's the thing about dogs, Charlie. They don't let you down."

"Could we talk?" he asked.

"What's there to say?"

"I've been a fool."

Can't argue with that, she thought.

"It was your choice," she said stiffly. "I asked you to

make a choice and I wasn't it. Simple as that. End of story."

He attempted another tentative step forward and she felt Hero's wiry shoulder muscles tense under her hand.

"I've been a fool," he repeated. "A monumental fool to think I could live without you."

He's doing it again, she thought, anger rising in her chest cavity. Same old story.

"Too bad," she said. "I've moved on."

He turned his head and looked down the street to where, in the distance, David was just turning the corner into Dame Street. "Him?"

Sally shook her head. "You don't get it, do you? This is nothing to do with David." She slapped her chest with her open palm. "This is about me. I've moved on, Charlie. Did you think I'd be sitting at home licking my wounds, pining after someone who stabbed me in the back?"

He looked anguished at that. "I know I don't deserve you. I know I've been a bastard, but I love you, Sally. I need you in my life."

She wanted to cry. Here he was, the love of her life, saying the words he should have said weeks ago, and she wanted to stab him, but at the same time rush into his arms. Her hands were shaking and her knees weak.

"I love you," he repeated.

"But not enough," she said, tears spilling onto her cheeks.

He shook his head unable to speak, too full of emotion. Then, exhaling and pulling himself together, he said, "I've left Imogene."

"What!"

He stepped forward, this time ignoring the dog, his

arms open to her. "I'm so sorry, Sally. Please let me make it up to you."

Shock rooted her to the spot. "You've left Imogene?"

He nodded, a wide grin spreading across his face. "Absolutely. Imogene's history."

"History?" She was stunned. "How did she take it?" Although she had only met Imogene briefly on a couple of occasions, she had gathered enough of an impression to know that Charlie Penhaligan's wife would not take kindly to being told she was history.

"Not well," he said, which, by the look on his face was a gross understatement.

She didn't know what to do. Charlie's declaration had knocked the wind out of her. He'd left Imogene. Scary Imogene, she who held the purse string, she who had him by the short and curlies, was history.

"Are you serious? You've left Imogene? For good? For ever?"

He nodded, then suddenly they were both laughing like fools and she was in his arms.

Chapter 41

Sally was a happy bunny as she headed out to work on Monday morning. She hadn't made it easy for Charlie. Why should she after the indescribable pain he'd caused her? She'd punished him, reminding him how badly he'd behaved, how disappointed she'd been in him, how much he'd hurt her, but the fact was he wanted her and he was begging her to spend the rest of her life with him. He had finally bitten the bullet and left Imogene, his old life and everything that represented, and he had chosen her. He'd begged for forgiveness, for a second chance. She knew it was a sacrifice for him as Imogene would surely make him suffer financially, but he didn't seem concerned. He wanted to be with her whatever it took. They had spent most of the weekend in bed, talking, planning and making love like new lovers, leaving the loft only to eat and let Hero out, until late on Sunday night when Charlie had dragged himself reluctantly away for the last flight back to London.

They had talked about setting up home together in her flat in Putney after the present tenant's lease was up. That suited her admirably as she felt an obligation to stay with Deadly at least until the end of the year; and she had also wisely decided that she wouldn't go back to Penhaligan, but find a job with another London agency which wouldn't be hard if her time at Deadly lived up to its promise.

Hero was waiting for her outside on Great George's Street. He'd loped off early on Saturday afternoon, presumably unhappy with Charlie's presence, so her heart lifted as she spied him sitting outside her door waiting.

"So don't beat about the bush. What do you really think?" she asked as they walked at a brisk pace towards the office. "He loves me, Hero. He's a good man. You'll get to like him, I promise."

I must stop doing this, she thought as a pedestrian gave her a weird look in passing. The dog glanced sideways but didn't offer any comment, obviously still in a minor snit. Thinking of snits it occurred to her that she hadn't called David and felt guilty about that, but wasn't sure what to say to him, figuring that the least she should do was to call him up and let him know that she was OK. She liked him. He was good company and a nice man and she hoped that he could accept the situation and still be her friend, particularly as it was on the cards that she'd be remaining in Dublin, at least until the end of the year. It's not as if he hadn't known about Charlie, she rationalised, at least in the abstract.

I'll call him as soon as I get to the office, she thought,

as she stopped off at Macari's for a takeaway low-fat cappuccino. As if reading her mind Hero caught her eye and, had she not known better, she could have sworn he gave her a sceptical sneer.

"I will call him and tell him the truth. Honestly, I will," she said, not caring if the other customers thought she was bonkers.

On the way into the office she bumped into Leo and they exchanged hellos.

"So this is the Dog of Legend," he said, reaching out his hand to pat Hero's head. "Big bugger, isn't he?"

"And a perfect gentleman," Sally said. "It's not a problem having him in the office, is it?"

Leo laughed then shook his head. "Like I'm going to argue with a fifteen-stone dog?"

Sally scratched Hero behind the ear. "He's a pussycat really. But if it is a problem . . ."

Leo waved her question away. "Not a problem. Anyway, he lends a certain je ne sais quoi to the building. A kind of Lord of The Rings ambience."

Hero closed his eyes and sighed.

"You think so? Maybe I should have called him Gandalph," she said, which occasioned the dog to give a snort of (presumably) derision.

"Well, maybe not . . ."

Entering reception they were greeted by Lily staggering under the weight of an armful of long-stemmed red roses, at least fifty, Sally estimated, comparing the bulk to the ones she had so viciously decapitated in the previous weeks. There was also another huge bunch of the same volume enveloping the top of Lily's desk.

"Are these for water or to be dumped?" Lily asked Sally, not wanting to take the trouble of hunting out suitable containers if she was going to bin them again, silently cursing all flash bastards of the world for causing her such inconvenience first thing on a Monday morning; while being honest enough with herself to realise that sour grapes figured largely in her annoyance.

Sally felt a flush of happiness wash over her. "Water of course," she said hurrying over to Lily and removing the card which was taped to the bouquet.

"Love you . . . C." it read.

"Spread them around the building," Sally said in a fit of magnanimity.

"Jesus! What the fuck did he do?" Leo said, and Sally grinned, so happy she was unable to take offence.

"The right thing," she said.

At four-thirty Lily buzzed Maggie to tell her Gavin O'Connor was in reception for the pre-production meeting.

"Our wonder boy's outside," she said to Tom, and they both headed out to meet him. There were two of them in reception, obviously brothers by the resemblance, one older than the other.

"This is Gavin," Lily said, indicating the younger one, "And this is his brother, Aaron."

Gavin was shorter than his photos suggested, about five nine at a pinch, two inches shorter than his sibling, but nonetheless remarkably cute in a boy-band sort of way. Maggie could also see why Lily had dallied, if only briefly, with Aaron as he was equally fit.

"Howya," Gavin said, giving each a hearty handshake, as Lily introduced Maggie and Tom, then Aaron gave them a nod.

"Good to meet you guys," Maggie said. Then to Gavin, "Mike Patterson, the director, and Herbie McFly, the producer, should be here any time now. How was your flight over?"

"Ah grand. Not mad about flyin', so you know yourself."

Tom suggested they go up to the conference room and Lily said she'd look after Aaron so, without further ado, the two creatives headed upstairs with the star of their campaign and a promise from Lily that she'd bring up coffee as soon as Mike and Herbie arrived.

The meeting was an informal affair, mainly an opportunity for Maggie and Tom, and Mike and Herbie to present Gavin with the concept, how it would be shot, and what was expected of him. He was pretty laid-back about it and a naturally funny guy, but very inquisitive about the whole process and not in the slightest bit prima-donnish which was a welcome relief. By the end of the meeting both Tom and Maggie agreed that he was a very good choice, with the added bonus that Tom would win mega brownie points and invaluable street cred from his daughter Jodie for the chance of meeting her idol.

The meeting broke up at just before six whereupon Herbie and Mike left. A short time later when Maggie, Tom and Gavin got down to reception Aaron was waiting with his coat on, as was Lily.

"We're going for a bite to eat and then on to The Loop later," Aaron said. "Do you guys want to come?"

Tom said he didn't want to deal with the embarrassment of being turned away by the bouncers for being too old, but Lily pointed out that that wasn't an issue as they'd be let into the Engine Room – the VIP area – seeing as they were with Gavin, so he could join the other VIP middle-aged farts.

"Put that way how could I refuse?" he said dryly, casting a jaundiced glance at Maggie. "Have to give it a miss, though. Things to do."

But Maggie knew well that it was because he'd rather stick his head in the microwave than go drinking in one of Dublin's trendier nightspots. Clubbing wasn't Tom's thing, full stop. He was more of a pub man.

Maggie said she and Aiden might see them there later, so to leave their names at the door, in the knowledge that the man in her life was a fervent Manchester United fan and would probably cut off her right arm, let alone his, to meet the footballer in the flesh. How saaad are men?

Sally passed through reception on her way out with Hero, and stopped as Maggie introduced her to Gavin and Aaron.

"Mighty dog," Aaron said, patting the dog's back. "Is he yours?"

Sally grinned. "Sometimes. When the mood takes him."

Gavin, who was obviously on for making a night of it, said. "We're going to The Loop later, Sally. Would you like to come?"

"I don't think they let dogs in," she said, patting Hero's back.

"They do if they're famous," Lily muttered which caused a general titter.

"Might see you all there later then," Sally said, then breezed out of the door.

She was in sparkling form, high almost, so much so that after she had gone, Maggie leaned in to Lily. "What's she on?"

"Did you not see?" she said, indicating the vase of roses on her desk. "Someone sent her a hundred. A fecking hundred. Imagine what that must have cost!"

"Was it the same guy whose flowers she trashed, d'you think?" Maggie speculated.

"Yeah, deffo, I'd say. Wouldn't you?" she said, adding under her breath, "How does she do it?"

For a Monday night, The Loop was busy when Maggie and Aiden arrived, but Lily, Aaron and Gavin, having turned up quite early, had nabbed a good table. As Aiden talked football with the lads, Maggie and Lily indulged in their favourite club game, Spot the Real Celeb – a must in the land of begrudgery, thought Maggie, where it is considered very un-cool to give the great, the famous and those who are but legends in their own lunchtime the satisfaction of even a hint of recognition. Many foreign members of this brother/sisterhood mistake this phenomenon for a form of politeness or respect for their personal space.

Lily was first to score as she indicated Lulu who was sitting at a table on the other side of the room chatting to Sally. Lulu was over-promoting her latest album and Sally was apparently (according to Lily's current information on the Creative Director) an acquaintance of the singer, having used her in a campaign a couple of years previously – In fact, it was a treble hit for Lily as they then realised that Samantha Mumba and her manager, Louis Walsh, who was now also managing Lulu, were also part of the group. Sally looked sensational in a clingy red Jersey dress and was still in cracking form, practically glowing with good humour as she chatted animatedly, reinforcing Maggie's assumption that her relationship with mystery-man must be on again.

For someone who had been away from the city for several years Sally seemed to be on friendly terms with a surprising number of people, and later Lily and Maggie noticed her flitting from table to table renewing social contact and generally networking.

Amongst others they spotted dancer Michael Flatley (one of the few whom Sally didn't appear to know), a pretty member of a generic boy band neither of them could put a name on, Nicole Kidman who was over shooting a movie and who stayed only briefly (Maggie claimed a bonus point for her), various minor Irish thespians, TV personalities and the statutory number of BPs (Beautiful People). In short, a quiet Monday night at the trendy Dublin nightspot.

Sometime later, while Gavin was giving it large on the dance floor, a leggy model wrapped round him, and Lily and Aaron seemed to be on quite friendly terms judging by how up close and personal they were dancing, Aiden went to the bar to get another round in so Maggie went off to find the loo where she bumped into Stephanie Valentine. She hadn't seen her since the debacle of the Super Savings voice-over, and felt uncomfortable with the fact that Anna had nicked her gig, so to speak. Steph however was OK about it.

"Hey, it's not your fault," she assured Maggie. "And it's not as if I'm short of work at the moment. Anyway, you give me plenty of voice-overs so I can't complain."

This was true. Due to Steph's versatility, Maggie did give her a lot of work. "I got a part in the new Jackie Chan they're shooting here," she continued. "I'm playing a lady cop."

Maggie grinned. "Excellent!"

"Yes, it makes a change from playing psychotic social workers, I can tell you."

After her cameo in Coronation Street, Steph had played a number of psychotic roles, and had confided in Maggie at one point that she feared that she was in danger of becoming psychotic for real if someone didn't offer her something different. There had even been talk of a storyline in her current Irish soap, *Liffey Town*, concerning her character taking a loopy turn.

"Speaking of psychotic," Steph said, lowering her voice, "that Gerry Starling guy gave me the creeps. Talk about harassment! In the end I had to get Tim to pick me up from a recording and introduce him as my husband, in capital letters."

"Are you serious?"

Steph nodded. "It was very awkward. He's way weird that guy and you'd think he had shares in a bloody florist's shop the way I had them arriving on my doorstep."

"You too! He's been like that with my mother," Maggie said. "He's smitten. He insisted on having her for the TV campaign, and he's doing the flower-showering thing. What a lounge lizard!"

"You can say that again."

"He didn't get physical, did he?" Maggie asked, suddenly concerned, and Steph shook her head.

"No. I didn't give him any encouragement. I nipped it in the bud, but I tell you, it wasn't easy. Particularly with me working for him, technically speaking, so in one way I wasn't sorry to lose the gig."

"But he took no for an answer in the end? He didn't turn into a stalker or anything?"

Steph laughed. "Oh, it was fine in the end," she assured Maggie. "Don't worry."

They parted company outside the loos and Steph went off to rejoin her friends.

The Gerry Starling revelation had suddenly deflated Maggie's good humour and she was worried now more than ever that Anna could get hurt. The fact that he hadn't got physical with Steph was no consolation either, on the grounds that she hadn't given him any encouragement, whereas Anna was sending exactly the opposite signals, judging by the number of times she'd been out with him.

But then is it any of my business? she asked herself. As Aiden had pointed out, Anna was an adult and how she chose to deal with Gerry Starling was her affair. But still Maggie felt uneasy. For the most part, and by her own admission, Anna had led a fairly sheltered existence up to now, so the question was, would she be able to handle it if Gerry did come on too strong? She didn't want to deal with the thought that her mother might actually welcome such a development in the relationship.

With this on her mind as she pushed her way through the throng towards her table, it was only at the last moment she saw Sinita. It wasn't the fact of seeing

Aiden's luscious ex that caused her to catch her breath and stop dead in her tracks, it was the small detail that she had her arms entwined around his neck and her tongue in his ear that was a tad unsettling.

Before she had time to react however, she saw Aiden unwrapping Sinita's arms and gently but firmly pushing her away. A huge wave of relief washed over her as it was obvious by his body language that he didn't want to play, but Sinita had other ideas and she lashed out at him, slapping him across the face then pummelling him with her clenched fists, her face twisted with fury, a stream of unintelligible abuse pouring out of her mouth. A small space cleared around them and a few onlookers paused in mid-sentence to take in the spectacle. When Aiden grabbed her wrists in an attempt to put a halt to the assault, she twisted free, then Aaron came up behind her and pinned her arms to her sides. All the time she was roaring abuse at Aiden, who was now standing back, his hands up, palms out in a "leave me alone, I don't want this" gesture. A bouncer came on the scene at that point along with some people from Sinita's party and they calmed her down, leading her back to their table still muttering and shouting the occasional obscenity in Aiden's direction. Then, show over, the onlookers lost interest and went back to their own conversations.

Aiden sat down and Maggie slid into the seat next to him.

"What was that about?" she asked.

Aiden shook his head. "She's drunk, that's all."

"Do you know her?" Aaron asked, sitting back down next to Lily who was giving Aiden a distinctly toxic glare.

"That was Sinita, Aiden's ex," Maggie explained.

With Maggie's recent experience of cheating men in mind, Lily gave him a sceptical look. "Your ex? Really?"

Aiden nodded. "She gets obstreperous with too much drink," he said, somewhat economically as if that explained everything, then he slid his hand out and grabbed Maggie's, giving it a squeeze. "Sorry about that," he said. "Are you OK?"

Maggie nodded. "I'm fine. I'm not the one she attacked. Another five seconds with her tongue in your ear and I might have been swayed towards violence though."

Aiden gave an exaggerated "Phew!" and wiped his brow and they both laughed, which lightened the atmosphere, Maggie's attitude towards the situation having changed the mood around the table.

"Does she have a drink problem then, your ex?" Lily asked.

"Not a problem exactly, but she gets weird when she drinks too much, particularly when she mixes it with coke." Aiden cast a glance over to where Sinita was now back on the dance-floor salsa-dancing with a short guy Maggie recognised from one of the Dublin-based production companies.

"I take it we're not talking cola drink here?" Lily said, and Aiden nodded.

After another round of drinks, with the following day's shoot in mind, Maggie decided to call it a night. Aiden looked relieved as it was obvious that despite his cool, laugh-it-off exterior, he was glad to get away from the now completely wasted Sinita for fear of another unwarranted scene, causing Maggie to revisit the notion that their parting may not have been as amicable as he had claimed.

Before leaving, she reminded Lily to make sure that Gavin got home at a reasonable hour as a car was booked to pick him up at his mother's house in Finglas at seven a.m. sharp. Lily responded with a crisp salute, which didn't fill Maggie with confidence. Suddenly, clubbing the night before a shoot didn't seem like such a good idea, particularly in light of the fact that Gavin looked as if he was only getting started.

"D'you reckon he'll be OK for the shoot?" she asked Aiden. "He was fairly milling into the beer?"

"He'll be grand," Aiden assured her, still endearingly chuffed to have met the Gavin O'Connor, Man United and Ireland soccer star.

Maggie needn't have worried, however, because when she, Tom and Jodie arrived out at Ardmore Studios early the following morning, Gavin was already there, in body if not in spirit – but it was nothing a couple of mega-strength Nurofen and a pint or so of water wouldn't fix. Jodie was thrilled to pieces to meet him and he was good as gold with her and posed for photos with her, though she was struck dumb with awe. Then, Denis Morgan, chief executive of I-Sport, arrived with his daughter Shona, and Gavin went through the whole rigmarole again without a grumble, impressing Maggie no end. He seemed like a genuinely nice guy, and she recalled Lily's remark about the family being 'dead on'.

As the make-up girl was giving him the once-over, one of the runners came in with a large mug of tea and a bacon sandwich which Gavin fell upon.

"How're you feeling?" Maggie asked.

"Didn't get in till gone four and drink always leaves me starvin'," he said. "I'll be grand when I get this down me."

And he was. The first shot was set up by nine and Mike explained again about the blue-screen background, showing him the actual footage they would shoot over; then they had a few rehearsals as Mike watched the monitor. Geordie, his assistant, from his vantage point halfway up a stepladder, out of shot, threw a soccer ball at Gavin's head and he had to head it to the left into a marked zone that would be the goal. Then Mike got Geordie to adjust the flight path of the ball a couple of times until he was happy.

Gavin was togged out in the Ireland soccer strip and looked great. Nudging Tom, Maggie whispered, "Now there's a fine pair of thighs."

"Down, girl!" he muttered in reply.

As Mike went for a take, they wandered over to the refreshment table and helped themselves to a couple of bacon rolls and some strong coffee. It was going to be a long day.

The first shot took seven takes until Mike was satisfied, then, Gavin went over to the refreshment table for further sustenance, as the crew set up the second shot. Tom and Maggie joined him.

"How's it going?" Tom asked.

"Could've done without headin' the ball so much," he

said, rubbing his forehead. "Bit delicate in that department today."

"Will you be OK?" Maggie asked, "There's more ball-heading in scene three."

Helping himself to a sausage roll he said, "I was thinkin' about that. How about I sort of scissor-kick it over my head instead? Would that do?"

Maggie looked at Tom, not certain what scissor-kicking over the head involved.

"Could the ball have the same flight path?" Tom asked.

Gavin gave a nod, then regretting it, winced. "Yeah. No problemo. What d'you think?"

"Yeah," Tom agreed. "I'll have to talk to Mike and the client to see if it's OK with them. But sounds good. Would look great. We'd have to get a couple of crash-mats in though."

Maggie had to take his word for it at that point, having no idea what they were talking about

"It's the shot where I save the Italy goal," Gavin said, full of enthusiasm.

Scene two was a kicking shot, so Gavin's head had a reprieve. Strangely this scene, though technically more straightforward, proved to be more problematic and it took ten takes to get it right, after which it was well after two and everyone was ready for lunch. While Maggie took Jodie and Shona to the canteen, and the crew prepared for the next shot, Tom talked to Mike and Denis Morgan about the changes for the third scene and both were enthusiastic about it.

It was a good call. The shot was spectacular and as

Maggie watched Gavin while he kicked the ball backwards over his head, hitting the target almost every time, she could see what all the fuss was about. It was pretty hard on Gavin, mind you, as each time he landed on his back on the thick crash-mats, but managed to do so, thankfully, without injury to life or limb.

Scene three, being a tad more complicated, took the rest of the afternoon to get in the can, but according to Mike's schedule they were on the nail, so they called it a day at seven. As shoots went it was pretty normal, and surprisingly snag-free with just two more scenes to shoot and the pack shot, with the links and end voice-over to be done the following week in post production.

After the previous late night, and the long day's shoot, Maggie decided to have an early one so declined Tom's offer of a pint and went straight home.

"How did the shoot go?" Anna asked as she muted the sound on the TV.

Maggie slumped down on the sofa beside her, and kicked off her shoes. "Great. Went like a dream and Gavin was brilliant."

"I had no idea it was so complicated," Anna said, "or that there'd be so much hanging around involved."

"You enjoyed it though? The Super Savings shoot?"

Her mother nodded enthusiastically. "Oh yes. Wouldn't have missed it for the world. But at least I'll know to bring a book the next time." She stood up. "I'll made you a nice cup of tea – then you can tell me all about it."

"Not much to tell," Maggie said, reaching for the

remote and clicking the mute button to restore the sound. "And with a bit of luck tomorrow will be the same."

Famous last words.

The following morning when Maggie and Tom arrived out at Ardmore Studios they were greeted by the news that Gavin O'Connor was missing.

Chapter 42

"Missing? How could he be missing?" Maggie's stomach muscles clenched with the first stirrings of panic.

Minty, Herbie McFly's assistant, sighed. "The car went to pick him up and he wasn't there." She was a thin gangly girl with orange dreadlocks, a naturally lethargic manner and jaded expression, which was probably an asset considering the way Herbie could go off on one without any advanced warning.

"Did the driver go to the right address?" Tom asked.

She hit her head with the heel of her hand. "Duh! Of course he did. Finglas. His folks' place."

"There's no need to be like that, Minty," Maggie snapped. "Did you try his contact number?"

"Mobile's switched off," she said. "I left a message." Her face registered an uncharacteristic hint of concern then. "Shit! How was I to know he'd need bleedin' baby-sitting?"

And Maggie thought, she's not alone there.

Tom caught Maggie's eye. "Where the feck is he?"

"Your guess is as good as mine," she replied, then took out her mobile and called Lily.

"Good morning. Deadly Inc. How can I help you?"

"Lily, it's Mags. Gavin's gone AWOL. Have you any idea where he'd be?"

"AWOL? Shit! No. Aaron and I had a pizza with him, then he went off clubbing, but I wasn't up for it so Aaron came back with me."

"The car went to pick him up at his folks' house but he wasn't there," Maggie said. "And he's not answering his mobile."

"Leave it with me. I'll call Aaron and see if between us we can track him down."

"Thanks, Lil. Do your best. The clock's ticking."

Apart from the fact that due to football commitments he wouldn't be available for an extra day's shoot, the astronomical cost of an extra day wasn't in budget so was unacceptable. They needed to find Gavin, and find him fast.

"Lily's going to call Aaron to see if he knows anything," she said to Tom, then to Minty, "Keep trying his mobile."

Aaron had no clue as to where Gavin might be, other than to speculate that he might have picked up a girl, which was of little help. However he phoned around all Gavin's old mates, while Lily, on the off-chance, tried the hospitals and the Garda stations. It was Lily who got a result first: Gavin was currently asleep in a cell at Harcourt Terrace nick after being arrested for public disorder. She called

Aaron and filled him in, then went to Dom's office and told him. He hit the roof for a full ten seconds until Lily told him sharply to shut up, that there wasn't a moment to lose and to get his act together, call Malcolm Tarpy, the company solicitor, and to get him to meet her at the cop shop where she was going to spring Gavin. Duly chastened, Dom ceased his rant and picked up the phone.

Aaron was in the Garda Station public office when she rushed in there out of breath.

"What's the story?" she gasped.

He cast his eyes skywards. "He was in a scuffle outside some club and they arrested him."

"Has he been charged with anything?" she asked, marginally horrified by the implications of Gavin having to make a court appearance before release.

Aaron shook his head. "They're not charging him. He was drunk and someone hit him so they just chucked him in a cell to sleep it off. I think they reckon it was for his own safety. He was completely twisted."

"Is he hurt?"

Aaron shrugged. "Dunno. Doubt it or he'd be in hospital."

A suited man, whom Lily recognised as Tarpy, Deadly's solicitor, walked past them to the desk.

"My name's Malcolm Tarpy. I'm acting for Gavin O'Connor. I believe you're holding him here?"

"Would that be a Gavin O'Connor, AKA Mr M Mouse," the desk sergeant said, a smirk on his lips and Lily cringed.

She stepped forward and touched Malcolm Tarpy on the arm.

"Hello, Mr Tarpy."

He turned his head. "Lily. How are you?"

"Good, thanks. But if they're not charging him, do you think you could hurry them up a bit. Right now Gavin's supposed to be out at Ardmore Studios shooting an ad."

A sheepish Gavin emerged from the bowels of the cop shop ten minutes later, in the company of two uniformed Gardai. They were all chat and by the sound of it Manchester United fans, but it was obvious that Gavin was still pretty much the worse for wear and had an angry-looking bruise and some swelling on his left temple.

"Howya, Aaro? Howya, Lily?" he said, unable to meet their eyes.

"Grand, Gavin. How's yourself?"

His hangover-befuddled brain didn't register the irony in her tone and answered her as if it were a serious question. "Not great. I had a skinful last night."

"No kidding."

Aaron gave his kid brother a clip across the back of the head in passing. "Eejit! You were supposed to be out on Ardmore three hours ago. No one knew where the feck you were!"

"Ardmore, is it?" one of the cops said as Gavin winced and rubbed his fragile head.

"He's supposed to be shooting a commercial," Lily said. "And it has to be finished today."

"I've got the car outside," Aaron said.

"Ah sure the traffic'll be only desperate at this hour," the other cop observed. "Isn't that so, Jack?"

"Ah, desperate right enough," Jack confirmed.

Great, Lily thought. That's all we need.

"Would you ever give us your autograph, Gavin, for

my young fella?" the desk sergeant asked, pushing a piece of paper and a biro across the counter.

"No problemo," Gavin said. "What's his name?"

"Roy . . . after Keano," the sergeant said, "but the wife's expecting again, so you never know we might have ourselves a wee Gavin this time round."

Gavin grinned, somewhat feebly, and picking up the pen signed his name. The other two cops wanted autographs too so that caused further delay. Then Gavin offered to get them tickets for the Ireland v Nigeria friendly match which would be the Ireland team's last game before they flew out to Japan for the Word Cup and that seemed to go down well, but all this was taking far too long. Lily looked at the clock. It was coming up for eleven-thirty.

"I suppose a police escort's out of the question?" she said, only half in jest.

"Should be there in fifteen," Lily said, finger in her free ear to block out the whoop of the police siren.

"What's that noise?" Maggie asked, barely able to hear her friend above the din.

Aaron, boy racer, was having the time of his life, foot to the floor in the wake of the cop car, all sirens and blue lights flashing .

"I got us a police escort," she said.

"What!"

"I'll tell you when I see you," Lily shouted. "ETA, twelve minutes and counting. Have make-up and Nurofen standing by."

The day's shoot commenced five hours late at two o'clock,

but only after Gavin had spent forty minutes in make-up having his distinctly grey complexion and purple facial contusions camouflaged with a thick layer of pancake. Even after that he looked rough, and a livid Denis Morgan insisted he down a whole litre of I-Sport to rehydrate him and to give him a bit of energy to complete the shoot.

In fairness it was an endorsement for the product because after about fifteen minutes Gavin noticeably perked up, but the rest of the day was a nightmare as his brain was experiencing great difficulty in coordinating his limb movement, so progress was painfully slow. Eventually Mike got the remaining two scenes and Gavin's end pack shot in the can, and the shoot wrapped by eight that night, after which they all repaired to the bar for a well-earned drink to soothe their collective ragged nerves. Maggie was the first to lift her glass to Tom and Mike and propose a toast to Lily for saving the day by finding their missing star and getting him there in record time.

"No better woman," Tom said, lowering his voice as he glanced over at Gavin who was quietly dozing on a sofa. "I'd say she gave poor Gavin a good roasting on the way though."

Maggie laughed. "I'd say that's more than a certainty."

Chapter 43

On Friday morning Sally was in bright and early as she had a meeting with Leo to discuss progress on the Shock FX campaign. He had been away in Paris for two days as a guest speaker at an international advertising seminar so she needed to bring him up to speed as the shoot was fast approaching. On her way in she passed a delivery boy who had just deposited a bouquet of lilies on the reception desk. A warm sensation washed over her as instinctively she reached out for the card assuming they were from Charlie, making a mental note to tell him that there was no need, but Lily beat her to it.

"For *moi*," she said, snatching the envelope away. "You're not the only one who gets flowers around here, you know."

"Oh!" Sally said, surprised and feeling a touch embarrassed. "Right you are."

Maggie, who was also on the way in, stopped dead in her tracks. "Who from?" she demanded.

"Aaron," Lily said, hugging the card to her chest, a huge grin on her gob. "We are once again an item."

Maggie grinned back. "Congratulations. Lunch. One o'clock. O'Neill's. Be warned, I shall interrogate you to within an inch of your life."

Leo was in Sally's office ahead of her with the two mandatory Macari's cappuccinos.

"Great couple of days," he said, as Sally dumped her briefcase on the floor and sat down behind her desk, picking a couple of fallen rose petals from the desk-top and dropping them in the bin. "Great hotel. Great food, but Irene spent a bloody fortune," he continued.

Sally laughed. "It's a tough job but someone's got to do it."

"Oh, by the way, Irene met a friend of yours – Charlie Penhaligan."

"At the seminar?" she asked surprised. Charlie hated going to seminars and hadn't mentioned that he'd intended to go to one, or indeed that he was in Paris when she had spoken to him the previous afternoon.

Leo shook his head. "No. He was on a shopping trip with his wife. What's her name . . .?"

"Imogene," Sally said, tight-lipped.

"Yes, that's it. Imogene. Irene knows her from way back when she worked in London. They bumped into each other at the Ritz, if you don't mind. Irene went in for a pit-stop to give her bloody Visa card time to cool down and the three of them had lunch."

"That's nice," Sally said, but her head was buzzing.

Charlie in Paris with Imogene? What was that about? It couldn't be right, but then why would Leo say it if it wasn't so? She was aware of her quickening heartbeat, of the traffic noise on the street, of Leo's voice, but not of what he was saying – it was as if he were talking down a tube. Then he stopped but her brain didn't register that he was waiting for her to say something, only realising that response was required when he said,

"So is that OK with you?"

"What?"

"The pack shot?" he said. "I've booked Aiden Dempsey."

"Oh right," she said, "fine," though the words again didn't register, her brain on overload. "Sorry. You're sure it was Imogene Penhaligan, and that she was with her husband Charlie. Charlie Penhaligan?"

Leo, whose mind was on Shock FX took a moment to switch channels. "What? Oh, yes. Irene knows them well. Now, about post production . . . I was thinking . . ."

Abruptly Sally had the sensation of wanting to vomit. Stumbling from her chair, with a perfunctory "Excuse me," she ran along the corridor to the ladies' loo, where she threw up. Then she knelt on the tiled floor, her head over the toilet, as she retched while her brain screamed. Charlie and Imogene. Paris. A shopping trip. How could that be? They weren't even together. It didn't make sense. At least it did, but she didn't want to face that reality. Charlie in Paris with Imogene, having lunch at the Ritz with Leo's wife, Irene.

I can't do this again, she thought. I can't face this.

She became aware of the door opening and footsteps, then someone touched her shoulder.

"Are you OK?" she heard Lily say.

Then Leo poked his head around the door. "Is she OK? Are you all right, Sally? What's the matter?"

"Of course she's not all right!" Lily said. "Can't you see she's sick?"

Sally raised her hand, in an 'I'm fine, please go away' gesture, a difficult concept to get across in the wave of a hand, so it wasn't surprising that both Lily and Leo failed to get the message. Sally just wanted to be alone. To curl up in the dark and be alone, but they wouldn't go away. Lily was behind her in the stall, one hand supporting her brow, the other across her shoulder, encouraging her to take deep breaths while Leo was shuffling from one foot to the other with no idea what to do.

Sally wanted them to go away. She hated Lily touching her, anyone touching her. She wanted to push her away, to stand up and scream. To scream with grief, with anguish, with sorrow, with anger. To lash out at anything that was in her path because of the realisation that Charlie had lied to her again. He'd used her. He'd used her and she'd let him. Believing everything he'd said, despite the fact that he'd lied to her before. But she had wanted to believe him, hadn't even entertained the notion that he would deceive her again. And what was the point? How did he expect to get away with it?

Struggling to her feet she pushed Lily aside, her mouth rancid, her eyes watery, and lurched towards the basin. Leo was still standing in the open doorway and she was aware of people passing along the corridor.

I have to get out of here, she thought. Rinsing her mouth out, she caught Lily's eye in the mirror.

"Seafood. Must have been off. Could you call me a cab? Must go home."

Pleased to be able to take some decisive action, Leo said, "I'll get you a cab. Lily, you stay here with Sally and make sure she's OK."

"Dodgy thing, seafood," Lily said. "Particularly mussels. Mussels can be really dodgy."

Sally nodded agreement. Her head was thumping now but the nausea had passed. She shivered, cold and clammy, her make-up streaked, eyes smudged. Then Lily went into one of the stalls. Unravelling a a long piece of toilet tissue, she folded it into a wad and ran it under the hot tap, then handed it to Sally.

"Here, this'll do to tidy up your make-up."

Sally took it from her gratefully and dabbed at her smudged mascara, then wiped off her foundation and washed her hands. She felt drained, but at the same time wired and it was a really weird sensation.

"How d'you feel?" Lily asked, breaking the silence.

How do I feel now that I know my lover is a lying manipulating toad and I've been a stupid, pathetic, gullible fool? Or how do I feel now I've stopped throwing up? she wanted to say, her throat full of bile, but she didn't. Instead she said through the mirror, "Better, thanks. I'll be fine, when I've had a lie-down."

"You're very pale," Lily said. "Will you be OK on your own? Would you like me to take you home?"

Sally was close to tears, touched by Lily's thoughtfulness as much as anything else, but she blinked them away with a shake of her head. Then suddenly the walls were closing in on her and she had to get out.

"I'll wait outside," she said, pushing past Lily and hurrying towards the stairs. "I need air." Overcome by the need to get away from the office, she didn't notice the dog as she rushed out of the glass doors and jumped into the waiting taxi.

The ride home was a blur, but at the same time seemed to take an age and Sally felt as if she was wading through treacle as she stumbled upstairs to the loft. Her brain could hardly cope with the task of unlocking the door and her fingers fumbled with the keys, dropping them twice before she succeeded. She was suffocating. Overcome by a need to be alone. Dropping her coat and bag she ran to the bedroom and threw herself on the bed, pulling the duvet over her head, before she broke down and howled on a cathartic tide of grief and sorrow but most of all, humiliation. Finally, exhaustion overtaking her, she fell into a deep, almost narcotic sleep.

He hadn't spoken to her all week and had been reluctant to take the initiative and make the first move to call her. It was obvious to a blind man that she had issues to resolve with Charlie the Stalker, so he felt that there was no point. If she wanted to see him she'd call. Hadn't she said as much as they'd parted the previous Friday night? "I'll call you," she'd said. But she hadn't, so that was that, and there was nothing more pathetic than someone who refused to get the message. He felt slightly irritated by the fact that she hadn't even bothered to pick up the phone to let him know she was all right though. How hard was that?

But by the Tuesday he had managed to put her from his mind and got stuck into the book, working all through the day, taking lunch at his laptop, and until late in the evenings making good progress. The plot was coming together well, and he was happy with his protagonist at last, after struggling to develop him from a one-dimensional cardboard cut-out, to an interesting but flawed character, who hopefully his readers would have sympathy with.

Occasionally his mind drifted towards Sally. It occurred to him that she had in all probability resolved her differences with the stalker or he would have heard from her, which caused him a stab of regret, on the grounds that, apart from the fact that she was a stunning-looking woman and that he fancied her madly, he really liked her. Granted she was weird, but it was this and her unpredictability that he found so appealing.

By the Friday evening he'd put down fifteen thousand words in total and felt justified in rewarding himself with a nice dinner and a few drinks.

Not surprisingly, with Thai being his favourite type of food, he found himself back at the restaurant he and Sally had dined at two weeks previously, so naturally she came to mind again.

Maybe I should give her a call, he thought. What's the harm? But then put it from his mind again on the grounds that he needed a complicated relationship like he needed a hole in the head.

The night air was chilly as he stepped from the restaurant, so he walked home briskly, his hands in his pockets, head down, and didn't spy Hero until he was right up to the entrance of his apartment block.

The dog stepped forward blocking his way.

"Hello, old fella," he said, surprised but pleased to see the mutt, assuming that his association with the dog had ceased along with his friendship with Sally. "To what do I owe the pleasure?"

The dog wasn't his usual self however, and instead of pushing his head into David's hand inviting a stroke, he seemed on edge, and kept moving away towards town, then stopping and staring at him, then returning and repeating the operation.

"What is it, Skippy? Are the boys trapped down the mine-shaft?" he said, then laughed out loud, amused at the comparison with the TV bush-kangaroo. But the dog was getting ever more agitated, until it occurred to him that he was indeed trying to tell him something, but what? That was the question.

One way to find out, he said to himself, then took a couple of steps towards the dog. "OK, fella. Show me," and they both set off at a crisp lick back towards town.

When she opened her eyes it was dark and it took her a few moments to register where she was, having no recollection of how she had got there. Her head was aching and her eyes sore and she had a raging thirst. Then reality kicked in and she remembered. She felt dead inside, no longer angry or even sad, just devoid of emotion.

Outside she could hear traffic passing and the ambient glow of the sodium streetlights seeped in though the muslin drapes on her window.

You got over him once, the voice of reason said in her ear. He's nothing to you. You can deal with this.

Yes, I can, she said to herself, I can deal with this. Then pushing herself up on her hands rolled off the bed and went to the bathroom, where she relieved herself, then cleaned her teeth and splashed her face with cold water. Catching her reflection in the bathroom mirror she barely recognised herself, her hair frizzy and every-which-way, her face puffy and her eyes red and swollen almost shut. Running her damp fingers through her hair, she sighed.

"You silly, silly cow," she said. "Being done over once is excusable, but twice by the same man is downright careless."

She reached for a towel and patted her face dry then smoothed out her hair. "What are you doing right now, Charlie?" she asked the mirror. "Congratulating yourself that you managed to talk me round, you lying bastard?"

The fact that she felt so calm surprised her after the last time, particularly in view of the way she'd felt the previous weekend when Charlie had declared his undying love. It was strange. Unaccountable. She deliberately thought back to her reunion with him, but couldn't raise so much as a tear. What's wrong with me, she thought, then said aloud to her reflection, "Charlie lied to you, you stupid cow! You're supposed to be heartbroken. Why aren't you still sobbing your stupid heart out?"

"Because I don't love him any more," she replied and she knew it was the truth. This time he'd crossed the line, and she was finally, totally, completely over him, and he had unwittingly helped her. She knew now that her tears hadn't been of sorrow, they'd been tears of shock, of anger and humiliation. Tears for herself, not tears of loss for Charlie.

Back in the living-room she picked up her bag and her coat, then checked her phone to find that she'd missed two calls, both from Charlie. She wondered if he had any inkling that the jig was up. Had he connected Irene with Leo and therefore with Deadly Inc? Had it crossed his mind that she might know now about his cosy romantic shopping trip to Paris with Imogene?

Accessing her voice-mail, she listened to Charlie's messages.

"Hello, cherub . . . you're probably in a meeting, so give me a call when you can . . . love you."

The second was timed at five fifteen that afternoon. He'd probably made the call on his way to Soho House for a drink before catching the train to the country for the weekend.

"Talk soon, cherub. Miss you . . . call me."

She deleted both messages, then scrolled through her phone book until she found the Gloucestershire number. Hesitating only briefly, she pressed call and waited.

When the door buzzer sounded, her first thought was Charlie, but unlike before, it wasn't because she wanted him, it was merely because she wanted to see his face when she told him what she'd done. She knew it wasn't Charlie, of course, as there had been no plan for him to fly over that weekend. Picking up the intercom, she was unexpectedly delighted, but at the same time embarrassed, to see David on the video screen. She felt bad that she hadn't called him, despite her promises to both him and to the dog, but it had slipped her mind, and anyway, she'd had no idea what to say to him. Nevertheless, she pressed the door release and then stood out on the landing waiting for him to come up.

Hero was the first up the stairs, followed closely by David.

"I've just done a terrible thing," she said as she knelt down on the floor to hug Hero's neck.

David stopped at the top of the stairs as he caught sight of her. She looked tired, her hair tousled, and her puffy eyes told the tale that she'd been crying, but she appeared to be in good humour now as she knelt next to the dog. In fact, her smile was warm and welcoming.

"You haven't killed anyone, I hope?" he said, half serious, and Sally laughed out loud.

"No. But you'll probably think I'm some sort of psycho when I tell you."

He faltered for just a beat, then grinned. "So what's new?" he said.

"I've never done anything like that before but I just felt he deserved it," Sally said.

David nodded. "Can't argue with that." He was thoroughly disgusted by Charlie's conduct.

She'd told him the whole sorry story from beginning to end, which was a first for her, but somehow she felt comfortable talking to him about it, sensing that he'd be non-judgemental.

"Don't get me wrong," she said, "I know I'm far from blameless, but as far as I was concerned it was over. That's why I left."

He nodded again. "A thoroughly understandable assumption, considering the circumstances."

They were lolling on the sofa in front of the fire, with Hero at their feet enjoying the warmth from the gas flames. David had his arm around her since a moment when she'd briefly broken down in mortification when recounting how gullible she'd been.

"So what exactly did you say to her?" he asked.

She turned to face him. "To Imogene?"

"To Imogene."

Sally gave a tiny smile. "I just asked her to tell her husband to stop harassing me. I said that I left Penhaligan in the first place because the situation was intolerable . . ."

"Not a hundred miles from the truth," David cut in and Sally nodded agreement.

"And I respectfully asked her to tell him to stop sending me flowers and to desist from calling me at all hours of the day and night."

"Desist? You actually used the word desist?" he said.

She giggled. "I believe I did."

Chapter 44

Late on Sunday afternoon, when Maggie, Aiden and Lily were all slumped on the sofa in the sitting-room watching a wildlife programme about gorillas in the Congo, and Anna was taking a snooze upstairs after the humungous roast-beef lunch she had cooked for everyone, there was a ring at the door.

No one moved, then Aiden said, "Can't get up, you're lying on my arm," so Maggie gave a groan and heaved herself up, certain that the effort would cause her to explode, after the heavy but scrumptious lunch.

Skye was standing on the doorstep, dressed in a long diaphanous hippy-style dress, flowers woven into her plaited hair, a crocheted shawl around her shoulders like a fugitive from nineteen sixties Glastonbury. She had a bunch of wild flowers in one hand and a cardboard box in the other.

"Hiiiii," she said in her usual languid way. "Is Anna home?"

"Come in," Maggie invited. "She's just having a lie-down but she should be up soon."

Skye followed Maggie into the sitting-room and the others stirred, Lily clicking off the TV, Aiden standing up and stretching himself.

"So how have you been?" Maggie asked. "Would you like tea or anything?" They hadn't seen her since the night in The Bleeding Horse when Ursula had died, though Maggie was aware that Anna and she had met up once or twice since.

"If it's not too much trouble I'd love a cup of tea," she said and, handing the flowers to Maggie, added, "I brought you these. I picked them in the Dublin mountains today." Then in one graceful movement she sat down cross-legged on the floor, the box between her knees.

"Thank you, they're lovely," said Maggie.

Aiden made for the door. "I'll make tea."

Skye gave a sigh. "Yeah. We went up to the Dublin mountains and held a Buddhist ritual for Ursula today."

"I didn't know you were a Buddhist," Lily said.

Skye shook her head. "I'm more of a pagan myself, but Ursula was a follower of the Buddha. And I know a Buddhist monk who lives in Rathmines so I asked him to do a bit of chanting and stuff . . ." She stared off into the distance.

"That was really sweet of you," Maggie said and Skye sighed again.

"It was amazing."

"So were there many of you at the er . . . ritual?" Lily asked.

"Just me and Shamus the Buddhist monk, and Conor. Dani couldn't make it."

"You know a Buddhist monk called Shamus?" Aiden said, somewhat bemused.

"Yeah," Skye replied, missing the point. "He lives in Rathmines."

Maggie sighed. "Only three people. That's so sad. If I'd known I'd have gone and I'm sure my mother would have liked to go."

Skye waved the retrospective offer away. "It was a kind of spur-of-the-moment thing."

Footsteps on the stairs announced that Anna was up and a moment later she walked into the room. "I thought I heard your voice," she said to Skye.

"Skye and Conor just had a Buddhist service up the Dublin mountains for Ursula," Maggie said. "Wasn't that a sweet thing to do?"

Anna smiled. "Yes. Very sweet," she agreed, then looked down at the box. "Oh, you remembered. Thank you so much."

Skye sighed. "No trouble," and placed the box on the coffee table. Aiden came in at that point with the tea tray of cups and saucers and put it on the coffee table next to the box, then tipped the Jaffa Cakes onto a plate.

"Your mother brought you up well, Aiden," Anna commented. "None of my boys would think of saucers."

"In our house even the cat had a saucer," Aiden said grinning, then handed the cups around.

"Did her folks claim the body?" Maggie asked after a pause, and Skye shook her head, her mouth being full of Jaffa Cake.

"No," she said, after swallowing. "The State had her

cremated. It's what she wanted. Couldn't bear the thought of being laid in the cold earth."

"I'm with her on that," Maggie agreed, giving a shudder. "So how come Dani didn't go?"

"She said she couldn't, that's all,"

"And how is she?" Anna asked.

Skye shrugged. "Oh fine, I think. I haven't seen much of her." Then, placing her empty cup back on the tray, she gracefully uncurled her lithe body and stood up. "I should be going now."

"I'll see you out," Anna said, and they walked out to the hall together.

When she returned Anna said, "That was sweet of her to take the trouble, wasn't it?"

Maggie nodded, "Yes. Poor thing. Sad to think there were only three people at the funeral though, and one of those didn't even know her."

"Well, the Buddhist service was sweet too, but I mean for her to take the trouble to bring Ursula's ashes all the way over here."

"Ashes?' Maggie said puzzled.

"Yes. Ursula's ashes. Her cremated remains."

There was a significant pause, then three pairs of eyes swivelled to the cardboard box sitting on the coffee table next to the plate of Jaffa Cakes.

"You don't mean . . ." Lily started, then trailed off.

A silence followed, broken by Maggie as she moved the Jaffa Cakes a fraction, so the plate of biscuits was no longer in contact with the box. "Mother, why have I got the ashes of a dead person on my coffee table?"

"Because I'm going to scatter them on my trip, silly," Anna said, picking up the cardboard box and cradling it protectively.

"Your trip?"

"My trip to India."

"Oh . . . that trip."

"Of course. And what better resting place for a yoga devotee?"

"But why you? Why can't Skye scatter them?" Maggie asked, a mental picture of Anna and Gerry Starling standing on the banks of the Ganges, hand in hand, sprinkling Ursula's ashes into the sacred river, flitting across her consciousness.

"Oh, didn't I tell you," Anna said, innocently. "I've decided to go at the end of June."

Maggie was stunned. "But that's less than two months away,"

Anna nodded. "That's right, pet. But you see Gerry managed to get me a really cheap deal through one of his contacts in the travel business. Isn't he a sweetie?"

At that precise moment Maggie could have come up with a number of words to describe Gerry Starling but sweetie wasn't amongst them.

A short time later Luke called to see if Aiden wanted to come out to play, and Anna decided to have a long soak in the bath, so Lily and Maggie went off to the pub.

Maggie was still mentally chuntering away to herself about her mother and Gerry Starling in India together, though the mental images had become a tad surreal with Anna dressed in a shimmering sari and Gerry all done up like a maharajah; even a couple of ceremonially decked-out elephants and the odd tiger had wormed their way into the picture.

"You don't even know that Gerry Starling's going for sure," Lily commented, irritated by Maggie's waspish humour. "Anyway, what if he is? It's time your ma got a bit of spoiling. No disrespect to your dad, Mags, but he doesn't strike me as particularly adept in the romance department."

"He sent her the irises," she replied, clutching at the lone straw, and Lily hit her forehead with the heel of her hand.

"Well, silly me! I forgot all about that."

"OK. I get your point," Maggie conceded. "He doesn't have a romantic bone in his body, but it doesn't mean he doesn't love her."

"Maybe not," Lily said. "But you can't begrudge Anna a bit of fun, can you? And whatever you say about Gerry Starling, he's obviously mad about her, and he's spoiling her rotten."

"I'm being childish, aren't I?"

Lily nodded. "A bit, but it's understandable. I wouldn't like it if my folks split up either."

"I suppose it's partly because it's all so out of the blue. I mean it would be different if I'd grown up with them bickering and fighting and stuff. But there were never any arguments in our house, at least no shouting matches. If there had been I'd probably be glad that they'd decided to call it a day."

"Maybe that's the guts of the problem," Lily offered. "They stopped communicating."

"Bit like Mark and me," Maggie said without regret. "I was thinking about it after that first weekend when Aiden and I got together, and I realised that I knew more about him in one weekend than I ever knew about Mark. It made me realise that I'd settled."

"How d'you mean, settled?"

"I mean I'd settled for Mark. When I look back, he didn't excite me – oh, we had great sex, but beyond that he didn't excite me. We'd practically nothing in common, and I haven't the first idea what his hopes and dreams are. Even when he moved in, it was almost a business arrangement, not because we consciously wanted to spend the rest of our lives together. I just kind of assumed we would. And it was something Aiden said too."

"What? That Mark's a wanker?"

"Apart from that. He was telling why he and his ex split up."

"Would that be the ex with stunning looks and the endless legs?"

"And the drink and drugs problem," Maggie said pointedly. "Anyway, he said the main reason why they split was because when she was away he realised that he didn't miss her. And it occurred to me that it was the same with Mark. I didn't miss him."

Lily raised a sceptical eyebrow. "So what was all the misery and the wailing and gnashing of teeth about when he left then?"

"That was just shock at the way he went about it. The thing is, any time he was away, on a business trip or at his mother's, I didn't miss him. In fact sometimes I was glad to have the place to myself."

"And what about Aiden? Do you miss him when he's not there?"

Maggie thought about that, then smiled and nodded. "Actually yes. Not in a clingy way, but my stomach sort of churns over when I see him or if he sends me a text during the day. I can't say that ever happened with Mark."

Lily shrugged. "So really the only thing you and Mark had going for you was great sex, then."

"I suppose . . . actually with hindsight, it wasn't that great."

"Compared to what?" Lily said, a gleam in her eye, and Maggie grinned.

"Compared to Aiden," she said. "But it's not as simple as that. I mean we didn't discuss stuff. Not even important things like kids. That's why I was so surprised when Conor told me he'd talked Dani into keeping the baby."

"There you are then," Lily said. "But at least you've moved on, and that's what Anna's doing. She wasn't happy with her life and she's moving on."

Maggie took a thoughtful sip of her drink. "I suppose if I'm honest, I'd just be happier if she hadn't chosen Gerry Starling to do her moving on with."

"You reckon that's it?" Lily asked. "You don't think you'd be feeling the same if it was, say, someone like Mike Patterson, or anyone else come to that?"

Maggie laughed. "When did you major in psychology?" she asked and Lily grinned back.

"I was just looking at it as if it was my ma and how I'd feel. But honestly, Mags, if you don't want to fall out with Anna, you have to let her get on with it. You'd go ballistic if she tried to interfere in your life. And at the end of the day, it's what she thinks of Gerry Starling that's important, not what you think of him."

"You reckon if she kisses him he might turn into a handsome prince?"

Lily shook her head. "Naaa! He'll always be a frog as far as you're concerned, but if he's Anna's handsome prince, that's all that matters."

Chapter 45

Both Maggie and Tom were out of the office at the post-production facility, Final Frame, for the edit of the I-Sport ads the following week. Gavin O'Connor was due to fly in on Thursday afternoon for the voice-over recording of the end line, and the Super Savings shoot was booked for the Friday, so it was all go.

The post-production edit was going well and they were happy with the way the ad was coming together. Gavin looked great and both were confident that he would have the desired impact.

Maggie brought Anna along on the Wednesday to see how it was all done when Jason Dwyer and Mike Patterson were doing the cut-downs.

"What exactly are cut-downs?" Anna asked as she watched them work in the editing suite.

"The whole ad is fifty seconds long," Maggie explained. "And that's shown for two weeks, then after that, when the public are familiar with it, we run shorter versions, or fifteen-second cut-downs. The viewer remembers the whole ad, yet it's cheaper to screen a fifteen-second version than it is to run a fifty-second ad, but the cut-downs have the same effect. Think Budweiser frogs. Though you only see a cut-down now, you remember the whole running theme."

"Oh I see," Anna said. "That's so clever. And is there a cut-down version of my Super Savings ads?"

"Oh yes," Maggie affirmed. "Though your long version's only twenty seconds and the cut-down will be ten."

"I'm dying to see it," Anna said. "When will it be done?"

"They're doing post on all three together next week after Friday's shoot," she said. "I'll bring you along to watch if you like."

Denying hotly that she was paranoid, but nonetheless deciding to take no chances of Gavin going astray between the airport and the Real to Reel recording studios, Maggie met him off the Aer Lingus Manchester flight at two-fifteen on Thursday afternoon.

He looked relaxed and well, his bruised face healed to a mere yellowy green tinge on his left temple, but it was of no matter because today he was over for a voice recording. He was in top from and good-naturedly stopped to sign a couple of autographs between arrivals and the taxi rank.

"So what's the ad look like?" he asked after they had settled themselves in the back of a cab.

"It's looking great," Maggie affirmed. "You'll see the footage at the recording studio."

As usual Maggie had booked Harvey Halliday and he

was his normal dour self as she introduced them, causing Maggie to surmise that perhaps he was the only other male of Irish nationality (apart from Paul Brody) who wasn't a soccer fan. Her opinion was overturned however when, as Gavin went into the booth, Harvey mumbled, "Uh . . . great game last Saturday, Gavin. Great game."

Gavin settled himself with his script in sight of the TV monitor on which they would run the footage he was to voice-over.

"Right, Gavin. Be natural but enthusiastic. I-Sport's the best thing since sliced bread – It's The Extra Man. OK?" Maggie said.

Gavin nodded. "Right. I-Sport. It's Isotonic. It's the extra man . . . that's the line?"

"That's the line, Gavin."

Harvey had been adjusting levels during Maggie and Gavin's brief exchange, so they were ready for a take.

"OK, Gavin. Let's give it a try. Wait until Maggie cues you. She'll count you in on her fingers, right?"

Gavin gave a thumbs-up to let them know that he understood, then Harvey ran the footage and Maggie counted Gavin in – three, two, one – on her fingers but, as Gavin delivered the line, her heart sank. He sounded stilted and mechanical. It had never occurred to her that he wouldn't be able to do it after seeing Jodie's video of him on the chat show, where he'd been funny and natural and relaxed. She cast a glance at Harvey.

"Shall we try that again, Gavin? This time try to relax. Think like you're talking to Aaron. Think like you're telling him how great I-Sport is."

Gavin gave her the thumbs-up again.

They waited for Harvey to set things up, then as the VT ran she cued him in again.

If anything he was worse the second time.

"How was that?" he asked, all enthusiasm like a playful Labrador puppy.

"He sounds like a fecking Dalek," Harvey muttered.

"Um . . . still a bit tense, Gav. Let's give it another go," Maggie said, though she had a sinking suspicion that this was as good as it was going to get.

Harvey chanted under his breath, "Ex-terrrr-min-ate. Ex-terrr-min-ate".

She was right. As the session wore on Gavin got worse and worse, despite Maggie's coaching. With about ten minutes of recording time left Tom poked his head in.

"How's it going?" he asked.

Maggie turned her back to the booth so Gavin couldn't see her face. "It's a fecking disaster," she said.

He looked over at Harvey who flicked a switch and played back the last take, and Tom's face fell. "Shit! Where's Doctor Who?"

Maggie nodded. "I know. From worse to worser. What are we going to do?"

"Get another voice-over?" Harvey suggested, which Maggie thought was particularly unhelpful, but Tom raised his eyebrow at her.

"Might be the only option," he said. "This is awful. What about Dudley Anderson? He has a great range and I'm sure he'd do a passable Gavin O'Connor?"

Maggie shook her head. "Passable ain't good enough. He has quite a distinctive voice. It'd be like Terry Wogan trying to do a David Beckham."

Then she had an idea and looked over at Harvey. "Run the tape and keep it running, Harvey. Tom, you get Gavin talking." She leaned over the desk and hit the talk-back mike, leaving it open.

"How's things, Gavin?" Tom said, copping on to her plan.

"Ah grand," the footballer replied, giving him another thumbs-up, delighted with himself, and no doubt thinking, this is a piece of cake; and, if Vinnie Jones can do it, so can I; and maybe I should give Guy Ritchie a call.

"He looks better than he did the other day at the shoot, doesn't he, Tom?" Maggie said pointedly to her art director, causing him to think, don't give up the day job, Maggie, and lose Guy Ritchie's number.

"Yeah. But the I-Sport helped him out then. Isn't that right, Gav?" Tom said.

Gavin grinned. "Too bloody right."

"So how was that, Gavin?" Maggie said. "Is it really so good that it sorted your hangover?"

"Yeah!" Gavin said. "It's isotonic, see. It rehydrates you. And that's way better than a fry-up for kickin' a hangover, any day."

"Right. I see," Maggie said, "So it is the Extra Man, then? We got that right?"

Gavin laughed. "It's the Extra Man all right. They should sell it as a hangover cure."

Maggie made a mental note to mention that to Denis Morgan.

Tom's eyes caught Maggie's, then he said to Gavin, "What is?"

"What's what?"

401

"The Extra Man?" Tom, asked.

Gavin grinned. "Feckin' I-Sport. You should know. You wrote the feckin' line!"

Maggie looked over at Harvey and he nodded that he'd got all he needed, so Maggie said, "We'll just do one more take to be sure to be sure, Gavin. Then we're done here."

"Right you are," the footballer said and once more did his Dalek to perfection.

Gavin's cab arrived dead on time and, after saying goodbye, he headed back to the airport to catch the return flight to Manchester. Then Harvey set about doctoring the tape with Maggie and Tom looking on, fingers, toes and every other extremity crossed, despite the fact that the session was well over time. But with Harvey this was a matter of pride. Eventually, due to the sound engineer's genius and dogged determination, he succeeded in splicing the words together, and they got Gavin enthusiastically delivering the line without a trace of Dalek.

"Artistry. Pure artistry," Harvey said, displaying his usual modesty.

Both Tom and Maggie insisted that he join them for a drink after it was done, despite the fact that he wasn't exactly the sociable type and, after some insistence, in the form of, "You will, you will, you will," he reluctantly agreed, but any casual onlooker could tell he was chuffed with himself.

On the way over to O'Neill's, Maggie gave Aiden a call and they agreed to meet up there for a couple of drinks, then maybe take in a movie.

"How did the recording go?" he asked.

Maggie laughed. "Like you wouldn't believe," she said, promising to tell him all about it later.

Lily didn't know what to do. An unusual occurrence for the PA, but it was a fact. She was sitting in a quiet corner casting an occasional eye to the door as she waited for Aaron to arrive, so he took her totally by surprise, being the last person she expected to see. At first she thought she was mistaken, he was so out of context; from the point of view that she knew that at that moment he should be asleep in bed on the other side of the globe. But it was the fact that he was in the company of that slimy little runt Tony Holland that made her realise that her eyes weren't deceiving her. There he was, large as life, slightly tanned and his hair blonder, but unmistakably Mark Beyer. Alive, well and drinking a pint of Guinness up at the bar not fifteen feet away on a quiet Thursday evening in O'Neill's.

After a 'what's wrong with this picture' moment she gathered her wits and took out her phone, but couldn't get a signal, probably due to the thick old stone walls of the former warehouse, and cursed silently to herself, then grabbing her bag stood up and made for the door. She glanced back to confirm to herself that it was really him, then bumped into Tom's huge bulk, on his way in.

"Lily. How's it going?" he asked, all smiles. Maggie was a few steps behind him in the company of Harvey the creepy sound engineer, sharing a joke. Lily suddenly found she was rendered speechless, her mouth flapping, no sound coming out, as she looked over her shoulder towards Mark and Tony Holland at the bar, then glanced over Tom's shoulder to where Maggie and Harvey were catching up with him, then back at the bar, then straight at the art director. *Ping – pong – ping – pong!*

From the look on her face Tom sussed that something was up, and followed her gaze to the bar.

"Oh fuck!" he muttered and stopped dead, as Maggie and Harvey dominoed into his back. Maggie caught sight of Lily, then took in her horrified expression, and Lily saw her eyes drift to the bar and rest on Mark's familiar back. Then her face froze.

"Is that who I think it is?" she said, and Lily managed a nod.

Without further ado, Maggie pushed past Tom and Lily and made straight for him, stopping one step behind and tapping him on the shoulder.

"Hello, Mark. Got your email," she said.

As Mark turned, the colour drained from his face. Even in the subdued pub lighting it was obvious, and Holland looked like a jaundiced rabbit, blinking uncontrollably as he gripped the bar for support.

"Mags! How are you?" It came out sort of strangled.

"How am I? Is that all you have to say?" She sounded calm though her body language was anything but, as she clenched her hands by her sides, her back ramrod straight.

Mark shuffled from side to side, taking in Tom, Lily, and the nerdy-looking guy in an anorak and a Fairisle tank top, then giving a quick glance around to see if any one else was watching.

He reached out his hand and touched her shoulder. "I never meant to hurt you," he said, and Maggie laughed out loud, shrugging his hand away.

"Really? Well, what did you think was going to

happen when you buggered off out of my life with half my furniture and no warning?"

"Uh, actually the sofas were . . . um," Mark started, then thought better of it. "I'm sorry, um . . . I didn't mean to er . . ."

"Does Dani know you're home?" Maggie snapped, not interested in his feeble attempts at justification, then before he had a chance to reply, she prodded his shoulder with her index finger to cause maximum irritation. "You remember Dani. The mother of your baby. The girl you dumped by leaving a text message on her phone? How feeble is that?"

Tony took a keen interest in his shoes as Mark's face flushed from putty to red, which infuriated Maggie as she knew without a doubt it was embarrassment at the scene she was causing rather than shame.

"I don't think this is the time or the place to wash our dirty linen," he said in a controlled tone, checking around, noting the interest of the other pub patrons, some of whom he knew by sight. "Would you like a drink and maybe you'll let me explain." Conciliatory now.

"I think the linen's all yours," she said. "Anyway, what's to explain?" Her voice was rising. "You were humping a student behind my back for a year, you bastard! You got her pregnant then ran away like the mean cowardly rodent you are!"

Mark took a step forward again in an attempt to put a containing arm around her shoulder, but she ducked out of the way with a look of utter distaste on her face.

"Don't touch me, you lizard! You didn't answer my question. Does Dani . . ." She glanced around at the increasing audience, playing to the gallery, revelling in his escalating discomfort. "You remember Dani, the student you knocked up and left to fend for herself without a penny. Does she know you're back?"

"As a matter of fact," he said, trying to scramble past her onto the moral high ground, "I came back to make things right with her and assume my responsibilities."

"Well, that's a very romantic way of putting it. What did you say to her? 'Dani, I want to assume my responsibilities?'"

There was sporadic tittering at that.

Maggie was aware that she was fast losing it. She had rehearsed this confrontation in her head in the days after Mark left, revising it after she found out about Dani, and in her speech she had remained detached and calm, but despite the fact that she was following her script almost to a T, she was far from calm now, and could feel the anger bubbling close to boiling point.

"That's noble of you, very noble," she snarled, wanting to hurt him, to punch him in the face, to see him bleed, barely managing to fight the impulse, reliving the pain and sense of worthlessness he'd caused her in the days after he left.

"Look. There's no need to make a spectacle of yourself. Can we talk about this somewhere else?" He sidled round again so he was between her and the silent but interested audience.

Then she felt an arm around her shoulder and was conscious of a familiar warm scent and heard Aiden say softly, "Come on, Mags. Let's sit down. The bastard isn't worth upsetting yourself over." It was a courageous move on Aiden's part. He had walked in just as Maggie had kicked off with Mark and was aware that she was close to completely blowing her top. "Come on, sweetheart. Let me get you a drink."

At that moment it was a toss-up between kneeing Mark in the groin, and elbowing Aiden in the stomach, mainly because she felt a fool and needed to strike out at something, anything, but she got a grip of herself and took a deep cleansing breath, thinking of Ursula briefly as she did, and suddenly things were back in perspective.

She leaned into Aiden and slid her arm around his waist. "You're right," she said. "He's not worth it."

In an effort to appear unconcerned and regain a bit of dignity, as they moved away Mark turned to Tony Holland and said, louder than he meant to, "Do you wonder why I chose Dani?" at which Maggie stopped dead in her tracks, slid Aiden's hand away and in one deft movement picked up Mark's almost full pint and emptied it over his head before he had time to register her intent and move out of the way. There was a brief silence, then a scattering of applause as Mark shook Guinness out of his hair and Tony Holland attempted to dab it off the front of his jacket with a paper serviette.

Brushing her hands together, she smiled at Aiden. "Now I feel better," she said. "Mine's a glass of Guinness."

"A Guinness it is," he said, suppressing a grin.

Tom led the way to a vacant table and the rumble of conversation around them resumed, then he went to up to the bar to help Aiden with the drinks order.

"Who was that bloke?" Harvey asked. "The one you doused in Guinness?"

"That was Maggie's ex," Lily said, then grinned. "They had issues."

"It was only half a sodding glass," Maggie said dismissively, then glanced over at the bar. Both Mark and Tony Holland were no longer in evidence, Tony's half-finished pint still on the counter. Delving into her bag she took out her phone.

"I think I'll give Dani a call to make sure she knows Mark's back in town."

"You reckon he was lying?" Lily asked.

Maggie shrugged. "I've no idea, but I wouldn't put it past him."

Outside the pub, Maggie sat on a low wall and, accessing Dani's number, called her. She answered on the third ring.

"Maggie!" She sounded anxious.

"Hello, Dani. How have you been?"

"Uh . . . great thanks . . . the thing is . . ."

"Look, Dani, the reason I'm calling is, I just bumped into Mark in O'Neill's and I –"

"I know," Dani cut in. "I've been meaning to call you, but I couldn't pluck up the courage. It's a sort of weird situation."

Maggie found herself smiling. "That's one word for it. The rejected lover calling the rejected mistress to make sure she knows their mutual former lover who dumped on both of them is back in town."

Dani wasn't laughing. "I'm sorry," she said.

"No . . . no. You've nothing to be sorry about," Maggie reassured her. "I was just calling to make sure he was telling me the truth when he said he was . . ." she hesitated for a beat and revised her words, "he was getting back together with you."

"Oh. I was afraid you'd be angry. You must hate us."

"For God's sake! I don't hate you. And as for Mark, well, I'm still angry with him for being a bollox, but I've moved on, Dani. I've no feelings for Mark at all on a personal level. Oh, I'm angry, but that's more to do with the way he left and the way he made me feel so shit, that's all. But, hand on heart, I don't hate him. That would require effort and he's not worth it as far as I'm concerned."

"I feel awful," Dani said. "But I love him, and I don't want to bring up the baby on my own."

Maggie shifted uncomfortably on the wall. The conversation was bordering on surreal, with her on the one hand telling Dani what a bollox Mark was, but at the same time wishing her every happiness with him. "It's cool, Dani. Honestly," she said, trying to wind up the call, "and I genuinely hope it works out for you."

"Thanks," Dani said sounding relieved. "I really appreciate that."

"Goodbye, Dani." She terminated the call.

"Do you really wish us well?" Mark asked. She hadn't heard him approach and wasn't sure how much of her conversation with Dani he'd heard. He stepped out of the shadows and stood about two feet away, his hands in his pockets. The front of his sweatshirt was stained with Guinness, but he looked unscathed apart from that.

"I wish her and the baby well, and I hope you're good to her and you don't let her down," she said, adding pointedly, "again. She's a nice kid. You don't deserve her."

"No. I don't suppose I do. I'm sorry I hurt you."

"Oh shut up, Mark, and stop trying to be Mister Nice Guy. It doesn't fit. You knew damn well what you were doing, but I don't care any more. I've moved on. It's old news. What were you thinking of, for God's sake?"

He shrugged, his hands still buried in his pockets. "I just lost it," he said. "I panicked. Dani was nearly seven months pregnant, things were iffy with us and —"

"Iffy? In what way? I didn't think they were iffy. I hadn't a clue."

"Well, it just goes to show how much effort you were putting into the relationship," he said.

Her hackles were up. "Don't you dare try and lay it on me, Mark! And if we're talking effort, you can hardly chuck stones considering you were humping Dani behind my back for a year. A whole sodding year! How do you think that made me feel when I found out?"

"Well, you couldn't have been that broken-hearted. You didn't waste any time hooking up with that guy from next door," he said, with a touch of sourness, which raised her hackles further until she realised that she didn't have to justify herself to him.

She looked up at him and smiled. "Yes. I suppose you did me a favour there. We'd never have got together if you hadn't been such a spineless git, and given him the job of telling me you'd moved out. I thought we'd been burgled."

"Burgled?"

"The furniture. You took the sodding furniture or had you forgotten?"

"Oh. Right."

The phone was still in her hand so she dropped it into her bag and stood up. This conversation's over, she thought.

He reached out and touched her arm. "Mags. Look, I'm sorry how things worked out, but can we still be friends? I'd hate for us to part on bad terms."

For a moment she was speechless at the audacity of it, the lameness.

Can we still be friends?

She laughed and shook her head. " I don't think so, Mark. I have enough friends." Then turning away, she walked back into the pub.

Chapter 46

On Saturday morning, Sally and David ate a late and leisurely breakfast then parted company on Grafton Street at noon as she had a hair appointment. Later, at around four, after a touch of light shopping, she wandered through the Powerscourt Townhouse Centre, window-shopping, stopping off at French Connection where she bought a groovy shirt for David and a strappy top for herself, then headed back to the loft.

It was a full week since she had discovered Charlie's duplicity, and in that time she had dumped all his calls and, when he attempted to get her on the office landline, had instructed Lily to tell him she was unavailable. By Thursday afternoon Lily had buzzed through to her complaining that Charlie Penhaligan was making a fecking nuisance of himself and was currently threatening to tie up all the lines if he wasn't connected immediately to her office.

"He doesn't believe that you're in meetings. He thinks

I'm involved in some conspiracy to stop him talking to you," she said, frustrated. "I can't get rid of him."

"So? I don't want to talk to him," Sally said. "Deal with it. That's what you're paid for. Oh, and do something about the flowers."

She stayed on the line and listened as Lily muttered, "Sod diplomacy," then said to Charlie, "Miss Gillespie said she doesn't want to talk to you, and you're to stop making a prat of yourself and to cease calling. Oh, and you're to stop sending flowers too. I've had instructions to forward them to the hospice and it's taking up too much of my valuable time." Large bouquets were arriving on a daily basis.

Sally now smiled to herself as she remembered his spluttered unintelligible response which was cut off as Lily hung up the phone.

She felt great. As if a huge weight had been lifted from her shoulders, at last certain that she was done with him. He'd shown his true colours and it hadn't been a very attractive sight, but she'd dealt with it in her own way and was quietly pleased with herself. It's amazing, after love dies, how many faults and flaws in an old lover's character suddenly become glaringly evident.

So it was that she climbed the stairs humming to herself. She dropped her packages on the floor and unlocked the door of the loft. Hero was standing inside wagging his tail when she entered.

"Do you want to go out for a pee, boy?" she asked, and as he padded past her, she put her bag on the granite counter and followed him back downstairs.

He had taken up almost permanent residence in the past week, accompanying her to the office and escorting her home in the evening, even following her into the pub on Friday night for the Deadly social get-together (but then he was virtually an employee) and Sally wondered if it was because he sensed that she might need the company. David too had spent a lot of time with her, she suspected for the same reason, but she hadn't made any objection, though was beginning to think that she should back off a little. Not that she was going cold on him, but she felt that if their relationship was to go anywhere, it would be a good idea to give each other a little space from time to time. She resolved to talk to him about it the following day when they were due to meet up with James and Catherine for brunch, confident that it wouldn't become an issue. David was the most up-front man she'd ever met. What you saw was what you got. He was confident and comfortable with himself and in no way needy. All the men she'd ever been involved with, even on a superficial level, had been needy, even Charlie in his own way (his ego needing constant stroking), so that was a welcome change and a breath of fresh air.

Taking a stroll up Great George's Street she followed Hero as he sniffed his way along the pavement, checking out lampposts and car tyres and lifting his leg along the way. The weather was noticeably warmer with the promise of a touch of real spring before it gave way to an indifferent damp Irish summer.

At the end of the street she turned and headed back, catching Hero's attention, thus giving him the option should he wish to return to the loft with her. In this instance he did, probably with dinner in mind, so they strolled back together.

Life is good, she thought, then placed her hand on

Hero's back. "I'm glad I made this change, Hero. It's working out really well. Serendipity. "

He stopped abruptly and at first she thought it was something she'd said until she felt his hackles rise and a low rumbling growl started up.

"What is it?" she asked, looking around.

The reason was standing at her front door watching her walk down the street.

Charlie.

It was a shock to see him. He was the last person she expected, and truth be told, she felt a little anxious, conscious that he wouldn't be best pleased that she'd called Imogene. She's seen his legendary temper in action, though never directed at her.

He stepped forward and the dog bared his teeth, prompting a pedestrian to give them a wide and swift berth. She was surprised, and a little perturbed to see that Charlie was smiling.

"Hello, cherub," he said, as if the previous week hadn't happened. "They wouldn't let me talk to you. And we have to talk."

"There's no 'they' about it, Charlie," she said. "And there's no conspiracy. The fact is, I don't want to talk to you. There's nothing to say."

He looked suddenly bewildered. "But why? What did Imogene say to you? Did she threaten you? She can be very vindictive."

"Threaten me? I don't follow you, Charlie."

He attempted another step forward, but had second thoughts when Hero gave a sudden savage bark, followed by a snarl.

"Can't you lock that beast up somewhere? He's dangerous."

Sally ran her hand along Hero's back. "Rubbish. He's a pussycat, aren't you, Hero?" Then she sighed. "It's over, Charlie. Face it. Show a bit of dignity and just go away."

"She got to you, didn't she?"

Sally was confused. "What are you ravelling on about, Charlie?"

"Imogene. She threatened you, didn't she? Somehow she found out about us and she threatened you?"

Unbelievable. He didn't know. He was so arrogant it hadn't crossed his mind that she might know the truth.

"Charlie. I told Imogene," she said. "It was me."

A look of total disbelief washed over his face.

"You? But why? We made plans."

Sally couldn't stop herself laughing out loud. "Plans based on lies. You told me you'd left Imogene. I know about Paris, Charlie. I know you lied through your teeth to me about leaving her, and I've had enough. You crossed the line, Charlie, and there's no going back."

"But I'm free now. Imogene's divorcing me. We can be together."

He still didn't get it.

She shook her head, saddened by how pitiful he looked. Imogene had chucked him out so he thought she'd come running. He just didn't get it. "Just go away, Charlie. Leave me alone. It's over."

She pushed past him to get to the door, unlocking it and stepping quickly inside, Hero ahead of her, but before she could close it, he put his foot in the way and shoved it in, his face now livid red.

"But I've given up everything for you! Everything!" He had little specks of saliva at the corners of his mouth.

"You gave up nothing, Charlie. That's the whole point. You didn't jump. You were pushed."

She wasn't afraid now, despite his change of mood. Apart from the fact that she only had to pull the door back and Hero would take a hefty chunk out of him, suddenly he had fallen from his pedestal and all she saw was an angry, sad little man.

"Go away! You're pathetic," she said with all the disgust she could muster. It must have been like a slap in the face because he backed off, and she closed the door. For a few moments she stood behind it listening, then glanced up at the security monitor to see what he was doing, but he'd already gone.

Chapter 47

On the way into the office on Monday morning Maggie bumped into the flower-delivery man on his way out. He'd been around so regularly lately that they were now on first-name terms.

"Hi, George," she said in passing.

He stopped for a beat and touched her arm. "Howya Maggie. Uh . . . I'm, um . . . sorry for your trouble." Then he patted her arm and scurried away as he spied a traffic warden who had just set course for his van which was parked on a double yellow.

Maggie frowned. "Sorry for my trouble?" she muttered, flummoxed for a moment by the standard form of Irish condolence, then carried on into reception where she was greeted by the sight of Lily examining a large funeral wreath of black and tulips and arum lilies. Maggie hurried over and put a consoling arm around her shoulder.

"Oh, my God! What's happened, Lil? It's not your gran?"

Lily's granny was ninety-three, so she seemed like the most obvious candidate.

Lily shook her head, her face pale. "No . . . it's Sally."

"Jesus! What happened?"

"I don't know. This wreath arrived just now, that's all I know." Reaching for the phone she called the conference room as Maggie examined the card. It read: *Sally Gillespie. RIP.*

Tom breezed in then and he too caught sight of the wreath. He stopped dead, giving Maggie a questioning look.

"Sally," she said.

His eyebrow shot up his forehead. "Sally? Bloody hell! She was all right on Friday. What happened?"

Maggie shrugged. "I don't know. This wreath just arrived in."

Meanwhile Lily was on the phone. "Dom. Could you come down to reception. I have to talk to you."

There was a pause, then she said sharply. "Dom, I wouldn't call you in the middle of a meeting if it wasn't urgent. Please. Just come down." Replacing the receiver she said, "It must have been some sort of accident over the weekend."

Tom shook his head. "But surely we'd have heard?"

Dom came down the stairs then, not looking best pleased. "What is it?" he barked at Lily, and she just picked up the wreath in reply.

"It's Sally," Tom said.

Dom's face paled. "Sally? What are you talking about?"

Maggie took the card from the floral tribute and handed it to Dom.

"It says: *Sally Gillespie. RIP.*"

"What?" Dom said, having some difficulty taking it in. "If there'd been an accident surely we'd have heard. It hasn't been in the death announcements in the *Irish Times.*"

Leo walked into reception at that point and taking in the scene asked, "Who died?"

"Sally," Lily replied.

Leo's jaw dropped. "Christ! When?"

"We don't know," Maggie said. "This wreath arrived and that was the first we heard of it."

Leo sat down heavily on one of the leather sofas. "Good grief. I was only talking to her yesterday."

"Well, someone sent a wreath, so it must be true," Maggie said, examining the card to see who it was from, but there was no indication, just the message. "She has family in Dublin. We should call to find out the arrangements."

The glass doors swung open. "Arrangements for what?" Sally asked.

The five of them stared at her open-mouthed for a beat, then Lily picked up the wreath.

"Your funeral apparently."

"Bouquet Man," Lily said across the table to Maggie. They were sitting in a small café on the quays having a fat 'n' salt (fish 'n' chip) lunch.

"You reckon?" Maggie said. "That's sick."

"I'd put money on it. I told you about the phone calls last week. It's obviously all off again and Mr Penhaligan's pissed about it."

"But sending a wreath's a bit strong. I think she should go to the cops. He sounds like a right weirdo to me. He could be dangerous."

"That's what I said to her, but she wasn't interested," Lily said, pinching one of Maggie's chips, having polished off her own. "Made light of it. Cracks on it's all a joke, but I think she was bothered by it, despite that. I mean who wouldn't be? It's creepy."

"Better than a horse's head in your bed, I suppose. Good job she has that big dog to protect her," Maggie pointed out, slapping Lily's marauding hand as it ventured over to her plate again. "Mind you, from the evidence it looks to be one of those volatile on/off affairs so we could well be back to bouquets in a day or two."

Lily shook her head. "I don't think so. I saw her with a cute-looking guy on Grafton Street last Saturday, so I think Bouquet Man might be history."

"No wonder he's pissed then," Maggie observed. "If only for his fiscal outlay on flowers."

Meanwhile at O'Neill's the late Sally Gillespie – reports of whose death were greatly exaggerated – was having lunch with David Heart. He was horrified by Charlie's sick joke and suggested making a complaint to the cops. She disagreed.

"What's the point? I've no proof he sent the wreath. Anyway, he's just trying to get back at me for telling Imogene. It'll blow over when he cools down."

"Well, until then, if you're nervous of being in the loft on your own, you can always stay with me for a while," he said.

"Thanks, but there's nothing to be nervous about,' Sally reassured him. "Charlie's bark's worse than his bite He's made his point now."

It was a sentiment expressed in hope rather thar certainty.

After lunch Maggie and Tom met with Denis Morgan, who was delighted with the finished ads and, after the screening, Maggie took the opportunity to mention to him Gavin's comments about the brilliance of I-Sport as a hangover cure. Being the entrepreneur that he was, that got Denis thinking and he, Maggie and Tom threw a few ideas around, the end result of which was that it was decided by Denis to market another I-Sport product under a different name, possibly with some form of analgesic added, in powder form in a sachet to be diluted with water, as a hangover cure. This was good news for Deadly Inc and Maggie already had the slogan too which Denis was tickled about, namely: *Better Than A Fry Up*.

As the meeting drew to a close Lily buzzed her to say that there was a call for her from her sister Lucy. Leaving Tom to see Denis out, she took the call in her office.

"Is it true Mum's going to India at the end of June?" Lucy asked, or rather demanded.

"As far as I'm aware," Maggie said.

"What do you mean, as far as you're aware?" She sounded distinctly tetchy.

"Just that, Luce. Her plans seem to change from day to day."

"And is it right she's going with this boyfriend of hers?"

Maggie, who had finally given in to the fact that Anna would do whatever she wanted, so there was no point in falling out with her over it, sighed.

"I honestly don't know. As far as I know she's going on her own. She might meet up with Gerry when she's there, but as far as I know she isn't actually going with him, so to speak."

Lucy didn't sound any happier. "Gerry? His name's Gerry?"

Like it made any difference. "His name's Gerry Starling actually. I'm not mad about him, and I was suspicious at first, but in fairness, he's been very good to Mum and he thinks the world of her."

"You're very calm about all this," Lucy said. "Our parents are a whisker away from divorce and you don't seem to give a damn."

"You're overreacting," Maggie protested. "No one's mentioned the D word yet. Anyway, it's up to them, and the way I see it Dad's not exactly fighting to save the marriage, is he? I haven't heard a peep from him in ages."

"So that means we have to do something."

"Like what?" Maggie asked. "The last time I interfered, he attempted GBH on a totally innocent bystander and stormed out."

Lucy made Anna's humphing sound. "Innocent, is it? From what I heard he was a drug-dealer."

Maggie burst out laughing. "He is not! He's a friend of mine and he was only doing her a favour. She wanted to smoke hash and Luke got her some. And before you kick off again, she wasn't that impressed with it, so don't start up about the slippery slope and the thin end of the wedge and all that guff. She's no intention of shooting up or anything."

Lucy was silent, as if thinking that over, then she said, "What's got into her, Mags?"

"I told you. She realised that there's stuff she missed out on and she wants to experience it before she's too old. That's all. As soon as she gets it out of her system she'll be grand. Trust me. It's just a mid-life crisis thing."

"But what about Dad?" Lucy said. "I was up there last weekend and he's got a housekeeper in, and Maura Hopkins is doing his VAT and stuff. It's like he doesn't need her any more."

This was news to Maggie. "He's got a housekeeper? Who?"

"Some young one," Lucy said.

"How young?" Maggie asked, younger women being something of a sore point.

"I don't know. Young. I didn't see her – she only comes in for a couple of hours three days a week."

"So who told you about India?" Maggie asked.

"Mum did, but I wasn't sure if she was winding me up or not. She's been totally weird lately, going on about yoga and karma and stuff. And this whole TV ad thing's gone right to her head. You'd think she was fecking Julia Roberts the way she's going on."

"Well, in fairness, she was only a couple of weeks in town and she managed to carve out a whole new career for herself. You have to give her credit for that! When she first turned up I didn't think she'd get any kind of job."

Lucy did the humph again. "You've changed your

tune. Last time I spoke to you, you were as worried as I am – now you don't seem to give a flying fuck."

Maggie sighed. "It's not that, Luce. But I've finally seen sense. Mum and Dad are adults and their relationship's none of our business. And just because they split up, it doesn't change anything as far as we're concerned. It's not as if they're asking us to take sides, or anything. It's not like there's any danger of a custody battle – some long-drawn-out international tug-of-love thing."

Lucy laughed at that, despite herself. "I suppose not. I just wish Dad would get his act together and do something. Deep down, I know he wants her back."

When Maggie got home Anna was preparing a pork stir-fry. "There's plenty if you'd like some," she said. "I put your name in the pot just in case."

"Dad's got a housekeeper," Maggie said. "And Maura Hopkins is doing his VAT."

Anna paused in her chopping, then resumed with added vigour.

"You're mistaking me for someone who gives a damn," she said, but Maggie could tell that she was bothered because one viciously shredded green pepper later she said, "Who?"

"Who what?"

"Who's his housekeeper?"

"I thought you didn't give a damn," Maggie said.

"Who?" Anna snapped, whacking down the knife, cleaving an innocent red onion clean in half and only narrowly missing serious injury to her thumb.

"I don't know. Some young one."

Anna sniffed then muttered, "Silly old fool."

"Did you tell him about your trip?"

"How could I? I haven't spoken to him since he attacked poor Luke."

"But you told Lucy."

"In the course of conversation. If either of you wants to tell your father, well that's up to you. But as far as I can see he wouldn't be interested." She picked up a handful of mushrooms and went about cutting them into quarters with gusto, muttering under her breath, "A young one, indeed." *Chop, chop, chop!* "A young one in my house!"

Maggie picked up a sliver of red pepper and popped it into her mouth. "Well, like you, Mum, I suppose he's moved on."

"Moved on? Humph. He didn't let the grass grow under his feet, did he?" *Chop, chop, chop!*

Maggie smiled to herself, amused by the spectre of the green-eyed monster evident in her mother's attitude. "Sooooo," she said, "I wonder who it is, this young one? Any ideas?"

Anna's lips were pursed as she poured oil into the wok and chucked the strips of pork in. "No. And it's of no interest to me. If your father wants to make himself the laughing-stock of the town, that's up to him."

Maggie was quietly amused by her mother's hasty jump to the conclusion that her husband was sleeping with his young housekeeper.

"You should really wait for the oil to heat up," she said. "That's the whole point of stir-fry."

Anna turned her head and glared at Maggie. "Are you trying to be smart?"

Maggie backed off, palms raised in submission. "Noooo. Just saying, that's all."

Dinner was a silent affair, and Anna didn't eat much, just moving her food around her plate, a stony expression on her face. Maggie ignored it.

"So are you off out later?" she asked.

Anna looked up. "What?"

"Are you going out later?" Maggie repeated.

Anna looked at her watch. "As a matter of fact I am." She pushed her plate away, and stood up. "I'd better go up and change."

She came down fifteen minutes later and popped her head around the kitchen door. "Don't wait up," she said. "I could be late."

After Maggie heard the front door bang, she called her father and by the background noise she deduced that he was propping up Mat Molloy's bar.

"Dad. It's Mags."

"How are you, love?"

Bypassing pleasantries she dived in. "Dad, did you know Mum's taking off to India in a few weeks' time?"

He laughed. "I know. Lucy told me."

"Dad. This is serious. And don't get me wrong, if you and Mum are determined to split up, then fine, but you do realise that if you want her back, if you don't do something soon, you could lose her forever."

"I have it all in hand," he said enigmatically.

"How do you mean, in hand?"

"I have it all in hand, Mags. Don't worry. Now, when are you coming home? Lucy tells me you've got a new boyfriend. It didn't take you long to get over the other fella ditching you, did it?"

Sensitive as ever.

"What do you mean, all in hand, Dad?"

He wouldn't be drawn, leaving Maggie none the wiser as to what his cunning plan was this time, but shrugging her shoulders she thought, I give up. Let them get on with it.

Chapter 48

"A young one," Anna muttered to herself as she drove along the Stillorgan dual carriageway towards Blackrock. "A young one in my house. How could he!?"

She was still simmering with rage at the thought of some young girl, younger than Maggie and Lucy, leading Dan by the nose. Do men lose all reason when they pass a certain age? she wondered. Was the silly old duffer under some illusion that a young one would want him for anything other than his money? It was flattery, of course, she rationalised. Some slip of a thing had seen her chance, had flattered and flirted with him and it had turned his head; but he wasn't Michael Douglas, and Catherine Zeta Jones certainly hadn't moved to town.

Bile rose in the throat as she thought of some floozy rooting through her things and rearranging the furniture, and Dan going along with it, completely beguiled. She'd probably have him going to the gym and making an eejitt of himself at the disco. A mental image of her husband of thirty-four years bopping like a Thunderbird puppet on the dance-floor, all got up in those baggy low-slung jeans the young ones wore these days, with a baseball cap backways on his head caused her to groan with embarrassment.

Behind the anger though there was a deep sense of disappointment. She'd thought he'd try harder. She'd thought her leaving would shake him up into realising how much he'd taken her for granted, and the apprehension that she'd been so wrong was hurtful. The discovery that she wasn't indispensable was a further blow. True it had taken two women to replace her, but that was of little consolation.

And in contrast Gerry had been so good, so thoughtful, so sweet, and her battered self-esteem had needed that. He'd had faith in her and given her a chance to shine, unlike Dan who no doubt laughed like a drain when Maggie had told him she intended to get a job.

"A job? Sure who'd give your mother a job?"

Well, Gerry had. And she hadn't let him down. She'd watched Mossie Hunt and Jason Dwyer editing the footage at Final Frame, and seen the finished ads and hadn't everyone said they were terrific? A wave of smugness washed over her.

Just wait till you see me on TV, Dan Fortune, she thought. That'll show you. You and your young one!

Pulling in to the side of the road she parked and switched off the engine, then sat in the dark, looking over at Gerry's house. It was a nice house. Detached, old, double-fronted, near the seafront, lovely garden, though Gerry had admitted that he got someone in do it.

Maybe it's time, she thought as she sat looking up at the house. He'd been so patient, despite Maggie's opinion that he had only one agenda, namely to get her into bed. Granted he'd been honest with her on that score, but when she had explained that although she was very fond of him, she wasn't ready to move their relationship on to that level just yet, he'd been very understanding, possibly because he too had experienced the pain and disappointment of marriage breakdown, so he knew where she was coming from.

She hadn't slept with anyone but Dan in the last thirty-four, no, thirty-five years and, although he hadn't been her first, she had only been with two other men in her whole life. The thought of exposing her middle-aged body to another man was difficult for her though and unconsciously she pulled in her stomach muscles and hiked up her bra-straps. Five children hadn't done her body any favours, but bearing that in mind she felt she looked in pretty good shape in her clothes, a standard size twelve, and her modest breasts, though having suffered the rigours of gravity, looked well enough considering. She'd always had good legs, a legacy from her mother's side of the family.

Pulling down the sun-visor she checked her hair and wiped away a wayward smudge of mascara, then took a deep breath. A few butterflies fluttered in her gut as she locked the car and walked up Gerry's drive to the front door.

"If you've moved on, it's time I did," she said aloud. "You might be sick and tired of me, but Gerry thinks I'm beautiful, and he'll be around long after that young slapper's sick and tired of you, you old fool!"

Gerry was surprised but very obviously glad to see her.

"Come in. Come in," he said. He had a tea towel in his hand and was in his shirt sleeves.

Anna proffered her cheek and he gave it a peck. "I hope I'm not interrupting anything. I just –"

"Not at all," Gerry insisted. "Just finished supper." He led the way into the kitchen where his lone plate, knife and fork drained on the dish-rack, beside a half-full glass of white wine. The cardboard wrapper of a Super Savings own brand cook-and-chill ready meal lay beside the empty plastic microwavable container on the beech worktop.

"Fancy a glass?" he asked picking up the remaining half bottle of Riesling.

Anna smiled. "Thanks," then sat up on a high stool at the breakfast bar. She was nervous as hell, not sure how to go about seduction, it had been so long.

"You look wonderful," he said as he handed her her glass, "But then you always do," and she found herself blushing as he raised his glass to her. "Cheers!"

"Cheers," she responded, then took a sip of wine to hide her confusion. She felt hot and bothered, anxious about what she had in mind. If only we could cut to the chase, she thought. If only we could skip all the flirting and kissing and undressing part and just be in bed, preferably in the dark. It wasn't that she was a prude about nakedness, but suddenly she wasn't sure she was ready to let him see her stretch-marks. He was talking but she was having difficulty concentrating as she tried to imagine what he would look like naked.

It was then that it occurred to her, with a certain amount of horror, that she wasn't attracted to him in the slightest. Oh, he was a lovely kind man, but she didn't find him even slightly sexually attractive.

Suddenly she missed the familiarity of Dan, the casual comfortable way they fitted together. Granted the passion had gone, but he knew how to please her, and had never been a selfish lover. An aching loneliness washed over her as she remembered how it used to be in the early years. When had it all changed? They had still made love, if somewhat mechanically, once or twice a month, and although it had become something of a chore he knew which buttons to push and always made her come.

Suddenly she saw that in a lot of ways she was as guilty as he, taking him for granted as much as he had her, and the thought of him with someone else was devastating.

I can't do this, she thought, looking at Gerry. I can't have sex with this man.

"Are you all right?" he asked.

"Sorry?"

"You look miles away."

She smiled at him, then placing her glass on the breakfast bar slid down from the stool.

"I'm awfully sorry, Gerry. I just remembered something really important I have to do," she said, averting her eyes as she told the lie.

"Are you sure you're all right?" he asked again, his voice concerned. "You look upset."

She waved his question away with a nervous laugh, hurrying from the room towards the hall. "There's somewhere I was supposed to be . . . and um . . ." She had broken out in a sweat and couldn't look at him, afraid he'd be able to read her mind and would be angry, or worse, laugh at her for being so pathetic. "I have to go," she said wrenching the front door open, and practically running down the drive. At the gate she looked back. "I'm sorry."

He was standing at the door, a bewildered look on his face. He raised his hand as she revved the car and accelerated away.

Around the corner she pulled into the kerb and parked. Her hands were shaking; she was hot, damp and emotional. I've lost him, she thought. Dan doesn't want me any more.

He'd given up on her and chosen a younger model, just as Mark had with Maggie. It wasn't suppose to end like this. But then when she thought about it, she hadn't really looked at the bigger picture when she'd decided to give herself some space. It was true she'd achieved a lot of what she'd set out to do, and there was still the trip to India, but somehow, at the end of it all, in an abstract sort of way, she'd imagined that Dan would always be there. Her stomach contracted as a wave of panic hit her. Winding down the window she consciously breathed deeply and evenly in an attempt to slow her heartbeat. Gradually it passed and she leaned her forehead on the steering wheel and closed her eyes. She could almost smell the burning wood of the bridges which were now but a smouldering ruin, and it was a daunting prospect.

After a moment she lifted her head, breathed in the night air and, loathing self-pity with a passion, tried to summon up something positive.

All right, so my marriage is over, she thought. Dan's swift onward move proves that. One phase of my life's over and another's just beginning. I am a single independent woman. I've started a new career and I'm going to India.

"Yes," she said aloud. "I'm going to India."

Turning the key in the ignition she let the engine idle for a few moments, than exhaled all the negative energy from her body and filled her lungs with the crisp sea air.

"I'm go-ing to In-di-a!" she sang. *"I'm go-ing to In-di-a!"*

As she let out the clutch and headed back towards the city, repeating the words like a mantra, she felt better, more positive, her excitement for the project renewed; but at the back of her mind there was a nagging regret at the certainty that she would, like Princess Diana, be sitting all alone on that marble seat.

Chapter 49

Dani was the last person Maggie expected to hear from so she was amazed when, on Thursday afternoon, she received a call from her with an invitation to meet up for a bite to eat at the Elephant & Castle. It was the last thing she wanted to do but, caught on the hop, couldn't think of a plausible excuse, so found herself agreeing.

Tom, who was obviously ear-wigging the call, had an infuriating smirk on his gob as she hung up the phone.

"Love to be a fly on the wall for that," he said, and ducked as Maggie threw a packet of Post-its at him.

"Well, she caught me off guard and I didn't want to be rude. Anyway, I like her. She's a sweet girl," adding after a beat, "if a little naïve."

"Do you reckon Mark'll hang around then?"

Maggie shrugged. "I honestly don't know, but I hope so for Dani's sake. Bringing up a baby on her own wouldn't be a load of laughs."

When Maggie arrived at the Templebar café at seven

thirty, the place was packed, but Dani was already sitting at a table, a glass of red wine in front of her. She waved and Maggie joined her.

"I was afraid you wouldn't come," she said as Maggie slid into her seat.

Maggie shrugged. "You caught me on the hop and I couldn't think of an excuse," she said, then laughed. "Well, it is a bit weird, isn't it?"

"I suppose," Dani conceded. "But I wanted to see you to say thanks for being so good about everything . . . I mean the way you called me to make sure I knew Mark was home and stuff. That was really nice."

"I just didn't trust that he was telling me the truth, that's all. I suppose you heard about the pint of Guinness I tipped over his head?"

"He did mention that. But they tell me it's good for the hair."

The waitress came over then, so Maggie ordered a beer, and they both ordered food.

"Mark goes mad if he sees me drinking," Dani said, as she took a sip of wine. "But it's not as if I'm overdoing it. Only the odd glass of wine or a Guinness. But he's so sweet. He worries about me and the baby, and he's taken to reading all the pregnancy books he can get his hands on, and next week he's coming to my antenatal class. He's really thrilled about the baby now. Really into the whole thing."

Maggie bit back the words 'Bully for Mark', instead laying it on Anna. "Well, as my mother would say, 'Pity but he wouldn't'. It's his baby too."

Dani looked down at the table top, blushing. "Oh, I

know. But at least he came back in the end. He just panicked. It was nothing to do with the baby; it was the whole thing with you and me. It all got on top of him."

"Deception's apt to do that," Maggie muttered, then felt bad for being so ungracious and reached across the table to touch Dani's hand. "I'm sorry. I don't know why I'm being like this. It's not as if I'm pining after him or anything."

Dani shrugged. "He did the dirty on you. You've a right to be a bit angry about it."

As the waitress returned with her beer, Maggie said. "He did the dirty on both of us," then raised her glass, "but he half redeemed himself so it's time I let go. Here's to the future!"

"To the future," Dani repeated, clinking glasses. She looked relieved.

"So where are you going to live?" Maggie asked as they were halfway through their dinner.

"For the moment we're going to move in with Tony on Haddington Road, and Conor's looking for a new flatmate, but when Mark's tenants leave at the end of July we'll move into his apartment."

"Very nice," Maggie said. "Have you seen Mark's apartment? It has a lovely view."

She realised then that she had let it go. She didn't feel even slightly resentful, but she was amused by the prospect of Tony Holland sharing his apartment with Mark, Dani and a new baby. Dani was with Mark now; and good luck to them. So Mark had left her for a younger woman, had been petty and mean over the furniture and stuff, but the truth was, he'd done her a favour. If he hadn't gone she wouldn't be with Aiden, and being with him made her realise how dead her relationship with Mark had become.

"So how are things going with Aiden?" Dani asked as if reading her mind.

"Great," Maggie said economically.

Dani smiled. "Good. That makes me feel better. He seems like a really nice guy."

"He is," Maggie agreed. Much as she liked Dani she had no intention of discussing the relationship with her. – that was way too weird.

"So how's your course going?" she asked to change the subject.

Dani enthusiastically filled her in on how her coursework was coming on and how she'd found out about a crèche for the baby so she'd be able to go back to college in October to do her final year. Then, over coffee, she went on to tell her how she hadn't said anything to her mother about Mark's brief trip to Australia and didn't intend to.

"So she has no idea?" Maggie asked astounded, there being no chance that she would have kept Mark's flight from Anna.

Dani shook her head. "I didn't want to upset her. Anyway she'd have pressured me to go home and, much as I love her, I couldn't imagine living with my mother."

Neither could I until she turned up on the doorstep, Maggie thought.

Dani pushed her empty cup away. "When's Anna off to India?"

Maggie told her and they discussed Anna's trip for a

while, and Skye, and then Ursula briefly. Then Dani called for the bill. She insisted on paying which Maggie found embarrassing but gave in gracefully in the end when Dani reassured her that Mark was supporting her now. So she thought, why not?

Outside in the street Maggie said, "I've got my mother's car. Would you like a lift home?"

Dani smiled. "Thanks. That would be great," and they set off together towards the carpark.

Sally was having a frustrating day, most of it spent out at Ardmore at the ShockFX shoot, but at six she'd had to schlep all the way back into town to an animation studio on Crowe Street to check on the progress of a twenty-second ad for fabric softener which was way behind schedule. By half past eight she was quietly cursing the fact that she and Leo had gone for animation in the first place, but it was too late and it would be too costly now to make a change. Besides, the client was more than happy with the concept so it was a case of sticking with it until it was right.

A further cause of frustration was the stream of vitriolic text messages she was in receipt of several times a day, all anonymous but all clearly from Charlie. From the first moment when the wreath had been delivered to the Deadly Inc offices, she had taken a conscious decision to ignore him, on the basis that if she reacted it would only dignify his actions and encourage him. However she had expected that by now he would have run out of steam, whereas rather than dying down he seemed to be gaining momentum. Resolutely though, she resisted the temptation to react, confident that his anger had to burn itself out sometime.

Her phone beeped a text-message alert, the sixth that day, as she was crossing Cope Street into Crown Alley on route to the car park to pick up her car. She gave a heavy sigh of irritation and opened it.

"Rot in hell, bitch," it read. She immediately erased it, then found David's number and called him.

"Hi, how are you?" He sounded cheerful.

"Been better," she replied.

"The stalker hasn't been in touch again, has he?"

"Only about half a dozen texts today. I think he's getting tired of the game," she said, trying to make light of it. The previous day she had received one every hour, on the hour.

"Well, it's his dime, as they say. Have you eaten?"

"No. But to tell you the truth I've no appetite. Apart from Charlie's little mind games, I've had a generally shitty day."

"How about you come round and I'll pamper you with a foot massage and a bottle of very good Soave I found at the back of the fridge?"

Immediately her spirits lifted. "Sounds like heaven. But I should drop home first to see if Hero's there. He wandered off before lunchtime so I didn't get a chance to feed him yet."

"Too late," came the reply. "He gave up on you and came over here."

She laughed. "So much for bloody loyalty."

"Ah well, I obviously serve a better class of dog food."

Feeling far more cheerful in herself, she ended the call

and, dropping her phone back in her bag, rooted for her carpark ticket.

As she entered the lobby she saw Maggie Fortune and a very pregnant girl standing together feeding coins into the pay machine.

"Hello," she said, smiling.

Maggie turned her head. "Sally! Hi . . . bloody machine. It won't take notes for some reason."

"Great," Sally muttered, conscious that her ticket should be around the ten euro mark and wondering if she had that much on her in change, before it occurred to her that she could use her credit card.

Maggie held the lift for her and they went up together.

"Which floor?" the girl asked.

"Three," Sally replied and the girl pressed the button. The lift ascended.

"How did the Shock FX shoot go?" Maggie asked, making conversation.

"Fine. But that crowd of wankers on Crowe Street are pushing it. They're already a week late with Silkysoft."

Maggie resisted the temptation to say 'I told you so'. She had warned Sally that the animators she'd chosen were unreliable, but Sally obviously hadn't listened. "Are you serious?" she said straightfaced.

The lights flickered and a moment later the lift juddered to a halt, flinging Dani against Maggie, and Sally against the back wall.

"Shit!" Maggie muttered, punching buttons to try and get some reaction, but the lift stayed where it was. They stood together looking at the ceiling, the way you do, waiting for something to happen, but the elevator remained totally static. After about ten seconds Maggie looked at the panel containing the buttons. "There should be an alarm," she said, then spotted it on the top row and pushed the bell.

"They'll be here in a minute, I expect," Sally said to the pregnant girl, who was looking anxious.

"I hate lifts," she said. "If I wasn't eight months pregnant I'd have used the stairs."

"It'll be fine. Someone'll be here soon," Maggie said reassuringly, but she was beginning to feel the first stirrings of panic. It was close to nine o'clock. Did the lift rescue people only do nine to five? she wondered, picturing a superhero type in a tight-fitting Spiderman outfit abseiling down the lift cable.

"All lifts have this safety brake," Sally reassured them. "It kicks in and stops it plummeting to the ground, so we'll be fine."

"Why don't I find that snippet encouraging?" Maggie said, finding the concept of 'plummeting' a tad unsettling. She had no wish to plummet anywhere.

"What's keeping them?" Dani asked. She had gone very red in the face and was leaning against the back wall of the lift. The bell stopped ringing, so Sally leaned over and punched the button, and it started up again, to little effect as other than the clanging nothing else seemed to be happening. She took out her phone. There was barely a signal but she dialled the emergency services, heard a woman answer, then the call dropped.

"Try yours," she said to Maggie, who already had her phone in her hand.

"I'll call Aiden," she said and dialled. The call connected

and he answered but all she had time to say was, "Aiden, I'm stuck in a lift," before that call too dropped.

"Must be the metal of the lift," Dani offered, then suddenly they all heard a rush of water and she wailed, "Oh feck! It's my waters. They've only gone and broken!"

"Oh my God! You're in labour," Maggie said.

"You're in labour? Oh my God!" Sally said.

"Shit! This can't be happening!" said Maggie. "You're not due for another four weeks!"

"Three and a half – pity no one told my baby the –" Dani broke off and clutched her stomach. "Oh, God . . . I think I'm having a contraction . . ."

The bell had stopped ringing again which was something of a relief. Sally banged on the doors.

"Heeelp! We're stuck and we have a woman in here in labour!" she shouted.

They all listened, but could hear nothing from outside. Maggie held her phone up and moved around the lift to see if at any point the signal was stronger. Nearest to the doors seemed better, so she dialled Aiden again. He answered immediately.

"Mags! Where are you?"

"I'm stuck in a lift in Templebar carpark," she said in a rush. "Dani's with me and she's in labour!"

"What? You're breaking up?"

"Templebar carpark. Stuck in the lift. Dani's in labour!" The call dropped again. "I've lost him," she said, shaking her phone. "Bloody lifts!"

"Let's shout together," Sally said and they banged on the doors again, shouting for help.

"Help! We're stuck! Help! Help!"

They stopped and listened but there was no response.

Dani lowered herself to the floor, choosing a dry area in the corner, and sat with her back to the wall.

"Are you OK?" Maggie asked.

Dani gave her a wry look. "Apart from being in labour and trapped in a bloody lift, you mean?" For someone in the aforesaid predicament and by whose own admission hated lifts, she appeared to be way calmer than the other two. Looking up at Sally she stuck out her hand. "Hi. I'm Dani."

Sally took her hand. "Sally. Sally Gillespie."

"Sally and I work together," Maggie said, as if that was relevant.

"Are you still having pains?" Sally asked.

Dani shook her head. "Not since that one."

Maggie banged on the doors again. *"Help! We're trapped! Help!"* then put her ear to the crack. "I think I can hear someone," she said.

She and Sally banged again: *thump, thump, thump!* *"Help! We're trapped!"*

This time they were answered by a hollow clang and a muffled voice.

"There's someone there!" said Maggie, a beaming smile on her face. "Won't be long now, Dani!"

At which point Dani had another contraction.

"Shouldn't you be breathing or something, you know ho-ho-ho-ha-ha-ha sort of thing?" Maggie said, feeling feeble, remembering Lucy's eighteen-hour ordeal in Kilkenny hospital, but Dani didn't comment, just gripped Maggie's hand like a vice. When it had passed, red-faced she loosened her grip.

"It's *hah-hah-hah-heeh-heeh-heeh*, actually," Dani said demonstrating.

"Well, try and remember next time," Sally encouraged. "I think it's supposed to help."

Maggie gave her a leery look over Dani's head, and Sally just shrugged helplessly.

Maggie banged on the doors again. *"Hello? Is there anyone out there?"*

A loud banging answered the question along with a muffled, "Hello? Are you all right? No one injured?"

No one injured!" Maggie shouted back. *"But we have a girl in labour here! She's eight months pregnant!"*

"OK. Don't worry. We'll have you out of there soon," came the muffled reply and Sally and Maggie hugged each other. "Don't worry about the noise, OK?" their rescuer continued. "You're all perfectly safe. We just have to work out the best way to get you all out of there."

The "just have to work out" wasn't particularly confidence-inspiring but Maggie didn't share that thought, instead she crouched down and took Dani's hand. "They'll have us out soon. Don't worry."

'Soon' was a relative term, and in the interim there was a lot of hammering and juddering which was a touch hairy. In fact it took the best part of an hour to open the lift doors, during which time Dani experienced more contractions. As the lift was trapped between two floor, the paramedics had to lower Dani to safety strapped to a chair. After she'd been successfully released, a hunky fireman assisted Maggie and Sally to the ground. Aiden was there with the emergency services and he hugged Maggie with relief when the fireman put her down.

"Please don't ever do that again," he said, kissing her. "You put the heart crossways in me."

"I'll try not to," she replied. "Will you come with me to the hospital? I want to make sure Dani's OK."

While the ambulance crew took Dani to the Rotunda maternity hospital, carpark employees accompanied Maggie and Sally to their respective cars, apologising profusely, then Maggie headed off to the Rotunda. Aiden was there ahead of her and had information that Dani had been admitted and was definitely in labour. Sally arrived at that point, much to Maggie's surprise.

"How is she?" she asked.

"Fine, thank goodness," Maggie said, then turned to Aiden. "I suppose I should call Mark?"

"Probably be a good idea," he said. "Would you two like coffee or something?"

"I'd kill for a coffee," Sally said, slumping down on a chair and Maggie nodded as she searched through her phone book for Mark's number. When she called it, however, it was out of service.

"Mark?" Sally said. "Your ex? So Dani's . . ."

Maggie nodded. "The other woman, so to speak."

Sally's perfectly shaped eyebrows elevated. "How bizarre! You in a lift with your ex's pregnant girlfriend?"

"I suppose," Maggie said, a tad irritated by Sally's observation. "How do you know about all that business, anyway?"

"Office memo," she said grinning, and Maggie laughed, despite her annoyance.

"Oh. Right. Magnus Nutter's office memo. That'll teach

Anna O'Malley

me to employ irony in the vicinity of a man who doesn't understand the concept."

It occurred to her then that Tony Holland might know where Mark was so she called him. The phone rang for ages but finally he picked up.

"Hello," he said, breathless.

"Tony, it's Maggie Fortune. I need to find Mark urgently."

"Um . . . how would I know where he is?" Tony said.

"Stop being a bollox, Tony. Dani's in the Rotunda and she's in labour, so if he wants to share the experience, tell him to get his butt up here fast."

She heard him gulp. "In labour? But she isn't due for another four weeks."

"Three and a half actually, Tony, but no one told the baby . . . just find him!" Maggie snapped, then hung up.

"That was a touch harsh," Sally observed.

"Tony and I have issues," Maggie said in reply and Sally eyebrows elevated once more.

Aiden returned with three coffees, so they all sat down and sipped gratefully.

Aiden grasped Maggie's hand, giving it a squeeze. "You OK?"

Maggie grinned at him. "I'm grand. I just hope Dani's baby is all right. She isn't due for another three and a half weeks."

"Well, she's in the right place," he pointed out. "Did you manage to get hold of Mark?"

Maggie shook her head. "No, but I got hold of that rat Tony Holland, so it's up to him to find the proud father now."

A nurse walked down the corridor at that point.

448

"Which one of you is Maggie Fortune?" she asked, and Maggie owned up by raising her index finger. "Danielle McGing's looking for you. Would you mind coming up to keep her company for a while?".

"How is she?" Sally asked. "Is she all right?"

"She's fine, but she has a fair way to go yet," the nurse said. "So there's no point in you all hanging round." She looked at Aiden. "Unless you're her partner?"

He shook his head. "No, I'm not. But we're trying to find him."

"No panic," the nurse said, then turning to Maggie added, "But she's a bit emotional right now so if you wouldn't mind keeping her company until her partner gets here . . .?"

Maggie shot a look at Aiden. Sitting on a hard chair in the Rotunda hospital holding Dani's hand for hours was the last thing she felt like doing, but she didn't have the courage to protest considering the poor girl's ordeal in the lift. "Um, OK," she said, then to Aiden and Sally, "There's no reason for you two to hang around."

"I'll stay with you," Aiden said. "Mark can't be that long. I'm sure Tony's passed on the message by now." Then to the nurse, "Is that all right?"

"Yes, that's fine. Would you two like to follow me?"

Sally look relieved by the opportunity to leave. "Right – I'll be off then, now I know she's all right."

Lucky you, Maggie thought as the nurse led them away.

Chapter 50

Dani was propped up in a bed wearing a faded hospital gown, and her face lit up when Maggie and Aiden walked into the ward.

"How are you doing?" Maggie asked.

"Happier now I'm in here. Didn't fancy having my baby in a lift."

"Where's Mark, do you know?" Aiden asked. "Maggie couldn't get hold of him."

"He's in West Cork on a job," Dani said. "And he so wanted to be here for the birth."

I'll bet he did, Maggie thought remembering how Mark couldn't watch *ER* or *Casualty* for fear of passing out.

"I called Tony Holland and told him to tell Mark to get his butt up here," Maggie said. "But you must have his mobile number?"

"I tried," Dani said, "but it's switched off, or maybe out of coverage. I left a message."

Not good news as that meant that they'd probably

have to stay until the bitter end which could take hours. Maggie glanced at Aiden.

"Then do you know where he's staying?" he asked and Dani shook her head, causing Maggie to foster doubts that Mark was in West Cork at all, but that doubt was sidelined as Dani's face contorted with another contraction. Unfortunately Maggie's hand was within reach and she suffered the vice treatment again.

"Breathe!" she encouraged. "*Hah-hah-hah*, Dani, remember?"

Dani nodded and started to huff as directed, and both Aiden and Maggie found themselves imitating her, sort of cheering her on so to speak, which left Maggie quite light-headed, and Aiden feeling a complete and utter prat.

"You're right," Dani said when it passed. "That was much easier with the breathing."

When she got to her car, Sally called David.

"Where are you?" he asked. "We were getting worried."

"We?"

"Me and the dog," he said.

"Would you believe, trapped for over an hour in a lift with two women, one of whom was in labour?" she asked.

"In labour as in having a baby? Are you serious?"

"Deadly. But the she's in hospital now and fine, so I'm on my way over, if it's not too late."

"It's never too late," David said.

By three o'clock in the morning, when there was still no sign of Mark, and the frequency of Dani's contractions had increased markedly, Maggie took Aiden to one side and said, "Why don't you go home?"

"And leave you here on your own? Mark can't be long now. It's only what? Four and a half hours max from there to here. I'll stay to keep you company."

"Mark might not even be aware that Dani's in labour," she said, "and if he is, he could well be lying low to avoid the actual birth. What better excuse?"

"You think he'd do that?" Aiden asked in a low voice glancing over at Dani who was perusing *HEAT* magazine.

Maggie gave him an old-fashioned look. "Hell-ooo – it's Mark we're talking about here. Mister Head-in-the-sand-I-can't-face-this-situation. That's why I think I should stay. I know it's not my problem, but she shouldn't have to go through this all by herself."

Aiden put his arms around her and gave her a hug, resting his chin on her shoulder. "As situations go, this is a touch surreal," he said and Maggie laughed.

"You could say that."

The midwife, a brusque and scary-looking Cork woman with over-bleached hair, came in then and asked them to "stip outside" so she could check up on Dani's progress.

"You really think he'd do a temporary runner to avoid being with Dani at the birth?" asked Aiden.

"He's the original man who wasn't there," Maggie pointed out. "I'm surprised he came back at all."

When the midwife reappeared it was to tell them that Dani was to be brought straight to the labour ward. "Are you her burting partner?" she asked Maggie, and it took her a moment to realise that she meant "birthing".

"Not exactly," she said, "but I think I'm all that's on offer right now."

"So are you game ball?" she asked and Maggie gave a squeamish nod. "Right, come wit me and we'll give you scrubs to put on," then to Aiden, "You might as well take yourself off. You're not needed."

The now redundant Aiden gave Maggie another hug and a kiss and she promised to call him with news, and he in turn promised to fill Anna in on what was happening. Then he left a trepidacious Maggie to get suited up for Dani's imminent birthing experience.

It was all over bar the shouting in just over an hour, when Dani was delivered of a six-pound baby boy after much effort, pushing, pain and five stitches on her part, and a bruised and squashed hand on Maggie's; and tears from both of them at the first sight of him, squawking and red-faced with annoyance at being brought into the world sooner than he expected. Being premature, after a quick peek, he was taken off to the baby unit as a matter of course, but Dani was assured that he had all the bits and pieces he was supposed to have, and appeared to be in fine fettle, of which Maggie had no doubt judging by his robust lungs.

They asked her to step outside again while they made Dani comfortable. Outside, she pulled the scrubs over her head and leaned against the wall to ease her aching back. A moment later she spotted Mark rushing down the corridor, a panic-stricken look on his face, clutching a wilted bunch of garage flowers.

"Great timing, Mark," she said making no attempt to temper the sarcasm. "Dani's done all the hard work and you have a son."

His face broke into a huge grin. "They're OK? It's a boy? I have a son?"

"After being trapped in a lift and carted here in an ambulance! Where the hell were you?"

"I was in West Cork, on business – I left as soon as Tony called."

Still sceptical, Maggie said, "You were really in West Cork? Not just keeping your head down out of the way?"

"Why would I do that?" He appeared mystified by the question. "She wasn't due for another four weeks. How was I to know she'd go into labour?"

"Three and a half, actually," Maggie said, feeling justified in her pettiness, but a smidgen childish all the same for trying to score points. "I'm going home now. The nurse will be out to get you in a minute. They're just making her comfortable."

She didn't wait for his reply and, shoving the scrubs into his hands, strode down the corridor without looking back.

The clock on the dash read four-thirty am and the first signs of the dawn were visible over the dark rooftops.

"Bizarre," she said aloud, recalling Sally's reaction.

If a fortune-teller had told me at the beginning of March that I'd be present at the birth of Mark's baby, that Mum was leaving Dad and would be the face of Super Savings, that she'd smoke dope, go travelling off to India, and that I was heading into a new relationship, I'd have asked for my twenty euro back, she thought. Then she smiled as she thought of Aiden and, picking up her phone, called him.

Maggie awoke with a start and peered at the clock through bleary eyes. 9:10. She could hear the muffled sound of music coming from the kitchen downstairs and lay there lazily trying to identify the tune until she did a double take on the time.

"Shit!" Leaping out of bed she stumbled to the bathroom and jumped in the shower, reducing the temperature to almost cold in an attempt to wake herself up. She felt groggy from lack of sleep, it being past five when she had fallen into bed, and having slept only fitfully, dreaming weird dreams involving babies and Anna and Sally, and for some unaccountable reason, the irony-deficient Magnus Nutter.

Wrapping herself in a towel, she cleaned her teeth then padded back to her bedroom to dry her hair, meeting Anna at the top of the stairs, a cup of tea in her hand.

"You should have a lie-in," she said, then a broad smile spread across her face. "Aiden told me about the excitement last night."

"That's one word for it," Maggie muttered, as she plugged in the hair-dryer.

"Well, I mean, trapped in a lift, then holding Dani's hand all the way through." Taking Maggie's face between her hands, she planted a kiss on her forehead. "I'm so proud of you."

"Me? All I did was be there. Dani did all the work, which is more than can be said for Mark. He turned up right on cue when it was all over."

"I heard," Anna said with a sneer in her voice. "Not that I was surprised."

While Maggie blasted her hair to get the heavy wet out of it, Anna sat on the end of the bed. "You should get back into bed when you've dried your hair," she said. "I'll ring

Lily and tell her you won't be in today. I'm sure they'll understand, given the circumstances."

If only, Maggie thought. "Can't," she said. "I have a client presentation at ten thirty."

"But surely –"Anna started, but Maggie cut her off.

"I have to be there," she insisted. "It's an important presentation," then seeing Anna's hurt expression through the mirror realised that she had probably been a bit abrupt, smiled at her mother's reflection and said, "But I promise I'll have an early night."

"Make sure you do," Anna admonished. "A girl needs her beauty sleep."

Noting the dark circles under her bloodshot eyes, Maggie was inclined to agree.

"I was thinking of going in to see Dani at teatime. Want to come?" Anna asked after a pause.

Maggie gave her a leery look through the mirror. "I don't think so, thanks. I've done my bit and the prospect of Mark and me on either side of Dani's bed is way too creepy."

"Well, I'll give her your love," Anna said.

Lily was full of it when she hurried into the office, out of breath, at a quarter to ten.

"So what's this about you being caught in a lift with SPOD?" she said, casting a belated glance at the stairs in case Sally was within earshot. "And what did Dani have, a boy or a child as my granny would say?"

"A boy," Maggie said. "And guess who didn't put in an appearance until it was all over."

Dom, Sally and Leo walked out of Dom's office at that point.

"Maggie! How's Dani? How did she get on?" Sally asked.

"She had a boy. Six pounds, and both of them are fine."

Sally smiled. "That's great. I was afraid for a while we'd have to act as midwives in that lift, and I wouldn't have had the first idea what to do, bar boiling water and tearing up sheets."

"You and me both," Maggie agreed, "but at least they didn't put me at the yucky end in the labour ward."

"Tearing up sheets?" Leo muttered.

"John Wayne . . . Westerns," Lily said, which left him none the wiser.

"You were there for the birth?" Dom asked, sounding impressed.

"If I'd had the choice I'd have given it a miss, but Mark didn't show up until it was all over. So what could I do?"

"Mark?" She could see Dom's thought processes ticking over by his changing facial expression. "Mark, as in . . ."

"Yes, as in my ex," Maggie said wearily, seriously considering asking Magnus to issue a bulletin to save her the bother of explaining over again.

Though it took less than an hour, the presentation seemed to take forever, as the client was particularly picky, making suggestions that were unrealistic for his modest budget, but she and Tom put up a good case for their favoured concept, and after some further minor quibbling the client went away happy.

After lunch she had a sound recording at Real to Reel with Steph Valentine. She was in good form, and asked after Anna.

"She's fine," Maggie said. "Heading off to India at the end of June, if you don't mind!"

"India? Excellent!" She wiped her brow and gave an exaggerated sigh. "My career's safe so!" and they both laughed.

The recording went fine, which was to be expected using a pro like Steph, but the day seemed endless, the minutes crawling by, and she felt light-headed the way you do after only a couple of hours' sleep. Thank God it's Friday, she thought as she headed out to Real to Reel's reception area where she bumped into Sally who was also on her way out.

"Finished?" Sally asked.

"Thankfully," Maggie said.

"You should go home," her boss suggested. "You look knackered." Then she paused. "Tell you what. I've got the car outside. I'll give you a lift."

Surprised by the unexpected offer, but nonetheless glad, Maggie said "Cheers. That would be great."

Sally's silver VW Beetle was parked a short distance down the road. Maggie was surprised by her choice of vehicle, assuming she'd have gone for something flashy and sporty like an MG or one of those little Beemer Z3 jobbies.

"So Mark turned up in the end," Sally said as they reached the car. "Happy ending."

"Assuming he sticks around," Maggie snorted. "I wouldn't hold my breath if I were Dani."

"Strange situation all the same. I'm not sure I'd be as understanding if I were in your shoes. I'd probably want to scratch her eyes out."

Climbing wearily in to the front passenger seat, she picked up Sally's Filofax, which was lying on the seat, and put it on her lap. "In theory yes," she said smiling. "But the flaw in the plan is that I got to know and really like Dani before I knew she was the other woman. And in fairness to her, she'd no idea either, so I couldn't just abandon her last night, despite any issues I might have with Mark."

"And do you? Still have issues with him, I mean," Sally asked.

Maggie gave it a nanosecond's thought, then laughed. "Actually no. Apart from thinking he's a complete bollox, that is."

Sally chuckled at her reply and started up the engine.

Chapter 51

After work Sally went along to the Deadly Inc, Friday night at O'Neill's thing. Truth be told she no longer found it an ordeal; in fact she rather enjoyed it as a ritual signpost pointing to the weekend, and even found conversation with her fellow women co-workers an agreeable change. It had been a trying week one way and another so she wasn't sorry to see the back of it. Charlie however seemed to have lost his momentum somewhat, having only sent one text that morning, and no further wreaths had turned up at the office which was, in itself, a relief.

Leaving at seven she drove home, parking in the underground garage. Hero had taken up temporary residence with David, seeing as she'd had to spend most of that day out of the office, but they were both due over later which gave her, she estimated, a good two hours to have a long relaxing soak in a lavender bath and a bit of time to herself.

It surprised her how quickly she'd become accustomed to having a dog around the place, which gave her a certain sense of empathy with Auntie Pauline. With that in mind she made a mental note to give her a call to see how she was getting on with Humphrey Bogart, secure in the knowledge that her esteemed aunt would have complained loud and long if she was having any problems with said puppy.

Her relationship with David too was a very different ball game from anything she'd experienced before and it made a pleasant change to be involved with a grown-up for a change. Men could be such babies, Charlie included, all ego and complex mind sets, whereas David was so . . . she searched for a word but could only come up with uncomplex (is that a real word she wondered) but in a good way. He made no demands of her, didn't go into snits or sulk if he didn't get his own way, didn't smother her with possessiveness, which was a consistent feature of all her prior relationships, but he was his own man at the same time, in no way a push-over or needy. It was an easy relationship in every sense of the word, "Laid-back," she said aloud as she reached the top of the stairs. "That's it. Laid-back and . . . nice." It was such an underrated word in her opinion. Nice was good. A warm feeling washed over her as she thought of him and, turning the key in the lock, she pushed the door open.

She was conscious of a scuffling sound then felt a thud in the middle of her back and the force of it sent her hurtling into the loft, stumbling with the momentum and ending up on her hands and knees, winded, in the middle of the room. Stunned, she took a moment to gather herself together before she heard the door slamming shut behind her.

"Bitch!" Charlie's voice full of rage.

As she scrambled to get to her feet he kicked her in the ribs, and she was thrown sideways onto the kitchen unit, whacking her head in the process. She screamed but it was stifled as another hefty kick knocked the breath from her lungs.

"Cow! Poisonous cow!" he spat, punctuating the words with flailing kicks which she tried to ward off by rolling onto a ball, her hands wrapped defensively over her head. Then she felt his hands in her hair and, as he yanked her to her feet, she screamed again, grabbing his wrists to prevent him pulling out clumps by the roots.

"Charlie! Get off me! Stop! Don't!" she shouted, but he wasn't in the mood to listen, instead he dragged her tottering across the room to the sofa and threw her down upon it.

"You've wrecked my life, you bitch! Why couldn't you keep your bloody mouth shut? But oh, no, you had to put the boot in. You had to get your pound of flesh."

He was standing over her, his face about six inches away, hands leaning on the sofa, his body half across hers.

"You did it to yourself, Charlie. You crossed the line," she said, engaging eye contact, and he replied with a stinging swipe across her face with his open palm. Instinctively she warded off the full impact with her hand, then started to thrash at him with her fists, kicking wildly with her feet, trying desperately to beat him off. She was both angry and afraid. Although Charlie's temper was legendary, she had never seen him like this, never witnessed him raising his hand in anger. He stood back and, relieved, she scooted back into the corner of the sofa pulling her knees up to her chest.

"What's got into you, Charlie?"

The question seemed to faze him for a moment and he looked perplexed, but then gave a humourless laugh. "You have to bloody ask? My life's in tatters thanks to you, and you have to ask?"

Her head was throbbing and she felt pain with every breath. Tentatively she pressed her side and nearly passed out with the resulting wave of pain. Broken ribs, she thought. The bastard's broken my ribs.

"I'm sorry," she said, attempting to cool the situation down. "You made me angry, lying like that."

He sighed and sat down on the arm at the foot of the sofa. He looked tired and dishevelled, a tuft of hair sticking up at the crown of his head, not his usual pristine self. "Why couldn't you just leave things the way they were? Why did you have to spoil it?" He sounded almost reasonable, which quelled her growing sense of panic.

"All I wanted was some commitment, Charlie, and you weren't prepared to give it to me."

He shook his head. "But why? Things were fine as they were. We were happy, weren't we? I loved you."

"Not enough, Charlie. I wanted more."

He stood up. "I could do with a drink."

"There's wine in the fridge." She leaned forward to stand, but caught her breath and cried out as her battered ribs protested. "I need to see a doctor – I think you broke my ribs."

He grinned at her, a scary sort of grin, all teeth and no humour. "You don't need a doctor," he said.

"I do," she protested.

Then he lunged forward and grabbed her by the hair again.

"Wrong," he said, his face only inches from hers. "You don't need a doctor, because the way I feel now I'm probably going to kill you."

When Maggie opened her eyes it was seven o'clock. She knew this because she could hear the *Emmerdale* music seeping up from the sitting-room. Still groggy the way you are after a daytime sleep, she could easily have stayed where she was, but she was thirsty and wanted to pee badly, so swinging her legs to the side if the bed, she got up.

Lying on the dressing-table she could see Sally's Filofax which she had inadvertently carried into the house with her after Sally had dropped her off. She'd placed it there before falling into bed, knowing that her boss was out of the office for the remainder of the afternoon, so was uncontactable as she didn't have her mobile number. I should get it back to her. She might need it, she thought, knowing how lost she'd be without her own personal organiser.

Sally Gillespie was a surprise. Maggie had expected SPOD, but so far her new boss had proved to be very reasonable and encouraging, which was a turn-up for the books, causing her to revisit the notion that the real Sally Gillespie must have been abducted by aliens. In any other situation this reassessment of her colleague could have been unsettling, threatening even, but Maggie was glad that her fears had been groundless as she loved her job, and if she and her immediate boss had a personality clash there was every possibility that she'd come out the loser. Thankfully that wasn't the case. In fact Maggie grudgingly acknowledged to herself that she quite liked Sally Gillespie, alien impostor or not.

Sitting on the end of the bed she flipped the leather-bound diary open, hoping to find an address. She was aware that Sally lived somewhere on Great George's Street, but didn't fancy schlepping the length of it knocking on doors. Her luck was in however when she spied a scribbled Great George's Street address with no other reference – she guessed that it must be Sally's place.

Anna was sitting on the sofa, feet up, watching *Emmerdale*, and the ads came on as Maggie entered the room.

"Not going out?" Maggie said.

Anna shook her head. "No. I felt like a night in front of the telly," she replied, then frowned. "And to tell you the truth, I felt I should back off a bit from Gerry. He's getting very keen and I don't think it's fair to string him along, if you know what I mean."

Maggie was gobsmacked, but at the same time delighted. She didn't want to make a big deal of it however, or get up any false hopes so she just nodded and said, "Right," and sat down on the sofa next to her mother. When the fifty-second I-Sport ad came on, they were both silent as they watched. Although she had seen the finished cut with Gavin's cobbled together end-line she was anxious how it would look on the small screen. She needn't have worried however, because it was terrific. Sighing with obvious relief she gave the air a minipunch.

"Yes!"

"That was wonderful," Anna enthused then there was a sharp intake of breath from her as she appeared on screen in living colour in the Super Savings commercial.

"I wonder if Dad's watching this?" Maggie said.

"Not right now," Anna replied. "He'll be doing evening surgery. But I suppose he'll see it later." She was beaming with pride, tickled to death to see herself on television. Almost as soon as the next ad was up, her phone rang. It was her friend Deirdre Joyce, calling from Westport. There was a flurry of excited high-pitched conversation about Anna's TV debut with a lot of 'did you really think so's" and "You don't think I looked fat?" repeated several times.

When it looked as if Anna was going to be there for the duration, Maggie caught her attention and mouthed, "Can I borrow the car?" gesturing outside to illustrate the point. Without breaking for a breath, Anna nodded and tossed her the keys from her handbag.

More accustomed to being a pedestrian, Maggie found herself taking the scenic route which was easier for her as she was unused to navigating Dublin's one-way system, finally finding a parking spot on Saint Stephen's Green which was but a brisk five-minute walk from Great George's Street. As she strolled down Grafton she did a spot of window-shopping, and when she spied a really sexy pair of silly shoes in Fitzpatrick's window, Aiden came to mind, and again as she passed Knickerbox. It's time I bought some new sexy underwear, she thought, resolving to pressgang Lily into an expedition the following afternoon. Though generally over the top with her own style, Maggie recognised that Lily had a good eye as to what suited and what didn't (she was brutally honest when asked her opinion). She knew what was cool and what wasn't, and most important of all, what was sexy and what was plain cheesy. With that decided, she turned left and headed off to return Sally's Filofax.

He's on a power trip, she thought. He's trying to scare me. It was working. Sally was pretty scared. For the last half hour he'd been rambling on about how his life was a shambles because of her. How he'd lost his home and his family. How Imogene was threatening to remove him from the board of Penhaligan (she was the major shareholder, it being Daddy's money that had started the firm), how humiliating it all was and how Sally was the sole cause of it. Reading between the lines she could see that it was the loss of face and status that was the most devastating part for him.

She found his whingeing pathetic. "You told me you'd left her," she snapped, all at once losing patience. "Had you any intention?"

He stared at her, calm now, but with hate and loathing emanating from his every pore. "Why couldn't you just leave things the way they were?" he repeated, ignoring the question. "Life was good. Why did you have to spoil everything?"

"Don't you think it's time to stop blaming me and take responsibility, Charlie? You said you'd left her. You lied to me. You made me believe that you wanted to be with me."

Without warning he completely lost it and lashed out at her, catching her a blow on the left temple which caused her to see stars. Instinctively she threw up her hands to shield herself and struggled against the soft sofa cushions trying to escape him.

The doorbell rang and they both froze.

"Who's that?"

"I'm expecting friends round," she said, her broken ribs causing her to wince as she slithered off the sofa and stood behind it, making a barrier between them.

After a short pause, the bell rang again. Please, please let it be David, she thought.

"What friends?"

"Friends from work," she said, not wanting to antagonise him further. "We're going out for dinner."

He was silent then, listening. She listened too, hoping that one of the other tenants might be leaving and would hold the door for David. But there was no sound of footsteps in the hall. No tap on the door.

After a short interval, he sighed and said, "They're gone."

Sally's heart sank. He was unbalanced. There was no telling what he might do and she had no intention of playing the victim.

"I think you should go, Charlie," she said firmly. "Go now and I'll forget this little incident."

It must have been the term "little incident" that did it. Again without any prior warning, he lunged at her, pushing her backwards until her back crashed into the wall, his face contorted with rage, his eyes wild and unfocussed, now completely out of control. Excruciating pain flooded through her body and her lungs cried out for air.

I can't pass out, she told herself. If I pass out it's all over.

Maggie recognised the dog, and vaguely recognised the man. The dog trotted over to her. "Hello, boy!" She rubbed his head, then thrust her hand out to David and introduced herself. "Maggie Fortune."

He looked perplexed by the unsolicited introduction until she explained, "I saw you with Sally at O'Neill's," then tickling the dog behind the ear, added, "And everyone at Deadly knows Hero."

His face registered recognition and he smiled. "David Heart," he said.

Maggie looked back at the door. "She's not there. I rang the bell."

He took a pace back looking up at the building. "Her light's on, so she must be in."

Maggie held up the Filofax. "I brought this back. I thought she might need it. I took it by mistake."

Suddenly Hero's ears twitched and he growled, bounding towards the front door of the building, barking persistently, very agitated, springing up on his hind legs, his two enormous front paws battering against the door.

"What's up with him?" Maggie said, jumping back, intimidated by the dog's sudden change of mood.

David, frozen by the unexpectedness of it all, suddenly had a very bad feeling.

"Oh shit!" he said, running towards the door. "Charlie Penhaligan."

"Wreath-Man?"

"Wreath-Man, poisonous-text man, sick bastard," he

said, pressing all the entry bells in the hope that someone would let them in. "He's been sending sick threatening texts all week." After what seemed like an eternity the lock-release buzzed and he slammed the door open, dashing towards the stairs, Maggie after him, the dog way ahead.

Maggie was horrified. "You really think he'd harm her?"

"I'm not taking any chances. Hero's not happy. That's good enough for me!"

They screeched to a halt on the landing and he thumped on the door.

"Sally!"

They heard a muffled scream and a crash, and David took a couple of paces backwards and ran at the door, crashing his shoulder into it. Maggie winced for him as it didn't budge an inch.

"*Sally!*" she shouted, banging her fists on the door panel. "*The cops are on their way!*"

Grabbing her phone out of her bag she dialled 999. "I need the police! We have an emergency here!" she said when the operator answered.

David stepped back again and took another run at the door.

Chapter 52

As Lily crossed over College Green and headed up Westmoreland Street she looked at her watch. She was very late, but thanks to the convenience of mobile telecommunications she'd been able to call Aaron up and let him know, seeing as they were only meeting for a quick drink before he went off to work at The Hanger. Aaron was a DJ.

It was all Dom's fault. A meeting with a client in London had been brought forward to early the following morning and she'd had to organise his travel arrangements for that night. Unfortunately he'd omitted to tell her anything about it until just gone five, so it was all go to get a flight and hotel accommodation sorted. But sort it she did, and had waved Dom off to the airport at seven-twenty for an eight-fifteen flight, instructing the driver to put his foot down.

It had been a long and irritating day, with everyday jobs taking longer than usual, simple tasks turning out to

471

be more complicated than she first thought and Dom's, "Did I not tell you? I'm sure I did," at five o'clock had raised it just one more notch on the bastard-day meter. One thing was for sure though. She needed strong drink to unwind.

Anticipating this eventuality, Aaron had a pint on the table when she arrived into the Palace and she slid into a seat next to him, gratefully taking a couple of large gulps, before coming up for air.

"Howya?" he said, grinning at her.

"Better after that," she said. "How's yourself?"

"Great. Gav's definitely in the Ireland squad. It was announced today." His excitement was palpable.

"Was there any doubt?" she said grinning back, a rush of his exhilaration infecting her. Hard to imagine Aaron's irritating snotty-nosed kid brother was a premiership soccer player chosen to play for his country. She could still remember at the age of thirteen, watching World Cup Italia 90 along with all the other kids, most of them, even the girls, dreaming of scoring the winning goal for Ireland.

It was weird to be back with Aaron after so long. She couldn't even remember why they'd fallen out. Whatever it was it must have been something trivial, because they'd always got on really well. Even at school when he was going through his smart-arse wide-boy phase, they'd still been pals.

"Your ma must be over the moon," she said.

He nodded. "You know yourself," then his eyes drifted, settling on something over her left shoulder.

"So were you waiting for me long?" she asked, but he

didn't react, just continued to stare into the distance. "Do tell me if I'm boring you," she said, her irritation returning. It had been that sort of a day.

His eyes flicked back to her. "Sorry? What?"

"I said, tell me if I'm boring you," she repeated, and he frowned, then shook his head, his eyes drifting past her again.

"Sorry. Don't look now but –" Immediately Lily craned her neck and looked behind her. "Don't look!" he hissed.

Lily turned back, none the wiser. "Well, you shouldn't say that!"

"OK. OK. Just be casual and glance behind you. Is that Maggie's fella sitting over there?"

Lily casually glanced over her shoulder in the general direction indicated by Aaron, then caught sight of Aiden sitting at a table in the corner and her jaw dropped.

"That's yer one, isn't it? The one with the . . ." He ran his nose along the back of his hand and Lily nodded, outrage building. The fact that Aiden was with the gorgeous Sinita wasn't the cause of her ire. It was more to do with the way he was leaning across the table, holding both of her hands in his and talking intently to her, that stuck in her throat. Sinita was equally intense and there was a lot of nodding and looking down at the table-top.

"The bastard? I never thought . . ."

"What?" Aaron said.

"Are you serious? He's over there practically snogging his ex and you say, what?"

Aaron leaned back in his chair and threw his hands up. "Hey! Nothing to do with me."

"I can't believe it," she said to no one in particular. "Aiden of all people."

"Can't believe what?" Aaron said. "For all you know they're talking about the state of the feckin' economy."

"Yeah right!" Lily snarled. "Any closer and he'll have his tongue down her throat."

She turned again in her seat and watched, as Aiden stroked Sinita's arm, talking intently. Sinita was nodding again and looked upset.

"I'm going over there," she said pushing back her chair.

Aaron put his hand on her arm. "To say what?"

"To ask him what he's playing at?

"Hold your horses," he said. "You don't know for sure it's anything iffy. What if it's business? He's a photographer, isn't he? She's a model."

"Business my arse," Lily said, pulling her hand away, but by the time she'd turned around again, the table was empty and two men were claiming it. Craning her neck she peered around the bar but Aiden and Sinita were nowhere in evidence. "Shit! That was swift. Where did they go?"

Aaron shook his head. "Search me. But to tell you the truth, judging by the other night I wouldn't fancy my chances with yer one if she took a pop at me."

"Why should she take a pop at you?" Lily asked, cross that she'd missed her chance to confront Aiden.

"Because she'd have to get past me before she could take a pop at you, my little scorpion," he said, grabbing her hand again and kissing it. What could a girl do? She sat down again.

Half an hour later Aaron had to disappear to set up for his night's work so he walked her to the bus stop.

"Don't go making accusations before you know the story," he warned Lily. "I remember how you can go off half-cocked sometimes and you usually come to grief."

"Cheek!" she said, giving him a playful cuff around the head. "As if?"

"Right. " He gave her a kiss. "I'd better be off. I'll call you tomorrow."

Watching him go, she dug her phone out and called Maggie.

"Where are you?"

"Would you believe in Saint James's A&E?" Maggie said. "Sally was attacked."

"What!?"

"Sally. Attacked by Wreath-Man. He beat her up, broke a couple of ribs and God's knows what would have happened it David hadn't smashed the door in."

"Who's David?"

"Sally's new fella. The cute bloke you saw her with on Grafton Street. Anyway, he broke the door in and Hero leapt on yer man, flattened him, then stood over him, a lump of arm in his mouth until the Guards came."

"Feck!" Lily said. "And how is she now?"

"The doctor's checking her over, but I think she's all right. Pretty shaken up though. The bastard went crazy. He'd completely lost it." She paused. "Where are you? I thought you were meeting Aaron."

"Um . . . that's why I called," Lily said. "We were in the Palace, you see. Now don't get upset, but I think it's only fair to tell you. You should know . . . the thing is. . ."

Maggie laughed. "What? What are you ravelling on about?"

Faltering, Lily told her.

There was a long silence from Maggie's end of the line. "Maggie?"

"He wouldn't do that to me," Maggie said. "Not Aiden." A leaden lump had suddenly formed in her gut.

"I'm sorry, kiddo, but I'm only telling you what I saw."

"No, there has to be some explanation. Aiden wouldn't cheat on me. He's not like that."

Lily sighed at the other end of the line. "You'd have said that about Mark three months ago, and look what happened there."

Maggie had stepped outside the door of A&E and was standing in the ambulance bay. "Aiden's nothing like Mark," she said, her hackles raised, but her heart was pounding and her hands sweaty and shaking. No. Please, not again. Not Aiden, a voice inside her head screamed. "Something must have happened," she said. "You said she was upset."

Lily tried to recall what she'd said. "Not upset exactly. More worried."

"There you are, then." Maggie was relieved to have found an explanation, however feeble. "Something happened to her and she called Aiden for help."

Lily wasn't convinced. "Such as?"

"I don't know . . . something."

"You're probably right." Lily was unable to hide her scepticism. "Something must have happened." She felt awful to be the bearer of bad tidings, but didn't want to see her friend hurt again. Better to tell her, she'd convinced herself. Better sooner than later, but now she wasn't so sure. "Look, you're right. It's probably nothing." She paused. "Maybe I shouldn't have said anything."

"No, no. You were right to call," Maggie said, wishing she hadn't, and with a heavy heart went back into A&E, the thought that Aiden might be seeing Sinita behind her back gnawing at her despite her denials to Lily. He wouldn't, she thought. Not behind my back. If he wanted to get back with her he'd be straight with me. I know it. The positive assertion made her feel better. "I trust him. He wouldn't do that."

"Do what?" David asked, and she realised that she'd been thinking aloud.

"Oh, nothing," she said. "Have you heard how Sally is yet?"

A nurse took them to see Sally a while later. She was sitting up in a cubicle, her temple badly bruised and puffy, her lip swollen. Her ribs weren't broken despite Charlie's best efforts, just badly bruised, and they were keeping her in overnight for observation. Charlie had been brought in to James's too to have his lacerated arm stitched and to have an anti-tetanus jab, then the cops had taken him into custody to the Bridewell.

"How are you?" Maggie asked.

"It only hurts when I laugh," Sally said, cracking a feeble smile, then wincing with the effort. David took her hand and gave it a squeeze.

"And have the cops charged Wreath-Man yet?" he asked.

"A detective asked me if I wanted to press charges and at first I was reluctant, until he reminded me that if Charlie hadn't been interrupted by you guys there's no telling how far he'd have gone. He was way out of control."

"The bastard could've killed you," Maggie muttered. "What a head case."

Sally nodded. "I had a sudden flashback to the moment when he pinned me against the wall. The look in his eyes . . ." She shook her head as if finding the memory hard to come to terms with – the fact that the man she had, such a short time ago, considered to be the love of her life could look at her with such hate and loathing. "That's why I decided to press charges."

"You were right," Maggie agreed. "He shouldn't be allowed to get away with it. If he did, he'd think that it was acceptable."

"Besides," Sally said, trying to bury the irrational feeling that she was being somehow vindictive, "he'll get a top lawyer and probably get off with probation, but the humiliation of a court case will be punishment enough."

"Not in my book," David commented, still angry; still harbouring his own feelings of guilt for not insisting she go to the cops as soon as Charlie had kicked off with the wreath and the subsequent vitriolic text messages.

Sensing this, Sally kissed his fingers and smiled at him. "Trust me. It's true. Face is everything to Charlie Penhaligan. Facing people will be a worse ordeal than six years in prison for him when this gets out."

David was still sceptical. "You think so?"

Sally kissed his fingers again. "I know so," she said.

The nurse came in then to tell Sally that she was being moved up to the ward, so they said their goodbyes and Maggie gave David and Hero a lift home, then drove back home herself.

It was very late, after two, by the time she got there and Aiden's house was in darkness, but his car was parked outside. She felt really down. Horrified by Sally's ordeal though she was, Lily's landmine had made it hard for her to dwell on it, as her mind kept drifting back to Aiden and Sinita. He wouldn't do that to me, she repeated, trying to convince herself, hoping that the more she said it, the more chance there was of it being true. Weary from the lack of sleep and the emotional rollercoaster that had been the last day and a half, she climbed into bed and fell into an uneasy restless sleep.

Chapter 53

Chatter and muffled laughter from downstairs woke Maggie up the following morning and looking at the clock she saw that it was past ten. She was stiff and sore and felt as if she'd gone ten rounds with Lennox Lewis. The night before, in the heat of the moment it had slipped her mind that Charlie's thrashing arms and legs had taken the feet from under her during the brief mêlée after Hero had bounded to Sally's rescue, and she'd fallen heavily to the floor, whacking her hip on the corner of the sofa as she'd gone down. Slipping her dressing-gown over her jammies she padded downstairs to the kitchen, her sore hip causing her to limp slightly.

He was sitting at the kitchen table with Anna, large as life as if nothing had happened, with a red-top tabloid on the table in front of them. They looked around as the kitchen door opened.

"Hello, pet, where were did you get to last night?" Anna asked.

Maggie looked straight at Aiden and said, "More to the point, where were you?"

He shook his head and exhaled. "Trying to talk Sinita out of skipping bail."

Anna held up the paper. "Look! It's here in the paper. She tried to score cocaine from an undercover cop and they busted her."

Despite her emotionally fragile state Maggie had to fight the urge to laugh at Anna's choice of words. "Busted?"

Her mother nodded. "Yes. And poor Aiden had to bail her out."

"You stood bail?"

"She called me from the cop shop, so I got her a solicitor, then went down there myself. She was in a state. After she was released we went to the Palace for a drink and she started talking about skipping bail, but in the end I talked her out of it. It's only a possession charge. Her brief reckons it'll be a fine at most, but Sinita was always a bit of a drama queen."

Maggie felt relief flood over her and she wanted to laugh again as she limped over to the table and sat down. Her instinct was right. She'd been right to trust him. (well, almost trust him). Something *had* happened.

Aiden noticed her limp. "What's wrong with your leg?" There was concern in his voice.

She was still trying to get her head around Sinita and her drugs bust. "Oh, a crazed stalker knocked me over while he was trying to kill Sally," she said. As conversations stoppers go it was pretty effective. Both Anna and Aiden stared at her open-mouthed.

"Well, that tops my story," he said after a couple o. beats. "Say again."

Maggie regaled them with the events of the previous night, skipping the part about Lily phoning, employing a smidgen of embroidery to improve the tale.

"Good enough for him!" Anna said when she got to the part about Hero almost gnawing Charlie's arm off (embroidery par excellence). "I hope they lock him up for ten years."

"He's more likely to get the probation act," Maggie said, repeating Sally's assertion that Charlie Penhaligan's expensive lawyer would, no doubt, Cite mitigating circumstances, severe stress, and promise that his client would attend an anger-management programme.

"Speaking of programmes," said Aiden, "Sinita's solicitor recommended she go into drug rehab. He says it'll impress the judge, so he's negotiating with the courts to change her bail conditions so she can head off and sign in to the Priory. So at least one good thing came out of it. Even by her own admission her habit was getting out of control." He reached across the table and took hold of Maggie's hand. "Are you OK? Your leg looks pretty sore."

Maggie shrugged. "It's not that bad. Just a bit stiff, that's all." Then she recalled Sally's words and smiled. "It only hurts when I laugh."

Anna frowned. "You should get it looked at. You never . . ." then she stopped and cocked an ear. "What's that noise?"

Both Maggie and Aiden turned towards the door and listened, as Anna got up from the table , hurried out to the hall, and pulled the front door open.

They heard her say "Oh my God!" and, glancing at each other briefly, jumped up from the table and ran (or in Maggie's case limped) out after her.

"Sweet Jesus!" they heard her say as she stepped out on to the pavement.

A small crowd had gathered. Not surprising. It's not every day a medieval knight in full armour rides down Gray Street. Anna was standing on the footpath staring up at her husband. He was dressed up in chain mail and full armour, with plumed helmet, and carried a lance complete with heraldic banner. The horse (his grey hunter, Major Tom) looked pretty snazzy too in brocade saddle-cloth and headpiece with a red ostrich feather. The neighbours were all out enjoying the show.

"I love you, Anna," Dan said, for all to hear. "And I'm sorry. Sorry I've taken you for granted and neglected you. Let it be known that I, Daniel Fortune, love you, Anna Fortune, need you and respectfully beg that you return to our own Camelot and take up your rightful place as my queen."

"Get down off there, Dan Fortune," Anna said, glancing around at the ever-increasing, greatly amused, audience. "You're making a show of yourself."

"I don't care," he said. "I love you. I'm your knight in shining armour and you're my queen."

Maggie was stunned but delighted by her father's romantic gesture. And a huge gesture it was for a man who was so deficient in the displaying-his-feelings department.

"I don't care how much of an eejit I look, Anna. I love you and I don't care who knows it. You're the only woman I've ever loved, and I don't deserve you, but please give me the chance to make it up to you."

Anna was red in the face, but Maggie could tell she was thrilled.

Then Anna's face broke into a huge smile. "Come down here, Dan Fortune, and let me give you a hug. I love you too, you old duffer!"

There was a round of applause at that, and Dan swung his leg over the back of the horse, but misjudged it. The weight of the armour succumbing to gravity, he overbalanced and fell to the ground with a metallic clash. There was pandemonium then. Anna was on her knees beside him all of a dither, but the weight of the armour made it impossible for him to get up, despite much effort from the interested onlookers, so Aiden took out his mobile to call the emergency services. "Is it the fire brigade or the ambulance?" he asked Maggie and after a brief deliberation they settled for the ambulance.

When the fuss died down and the ambulance arrived, as they were loading him into the back, with Anna holding his hand, Dan said to Maggie. "I don't know how they fought battles in this fecking get-up in the olden days."

"Maybe not," Maggie said, squeezing his hand, "but it didn't stop you winning this one." He grinned at her and winked as the doors closed, and as the ambulance pulled away, his words came back to her: "I have it all in hand." She chuckled quietly.

Maggie spent another few hours in A&E. She was beginning to feel quite at home there after the past couple of days. She and Aiden had followed the ambulance down after putting Major Tom back in his box, which Dan had parked around the corner. They couldn't fathom out how he had managed to hoist himself up on the hunter's back in the first place though. Dan made the front of the *Evening Herald* – a full page with him on the back of Major Tom, his arm plastered and in a sling, and Anna did an interview for the *Six One News* (where she was referred to as 'actress Anna Fortune') before they set off that evening back to Westport, towing Major Tom in his box.

It had been a hectic couple of days for Maggie, between Dani giving birth, Sally's assault and her father's epic plan.

"We've got the house to ourselves," she said to Aiden as they waved her parents off. "Any suggestions?"

Sweeping her up into his arms he carried her back into the house.

"Oh, I'm sure we can think of something to while away the time," he said.

Epilogue

Six weeks later Maggie saw her parents off at Dublin airport as they departed together for an extended trip to India, having left the practice in the capable hands of Dan's junior partner. Dan had decided that there was more to life than work, and he wanted to make up for lost time with Anna. She'd never seen them so happy together, and hoped that it would last and that her father wouldn't start taking Anna for granted again; but knowing her mother's determination, she was quietly confident that all would be well. Due to the success of the Super Savings ads, and despite the fact that Gerry had been kicked into touch so to speak, Anna had been offered a new contract for the Super Savings Christmas campaign.

As Maggie drove back to the city in the taxi she was amused but delighted when the cabby, in the course of telling how he'd just got a digital satellite dish, called it "the extra man".

"Sorry?" Maggie said, not sure she'd heard right.

"The satellite," he said. "It's deadly. It's the extra man."

"Is that right?" she said, tickled to death that her slogan had suddenly become an accepted expression of excellence. I must tell Aiden, she thought and a warm glow settled over her as he came to mind. This is nice, she thought. Very nice. In fact . . . it's the extra man.

THE END